In the Footsteps of Harrison Dextrose

Nick Griffiths

Legend Press
Independent Book Publisher

Legend Press Ltd
13a Northwold Road, London, N16 7HL
info@legendpress.co.uk
www.legendpress.co.uk

British Library Cataloguing in Publication Data available.

ISBN 978-1-9065580-0-0

*All characters, other than those clearly in the public domain, and
place names, other than those well-established such as towns and
cities, are fictitious and any resemblance is purely coincidental.*

Set in Times
Printed by J. H. Haynes and Co. Ltd., Sparkford.

Cover designed by Gudrun Jobst
www.yellowoftheegg.co.uk

Legend ▌Press

Independent Book Publisher

This book has been published by vibrant publishing company Legend Press. If you enjoyed reading it then you can help make it a major hit. Just follow these three easy steps:

1. Recommend it
Pass it onto a friend to spread word-of-mouth or, if now you've got your hands on this copy you don't want to let it go, just tell your friend to buy their own or maybe get it for them as a gift. Copies are available with special deals and discounts from our own website and from all good bookshops and online outlets.

2. Review it
It's never been easier to write an online review of a book you love and can be done on Amazon, Waterstones.com, WHSmith.co.uk and many more. You could also talk about it or link to it on your own blog or social networking site.

3. Read another of our great titles
We've got a wide range of diverse modern fiction and it's all waiting to be read by fresh-thinking readers like you! Come to us direct at www.legendpress.co.uk to take advantage of our superb discounts. (Plus, if you email info@legendpress.co.uk just after placing your order and quote 'WORD OF MOUTH', we will send another book with your order absolutely free!)

Thank you for being part of our word of mouth campaign.

info@legendpress.co.uk
www.legendpress.co.uk

There is something to be said for a woman's company, outside of the bedchamber. When I was feverish, Mrs Dextrose mopped my brow; when the minking bailiff came for my possessions, it was she who barred his way, with flabby upper-arm and kitchen implement; when I vomited across the dining table, it was she who binned the ruined food, wiped the table, sprayed air freshener and called the guests telling them not to come after all.

Did Mrs Dextrose moan? Of course the minking horse's hangdown did! For three solid days!

How I wish I could hear that barking now. It would be music to these ears.

Must get a grip on self... Yes, that should pass some time and quell this mithering mood.

Bring on the whores!

Well, there could be no doubt about it. The photographs were from the same negative: one, Dextrose had carried around in his pocket for the past 32 years; the other, a direct copy, must have been given to my mother at the time of my adoption.

So I had been adopted. Mother and Father weren't my real parents after all. At least that explained the emotional distance I had always felt from Father, and vice versa.

It really was too much to take in. I had come all this way, through so much struggle and adventure, to bump into the man responsible for my efforts, Harrison Dextrose, whom I now discovered had sired me.

And I had another name. I wasn't Alexander Grey – he had been a lie all along. I was Pilsbury Dextrose.

What a stupid bloody name.

The telephone rang.

I didn't answer it.

Pilsbury and Harrison Dextrose will return in
Looking for Mrs Dextrose

For Lillian

With thanks:

For Dextrose encouragement over the years: Jane Hill, Anne Jowett, Lucy Naylor, Malcolm Pugh, Nick Sayers, Shelley Weiner.

To Tom, for publishing, and Robin, for representing.

Harrison Dextrose's "Too many cooks" pun (see inside) was first uttered by Paul Merton in the excellent *Paul Merton in China* on Five. I laughed so much, I had to get it into print. Acknowledged with thanks.

As ever, vast gratitude to Mum & Dad – bless. And to Sinead, a star, for ceaseless support.

The Dextrorian Quest
(as followed by Alexander Grey)

Not to scale

How It Began

It was my 18th birthday when I chanced upon Harrison Dextrose's *The Lost Incompetent: a Bible for the Inept Traveller*, little knowing that it would one day lead me to kill a man with a dead penguin.

I regularly visited Second-Hand Books in Glibley, my hometown, being a voracious reader of anything from fiction to manuals on making furniture (though I never actually made any). Each time, I would rifle discreetly through the vintage pornography tucked into a hidden corner – dog-eared copies of *Girl Illustrated* and *Lost in Bloomers*, their covers featuring demure girls with dark curls and wry smiles who had forgotten to wear any clothes.

It was while flicking through the familiar magazine covers, as a birthday treat to myself, that I found Dextrose's book. Perhaps someone had changed their mind about buying it and had dumped it there, or they'd had insufficient funds and *All Gussets and Garters* had won.

I picked it out, realising that fate had meant me to read it.

Fate did not let me down.

The edges of the pages were brown and gently undulating. On the cover was a black-and-white photograph of the author's head. Harrison Dextrose stared defiantly into the camera, eyes alive with rancour. What manner of man was this? A full, dark beard festered around his jawline and encroached on his cheeks. His hair was a mop of curls, greased down in a futile attempt at neatness. Tiny broken blood-vessels coursed between the blackheads on his nose.

Flaunt the imperfections – I loved Dextrose on sight.

The back-cover blurb read:

Harrison Dextrose is the last of the great British explorers. This is his first book, a cornucopia of strange incident, concerning his journey from Blithering Cove in England to Mlwlw in Aghanasp, tracking down his former acquaintance, the philanthropist Livingstone Quench. Dextrose names this his Dextrosian Quest, a justly grandiose title. It will take him through lands rarely written about, because they are considered unfashionable. However, the author never ceases to find colour, even if he must inspire it himself. Which he often does.

Dextrose had clearly lived. The eyes said 'early 40s', the features said 'add ten'. Stuff the Walter Raleigh of history books, who returned to these shores fawning and proffering root crops. Here was a real sea-faring hero, ravaged by alcohol and sexually-transmitted disease, who probably couldn't remember the name of the ruling monarch. Were his parents alive, I felt sure they would have long since disowned him. Was there anything of me in him, I wondered? I liked beer and had always been an embarrassment to my parents.

Inside, the publication date: 1973. My 18th occurred in 1983, a full decade later. I sought the Foreword:

I would always hook up with Livingstone Quench when I returned to England from my ground-breaking travels. It beat talking to Mrs Dextrose and inevitably took in a public house and lechery. We also shared a sense of humour. I saw plenty of myself in Quench, by which I am not suggesting that we mated.

Besides myself, Livingstone Quench is the only human being

I admire. What made him disappear off the face of the earth, I do not know.

We had been imbibing in The Crock of Shit, niggled as usual by the crackerjack barnacle Wilson Niff, who could not take his alcohol. Friend Quench had had a trick up his sleeve to relieve us of the bowler-hatted mink[†]. That morning, he had bottled his pungent first urine, treacle-coloured and of a similar consistency, and had lightly carbonated it in his Sodastream. When Niff excused himself, Quench swapped this foul brew with the minker's scrumpy.

We could barely control our glee. Disgracefully, Niff sank the full pint in one and demanded to know whose round it was next. Quench took umbrage and stormed out and that was the last I saw of him.

No rumour, no postcard, nothing. Eventually, I heard tell he had opened his own hostelry in Aghanasp, in the middle of nowhere, and had named it Gossips.

Gossips?! Unutterable twaddle! Only a goose names his bar after the idle chatter of women! I assumed that devils were abroad and set out to find Quench myself, to void this slander.

Thus began my great Dextrosian Quest.

[†]Editor's note: without wishing to curb the author's way with words, in the interests of non-offensiveness, we have substituted Mr Dextrose's multiple profanities with the word 'mink', which seems harmless enough.

The price was pencilled inside: *5p.* I needed no further enticement and strode boldly to the till. Well, no one else was going to buy me a birthday present.

I must have read *The Lost Incompetent: A Bible for the Inept Traveller* a dozen times a year since I bought it, inspired by Dextrose's aggressive prose, his strange adventures and his dislike of almost everyone else in the book. It was as if the word 'curmudgeon' had been invented just for him.

With each passing year, the Quest seared itself into my brain. The characters assumed vivid, human form; I could hear their voices and recognise their frailties; I knew their words off by heart. The book became a movie in my head and, at its heart, was the enigmatic Dextrose.

I admired and adored the man. He seemed to me a free-floating island of bile, flicking Vs at social etiquette, representing the antithesis of myself, a polite product of an empty suburban upbringing. I had often wanted to flick Vs at people, but worried that an authority figure would tick me off.

I had been brought up and still resided in Glibley, in Surrey, a commuter-belt wasteland that imagines itself as a garden fete where the sun perpetually shines and ladies in hats swat wasps. Its residents competed with one another, for the newest car, most outrageous topiary and most educationally accomplished son.

It was why, no doubt, Mother and Father sent me to boarding school, St John the Short's, in the neighbouring town of Elmwood – to excel in academia. Instead, much to Father's chagrin, I achieved only mediocrity and an aversion to contact sports.

I made a few friends there, none of whom lived anywhere near Glibley, so my holidays were spent moping around at home doing horticultural chores, or annoying Father with my inertia. He was a small, greying man with a ginger moustache and a thin, stern face. He taught at Glibley Secondary and made up for his ordinariness with snide remarks and an explosive temper. Mother, hair tied in a bun, mimsied around him in a selection of aprons.

There was one friend who lived in our street of mock-Tudor detached housing and cherry trees. His name was Benjamin Grebe and his father was a travelling sports equipment salesman. On the few occasions the Grebes visited our house – Father deemed them proletarian – Benjamin's father would drop into conversation that he "sold goals to Newcastle". Everyone would laugh politely, besides Mr Grebe who found himself hysterical.

Benjamin was a shy youth with a lisp who began showing signs of baldness at 16. We grew up together, playing soldiers – using sticks for guns and beating aimless trails through the local woods. When we hit adolescence we changed tack and instead found new ways of secretly ogling his next-door neighbour, Suzy Goodenough.

We wore corduroy and stiff shirts that buttoned up while she wore comfortable clothing and chewed gum. Sometimes, she would sit seductively on her garden gate, clutching a radio, shaking her pony-tailed bronze hair and pretending not to realise that we were watching. Pop music was frowned upon in my house, where the compositions of dead Russians drifted along the corridors among the chintz.

Suzy Goodenough was our goddess and Benjamin and I were rivals for her affection, though we never actually plucked up the courage to speak to her. Instead, we cycled past her repeatedly, attempting to pull wheelies, and watched her breasts grow as if in time-lapse photography.

Two events led to my venture in the footsteps of Harrison Dextrose. The first was the untimely death of my parents. The second was Suzy Goodenough's challenge to copy Dextrose's feat, with sexual favours as the carrot. There were psychological factors, too, I realise now, most obviously my need for self-respect.

It had been my final term at St John the Short's when my solemn headteacher, Mr Tremayne, had called me into his office and told me of Father and Mother's demise. Father had electrocuted himself cutting through the cable of his new electric mower and Mother had suffered a similar fate, trying to rescue him. They were spotted over the garden fence, locked together in death's grip, having massacred the petunias.

Distant relatives of whom I had no knowledge attended the funeral, offering blithe condolences. No one cried, not even me. Although I missed Mother's bosomly shelter, she had been in such thrall to Father that her personality had been subsumed. He, I came to realise, cared only about me as a reflection of his social standing. His loss meant freedom to me, and it cast no shadow.

Happily, Father had also alienated the rest of the family, making me the only available heir. So I received, some months after my 18th birthday, the house and his money: a considerable sum, accumulated through wise investment and stingy saving. The accountant explained, using graphs and sums easily ignored, that I could live off the interest for some years to come – and I required no second bidding.

It seemed foolish to seek higher education afterwards, being no longer ordered to do so, and with poor A-levels anyway. Gallingly, looking back, I translated the freedom I had fallen upon into wanton lethargy of such duration that I find it embarrassing to recall here.

For 15 years I frittered away my existence and inheritance, watching television into the smallest of hours, rising in the afternoon, then reading perhaps, and making something on toast; over and over again, until days, weeks and months rolled into one and my existence became largely pointless. Only now on reflection, having dragged myself – with great success – out of that cycle, can I recognise the blinkered stupidity. At the root of the escape stands one man: Harrison Dextrose – to whom I owe everything.

At least I did not become a hermit. My accountant's first 'allowance' cheque in hand, I had discovered The Goose, the local public house, and would visit regularly with Benjamin. He had also left school, being thick, and was following in his father's footsteps, or at least in the wake of his Ford Sierra.

We'd drink the night away every Friday and Saturday, and on varying weekdays depending upon Benjamin's availability. The locals tended to avoid us since they were snobs – Benjamin was a salesperson, while I was unemployable and sported a tangled beard and flip-flops.

One night, to our incredulity, Suzy Goodenough walked into The Goose, plonked herself beside us and insisted upon conversation. Though it had been 15 years since we'd last gazed upon her form, Suzy and her mother having left Glibley when her father's affair had become public knowledge, she was instantly recognisable. Long, sleek, bronze hair streaked with blonde, eyes of azure, an oval face of perfect complexion with dimples mid-cheek, curves that one could melt into, and wrapped in a red dress that exposed cleavage as tempting as any diving pool. Suzy Goodenough.

On arrival, she had made straight for us, sat down and demanded that I buy her a drink. Her estuary English, picked up no doubt in some grim new town, failed to tally with her image but it didn't matter. She was back, she said, and intended to make the best of it. Her mother had lost her job and had been offered one by her old employers in Glibley, which she had been obliged to accept.

There was no mention of the affair all those years ago and the subsequent night-time flit, which had caused such a stir. I still recall the *Bugle*'s headline: 'Glibley Too Good For Goodenoughs'.

Since that night in the pub, an acquaintance had developed and we three met regularly, on the condition that I paid for the drinks. Suzy rarely offered much; however it was still she who provided the second inspiration for my trip.

When Suzy and I were both 16, unbeknown to Benjamin or

any others, there had been one afternoon during which she had encouraged my attentions, being bored and desperate, although our fumblings had ended in such ignominy that I still cringe at my ineptitude.

A few weeks after Suzy's return to Glibley, with that lost tryst an uncomfortable memory, she, Benjamin and I had gathered inauspiciously in The Goose.

I often talked of Harrison Dextrose and *The Lost Incompetent* in glowing terms, causing Benjamin, and later Suzy, to glaze over. That night, instead of glancing away in boredom, she snapped: "If you're so fucking in awe of the old fart, why don't you get off your arse and do it yourself, rather than sitting around droning on about him, boring the crap out of us? You might even bump into him and get to suck his knob."

Which was charming.

I can't pretend that the thought had ever crossed my mind. Dextrose was the world's finest adventurer. Were I to do so – follow in his footsteps, that is – it would require planning, supplies, enthusiasm and energy. All strangers to me. Yet there was something appealing, under the warming spell of alcohol, about the prospect of emulating my great hero. Who was to say that I wouldn't be able to manage it? Not my previous five pints of lager, that was for certain. Hell, I might even gain a personality!

I had the necessary finance and such a journey could become an enlightening antidote to my life of bedsores and baked beans. Despite my physical inactivity, I still devoured books – I had not become braindead – and it was Dextrose's tale that had always captured my imagination. I had recreated his travels in my mind, soaking up his words as if I were there with him (from the safety of my lovely, slightly stale, duvet). Perhaps it wasn't such a bad idea?

"I couldn't possibly."

"Listen, hotpants," Suzy sneered. "If you complete the same

stupid journey quicker than the old fart managed it, I'll let you screw me. Properly, this time."

Benjamin stared at me meerkat-style, stunned by the news of the unconsummated adventure.

"I'll go!" I exclaimed in beer fumes.

Over the following weeks, the idea did begin to make perfect sense. It became time to throw off the bedding, to introduce myself to the world. 'New me' was a sexier fellow who strode with purpose. I shaved off the beard and bought some shoes. Alexander Grey had become inspired!

We worked out how it could be done. Harrison Dextrose, who was not one for factual detail, had written no contact information into *The Lost Incompetent.* So we called International Directory Enquiries and to our astonishment were given a number for a Gossips, Mlwlw: (00347 18) 12. Small place, presumably.

According to Dextrose's book, he had reached Livingstone Quench's bar at 1.32am on his 24th day of travelling. Mlwlw being five hours ahead of England, Suzy would call the Gossips number at 8.32pm, her time, on my 23rd day. If I answered, it would prove that I had beaten Dextrose and could rightfully claim my libidinous prize.

There was a brief debate over my potential to deviate from the route, silenced by Suzy: "Sod it. I'm not worried. He doesn't have the imagination to cheat."

Such a tease.

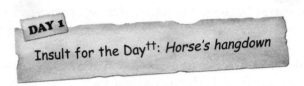

DAY 1

Insult for the Day[††]: *Horse's hangdown*

[††] *extracted at random from the multiple insults used by Harrison Dextrose in* The Lost Incompetent: A Bible for the Inept Traveller

The start of an epic journey can be fraught with emotional trauma. All those painful goodbyes and sobbing loved-ones. Perhaps it was lucky, then, that no one turned up to see me off.

Blithering Cove is a decaying harbour town on England's North-East coast: the setting for the start of the Dextrosian, and therefore my own, Quest. I was determined to follow Dextrose's route to the letter, to become methodical, resourceful, knowledgeable, even charismatic.

It was a late-autumn afternoon. The sky was overcast though the winds were light. I leaned on rusted railings and gazed out to sea, seeking the arrival of The Unsmoked Haddock, the vessel I had chartered to take me to Skaramanger, the main port on Emo Island and its capital. So that its captain could recognise me readily, I wore a jester's hat, purchased for the Glibley Carnival but never used, Father having shortly deemed carnivals unnecessary.

Children pointed at me and laughed then continued smoking. Behind me, shop-fronts were boarded up and people swore freely. I felt that I didn't belong, manners having been drummed into me since my earliest years.

A seagull swooped down from a hover to land beside me, eyed me as if I were insane, then flew off. I was determined not to be unnerved by an outsized bird. Besides, it was far easier to be unnerved by the fishing boat that chugged towards me, its captain gesticulating in my direction. That must be The Unsmoked Haddock, I thought, and its skipper, one 'Mad Dog' Mahaffey. Yet the boat appeared so small and battered, and, to the untrained eye, unseaworthy that I considered hiding the hat and scarpering.

It shuddered along belching pollutants with Mahaffey on deck saluting, as if I were some pompous committee welcoming him back from a war with oil people.

As he reached the wall he threw across a rope, calling out, "Catch it, matey!" – the salty vernacular leaving me quietly amused.

Sadly I dropped it. The rope uncoiled towards me, one end thwacking across my cheek. As I suppressed a weedy "Ow", co-ordination deserted me further and it unfurled into the water below. Mahaffey cursed in mutters, something involving the word "landlubber", recoiled the rope and tried again. On the fourth attempt, I caught it, by which time his eyes had become bloodshot.

As I made fast The Unsmoked Haddock, Mahaffey hauled himself, wheezing, up a rusty ladder barely fastened to the harbour wall. He greeted me with a firm handshake and something that sounded like, "Lost the dog in the lift-shaft".

He had voluminous grey whiskers, matted by the winds and unkempt, his skin was raw and flaky and his nose resembled a prize radish. The obligatory sailor's cap, white with black band, bore an official-looking insignia that he must have purloined, while his garb – black roll-neck sweater, yellow waterproof trousers and large rubber boots – was as scarred as his sea-addled mind must surely have been.

As Mahaffey spoke, he rolled silvery eyes and chewed on

what looked to be a dried frog's leg, plucked from a paper bag in his trouser pocket.

"Are those dried frogs' legs?"

"Aye," he replied, again rolling his eyes. "Job lot."

Perhaps he was playing up? Or his eccentricities were an affectation?

I asked, "Why do they call you 'Mad Dog', Mr Mahaffey?"

He turned and pointed down into The Unsmoked Haddock. "Mad Dog," he said.

There, in the back of the boat, lay an old black Labrador, drenched and greying. It might well have died of drowning without its owner having acknowledged the fact.

"Ahoy there!" I called out, hoping to impress the captain.

The Labrador raised its head briefly, shot a look of resignation and slumped back into its reality. There was nothing mad about that forlorn mutt.

"Supplies," said Mahaffey, crunching on the latest frog's leg. "Gots to get 'em. Meets I here at eight bells." And off he went, limping.

I stood at the harbourside bewildered, until he called backwards, "Needs plenty of booze, young 'un." The man seemed unstable enough as it was.

Should I quit now, I wondered, while I was ahead? I dismissed the idea as cowardly… But I *was* a coward! I had to dismiss that idea too.

Give it time and I felt certain myself and the sea-dog could bond. How he would love contrasting his fruitful, outdoor life with my pathetic endeavours. People like him undoubtedly loved boasting. Failing that, I could always keep out of his way below-deck.

I had already packed. Harrison Dextrose, in *The Lost Incompetent: A Bible for the Inept Traveller*, had provided a list of recommendations:

Supplies
When in doubt, I take everything and have someone else carry it. There's always some minking local with a hook for a hand who'll porter for you, for the price of a bean, if your crew has deserted. Creating employment in this way, I consider myself to be a philanthropist, as well as Britain's greatest living explorer.

These are the supplies I pack for any long journey:

* *Trousers, rugged x2 (1 waterproof)*
* *Jackets x2 (ditto)*
* *Shirts x3 (nothing poncey, you're not a minking fashion statement)*
* *Jumpers x1*
* *Underwear (5 prs each)*
* *Boots x2*
* *Hat (optional)*
* *Sleeping bag*
* *Toiletries (says Mrs Dextrose)*
* *Swiss Army knife (I once served in the Swiss Army)*
* *Notebook and pencil*
* *Passport (though everyone knows me)*
* *Currency/travellers' cheques (drink and whoring)*
* *Compass (you may need one – I smell directions)*
* *Billy can (no he can't! My little joke)*
* *Matches*
* *Chocolate*
* *Pornography (when a region is devoid of whores)*
* *First-aid kit (mine consists of haemorrhoid cream and bandages)*
* *Whiskey (fill all remaining space with this)*

Obviously, the '*Inept Traveller*' of Dextrose's title refers to the reader not the author, who regularly refers to himself as

'Britain's greatest living explorer'. He believes this and I would concur. Such boundless self-confidence, being the antithesis of my mealy-mouthed reticence, only impressed me further.

All of his recommended items I had duly packed into an expansive rucksack, besides whiskey, which makes me gag. Instead, I took a Walkman and a selection of cassettes for any dull sections of my journey. Thus prepared, I headed for a pub, to calm my tender nerves.

I chanced first upon a market square, devoid of any stalls and featuring a smattering of pedestrians, all octogenarians bemoaning the weather. In its far corner stood The Severed Head public house.

The exterior looked quaint enough: thatched roof, window boxes and a sign that swung rustily depicting Charles I's last moments. Inside was all dark wood and old beams, the walls and ceilings pestered by sea-faring paraphernalia. The place reeked of spilt wine and sawdust, though there was no sawdust in evidence. Perhaps hordes of peg-legged sea-dogs lay rotting in the cellars, having stumbled there in a quest for the urinals decades earlier? I needed a beer, but this was not the place.

Turning to leave though, I was halted in my tracks by a shrill voice.

"You!" it went. "You!" (And it could only have meant me, being at that moment The Severed Head's only patron.)

There, behind the bar, was a large-boned woman. "No one leaves my pub," she said, all grim-faced.

"What, ever?" I asked, hopefully humorous.

"Don't be facetious with me," said Fat Landlady. "No one leaves my pub without first taking a drink."

Now, I knew my consumer rights but, before I could exercise them, she was pouring a pint of something.

"You'll have a real ale," said Fat Landlady. "You'll like my real ale."

Was this a first stab at friendliness or a threat?

"Thank you," I said, "but I prefer cider."

"We don't do cider. Only real ale."

"Then could I have a spirit, please?"

"You'll have a bloody real ale!" screamed Fat Landlady. "And take off that bloody hat. I won't have jokers in my pub."

Approaching the bar, I removed my jester's hat and scrunched it into my wringing hands as some oik might do in a Dickens novel before asking for something food-wise.

Fat Landlady had a laughably rotund face, ruddy cheeks and permed mousy locks with a nicotine highlight. Her vast upper arms looked like twin piglets protruding from a voluminous blue-and-white checked summer dress. Put her in a Forties-style bathing cap and suit and she could have inhabited one of those saucy seaside postcards, beside a weasely little man making innuendo about erections.

She must have caught me looking her up and down, which admittedly took a while. "I hope you're not imagining me in one of those saucy seaside postcards," she said. "The last customer did that."

Thankful that the pint had been poured, I silently handed over some change and made to sit down.

"Not there!" she thundered. "That's Harry's seat!"

"But Harry's not here," I muttered.

"Never you mind where Harry is. God rest 'is soul. You sit where I says!"

So I found a place elsewhere and shrank into it, cradling the ale and inspecting the glass for signs of anything interesting. There were none.

Looking up, I noticed that a rowing boat had been nailed to the ceiling.

"Stop that!" shouted Fat Landlady.

The Lost Incompetent has a section on the origins of

Blithering Cove, which I turned to, hoping to stay out of trouble. I knew its tale off by heart, but always enjoyed it.

BLITHERING COVE

Set sail yesterday but turned back by gales. Drowning sorrows, holed up in The Hapless Traveller, taking full advantage of Happy Hour.

No other minker in the place. In the absence of banter I rifle through a display of leaflets, hoping for lingerie shots. Instead find Tourist Information Leaflet no 12A: Origins of Blithering Cove. Background waffle interests me not, but I am short of news so here is the information, reproduced verbatim, with no concern for copyright.

'The small fishing port of Blithering Cove grew up in the early Seventeenth Century, when locals reported lights out at sea come nightfall, and rumours of mermaids basking on sandbanks spread throughout the region. A bounty of eight gold sovereigns from the local mayor, William Cholmondley, was laid on the head of the first mermaid to be slain, and fishermen from miles around took to their boats, hoping for a prize catch.

History tells that the locals, bored of having no industry, had made up the stories, and the fishermen stayed anyway.

Naturally there was a price to pay for this deceit. Cholmondley's 14-year-old son, Charles, had been central to these mermaid untruths. To add credence to his tales, he would wade out at low tide in the dead of night to find a sandbank, where he would slip into a silken fishtail (sewn by his mother) and wave a lantern. At the first sign of approaching hunters, young Charles would extinguish the light, pack his tail into a rucksack and, being a stout lad and strong in the water, would swim unseen back to dry land.

One night, it is said, a genuine mermaid lured the youth to

*his death amid the waves with promises of eroticism. More
likely, he had grown too fat for the costume and could not slip
out of it as the waters rose. Records show that he was found
washed ashore three days hence, tail attached, in rigor mortis
clutching an empty ice-cream tub.*

*Around these parts, it became known as the story of The Boy
Who Cried Mermaid, and served as a warning to others never
again to fabricate tales about fish-style beings.'*

Author's note: Sounds like mink to me.

According to my plastic Torquil the T-Rex Dino-Explorer's
Watch, free with tokens from packets of sugar-frosted breakfast
cereal – which told the time *and* featured a compass – it was
19.50. Assuming that Mahaffey's 'eight bells' translated to
8pm, I had better hurry.

The captain was waiting at the harbour when I arrived, the
dog asleep at his feet. He looked annoyed.

"When I says eight bells, matey, I means eight bells!" he
snapped.

The Labrador twitched.

I glanced at my watch. "I thought this was eight bells, Mr
Mahaffey."

"Eight bells is when I rings the bell eight times. Did 'e not
hear it?"

"No, sorry," I mumbled. "I was in the… pub."

Mad Dog's face lit up. He slapped me on the back then
flinched. "War wound," he explained. "Don't 'e worry, young
'un. Anyone who drinks warrants leniency. Now, let's get 'e
aboard sharp. The winds is in our favour. Come, Mad Dog!"

The hound rose reluctantly, turned and leapt into The
Unsmoked Haddock where it skidded on the sodden deck, went
nose first into the far side, somersaulted and flew over the side
into the water.

Mahaffey tutted. "Always does thats! Mad bugger!"

I followed the captain into his craft, jumping the final few feet and toppling under the weight of my rucksack. Though it hurt, I dared not show it.

So I was on deck! It was really happening. Cowardly, lazy Alexander was embarking upon a voyage that would take him into barely charted regions populated by colourful natives. Everywhere I trod, Harrison Dextrose would have trod before me. Except on this rotting boat.

While Mahaffey heaved his sodden mutt from the harbour by its collar with a gaff hook, I breathed in vitality. Seagulls wheeled over a departing trawler, squawking for dinner. If the fish made a pact to turn in early, trawler-folk could reasonably fish at more godly hours. But the fish are not our friends, or they would have been fashioned with prettier faces.

It would take almost two days to reach Skaramanger, on Emo Island – renowned for its fishing, rugs, an odd theme park, but little else. It was, however, a useful stopping-off point on the sea journey to Klütz, capital of Klükamüs, where Dextrose had travelled. I was nervous, exhilarated, and concerned about the dog, which had found a dead octopus and was wearing it as a hat. If it was a mad dog after all, perhaps Mahaffey was sane?

"Brought along a pair of antlers, case we gets bored," said Mahaffey.

"Sorry?" I replied.

"Never travels anywhere without 'em. Pair of antlers always whiles away the hours."

I couldn't think what to say.

"Game called Antler Music," Mahaffey explained anyway. "Invented by Cap'n Jake 'Bonehead' McCoy back in the 1600s to quell a mutiny aboard his vessel the Distant Relative…"

I could feel a salty tale coming on, rife no doubt with 50-foot waves and scurvy.

"T'had been a shocking trip: 50-foot waves and decks rife with scurvy. Galley crew reduced to serving gull gizzards on accounts of everyone having eaten the gulls. Lost in the Pacific with only a pair of antlers for amusement, which the Cap'n had procured from an ancient elk. There was mutinous talk that he comes to hear of. Talk of throwing the Cap'n to the sea beasts. So he invents Antler Music, like pass-the-parcel, but with antlers instead of a parcel."

"When the music stops the sailor wearing the antlers is out?"

"Aye."

"And how will that work with just two people?"

After some thought he concluded, "It'll be a short game, matey."

"And who'll be playing the music?"

This had not occurred to the illustrious captain. "Mad Dog here whines at the sky. We coulds play until he stops?"

A thrill, I imagine, not dissimilar to embroidering for one's country.

Then Mahaffey trumped his own idea. "Or," he continued, in the tone of one about to present a great scientific discovery to envious boffins, "we coulds play along to the shipping forecast!"

He beamed and popped a frog's leg.

I was despondent. Here I was, setting out on a sea journey in a boat that might sink if struck by a pilchard, with a lunatic and his octopus-hatted dog, and the heartiest form of amusement yet devised involving continually swapping a pair of antlers while some weather-type wittered on about Dogger East by Walter Ten or whatever.

Luckily, my mood brightened once we set sail. The weather was not unkind and a crescent moon provided reflections that danced on the waves, like shiny bras on swinging breasts. Ahead of us stretched water; behind us, the land faded away as if it had never existed. I was no longer a citizen, but a traveller.

For this trip to Emo Island, including 'food' and 'lodging', I had paid Mahaffey £150. This was no luxury cruiser, and as Mahaffey had put it when I telephoned him on a Tourist Office recommendation, "Dependings on the weather, could be a lusty trip. Mights end up dead." I had laughed it off as black humour at the time.

So what should I do to pass the time, I thought? Being previously unemployed, I should have been adept at killing time, however there were few noticeable distractions aboard The Unsmoked Haddock. So I found my Walkman, inserted a Sex Pistols tape, which seemed suitably energising, and stared out to sea.

Punk had passed me by while I was at public school. Such establishments are supposed to foster intelligence, yet deprive pupils of any outside influence or culture. They're a mental institution in which everyone considers themselves normal. Father had me wearing a bowtie on weekends at the age of 16.

Johnny Rotten, meanwhile, had been famed for wearing a Pink Floyd t-shirt on which he had scrawled the words 'I hate…" How could anybody hate Pink Floyd? So they had long greasy hair and tracks that took up a whole side of a record, but they made *Dark Side of the Moon*, the soundtrack to my adolescence. And *Animals* and *Wish You Were Here*. (I never got the psychedelic stuff, perhaps because the only acid I had encountered was in a chemistry lab.)

Father's one concession to my youth had been to buy me a second-hand stereo (so old it had options for 78rpm), which I was allowed to take to school. Its stylus was so lengthy, people started calling it 'The Hypodermic'. One thing then led to another and I became 'The Doctor'. It could have been worse. In fact, it was. The really cool kids called me 'Twatface'.

God, I loved Pink Floyd. *The Great Gig in the Sky, Money,*

Us and Them, Brain Damage. I'd sit in the dormitory, sound down – no loud music allowed and Father's concession to my youth hadn't stretched to headphones – my ears between the speakers, taking in the soundscapes.

I wrote up all the lyrics in fountain pen and pinned them behind my bed. The one about staying home to watch the rain had offered particular resonance.

I had always known, in the back of my mind, that I wanted to achieve something one day (sex with Suzy Goodenough withstanding). It was just a matter of realising what that something was. Thank heaven for Harrison Dextrose.

Lounging around after my parents had died, too lazy to work, reading, watching telly and lobbing things at mice making whoopee in the overflowing bins, had gradually lost its appeal. Fortunately, reading *The Lost Incompetent* was to plunge a bare foot into the icy sea of a distant, eerie isle, and to have it bitten by an irate seal.

Take this passage, for instance:

Attempt to brush teeth. Oral hygiene is not normally my priority, however last night met an edible goer in the alehouse, name of Mnestrina (or somesuch), who recoiled when I repeated her name while sighing.

Minking tap delivers no water! Ring the bell for service – Tinkle! Tinkle! – mistress of the hostel deigns to appear, wearing curlers, night-gown and a face resembling a monkey's groin.

"Get out!" I yell, having something against women with faces like a primate's privates.

By my fifth or sixth read, I was there with Dextrose in spirit and familiar with his every footstep.

After Suzy had challenged me to follow in Dextrose's

footsteps and the madness and audacity of accepting had sunk in, the journey had begun to take shape in my head.

I pictured myself mingling happily with drunken revellers in the fairy-lit town of Klütz, swapping tales of adventure, or shopping until I dropped in the giant malls of High Yawl.

When Dextrose encountered anything remotely dangerous, he skirted around it. There was no reason why I couldn't do the same. It wasn't just that I needed a dose of character-building; I also needed to get out of the house.

The Unsmoked Haddock was an old vessel, held together by barnacles. If they joined a barnacle cult and committed mass suicide, we'd be left clinging to planks.

Nets, baskets, ropes and trawling paraphernalia were stacked around the sides, while Mahaffey and the dog stood in the cabin up front, the captain muttering to himself, staying upright only by clinging to the wheel. I presumed we had satellite navigation and wondered whether Sputnik was still functional, such must have been the age of the cosmic crate guiding this floating timberyard.

Central in the deck was a hatch that led to sleeping quarters below. I lifted it and climbed in, lugging my rucksack down steps angled like the Leaning Tower of Pisa. There was a campbed and dog basket, charts, provisions – including a stack of 'Croaky Jacques's Dried Frogs' Legs' boxes, a truncated hat stand, a barometer with its pointer nailed to 'Fair', shelving on which musty ephemera jostled for space with a single novel (*Three Men in a Boat*) and a seemingly oily rag which, on closer inspection, turned out to be underwear. The place smelled of salted grandparents.

A tiny door opened onto the toilet-bucket, contents of which were sluiced into the depths below. I shall refrain from describing the smell.

I eyed the campbed. The evening had been all go, far more

go than I had experienced of late. Forty winks seemed in order; however Mahaffey's sheeting resembled the Turin Shroud, though his creeping stain surely had no religious significance.

I unpacked my sleeping bag, unfurled it over the campbed and climbed in. I zipped the bag up to its furthest extent, tugged the hood over my head and pulled tight its cord. Keep any lurking nasties out.

I was asleep within seconds.

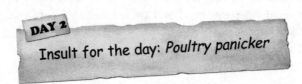

I was woken by a fearful noise. The hound was howling, accompanied by Mahaffey on harmonica. I buried myself into the furthest recesses of the sleeping bag, caught amid daydreams of banshees scurrying for cover, and wished that the cacophony would cease.

I checked my watch using the Dino-light feature: 13.12. Afternoon on my second day!

Instantly enthused, I lofted the hatch to emerge into a chilling wind.

"Lovely music!" I lied, hoping to crawl towards Mahaffey's good books.

"T'was to ward off evil spirits!"

Something compelled me to joke. "Ward them off? You assaulted their womenfolk, burned down their village and departed on horseback, whooping insanely!"

Mahaffey didn't laugh. "Watch that lip, young'un. Many an oik likes 'e has found his way to Davy Smith's locker."

"Don't you mean Davy Jones's locker?"

"Not if it were Smith's locker I threw overboard."

With that he went about his business.

The incident gave me the creeps and I retreated among the netting. The dog padded over at one stage and lay at my feet, until I kicked it square on the nose so it padded back to Mahaffey, sullen and dejected.

Gradually too bored to be nervous, I retrieved my rucksack and took out *The Lost Incompetent*. The entry for Emo Island began:

EMO ISLAND
Population: No idea
Capital: Skaramanger
Currency: Emoti
Principle industry: Fishing, rugs
Whiskeys drunk: Stop pestering me, woman

Arrived yesterday in Skaramanger with Caribou Tench and the crew of two loafers, Shark and Skink, the purting glumpots. By mink, it's small. Three bars, general store, post office, harbour with a dozen fishing boats and repellent natives everywhere making rugs. Can't move for minking rugs. They could carpet the minking island ten times over, and look to have done so. Haddockfesters. Must go elsewhere. But there's only a ludicrous theme park several miles hence, and for now tiredness overcomes me. Yes, tiredness. You try circumnavigating the minking globe.

All useful stuff, if you read between the lines – and took with a pinch of salt the idea that Dextrose is circumnavigating the globe. His Dextrosian Quest is in truth a more modest goal.

As for Caribou Tench, who is explained elsewhere in the book, he was Dextrose's trusty guide and sidekick, a tracker from the Western Plains, so named because the first thing his mother saw after he was born was a caribou eating a tench.

I discovered his fate in an archive journal, while researching Dextrose and his Quest in Glibley Library. During a later expedition, Tench had been swept overboard in high seas during a crossing of the mighty Gimp Straits, infamous for their unpredictable weather.

Ironically, given his name, Tench had drowned. His body was found washed up several days later at the place where Dextrose landed, Fort Knott. Wrapped within his fist was a note that read 'Dextrose is great'. However, the author of the article suggested that an 'i' had been crossed out and 'rea' squeezed into its space. Britain's greatest living explorer had declined to comment.

Whatever one's take on the entry in *The Lost Incompetent,* it gave little hope of laughs aplenty on Emo Island.

A significant while later, having remained resolutely motionless in the attempt to quell nausea, I was approached by a grinning Mahaffey. The sun had set and the sea resembled a glittering padded quilt.

"Cares to join I for some fishing, young landlubber?" he asked.

"Why not!" I replied, having never fished before but wishing to keep him happy. "Who's going to steer the boat?"

"Mad Dog takes over tonight, matey," Mahaffey replied.

Sure enough, the mutt was in the cabin, propped up on its hind legs, forelegs draped over the wheel, tongue lolling stupidly.

"But it's a dog!" I protested.

"Aye. And your point be?"

"Dogs can't steer boats!"

"Mad Dog can."

My tone became hysterical. "Name me one famous sea-faring dog!"

Mahaffey popped a dried frog's leg and scowled. "Your attitude tires me, young 'un. And when I tires, my eyelids droop. Mad Dog here can steer a boat as well as any sailor. I points him at a constellation – this night Orion, the hunter – and he sets course for that until it disappears with the dawn. Now, lets us fish. My stomach hungers."

That seemed to be an end to the argument. (I had argued that dogs can't steer boats and seemed to had lost.)

The captain set up a pair of hand-lines, all nylon and knots, and we threw hooks baited with dead fish-bits over the side, which hung among a shoal of mackerel, depleting its number with each cast.

He said nothing, staring into the waters. His presence gave off a tinge of melancholy, such that I warmed to him slightly. His moodswings had perturbed me but now he was calm. And if he knew his skippering as well as he knew his fishing then perhaps I was in safe hands, after all. I decided that my concerns about the dog's navigational skills might even have been unfounded.

"How did you come to be a sailor, Mr Mahaffey?" I asked.

"T'is all I knows, matey."

He launched into a protracted tale of poverty, herring and sectioned relatives. Mahaffey had grown up in Blithering Cove, one of 14 children, five of whom had perished in the same sea-faring disaster. Their father had been a famous trawlerman, called up during the First World War to serve in the navy. He had been honoured for his bravery after dragging three wounded colleagues from violent seas, but had gone AWOL soon afterwards, his crewmates maintaining that he was abducted by crabs.

The offspring had mourned Mahaffey Sr greatly, leading a couple of them to go off the rails. Mad Dog himself had gone to sea, to fashion a living.

"Have you ever married?" I asked. It silenced him briefly.

He sniffled, wiped his beard and inspected a portion of dried frog's foot that transferred itself to his palm. "There was once a woman. Hair like a sweep's brush and the eyes of a plaice. Name of Vera. I dids love her, though she left me for a landlubber."

He trailed off. I left it there.

A hearty catch of mackerel had been assembled. The captain set up a burner and we gorged ourselves on the delicious oily fish, washed down with rum, while a Labrador steered us towards Emo Island.

This would do.

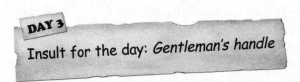

I woke around noon the next day to a hangover, made worse by the Unsmoked Haddock's undulations.

Mahaffey was back at the wheel and the sea was choppier than I had yet experienced. Ashen cloud scudded across the skies. The dog lay curled up asleep at the bow, showered by surf yet unperturbed.

The captain pointed ahead. "Shoulds be making land soon, matey!"

Towards the horizon, a hilly, bleak land mass was indeed visible. The journey had passed more quickly than scheduled; I had expected to reach Emo Island only by evening.

My spirits lifted. "Were the winds behind us last night?"

"Dog took us off course," said Mahaffey matter-of-factly.

So that wasn't Emo Island. Elation drained from me like liquid from a bottomless bucket. Where were we? I could muster neither the indignation nor the heart to ask.

What had I been thinking? A dog steering a boat!

I had been taken in by a man who numbered flatfish eyes among his preferred female qualities. I felt like telling him what I thought of him, but that would have hurt Mahaffey and he in turn would have hurt me.

I slumped down as a tear of exasperation (and possibly patheticness) escaped one eyelid. Of course I wasn't cut out for adventuring. Harrison Dextrose was a professional. The furthest

I had previously travelled was to school in the next town.

Had I been able to wave a magic wand, I would have gone home that instant. But there were no wands, magic or otherwise. I realised how comfortable my life in Glibley had become.

Looking upwards, I sought divine intervention. Instead, I caught a wad of shit full in the face from a passing seabird.

"Shit!" I yelped, scraping frantically at glop that stank more than bite-sized bird excrement had a right to do.

Mahaffey roared with laughter. Even the dog was up on all fours, wagging its tail, barking excitedly.

"T'is a good omen!" bellowed the captain, reciting: "Shoulds a bird shit on deck/Beware ye of wrecks, Shoulds a bird shit in yer eye/Yer ship she will fly!"

"It doesn't even scan properly," I pointed out sulkily.

"I knows!" said Mahaffey, bent double at such hilarity.

The captain slapped me on the back and the dog licked my face, developed a taste for birdshit and wiped me clean. Suddenly we were one happy family. Amazing how travel can broaden the mind.

When we had all calmed down, I felt able to ask the captain where we were actually headed.

"Frartsi. Fear not, young'un, t'is the island next to Emo."

"We couldn't just change course and head to Emo Island anyway?"

"Daren't risks it. I has enough fuel to gets me home, and not a gallon more. Blame Mad Dog here. T'is the first time he ever tooks me off course. Well, not the first. Maybe the 20th."

A flush of anger rose within but I didn't want to spoil the mood. At best, I pushed my luck. "How am I expected to get to Emo Island?"

"Finds a local. Tells 'em where 'e wants to go and tells 'em Mad Dog sent 'e."

"Really? You're known in those parts?"

"Well, no."

So we were headed for Frartsi, a place I knew nothing about and that wasn't even mentioned in *The Lost Incompetent*. On the first leg of my journey, I was already deviating from the route of the Dextrosian Quest.

Looking on the bright side, Dextrose's route had been formed quite randomly, more a result of the nearest ale-houses and loose women than based on geographical design. His sole imperative had been to terminate in Mlwlw, where Livingstone Quench, Dextrose's bar-owning friend, had been rumoured sighted.

For instance:

Had planned to go to Yi-Haw but Caribou Tench tells of a whorehouse the size of minking Wales in High Yawl, which calls for a diversion. Tell crew, 'Pack yer antibiotics, lads! We're off to knob for Queen and country!'

And yet Dextrose dedicates his book: *To the wife*

Mahaffey weighed anchor in a cove before a brief beach, which led to a steep, gorse-lined slope, over which I could spy a few peaks of unwelcoming hills. To the right, the shoreline curved away and there was just sea; to the left, a modest range of hills that continued into the distance.

"T'is Frartsi," said Mahaffey, stating the bleeding obvious, before popping a dried frog's leg with satisfaction, as if getting us here were the accomplishment of his task.

He lowered the dinghy – a smaller version of The Unsmoked Haddock, so no less dangerous – and we climbed into it down a rope ladder. I sat, silent and moody.

When Mahaffey rowed, it was impossible to tell whether it was the oars creaking or his bones. The dog stayed aboard The Unsmoked Haddock, erect at the side, snout towards us, howling forlornly.

Our ride towards a remote settlement brought to mind such films as *Treasure Island* and *Mutiny on the Bounty*, in which devious sailors filled with greed land on virgin beaches to slice and dice unsuspecting natives, steal their gold, argue among themselves then kill each other, leaving the most handsome one to sail away with a busty native girl and the loot.

This was unlikely to happen here. In *Mutiny on the Unsmoked Haddock*, the captain falls asleep in a drunken stupor, leaving the ordinary seaman staring at a gorse bush and not a lady in sight.

We beached and Mahaffey helped me with my rucksack. I clambered overboard, submerging boots in chilly sea, just avoided toppling, and off he rowed with a cheery wave.

"Good luck, young'un. 'E'll needs it! Hohohohohoho!"

Cheers. I considered waiting until he was a safe distance away then shouting abuse, but decided otherwise. Heroes get the girl but often die young; cowards can masturbate into their dotage.

This was the loneliest I had ever felt. I watched Mahaffey recede towards his vessel, haul himself aboard and chug away with one final wave.

I thought of Benjamin and Suzy – mainly Suzy – of Mother and even Father. What would he have said if he could see me now?

Something along the lines of: "Stupid boy! Get to your room!"

It fired me into action. Inactivity might be the easiest option but it would not find me shelter and food. At least last night's mackerel still filled a space in my stomach.

There was nothing for it but to trudge, upwards, over the sandy slope to see what lay beyond – hopefully, a neon-lit hamlet with welcoming bars and bus-rides to Emo Island.

The wind was cold and the sky watery grey. I consulted my

watch: 16.52. Night would fall, the temperature would drop further, and I would be in trouble.

I realised only then, with sickly horror, that Harrison Dextrose's recommended list of supplies had not included a tent. Of course such a distinguished traveller would not be seen dead in a flimsy construction of poles and canvas. He had been known to sleep in vehicles, but that was the lowest he would sink. Usually, it was the hostelry or the whorehouse.

Startled into reality, I set off at puffing pace.

The sandy beach proved hard going. I found a narrow uphill path through the gorse bushes, prickly spurs catching my fleece jacket and tugging me backwards. I prayed for signs of life over the hill and listened for sounds. All I heard was the wind through the gorse.

Nearing the top of the sandy ridge I strained my neck to see over. Tops of hills a mile or so away... their slopes heading down into a valley... and at the bottom... three stone cottages!

"Oh thank Christ!" I exclaimed aloud.

The dwellings were spaced apart in a triangular formation. Sheep grazed on the slopes around them. I strained my eyes for sign of a shepherd, without luck. Perhaps he was inside, brewing tea?

This was, at least, civilisation, and I headed into the valley with undue optimism.

The first cottage was an ancient thing constructed of rocks cemented together. A weather-stained timber roof sloped downwards, with something resembling seaweed swinging from its eaves. There were gaps between the door and its frame where the wood had become bowed.

I knocked, realising that I had never spoken to a foreign person before. For me, they existed only in movies: moody types, generally with firearms.

No one answered.

I tried the other two cottages. Still no one.

Releasing myself from the rucksack's burden, I sat on the doorstep of the third cottage and checked the sky, which had grown purple. Eventually, devoid of resolve, I lowered my head and tried to sleep.

A woman's voice broke into my subconscious and made me start. "Hll!" it went, slightly butch.

I looked up. She was striding towards me, dressed in long white coat and matching hat, carrying a stick as tall as she, and pursued by sheep.

What to do? Run and hide? But she had already seen me. Her voice sounded friendly enough, but what if that were purely to lull me into a false sense of security and she planned to poison me and cut me into pieces while I slept? It would be bad enough if she only planned to talk to me. She was a complete stranger.

At least she was a woman. A man would be scarier. Oh God, she was almost here. Appeal to her maternal instincts…

"Hi!" I called out. "Could you help me, please?"

"You no Frartsi!"

"No no! I'm from England! English! Well, British! Great Britain." I was beaming for no reason. "I've gone travelling by mistake!"

She had the build of a female boxer, with a strong jaw, narrowed eyes and brittle, red, spiky hair. Her coat and hat were woven from wool and on her feet she wore sturdy, ankle-high boots.

"Could you help me, please?" I repeated out of nervousness.

"You been welcome go in," she said, opening the door, which hadn't been locked.

How stupid of me! Residents around here were unlikely to see other people, let alone burglars.

But would I have dared enter uninvited? Of course not. "Rules are made to be kept," Father used to say. "Spirits are made to be broken." Long after his demise, I still feared the wrath of authority and like a child would toe the line unquestioningly.

I suddenly noticed that I had become surrounded by poodles. So, those were not sheep trailing her, but some kind of outsized hill poodle: sturdier, shaggier and more menacing than the domestic version. They stared as one, baring teeth.

I bolted indoors.

"I Mdra," she said. "You have luck I spick your lingwidge."

The house was on one level, four rooms leading off a hallway that ran the modest length of the building. The interior walls had been flattened by something resembling mud, cracked and powdery brown in places, and perfunctorily whitewashed. Three black-and-white pictures lined the hall, each fashioned with the skill of a child armed with coal. There was Mdra, looking deformed, out tending poodles; the head and shoulders of a stern-looking gentleman with blazing eyes – husband? I was too shy to enquire. And one of a child with way too much hair – a son? Again, I did not ask.

Mdra gave me the tour. Lounge, main bedroom, guest bedroom. "But not m'ny guest," she laughed apologetically. "What your nom?"

"Nom? Oh, sorry, name! My name is Al-ex-ander."

I was speaking slowly and shouting. This woman came from a country I'd never heard of, yet spoke my language very passably and *I* was patronising *her*!

She motioned me through a door at the end of the corridor into a kitchen-cum-dining-room, which was rather cramped for that dual purpose.

A single square window looked out over gorse and hills, now shrouded in gloom. The walls bore the brunt of a series of ill-fitting cupboards crudely fashioned from unpainted wood. A table and two chairs were in one corner, all equally rickety.

The cooker was a bulbous blackcast-iron affair with space for just one pan. Next to this was a desk stacked with root vegetables and a metal bowl filled with washing-up. Mdra explained that water had to be carried, two buckets at a time, from a river some way away. Since she could not afford transport, she walked everywhere.

As she spoke, a brown rat poked its snout out from among the unwashed dishes in the bowl and sprinted for the door. I yelped, pointing.

"Make we nice meal," said Mdra.

What on earth was I doing here, in the middle of nowhere with a poodle-herd who roomed with rodents? Be brave, I told myself. Or at least don't be weedy.

What would Harrison Dextrose have done in this situation? Oh. He'd have made a grotesque pass at Mdra. The thought tickled me, enough to calm my nerves.

While I waited at the table, Mdra loaded two plates with bread. Next, she chopped what looked to be a turnip and shared that out. As she went to the farthest cupboard for more ingredients, one of the other cupboard doors opened slightly and another rat's head appeared. The rodent spotted the food, jumped down onto the table and began chomping away.

I sat there horrified, unsure whether to say anything. While I watched, another two rats joined it.

"Um, Mdra..."

"Yes," she said, her back to me.

"I think you have rats."

"Yes," she replied, unconcerned.

"They may be eating our food."

She turned and tutted. "N'thing can do. In Frartsi, no touch rat. If hurt, lond become infertool."

"Your land becomes infertile?"

"Yes."

"But your lands look pretty infertile already."

"Yes."

I tried to sound wise. "In our mythology, we have a character called the Pied Piper of Hamlin."

She ignored me.

The evil rodents eventually returned to their hidey-holes and Mdra prepared a second meal, which the rats were too full to eat.

When she joined me at the table I braved asking about transport to Emo Island. Mdra said she knew of someone who would hire me a pony and cart the next morning. At least that's what it sounded like.

"Pony and cart?" I queried.

"Yes."

But Mahaffey had told me that Frartsi was an island, and presumably Emo Island was too, the clue being in the name? How could land-based transport make a sea journey? I asked Mdra.

She looked puzzled, causing flesh to mass between her eyebrows. "You not hear of Unknown Tunnel? Go through hill to Emo Island, for twenty-and-one mile. Builded by incestor."

"Your ancestors built it? Amazing," I replied. "In England we built an underwater tunnel 21 miles long, employing thousands of surveyors, engineers and labourers, using the latest laser technology and a drill the size of a house."

"Oh," said Mdra. "Two incestor, boy and father, they build Unknown Tunnel with axe and pointy bone."

After dinner, Mdra showed me to a bed of poodle pelts in the guest room, blew out the single giant candle and cooed from the doorway, "Sleep good, Alexindra. Not let bed-bug biting."

"Night," I mumbled back, already sleepy and deliriously cosy.

The door opened and Mdra reappeared. "Not joke about bed-bug."

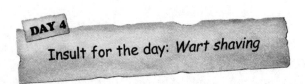

It was a night of fitful slumber during which I imagined I could hear the tiny sniggers of approaching insects. Every part of me bristled and much time was spent slapping at sudden itches.

Mercifully, Mdra let me sleep in and it was gone noon when we took our breakfast of rampant carbohydrate. The woman was kind enough, but from a different place that luxuries did not trouble. The language barrier made conversation stilted until it dwindled and was replaced by exchanged smiles.

When we had finished eating, Mdra walked with me to meet Ogr, the pony and trap man, who lived in a neighbouring valley.

We first encountered an ancient, stooped, bald fellow in rough brown robes, carrying a cabbage. When he saw us he smiled and circled his head three times with the vegetable.

"Hll, Mdra," he said in a thin voice.

"Hll, Cdfl," she replied and spoke to him in Frartsian, the only word I could understand being Alexindra. Then she said to me, "Cdfl is Frartsi monk. He know all."

Cdfl eyed me with displeasure. "Hole in sky make the birds heat up," he snapped.

A reference, I assumed, to global warming, which was hardly my fault.

"Bah! Cdfl must go," the tetchy bald man said pointedly

to me. "Much monking to do. Gdbi, Mdra."

Mdra and I trekked over the next hill line to see another triangle of cottages. The exercise was punishing and my guide had to stop on several occasions while I rejuvenated.

Ogr's place was similarly constructed to Mdra's, if more run-down. Cart parts lay scattered around its grounds and there were grease-stains on the woodwork.

The owner answered his door looking as if he had just woken up, wearing only long-johns. His chest was pale, troubled only by three hairs, and his stomach protruded.

It is said that owners grow to resemble their pets, and Ogr certainly looked like a horse. His face was long, his nostrils flared, and an ill-conditioned reddish fringe threatened to obscure his view.

Mdra chatted with him in Frartsian. Every now and again, he would eye me without moving his head.

"Ogr say hire Alexindra pony and trap and he drive to Emo. This cost is 200 Frar."

"I'm afraid I don't have any local currency. Does he accept Visa?"

She looked puzzled. "Visa?"

"It's a credit card. The bank pays you, then you pay them back with interest."

"You find pay money interesting?"

I assumed that Ogr didn't take Visa. "Perhaps I could trade with him?"

Mdra communicated this in the local tongue. I sensed that Ogr's command of English matched mine of Frartsian.

"What hoof, Ogr like?" Mdra asked.

I opened my rucksack and Ogr was into it like a pig after truffles. When he retrieved the Walkman, I held my breath. Music was an invaluable travelling companion.

I need not have worried. He sniffed at it, pressed a button at random and dropped it with a look of panic when *Anarchy in the UK* hissed from the earphones.

His goal turned out to be my Squid and Kelp Bath Essence. Ogr studied the bottle and its green liquid with wide eyes, clutched it to his sweaty bosom and began to unscrew the cap.

"It's not alcohol," I warned him, but too late.

He took a swig of the soapy glop, looked briefly confused, then laughed delightedly, rubbing his stomach. "Mmm!" he declared, foaming at the mouth. The deal was done.

Mdra walked me to the entrance of the Unknown Tunnel, where Ogr was to shortly meet us with his pony and cart.

The single-minded hike proved uneventful – along the valley floor, beneath oppressive black clouds like cotton wool used to clean ashtrays, punctuated only by the sort of small-talk that old ladies with bone china and scant memories might indulge in.

The Unknown Tunnel alone was impressive: a black hole gouged into a looming hillside, which became visible long before we reached it.

Ogr arrived eventually, towing an animal that looked sorrier than a reformed murderer. The trap, however, was pristine and the sort of thing that might be found in one of those interminable BBC costume dramas, in which hordes of sexually frustrated women giggle provocatively at the sight of a man's hat.

I tried patting the beast on the head, introducing it to the concept of affection. It stared back, unmoving. I decided to call it Eeyore.

It would have to do.

"Right!" I trilled with feeling. "Better be off!"

Harrison Dextrose, who sailed directly to Emo Island from Britain, had arrived aboard his own vessel, 'Dextrose I', during the afternoon of his fourth day, having lost some 36 hours to a hangover, courtesy of the inns at Blithering Cove. Already I was lagging behind him, thanks to Mahaffey.

I write this from the cabin of 'Dextrose I', where turbulent seas batter my head, forcing my pen to skate stupidly across the page. The previous day is a stranger to me and the thought of rum excites me only vaguely.

What happened in Blithering Cove? I recall just two events: deciding that it should be my birthday, with cake; and attempting to urinate into crewman Shark's ear, while he was in the Lounge Bar and I was in the Public.

My body is bruised and the tip of my left index finger is missing. I can only assume there was a skirmish.

Caribou Tench, the teetotal minker, won't confirm or deny this. He sits moodily saying nothing, staring down his nose at me. I'll show the plum-pickle minker. Just as soon as this throbbing passes.

It was time to bid farewell to Mdra. Being unaccustomed to goodbyes, I could only stare at the ground, scraping my feet.

"In Frartsi we say 'Gdbi'," she explained.

"Gdbi," I mumbled, blushing.

She had gifts for me: cold meats, bread and a poodle-wool cardigan, which was warming but made me look like an easy-listening crooner who had lost his stool.

I climbed aboard the trap next to Ogr and as we departed I turned to wave to Mdra, who had already left.

Progress was painfully slow; the nag wheezed with each breath and kept turning around as if to ask, "Are we there yet?" At that pace it seemed we might cover the 21 miles in as many hours.

As we ventured further into the tunnel, darkness enveloped us until I could no longer see Eeyore, only hear his exertions.

The clip-clops of his hooves had begun to echo around us, at least making it sound as though several beasts were labouring on our behalf.

Ogr lit two oil-lamps and attached one to each side of the trap with string. He was a silent type and I was loath to attempt conversation.

The sense of freedom that had visited me as I had left Blithering Cove, though lightly battered, at least remained. There would be wonders to behold in the journey ahead. I already longed to witness Emo Island's rugs, which seemed ironic. Put a selection of rugs in my garden and I wouldn't even have glanced out of the window at them. Yet put the same carpetry abroad, call it a tourist attraction, and here I was, having made a hazardous sea journey, keen to witness it.

I pondered briefly the merits of common proverbs and became troubled by 'A bird in the hand is worth two in the bush'. Why is it? How many people went around cradling a bird and thinking to themselves, 'Aha, two birds over there in that bush... No, I'm better off as I am.'

At a peak of boredom, mercifully, we stopped to eat. I broke out Mdra's bread and cold meats, and shared them with my driver. He, in turn, broke out my Squid and Kelp Bath Essence, took a healthy slug and offered the bottle to me. When I refused, Ogr laughed, involuntarily blowing bubbles.

The journey continued in relative peace. Ogr handed me an itchy blanket and the metronomic clip-clopping of the nag's hooves sent me into a bleary trance, until soon I was sleep.

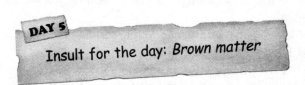

It was becoming apparent that this was no trip from one sumptuous meal to the next. Perhaps that is what triggered my dream of a carnivorous banquet at which I gnawed voraciously on a great hunk of roast pork. That, or the fact that I woke to the smell of burning flesh.

We had reached the other end of the Unknown Tunnel, its aperture threatening the arrival of a gloomy dawn. There, a shadowy group had gathered around a bonfire, rubbing hands. One burly figure was adding a yelping poodle to the flames. When they noticed our arrival, they began advancing, waving arms and placards, and shouting.

It seemed to be some sort of picket line. The Emo Islanders were protesting, which was a bit much. Frenzied barking in the background suggested that further fuel was available for the protestors' inhuman fire.

Unused to this sort of thing, I turned to Ogr for advice, but he looked spent and somehow sozzled, and the nag was on its one-after-last legs.

Confused and petrified, I pulled Ogr's blanket over my head, adopting the ostrich approach. The Emo Islanders were not taken in. One swiped the disguise from my head.

"Ynn! Fr ynn?" he bellowed. He had the tone of someone in the Russian Mafia and looks to match: sockets so deep his eyes were in shadow, perfectly square jaw, slicked-back dark hair, unshaven, with a moustache so vast it was more a beard with a bald patch. Covering his sizeable bulk was a black, woollen suit, stained and torn, unlaundered in a decade.

My eyes worked – he was an ugly brute, about seven-feet-tall, well into middle-age – but my vocal chords were numbed by fear.

"Ynn!" persisted Russian Mafia, poking me impatiently.

I felt my bowels turn over.

"I'm with him," I said, motioning towards Ogr, whom I noticed had curiously bound his own wrists with string.

The driver then began jabbering away in Frartsian, all gestures of innocence and wide eyes. My mind reeled. What was happening?

"So!" declared Russian Mafia with a sneer when Ogr had finished grovelling. "English smuggler!"

He grabbed Mdra's gift, the poodle-pelt cardie, and wrenched it off my shoulders, twisting my arms backwards in the process. I made no effort to resist. He flung it contemptuously to the ground and spat at it, but missed. He tried again but didn't seem able to raise the spittle. Then he tried to stomp on it, but there was something gammy about his leg.

"And this?" he enquired, clasping my left wrist in his big hand, wrestling free my Torquil the T-Rex Dino-Explorer's Watch.

"I got that free with breakfast cereal," I explained toadyingly.

Russian Mafia launched it into the Unknown Tunnel's blackness.

I watched in mute horror, so petrified that I would have happily let him burn all my possessions.

"You!" he snapped, and I flinched. "You come to our land at dark, steal poodle, send to England and make own knitwear – then sell to us! You is smuggler!"

"I'm not," I protested weakly.

"You is!"

"Really, I'm a tourist. Sir."

"You is smuggler!"

Russian Mafia clamped his fingers around my chin, making my cheeks puffy. "If not true, why take driver and tie hands?"

At last I found full voice, so indignant was I at Ogr's betrayal. "I didn't!"

"You did!"

"I didn't! He did that!"

"Why he do this thing?"

"Because he's a two-faced coward!"

"Ha! Now you lie for sure! He have one face!

"Ah, right, no, that's a figure of spee…" I didn't finish.

"One face! No two!"

"Yes, that's right, but…"

"*You* is coward, England person! You know what do with coward?"

I didn't.

"We roast coward!" shrieked the brute, at which point the rabble of pickets surged towards me, shouting angry nonsense, hoisted me above their heads and began carrying me towards the fire. I could smell my own fear and their hair pomade. The situation had taken a grave turn.

"Wait!" I shouted in desperation, and incredibly they stopped. Except I hadn't thought of a follow-up.

Panic necessitated action. As confusion reigned, I rolled off the lofting hands and hit the ground running.

Before me was a dirt road stretching towards a forest of firs; a number of poodles, penned in; three horse-and-carts, the animals in no better condition than Ogr's (the quisling); and a pick-up truck, black and shabby. From behind me came the sort of commotion made by disorientated radicals.

My mind raced. Escape on a poodle seemed out of the question and, since my only experience of the horse and cart suggested that it was ill-suited to high-speed chases, I made for the truck. As I did so, I wondered how I planned to start the thing.

The passenger's side being nearest to me, I leapt onto the footplate, scrabbled for the handle, wrenched open the door and swung inside with the intention of leapfrogging the gear-stick into the driver's seat... which was already occupied by a dwarf with a quiff sitting in a child's seat.

Undeterred, adrenalin pumping, I slapped down the door-lock on my side and leant over to do the same to his. As I did so, I noticed the stilts attached to his feet, allowing him to reach the pedals.

"Please go!" I yelped.

"Hundred seex mile Cheecago, haveeng fool tank gas, ceegarette, ees dark, weareeng sunglass…" said the dwarf, and looked at me expectantly.

"What ze line?" he demanded.

Protestors had reached the truck and were swarming over it, tugging at door handles, pounding fists on glass. One climbed onto the roof of the cab and was leaning over the windscreen, grinning like a hungry psychopath. His head was square, like Frankenstein's, and he had ruddy, pitted skin and no teeth. He began motioning between his mouth and mine, as if to suggest that he would be having my teeth when all this was over.

"What ze line?"

"Please just drive! They'll kill us both!"

The dwarf remained impassive. "Ees so! Ze line?"

I was going to have to humour him.

I had some clue. We'd watched *The Blues Brothers* a couple of times at boarding school and I recognised the line from when Jake and Elwood piled into the car. Something like, 'It's 106 miles to Chicago, it's dark, we're wearing sunglasses…' But what came next? It didn't encourage productive thought to have men who looked like they had been recently released from ice tombs hammering near one's head.

I hazarded a guess. "Let's go?"

"No!" said the dwarf, folding his arms.

"I *don't know*! *Please drive*!"

Cold, menacing faces peered at me from all angles.

"What ze line?"

A lucid moment; something clicked. "Hit it!" I yelped, just as one of the mob shattered the windscreen with a pick-axe. The surprisingly tough glass buckled outrageously inwards – towards the dwarf, happily – to resemble crazy-paving in ice.

We sped away with an unearthly revving noise, scattering enraged types who howled in frustration.

We were safe, I thought. Then I noticed, at the top of the windscreen, whitened fingertips clinging to the roof. A stowaway had found a grip despite the dwarf's silly speeds. The fingertips became fingers, then huge hands, and an upside-down toothless grimace appeared beneath a noticeable moustache.

"Eet Durhed," said the dwarf.

This wasn't how it was meant to be. By now, I had hoped to be admiring a succession of rug designs, not chauffeured by a dwarf at breakneck speed, hounded by psychotic pickets.

Durhed had started pawing at my undamaged half of the windscreen, trying to get at me, unaware of the solidity of glass, while cursing in Frartsian.

"What wanteeng, Mary? Wanteeng ze moon?" the dwarf taunted him.

"What's he saying?" I asked.

"Sayeeng cut off leg zen arm zen head, zen playeeng weez teetz."

"What tits?" I squealed, pressing backwards into my seat.

"No teetz," he said, pointing at his chest. "*Teetz*!" He pointed inside his mouth and broke into a cackling laughter. "He ees travelleeng weez lady!" the dwarf hooted, seemingly enjoying the peril.

He wasn't from around these parts, where the natives appeared thick-set, frosty and pale. This one was all perma-tan and perma-grin, sturdy and confident, aged anything from 30 to 50, and his dark, thick hair was fashioned into an outrageous quiff that spilled from his forehead like cornet ice-cream. Complementing this, he boasted thick, bushy sideburns in which sandwiches might have become lost. The face was proud, handsome.

I decided to make friends with him. "I'm Alexander. What's your name?"

"Detritos," he replied, offering a hand. His grip was firm.

Durhed still clung to the windscreen. He seemed to have become used to the situation and was humming to himself, presumably biding his time.

"Please can we get rid of him?" I asked.

"Why no sayeeng?" replied Detritos, and retrieved a sawn-off shotgun that had been hidden beside his child seat, aimed it at Durhed, who looked momentarily bewildered, and fired. The windscreen went red and blew inwards, showering the cab with sticky shards as I shielded my face with my sleeves. A briefly bumpy ride suggested that we then ran over the unfortunate lunatic.

"Zees one beeg pile off sheet!" laughed Detritos, covered in bloody glass.

Though we were travelling at 60 miles-per-hour, I scrabbled for the door lock. Bailing out at speed was preferable to being trapped in a vehicle with a homicidal, armed dwarf.

He seemed shocked. "Pleeze, no. Detritos no keel Meester Alexander!"

"You just killed him!" I squealed, motioning where Durhed had once been.

"Ees Durhed!" Detritos laughed. "Nobody likeeng! Detritos likeeng Meester Alexander. He crazee. Ees good!"

I forced this to sink in. Perhaps, for now, I was safe. I could consider escape later, when the miniature assassin was at a safe distance.

"We luckiest son off beech een world! Knoweeng zees?" announced the dwarf, beaming.

We drove on a dirt road through dense forests of pine for maybe an hour. The bittersweet smell of the fir reminded me of my childhood perched in trees in the back garden. I noticed that it was getting chillier, perhaps because we had no windscreen. At least I had a few layers on, including a fleece, despite the loss of Mdra's cardigan.

When we left the forests behind, the terrain became hillier – outcrops of rock dotted among coarse grasses. The sky had become a deep shade of purple. To capture the scene adequately in oils would have required a deranged painter with a headache.

Like Frartsi, Emo Island appeared unforgiving. The dwarf had become contemplative.

On the odd hill would be a distant herd of poodle, or possibly sheep, and a stone smallholding, but there were no signs of human life. I felt homesick. What had I got myself into? This trip was meant to be fun, if challenging. Lately, it had begun to resemble a survival gameshow.

Eventually we hit a flat coastal road and the first sizeable – though still small – settlement came into view, by which time I had regained my initial suspicions of my chauffeur and was determined to escape him.

A smattering of fishing boats was visible in a harbour off to our left, bobbing with conviction under the momentum of a biting wind that blew in from the sea. Though the sun occasionally broke through the clouds, it was having little effect.

Perhaps I could persuade a skipper to take me off the island?

Anywhere would do; balls to my Quest, balls even to sex with Suzy.

"Where's this?" I asked Detritos.

"Skaramanger," he said.

According to a local on a barstool, this place used to be called something innocuous until one former mayor, a James Bond fanatic, proposed that the town be renamed. The power-crazed mink originally wanted to call the place 'Pussy Galore', but the stiffs hereabouts protested and settled on 'Skaramanger'. Would've been a mink of a misnomer, anyhow – Emo Island women are built like puddings and not remotely delectable, and our enquiries after whorehouses have met blank stares.

Crewman Skink went AWOL yesterday, which leaves just Shark, Tench and myself. Farthing-faced chit said he was off for a nightcap. Shark, not the brightest button in the box, assumed he meant a warming hat for bedtime, accused him of being a ponce and a fight broke out. No harm done though Skink declared himself offended, walked off and is yet to return. Tench says he saw him board a boat at dawn.

Secretly couldn't give a monkey's mink. One less wage to pay and the rest can share his load between them. In fact, I should have fired the whingeing gibbon-dribble ages ago.

Skaramanger! By chance, I was back on track. Dextrose came here before me. I fancied I could sense his after-image. Was there fortitude and adventurism within me, which had previously lain dormant? Was there more to me than I had imagined?

Then it struck me: the book! Where was Dextrose's *Bible for the Inept Traveller*? And where, for that matter, was the rest of my stuff? Panic gripped me so hard that my head swam. My rucksack was still in Ogr's cart! The only belongings I had left were on me now. I felt sick.

Frantically, I stuffed hands into pockets. First out was my wallet – such sweet relief. I rifled through its contents: traveller's cheques, credit card, buckled passport, miscellaneous receipts – all useless, a spoof business card suggesting that my job title was 'International Stud' and two monochrome photographs, one depicting my parents standing stiffly, the other, more faded, of me as a bawling baby, aged perhaps six months – an item of sentimental value that I had rescued from Mother's belongings – and a Swiss army knife. I had never actually used my Swiss army knife but it had 15 blades and therefore potential.

Back pockets. Something book-shaped. *The Lost Incompetent: A Bible for the Inept Traveller*! I'd stuffed it into my back pocket without thinking. Dextrose's writings were the reason I was here; without them, I would have become a navigator without charts. More than that, I had a sense of the man whenever the book was near me. It sounds almost religious, which would be an exaggeration, but 15 years alone in a house can do things to the mind.

That was it for the belongings then: wallet, penknife, book. I felt out of my depth, gripped by the realisation that I was hundreds of miles from home, in peril and friendless. My mouth went dry.

A weak man would wish for his mother. I tried, but Mrs Mildred Grey was a timid woman who wore floral dresses with lacy collars and a forced smile. She was prone to tears and I once witnessed her crying when she had over-boiled Father's breakfast egg. Much use she would be out here. I stopped wishing for my mother and resolved to find strength from within.

Among the outskirts of Skaramanger, beside a block of run-down housing, the dwarf parked the truck, grinned at me and unhooked the stilts from his feet. "Meester Alexander carryeeng

Detritos," he said. "Ees beeg queek."

My heart sank. How was I to slip away unnoticed from someone who was clinging to my head?

We left the truck, the dwarf on my shoulders. He bent over my face until the stupid quiff tickled my nose, grinned once again and said, "Louis, sinkeeng zees begineeng off beautiful friend's hip."

He was a madman.

As we entered the narrow streets in this housing quarter, I became aware of a strange sensation, as if I were walking on air. I looked down. The streets were carpeted with thick-pile rugs. I had found them! This meant more to me than it should have done.

They were all majored in red or green, with motifs woven in. Some designs I recognised: poodles, penguins and crows, cast as omnipotent beings. Elsewhere were giant, naked humanoids, gods possibly, mostly with vegetables for heads.

"Queek!" snapped the dwarf, as I had stopped to gaze. The sightseeing was over.

Detritos said it was too dangerous to go to his house, because Russian Mafia, whose name was Borhed, knew where he lived and might seek revenge. But Skaramanger, as Dextrose had astutely pointed out in his book, comprises three bars, one general store and a post office, plus sparse housing and a theme park some ride away. So where to hide? Not the bars – too obvious – and one can only hole up in a general store or post office for so long without drawing attention to oneself. Then the dwarf spotted a flyer in Frartsian, taped to a wall.

"Haha!" he cackled. "Detritos showeeng."

I was directed past grey stone buildings with small darkened windows, flat tarmacked roofs spattered with the birdshit of ages, and imposing wooden doors, such as one might find on grander properties.

We stopped at one. From inside drifted sounds of women

nattering.

"Wimeen's Group!" announced the dwarf, clearly amused. "Borhed no sinkeeng look here!"

"But I'm not a woman!" I protested.

"He wanteeng die, or he wanteeng talk wimeen sings?"

It was a compelling argument.

Sheepishly I knocked while Detritos clambered down my back. A wizened crone in a woven dress with fur collar answered and ushered us into a spacious living room obscured in a haze of cigar smoke. The walls were carpeted, floor to ceiling, with rugs: further vegetable gods, poodles, penguins and crows, with one larger example on the far wall bearing an outline map of Emo Island (whose shape resembled a boomerang) and the English legend: 'Boyfrend Go Emo Island, Get Me Shit Rug'. Central was a solid square wooden table, with a grey-haired woman at each side.

"Hello ladee!" triumphed the dwarf.

Their table was cluttered with beer and ashtrays, and the fat stump of a stogey was clenched in the bulbous chop of each woman.

"Detritos!" they chorused, genuinely pleased to see him.

They chatted briefly in Frartsian, then Detritos introduced me.

"Oooh!' they said, all ogling.

They announced their names. All four of them were called Frihedhag. Since that was confusing, I mentally attached a nickname to each one.

There was the original Frihedhag, the crone who had answered the door – aged maybe 90, short and wiry, who looked as though miniature farmers had ploughed her face. I named her Original. Another was her identical twin, though who helpfully wore a neck-brace so wide that she was forced to stare down her nose and speak through gritted teeth. She, I called Neck-Brace.

Perhaps five years younger but no less haggard was the Frihedhag with the worst teeth. If Emo once had a dentist, he or she had died and crawled into this one's gob to decompose. She became Teeth.

And the fourth Frihedhag: probably mid-50s, so youthful by comparison but no beauty. Grease stains around her mouth suggested that she had binged on lard. Her head looked like a pig's trapped in a pink moon. Piggy Frihedhag.

I offered an embarrassed wave. The Frihedhags giggled like teenagers, hiding their mouths behind hands ravaged by scabs.

"Hello, I'm Alexander," I said, though they knew this already.

They were sisters, they explained in reasonable English. Frihedhag meant daughter of Frihed, which meant son of Fri. Neck-Brace had a great, great grand-daughter named Frihedhaghedhaghedhag, which they admitted was a mouthful. Then the conversation ran out.

The dwarf broke the awful silence. "Detritos goeeng. Meester Alexander safe weez ladee, yes?"

"Ooh yes, Detritos!" they chorused.

"Bye-bye!" he called to them with a wave. Then to me, "Comeeng back here! Comeeng back here, eenstall fuckeeng juke-bock!"

The door slammed shut.

"Ooh, I know it!" said Piggy.

"Sorry?" I asked awkwardly.

"I know it!" she repeated, as if I hadn't heard. "Detritos often speaks the lines from films. That one I know but cannot place!"

Teeth explained: "Detritos is not from here. He came two years ago from Green Golan, many miles away. He never says why, but we like him because he has thick hair and much laughter. When Detritos came, he spoke only Golanese, no

Frartsian and little English. So he spend time in Frartsi with teacher, to learn Frartsian, and he learn English by seeing film at Picture House of Daghaghaghed. This why many thing he say are from film!"

It made sense of sorts.

Piggy said, "Come, sit down. We like you also."

But there were only four chairs, each occupied, and no Frihedhag made a move to find another.

Sensing my confusion, Teeth said, "I am sorry, there are no more chairs. You choose one of our laps."

They all giggled, which would have been provocative had the Frihedhags not held the collective sex appeal of a hollowed-out turnip.

Hastily I chose Piggy's, as the most padded. She offered a knee and I sat. "Ooooh!" gasped the other three, eyeing her enviously.

Neck-Brace Frihedhag offered me ale, which I accepted, and a cigar, which I declined – pointlessly, it turned out, as the ale tasted of cigars. Then the Emo delicacy 'shoki pnti' ('surprise bread', one translated) was broken out, the surprise being that it boasted a baked insect inside a hollowed-out centre. Mine was a millipede, a blackened thing with legs, which I declined to eat, risking offence. I need not have worried; Piggy snatched it and wolfed down its lengthy grossness with gusto.

The Frihedhags wanted to know where I came from and why I was here, my every tale being greeted with a chorus of "Ooohs". I explained about Harrison Dextrose and Original had hazy recollections of his visit some years back.

"He had red face and too much beard. Either he was asleep in bar or tell stories of bravery."

That'll be him, I thought.

None of the sisters had visited Britain, but had impressions of the place from travellers. They asked after Roger Moore.

James Bond, the Frihedhags explained, is an icon and hero to many Emo Islanders, for whom film is the primary escapism (English is taught in school here, purely so the natives can indulge their passion unsubtitled). As Dextrose had written, Skaramanger was indeed renamed after the celebrated villain.

Remembering manners, I asked after them. Each sister was a part-time rug-maker, their wares exported to neighbouring countries (though not to the neighbouring Frartsians, who considered rugs to be an unnecessary luxury).

Both Original and her twin Neck-Brace were married to the same man, Blog, monogamy being frowned upon because infertility was common.

Each twin had a daughter – both named Bloghag – who were grown up with children of their own (Blohhaghags and Bloghagheds).

Piggy had never married, and no one could understand why. Teeth, however, wedded Nob, a fisherman. He died in a trawling disaster. They had two sons, both Nobheds, whom no one liked.

Desperate to stop them talking about relationships, I mentioned the story of Borhed and his creeps, to much sympathetic head-shaking.

"Borhed is most evil," Original Frihedhag said.

"Emo's inhabitants are peace-loving and respectful of others. If there is a crime on the island, there can be only one man behind it," she continued. Smuggling, extortion, GBH, burglary, arson, fraud... Over the years, Borhed had apparently accumulated a band of ne'er-do-well followers, lured through loot.

The one-man justice department, there having not been much call for policing, was Sheriff Gmi. Some years back, while attempting to bring Borhed to trial, he had been murdered. Afterwards, the murder weapon had been found in Borhed's pocket and he had gone around in a t-shirt bearing the legend,

'I KILLED GMI'. However, with the sheriff dead, no one could get the charges to stick.

As a result, the Emo Islanders put up with Borhed because no one was prepared to raise their head above the parapet, lest he lopped it off.

"What made him so evil?" I asked.

"Borhed was abused as child," Original explained.

"One time," added Teeth, "when Borhed parents were cold and there was no wood for fire, they chop off Borhed legs as fuel. After this, he is bitter."

"Oh my God!" I almost felt pity for the man.

"Do not feel pity for Borhed," said Original. "He then chop off our father's legs to use as his own."

"Borhed himself attacked last week with axe and chain, taking chunk from bosom of our youngest sister. Show him!" urged Teeth.

"Actually, I'm squeamish!"

"He is shy," said Teeth.

"I like him," said Piggy.

"I like him more," said Teeth.

"My pubic hair fell out," announced Neck-Brace. "Yet my facial hair still blooms."

"This happened to me, too!" Original declared. "We are of certain age. Our bodies think maybe musty scent of our sex parts no longer needed…"

The Frihedhags gazed at me lasciviously.

Without warning, there came an almighty crash, the front door split open, and there was the towering, black-suited Borhed, backed by henchfellows. Tales of geriatric sexual conquests suddenly seemed appealing.

"Grat smnki, Frihedhags!" thundered Borhed.

The sisters stood up, defiant. Piggy hurled me into a corner, away from danger, where I cowered, happy to let the old women protect me.

"Dg nbitz, Borhed!" screeched Original, fists clenched. Yet she was a decrepit-looking thing and under-nourished – this would surely be a brief, one-sided confrontation.

Borhed and his dozen thugs adopted menacing poses. Original Frihedhag quickly span on one foot, launching the other into Borhed's face. No sign of arthritis there. Her victim staggered backwards, nose and lip split open, hand flailing for the wounded cakehole.

What followed was like a blurred fight scene from a Kung Fu movie, in which nimble types (the Frihedhags, somehow) take on multiple opponents who are lame-brained and often disorganised.

These women knew how to handle themselves. Even Piggy exuded a certain grace when flying through mid-air.

However, in Kung Fu movies the multiple opponents do occasionally win, due to sheer numbers, as proved to be the case here.

The last Frihedhag to go down, pinned beneath several assailants like her sisters, was Teeth – though not before she had removed one man's eyeball with a bare hand and rolled it along the floor to trip another, who fell backwards into two other attackers, who fell backwards into a further three, and like bowling pins they tumbled.

When everywhere was piled humanity and heavy breathing, Borhed turned to me with a sneer.

What to do? I felt for the Swiss Army knife in my pocket and found it. But what chance would I have against all these men? Come to think of it, what chance would I have had against just one of their grandmothers?

"You think escape me here, fool?" taunted Borhed. "When spies are all over? You hide among old women, let them fight for you! I spit in your direction!" He did so but missed. Borhed wasn't a terribly accurate spitter. Wishing to appease him, I scraped up some of the phlegm with a finger and wiped it on my fleece.

"He disgust me!" Borhed thundered. "Take him!"

I was set upon, bound, and a sack tied over my head.

"Now come with us, snake!" cackled Borhed.

I was then hit over the head with something blunt and heavy.

Never trust a native. That is my golden rule, which has seen me through three decades of exploration. If someone offers hospitality, I ask them, "Why?" What is in it for them? I have never offered unconditional kindness and I do not expect to receive it.

Backstabbers wear politicians' faces. Heed this tale of my encounter with the Mortivika tribe, during my first expedition to the Parrish Isles.

I was green in those days, and close-shaven. Caribou Tench and I arrived on one sun-soaked beach of the Parrish Isles aboard a chartered vessel and were greeted by grinning gushers the colour of burnished walnut, wearing beads and nought else.

Tench communicated with them using hand signals and drawings in the sand. They seemed friendly and helped offload our supplies before taking us to their village among trees, where they implored that we tarry the night. We saw no reason not to.

Come evening, when the cold came, we shared their campfire and their local brew, a fearsome blend, swapping long-winded tales of derring-do.

I wondered aloud why there were no women present. Tench enquired and was told that the genders did not mix on a Thursday.

I was young, unused to alcohol's demons, and I blanche now to recall that I passed out. When I woke, I knew instinctively that something was missing.

Tench, a dab hand at rudimentary medical procedure, offered his prognosis. The previous night, he said, someone – possibly more than one person – had stolen my dignity.

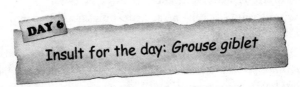

My pounding headache threatened to crack an eyebrow. I was in a darkened, chill room, legs bound, arms tied behind my back, lain against hard stone. I could make out looming inanimate shapes and walls. The room was small. Inside was eerie silence, but from the outside came a strange muffled, repeated sound, like kazoos played at random.

A wave of loneliness and self-pity overcame me. What was happening? Were my travels to end here, in confinement? Or worse? It didn't bear thinking about. Nothing this disturbing had ever happened to Harrison Dextrose. I began to sob.

"Bngi?" said a weak, weasely voice from the shadows.

"Hello?" I replied, with sudden hope. A friend?

"Bngi?" repeated the voice.

"I'm not Bngi," I said.

"Eh?" said the voice.

"I am Alexander. Who are you?"

"Eh?" said the voice.

"Alex-ander. From Eng-land. Who are you?"

"Eh?"

"What is your name?"

"Eh?"

"WHAT'S YOUR NAME?"

Someone outside hammered on a door to our dungeon and shouted in Frartsian.

Shuffling painfully sideways, I edged towards the voice, my sole source of hope. "My name is Gydi, I cannot hear," it said, "for I am old and my ears are broken."

Great, I thought. How does one conspire secretively with a person who is hard of hearing?

"Where are we?" I asked, as loudly as I dared.

"Eh?" replied Gydi.

I edged closer. "Where are we?"

"I am old and my ears are broken."

Giving up any attempt at communication over small distances, I continued the tortuous shuffle around the room, knuckles grazing on concrete floor, until I had sidled far enough that our arms touched. My fellow prisoner felt clammy and smelled of wee.

"Where are we?" I repeated.

"I am old and my ears are broken," said Gydi.

I exploded in frustration. This was no potential great-escape committee but an ancient, urine-sodden muppet. "I KNOW!"

Keys rattled, the door was flung open and artificial light flooded in, hampered only by the substantial figure of our guard. While he bellowed something menacing, I glanced sharpishly about me: a rusted iron tank the size of a garden shed, a giant engine-type contraption, thick pipework and gauges. I turned to see Gydi and instinctively shrank away. The man looked like Merlin the magician after years of persistent attack by moths. His hair was grey and everywhere, and his drooped face might soon have dripped into his chest and been lost forever.

The once-muffled kazoo noise now pestered my ears and... what was that behind the guard? It looked like a penguin suspended in mid-air. Wait, it *was* a penguin suspended in mid-air. Of course! The racket was supposed to imitate the birds calling. So this was the deceased-penguin theme park on the outskirts of Skaramanger, of which Dextrose had written. I had

67

been brought here by Borhed and imprisoned in some kind of pump room!

Which was no reason to get excited.

Some hours passed while I sat in the darkened pump room, now secured to piping opposite Gydi to stop us conspiring. The irony was not lost on me. Short of being supplied with megaphone and ear trumpet, we would make a poor debating team.

I tried to recall Dextrose's writings on the theme park, wondering if there might be some back exit mentioned, but nothing workable came of these mental exertions. I did at least recall the origins of the place.

Emo Island had once been snowbound for eleven months of the year. Summer, in July, had been just bastard cold. Then, some half-a-century ago, during what should have been the height of winter, the snow melted. There remained a nip in the air, though not enough to comfort the resident penguin population.

The Indian summer became an Indian decade. The penguins died. Since the islanders considered the birds to be worshipful beasts, they refrained from consuming the carcasses.

Instead, the Emo Islanders stuffed the birds and set them into a theme park as a tribute.

Author's note: In all my travels, I had never encountered a bigger bunch of mackerel-snappers. Mink to the lot of them.

A commotion began outside, sounding like some kind of a celebration. A key turned in a lock, the door once again swung open, and Borhed himself appeared, grinning widely. He stood in the doorway, unnervingly muscular arms folded at his chest, his sunken eyes so lost in the shadows that they might have been merely skeletal sockets. I imagined the Frihedhags' father's legs, turning to mould inside the villain's trousers, and shuddered.

"So, friend!" he declared, clearly insincere. "I bring you outside, show how other friends desert you!"

To Gydi, much less fake-jocularly, he shouted something Frartsian.

"Mn nski n'mnt rkni grtti," replied Gydi.

Borhed slapped him across the face.

I found new sympathy for the frail old goat. "Hoi!" I blurted out in a schoolboy voice, instantly wishing that I hadn't.

Borhed hobbled across – the brutally stolen legs seemed to be failing him. His evil eyes bore into me.

"Hoi?" he thundered, showering spittle. "Hoi? You tell me this!"

I kept wisely silent, quivering inwardly.

"This old fool, he owes money!" screamed Borhed, at such volume that even Gydi must have heard. "I chain him until he pay."

How then was Gydi expected to hand over the debt? Still, no sense in pointing out this flaw in an otherwise perfectly maniacal plan.

Borhed freed me from the pipework and, feet still tied, hefted me over a shoulder fireman-style. A wave of nausea flowed through my body, returning a mouthful of bile that dribbled down Borhed's back.

I was propped against the wall of the box office, affording my first view of Emo Island's famed deceased-penguin theme park... although these were not the circumstances under which I had intended to visit.

It was a rather beautiful structure, unlike the functional Emo architecture I had previously witnessed. In the centre, a vast ice-blue pool of water, bounded by shapely curves. Above, a curved ceiling of wooden white-painted planking, inset with hundreds of lightbulbs, each giving off a faint glow. As a celestial dome, it was most beguiling.

The *pièce de résistance*, however, was the penguins.

There were maybe 100 of the creatures, stuffed and posed, as if captured in a photograph. Some had been gathered in groups at the pool's edge; others floated inside it; some were caught in mid-leap towards the water, suspended by nylon from the roof; while others – artistic licence employed – swooped down from the ceiling as if part of an RAF attack squadron. All the while, the penguin-noise chattered over loudspeakers set around the walls. The scene was impressive. And I had got in for free.

"You!" shouted Borhed, interrupting my reverie.

He and several cronies were gathered around a large wooden crate, grinning like youths who have hatched a plan.

"Have present from Frihedhags!" he declared.

So my libidinous protectors were still alive. A glimmer of hope.

"Listen, I read," continued Borhed. "'Dear Borhed. It mistake fight you. We wish no more. Here gift, say sorry. Please burn Britain boy. Love, Frihedhags.'"

The lid was levered off with a crowbar and the crate tipped onto one side. Out rolled a large wooden hobbyhorse on wheels, with a barrel belly, plank legs and crudely carved head. Borhed looked confused.

Much muttering went on until Borhed let out a roar of laughter and, being easily led morons, the underlings followed suit. The maniac then mounted the wooden steed and raised a fist in triumph.

"I am perhaps King!" he announced.

Any king riding into battle on a horse so fantastically undersized could only hope that his enemies might die laughing. Again, though, I decided against pointing this out.

"So, snake," he said. "What do with you?"

"Perhaps…" I began, but was too scared to finish the sentence.

"Hahahaha!" guffawed Borhed, not really laughing. "I like your spirits. But already I plan death!"

A hand squeezed my heart.

He snapped his fingers and a minion scuttled forward, carting a cardboard box that was placed at Borhed's feet.

"The next day," bellowed Borhed, "we play Insect Race To Death!"

I had never heard of it.

"If you lose, you die!"

I chanced an arm. "And if I win?"

The option did not seem to have crossed his mind, so he stopped to ponder it, massaging his giant moustache. Finally, he announced, "You win, you go!" This caused mutinous mutters. "I say this," he added, pausing for effect, "because you not win!"

How everyone laughed.

Borhed extracted seven jars from the box. In each nestled a repellent creature, all larger and more menacing than their British equivalent: earwig, cockroach, centipede, millipede, dung beetle, woodlouse and a large black thing I failed to identify, involving multiple legs, shiny carapace and twin claws. Had he been cross-breeding his cockroaches with crabs? I would not have put it past him.

"You choose one, I take rest," my captor explained, picking out the millipede and stroking it like a favourite pet. "Which one you think most quick?" he sneered. "Pick right, snake! Hahahahaha!"

The need for crucial decision-making elbowed aside my fear. But I was buggered if I knew. The tortoise and the hare were celebrated rivals, and the outcome of their race well-documented. Sadly, Aesop had failed to write a fable entitled *The Earwig and the Dung Beetle*.

Was this, I wondered, what it took to achieve copulation with Suzy Goodenough? Just six days into my ideally 24-day journey and already I was required to cling to life through an intimate knowledge of insects.

I was thrown back into the pump room and chained next to acrid Gydi. My situation was dire. What I knew of entomology could be written on the back of a passing ant. Even if, by some fluke, I picked the fastest insect, there was no guarantee that I might be allowed to live.

Still I had to try, and I clung to mentally preparing for the race, rather than fearing its consequences.

I recapped the field – earwig, cockroach, centipede, millipede, dung beetle, woodlouse, large black thing with claws – and tried to be scientific. (Having failed O-level Biology, the omens were not good.)

Was number of legs directly proportional to speed? If so, the millipede had the race sewn up, with the centipede an obvious second. But carting about all those legs must be cumbersome, and the co-ordination required monumental. Humans have enough difficulty learning to walk on two legs; imagine the problems of the toddler millipede.

Then the earwig. What was that awful pincer thing at the back? To make it look more horrific... or, to act as a spoiler? An intriguing proposition.

Cockroaches. Eugh. And there my knowledge of these creatures ended.

Dung beetle. I was likewise in the dark, though one could make assumptions about potential fitness from a cursory analysis of lifestyle and dietary habit. The dung beetle ate shit. Shit was waste – all that unwanted overmatter after the goodness had been absorbed. Therefore there was no nutritional value in shit. The dung beetle stood no chance.

Woodlouse. Impossible to determine, since it hid its legs. There might be tens of the things, or hundreds. Was that weird outer shell aerodynamic? I imagined launching one like a paper dart, this mental experiment resulting in the woodlouse plummeting to earth. However... if one could be encouraged to roll into a ball, then flicked... possible race winner!

But what of the large black thing with claws? Definitely an unknown sprint quantity. Perhaps a ringer?

My conclusion: pick any entrant, bar the dung beetle, based on various assumptions that may or may not be correct.

It was hopeless. I sighed the juddering sigh of the condemned.

"What wrong?" whispered Gydi.

"Hnn?" I replied, stung by his sudden lucidity.

"What wrong?" he repeated.

"Can you hear me?" I asked, taken aback.

"For sure."

"You git," I said, more loudly.

"Shhhhhh!" he spat, suddenly animated.

So Gydi could hear. My banged-up, stained colleague had been faking it all along. But why? Did he have a cunning plan?

"Why didn't you tell me you could hear?"

"How know trust? Maybe you are with Borhed – a flower?"

"Plant."

"A plant. But then help Gydi from Borhed, so maybe trust."

"But *why* do you pretend not to hear?"

"I tell. When Borhed and men come, Gydi make play not hear. Is trick – like your James Bond!" He hummed the Bond theme tune. "But then it not help, make play not hear, but late now. If now Gydi tell, Borhed make play, maybe kill."

"You might have been able to talk your way out of this!"

Gydi's chapped, bloodless lips curled downwards. "Am I old

and stupid?"

"Do bears shit in the woods?"

"I not know. What is bear?"

Gydi told me the tale of his incarceration.

Borhed, besides his many other criminal activities, illegally sold starlings on the black market. (The birds, when roasted, are considered delicious on Emo Island but may only be shot by licensed hunters.) Gydi had ordered a dozen of the birds through a contact of Borhed's at market; however, when the birds arrived he found them to be crudely dyed pigeons, coloured to look like starlings. So the invoice went unpaid.

An outraged Borhed had visited Gydi in person, when our hero had the bright idea of feigning deafness. Getting nowhere with the old duffer, Borhed had suggested physical violence and Gydi, being less unhealthy back then, raised his fists, challenging the bully to a fight.

Borhed then sent in three of his burliest henchmen, who kicked the crap out of our champion of consumer rights. Feeling doubly cheated, and being a man of principles, Gydi refused point blank to cough up the cash. The rest is history. Ancient history, by the look of my companion.

A guard entered, bearing food. "Who speak?" he demanded.

"The rats," I replied, not thinking the excuse through.

"OK," he said, only slightly distrustingly.

He released mine and Gydi's left arms and handed out plates of lumpy food, which we balanced on our laps.

Happily, when the door shut and gloom descended, we were unable to see what we were eating. It tasted like rancid banana mush, but I was starving and wolfed down the lot.

The old man elbowed me gently. "What Borhed plan?"

Incredibly, I had forgotten all about tomorrow's race, which I explained to him, along with my dire chances of winning. Gydi chuckled and, with the free hand coated in gruel, squeezed my thigh.

"Gydi help!" he declared.

I was prepared to clutch at any straw.

He went on, "When Borhed take you out, two guard come in for smoke. They talk of race, not know Gydi hear. Say dung beetle most slow, every person know this. So Borhed play trick – not let beetle eat shit. Feed only salad leaf and low-fat cheese."

"My God!"

"So dung beetle win!"

Were we not chained down we would have danced a jig of delight.

Hours passed while I was too tense to sleep, until finally Gydi and I were unshackled and led outside. This was a rare treat for my companion who had earlier revealed that he had not stepped outside his prison since one Christmas several years previously. Borhed and his henchmen had been plastered at the time, so were unnaturally generous. One of the henchmen had dressed as Santa Claus – here, known as 'Partli Portli' – and, to Gydi's delight, had presented him with a stocking. Childlike glee overcoming his usual suspicion, the old man had reached inside and retrieved a vicious mousetrap that had taken off three fingertips, much to his tormentors' amusement.

I had tried to blank my mind of the cursed race. Though I knew the supposed winner, I was also aware that there could be no certainties in insect racing. I merely had the upper hand.

What if the unidentified large black thing with claws was indeed a ringer? What if the dung beetle sustained an injury? What if it didn't even realise it was in a race? The starting whistle would go, and the dung beetle might settle down for a snooze…

Gydi did his best to cheer me up with matey nudges, but my nerves were in tatters.

Borhed and a dozen morons, waving sticks and spears, had

76

gathered under the starry dome of the theme park, tense and excitable. A crude racetrack had been fashioned from strips of wood, forming seven lanes of perhaps ten metres, each with a jar containing the respective insect at one end.

Borhed himself sat astride the ridiculous hobbyhorse, playing king, his dark attire capped with a robe of bleached-white poodle-wool. To his left was a pile of firewood, an Alexander-length stake protruding from its core. Behind me lay the chill blue pool. All around us was a silent, unseeing audience of penguins, their faked chatter ringing in our ears.

My blood ran cold. This, somehow, was for real. I might endure a terrible death. Bravely, I fainted.

I came to at Borhed's feet. My hands and feet had been untied, though my arms and legs would not move through numbness. My head swam and my pulse pounded in my temples. Everything went red. I understood pure terror.

Borhed looked across at Gydi, slumped against a wall, and called to him in. Frartsian, "Mnsk trgi glot hnki pnki spin ragni!"

Everyone cheered.

"Mn nski n'mnt rkni grtti," countered Gydi.

"I tell your friend," Borhed explained to me, "that today you die! He reply, he old and ears not work."

My voice would not work, and my face had become its own death mask.

"So," he continued. "Which insect to choose? Think good!"

He laughed a belly laugh. Everyone followed suit.

A hand grasping each shoulder, all seven feet of Borhed hoisted me off the ground and carried me towards the racetrack. We gazed down at it. Each insect was attempting uselessly to rear out of its glass prison, except the dung beetle, which looked to be either dozing or dead.

Doubt confused my mind.

"Choose now, snake," ordered Borhed.

What had Gydi and I agreed? I couldn't remember. My brain refused to function. Oh sweet Jesus. My bowels rumbled like thunder, and it reminded me…

"The dung beetle!" I exclaimed.

"No!" snapped Borhed. "Choose again!"

The oaf's patent panic shifted the power base. Confidence caressed my nerves. "The dung beetle," I repeated calmly.

"No!" responded Borhed, his gang now strangely quiet.

"Yes," I said.

Borhed thought. For frozen seconds the echoing penguin calls were the only sound. Eventually, he said, simply, "OK." Was he up to something?

Preparations were made for the race. Seven shadowy minions came forward, each to kneel behind a lane of the track holding an insect jar. Borhed sat beside me on the toy horse, an arm around my shoulders like some malevolent gameshow host. When he blew a whistle, the jar-lids would be uncapped and the creatures released to scuttle along their trackways.

"Insect Race to Death!" announced Borhed. In the artificial half-light, his gang thumped sticks and spears against the floor.

A terrible tension overcame me.

"Now!" Borhed boomed in my ear. "We put you out of mystery!"

"Misery," I mumbled under my breath.

"On tree!" he called to the seven keepers of the jars. "One! Two! Tree!"

The whistle emitted its harsh shriek.

Off came six lids, out dropped six eccentrically limbed creatures. However, the seventh lid, retaining the now-frantic dung beetle, remained firmly in place, its filthy keeper a picture of cartoon innocence.

"Hoi!" I yelled.

"Hahahahahahaha!" laughed Borhed, throwing back his big head.

The unidentified black thing with claws had tumbled onto its back and was trying desperately to right itself, legs flailing in thin air.

The woodlouse, rather than travel forwards, had scuttled sideways and was attempting to scale the wall of its lane.

The earwig seemed to be having a scrap with itself, curled into a writhing ball of shiny undesirability.

Both millipede and centipede were striking out at an amble, the latter having the early advantage.

It was the cockroach that was winning, making methodical tracks towards the finish line.

"Let the beetle go!" I screamed. *"Let the beetle go!"*

Borhed laughed. The lid remained in place.

"You cheat! He's cheating!" I pointed out, as if anyone would care.

But one person did. Gydi came running towards us, hands behind his back, head craned forward, hair billowing behind him like a tattered windsock. This once hunched tangle of grey stopped before the racetrack and, although his spinal column protested, stood tall to cry out: "Let go beetle!"

The booming command seemed disembodied from the wasted human that issued it. Such was the shock of Gydi's dramatic transformation that the jar keeper obeyed.

"You!" Borhed yelled at Gydi. "Stop it!"

"No!" replied the wizened one.

"Take him!" Borhed screamed.

Within moments, Gydi disappeared beneath underlings, punched and kicked then dragged to one side. "I kill soon!" Borhed called after Gydi's once again defeated form.

Back at the racetrack the woodlouse had gone AWOL, scuttling across the floor and straight into the pool, where it floated, floundering.

The centipede, meanwhile, had crawled over its barrier into the millipede's lane where the couple seemed to be engaged in coitus.

The large black thing with claws remained on its back, having given up the struggle to turn over, and was staring at the ceiling, indulging in a moment of introspection.

The earwig had stopped fighting with itself and stood, exhausted, wondering where it was and why it was there.

However, the cockroach had continued its inexorable journey and was now just a couple of metres from its goal.

The dung beetle was a revelation. It zipped up its lane like a streak of black, already overtaking the cockroach. Unhappily, though, this exertion had substantially tired (or perhaps bored) it and, although tantalisingly close to the finishing line, it was now horribly stationary. The cockroach drew level. In response the dung beetle got back up and pottered forwards.

Neck-and-neck, centimetre-by-centimetre, the repulsive foes inched towards their target until, half-a-metre from the line, my beetle stopped again. Either it had given up the ghost or was having another rest. It was impossible to tell on a face so small. On went the cockroach, painfully slowly but with reserves of stamina that the beetle seemingly could not match.

"Run! Bloody *run*!" I urged, waving my arms like a madman. Beside me, Borhed watched smugly.

The cockroach came within an inch of the finishing line. Then it too stopped!

"Now's your chance! Go! *Go!*" I pleaded at volume. Something, not my exhortations I imagined, roused the insect from its inaction. Off it went.

Down on the line the dung beetle bore. Off his wooden hobbyhorse Borhed hopped, and strode across to the racetrack. Just as the beetle was about to claim victory, he trod on it with Pa Frihedhag's stolen foot, twisting and grinding a toecap into its body.

Where once raced a hero, now lay reddy-black mush. With a mutter, Borhed nudged the cockroach over the line.

Odd, but I swore I could hear a muffled thumping and cursing.

"Haha!" taunted Borhed, childishly pointing. "You lose!"

His followers broke into an ecstatic applause.

I *did* hear a muffled thumping and cursing. Coming from the wooden hobbyhorse.

"Now you burn!" thundered Borhed.

But I was no longer paying attention to the process of my demise. Someone was inside the horse, banging about. I caught a phrase: "Fuckeeng Frihedhag!"

"Hey, snake!" called out Borhed, but puzzled.

An eerie hush descended upon the crowd. Something was wrong.

A burst of machine gun fire shattered the silence, blasting holes in the side of the wooden horse. The upper half of its barrel belly swung upwards and up popped the dwarf Detritos, clutching an Uzi.

He glanced at me, grinning insanely. "Frihedhag lockeeng outside!"

Standing upright in the horse the dwarf span, spraying automatic fire into Borhed's gang. Armed merely with pointy sticks and tiny minds, they stood no chance. Feckless, they tumbled. Not one mounted any sort of challenge; they just fell.

I dived for cover, ending up in Gydi's lap, which was no place for a person with a working nose.

So came the showdown. Detritos turned to face Borhed, still at the racetrack, and levelled the Uzi. Borhed remained impassive.

"Go, Detritos," he taunted. "Shoot Borhed." (All deranged megalomaniacs refer to themselves in the third person.)

Wordlessly, without emotion, the dwarf pulled the trigger.

Nothing happened. His expression of cocky superiority turned to one of confusion.

"Fuckeeng gun," he muttered, shaking the thing as if that might mend it.

"Not worry," said Borhed. "I count bullet. All away, small person!" A sickly grin split his face.

Slowly, with considerable menace, he reached into an inside pocket of his tattered black suit and withdrew an ancient flintlock pistol. He aimed it at Detritos, cocking the weapon.

The dwarf was helpless. Though Borhed had but one shot, it would take Detritos a good while to reach him on those legs, by which time he would be dead. A gnawing sense of debt and honour invaded me. I had to help the dwarf, and instantly.

My Swiss army knife! No one had thought to rifle through my pockets upon capture, because they were all more stupid than a pork pie. With my hands bound, I had been unable to retrieve it – no longer! Though the cumbersome weapon was hardly weighted for throwing, it did allow for attack from a reassuring distance. It would show willing.

Fumbling and panicked, I retrieved the knife from a back pocket, tugged open the main blade with a thumbnail and in one arcing movement of the right arm, tossed it all too eagerly in Borhed's direction.

My quarry, spotting this out of the corner of an eye, swivelled to watch with evident amusement as the knife tumbled pathetically upwards, on a trajectory that would take it way over his head.

Myself, Borhed, Gydi and Detritos looked on in wonder as the Swiss army knife made its ungainly way roofwards, where by some incredible fluke it severed the aged string holding up one of the dive-bombing stuffed penguins, which, free of its restraint, dropped like a Stuka, to land beak-first between Borhed's deep-set eyes.

Time stood still as the hulking sadist tried to take in the

situation, mortal terror etched into his features, as indeed was the penguin.

With almighty tenacity, Borhed raised a giant hand and, as the wounded cowboy wrenches the arrow from his leg, plucked the penguin from his forehead.

An impressive spray of blood shot out from the resulting hole, landing just before my feet and flecking my trousers.

Borhed, squealing like a stuck pig, dropped to his knees. Though blood careened down his face, forming a ghastly mask, life having all but deserted him, he shot me a haunted, defiant look of pure hatred. Then he toppled forwards, dead.

"Man defineet haff corncob up ass," noted Detritos.

In that moment, the hours of deathly tension were spirited away. It was over. Borhed, murderer, sadist, psychotic, starling smuggler, was dead. Good riddance.

Numb yet elated I rose, wandered across to the lifeless form and kicked it disdainfully. My foot connected with Borhed's left leg, which shot out of his trousers. Pa Frihedhags' limb, stiffened with a wooden pole strapped around the decayed flesh, pivoted at the knee, skittered across the stone floor and slid into the pool, where it floated serenely towards freedom.

We three survivors trod wearily to Detritos's abode in Skaramanger, a half hour's journey, while night set in. The dwarf's place was not unlike the Frihedhags', only filled with weapons rather than rugs, and involving shorter furniture.

I dropped immediately onto the living room sofa and became immersed in intense slumber.

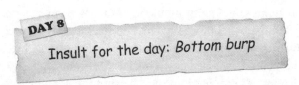

It was early afternoon when Detritos nudged me awake, bearing food.

"I luff heem, Jack," he said.

Propped on a stool at his kitchen table, I feasted on bread and boiled cabbage, which stank like the contents of a bin. Detritos sat silently opposite me, greased quiff matted by sleep, dribble on chin, head in hands, staring dreamily.

He had saved my life, but then I had saved his. He seemed enamoured of this bravery.

"Where's Gydi?" I asked, anxious to stop him simpering.

"Gydi go," said Detritos. "Sinkeeng wife forget heem."

He handed me a note. It read: '*Man. (Not no naym. Sore.) Fank u. Gydi go. Gydi.*'

The old man had played his part, too, and might have paid with his life. I became lost in an affectionate respect for the occasionally friendly foreigner. Detritos caught me staring thus and gazed at me in kind.

Shortly, he was hugging my right leg.

"Makeeng hornee, babee?" he leered.

"No, you're bloody not!" I exclaimed. But I was curious about something. "Why did you risk your life to save me?"

He shrugged. "Mdra askeeng."

"You know Mdra?" I spluttered.

"Yes."

"How?"

"Friend."

"How?"

"Mdra show speakeeng Frartsi."

"So you know her well?"

"Mdra sayeeng, 'Detritos like son'."

It returned to me in a flash: the childish portrait in Mdra's hallway of the short fellow, whom I had imagined to be her son. Detritos! So they were friends. As I rode with Ogr, Mdra must have contacted the dwarf, knowing Emo Island to be potentially perilous, and had asked him to ensure my safety. It would explain why he had been at the exit of the Unknown Tunnel, yet unconnected with Borhed. And when I was captured, he must have conspired with the Frihedhags to plan my release. It was only unfortunate that they had locked him inside the horse.

It was all starting to make sense.

It is during our second full day on Emo Island – our sixth on the Dextrosian Quest – that crewman Shark arrives in Paphed's Bar with mucous dribbling from his eyes, and hustles myself and Tench into a corner away from minking earwiggers. I have not seen him so excited since the repeal of the licensing laws on Puritania in '66.

He had been woken up, he claims, by the Lord himself, with halo, entering his quarters. This vision had told him: "The grail! The grail! Is here by the quarry!"

I mock the simpkin mercilessly. Even Tench, a sensitive minker, is given to join in. Shark has rum for blood and has hallucinated in the past, but he is convinced that the message is kosher and spells fame and fortune for us all.

Of course I am not one for ostentatious display or global renown – discovery is its own reward – but he is so insistent that I begin to take him seriously and we call for fresh ale and a potato juice for Tench.

We fathom a handsome way to test the authenticity of Shark's burbling: is there actually a quarry on the island? If not, we can rib Shark some more and force him to undertake the Seventh Dare.

It is decided that Tench, who has a smattering of most lingos, should ask the barmaid. Minked if she says there is a quarry, now disused, just north of Skaramanger.

Shark shakes me until my upper dentures come loose and I am forced to cuff the over-eager dipswill. But I admit that I am becoming intrigued. If I'm able to find the Holy Grail, which has eluded the greatest adventurers for centuries, it would be the most important discovery in history. I, Harrison Dextrose, would be responsible and could with modesty allow myself the resulting celebrity.

Shark finds shovels but Tench, ever the sceptical mink, refuses to help. "Shark speak with fat tongue," he ninnies.

"Mink him," I say, so the two of us set off.

We find the quarry easily. It is well signposted and the Frartsian for 'Quarry' is 'Qri'. It looks manageable enough in diameter and depth, chalky with ingrowing plants, and half-surrounded by bush.

It occurs to us then that we do not know what the Holy Grail looks like – history books are not my forte, since I prefer to make history. Shark suggests that it would be ornamental. Knowing that it would be more functional than that I overrule him and we agree to search for crockery or storage jars, and split up to double the eyes.

It is tiring work, beating aside minking bushes. I find a handful of discarded tools and a cracked green pot that excites me, until I notice a date stamped underneath that is significantly after the start of the first millennium.

We abandon the hunt at nightfall, having forgotten to pack torches in our haste. My fervency has diminished and I am given again to doubting Shark's reliability.

When we return to Paphed's Bar, Tench is sitting where we left him, looking smug. He asks us to go to Shark's quarters at Naghag's guesthouse, which we do after ales.

Tench rings the bell at reception. An old woman appears wearing well-established facial hair and a white hat, at which Shark drops to his knees, calling out, "Lord! Lord! You have returned!"

Smelling a rat, I kick the minking mouse's gurnard and he falls forward snivelling.

Tench explains that she is the washerwoman. He had questioned her earlier and gathered that when she entered Shark's room that morning, she had said, "Ygrjl! Ygrjl!...S'yrbi, kwr'i!", which is Frartsian for "Laundry! Laundry!... Sod that, he smells!"

Author's note: I did not enjoy being made to look foolish, least of all by Tench, but I recounted the story for two reasons: it shows that I am only human; and because Shark, when he reads this (if he ever learns to read), will understand why I docked him three months' wages.

So here I was, already lagging behind Dextrose, who had left Skaramanger in a hurry on the morning of his seventh day, bound for Klütz in Klükamüs aboard the Dextrose I. Of course, the esteemed explorer had had neither Mahaffey nor Borhed to contend with.

In order to claim Suzy Goodenough's prize, I was required to beat Dextrose to Aghanasp. At this early stage in the Quest, all was not despair. Having lost crewman Skink to sulking, Dextrose's sea journey had been under-manned. If I could charter an efficiently crewed vessel at once, I might be able to make up the lost time.

I thought of Suzy and imagined myself locked into her hero-worshipping embrace.

It was time to leave Emo Island. I should inform Detritos, the leering pervert, immediately. Our acquaintance was reaching its natural conclusion.

The dwarf was still clinging to my leg, begging me to stay, as I dragged him across the floor to answer the knock at his door. It was Original Frihedhag, bearing gifts.

"These for you," she said, handing over piled clothes, "for kill Borhed."

The Frihedhags had obviously been knitting furiously. They gave me woollen jumpers and cardigans, woollen shirts, even woollen trousers, each with a repeated motif: penguins, cabbages, that sort of thing.

"Gosh," I faltered. "Thank you very much."

"He goeeng!" came Detritos's strangled squeal.

"Oh, hello, Detritos," said Original, having not noticed him down there.

"Meester Alexander goeeng!" squealed Detritos again.

Original looked up at me. "Are you leaving, Alexander?"

"Yes, I have to go, I'm afraid. I'm well behind schedule already. Sorry."

The Frihedhag, in her woven dress with her lined face and puckered lips, looked crestfallen. The dwarf, still clinging to my ankle, seemed about to burst into tears. Why on earth did these people care about me? I knew myself far better than they did, and I could barely be bothered.

"Lookeeng daddee!" implored Detritos. "Teacher say eef bell reeng, angel, getteeng weengs."

"Right," I said. "I have to go."

Original took my hand in her far bonier version and smiled as pensioners do. "Alexander," she said, "if you must leave tomorrow, this evening we have party for you."

I hadn't said anything about 'tomorrow'.

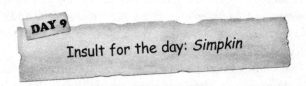

DAY 9

Insult for the day: *Simpkin*

The blanket wrapped around my arm seemed oddly clammy. Willing open my left eye – the right being otherwise engaged, playing host to a thumping drumbeat – I spied the comatose form of Piggy Frihedhag in adjacent slumber, and realised that my limb had in fact become trapped between her buttocks.

I should have whipped it away with a shrill scream, but my whole being was numbed by last night's alcoholic intake. My flesh felt leaden.

With extreme effort I grabbed the encumbered wrist and tried to tug it free from the dank crevice. But it remained there, trapped in some terrible vacuum, and instead I dragged Piggy's bulk towards me. I felt the hot breath of a nuzzling lover before realising she had farted involuntarily on my arm.

"Mmmm?" murmured Piggy, still asleep.

As my brain began to function, panic gripped me. Why had I woken next to her? Where was I? How had I got here? Please, no. Surely not.

The Frihedhags had staged my leaving party at their home, each garbed frivolously. Original and Neck-Brace wore short, woollen dresses in garish orange, and looked like Flintstones. Their sister Teeth bulged from a white trouser suit that had belonged to Nob, the outfit having been dramatically let out to fit her. Piggy, ever ostentatious, wore bondage gear fashioned from bin-liners and netting.

Detritos was there, wearing leather and leering, alongside various other Emo Islanders to whom I was introduced, and instantly forgot. Word had been sent to Gydi, Original said, but his wife was making him stay in to make up for lost time.

Initially a reluctant guest, I was quickly relaxed by a powerful alcoholic punch. Even the bitter cigars and ochre-coloured ale, with its slimy precipitate that went down like phlegm, had begun to taste reasonable.

I was under-nourished and the booze so potent that memory had deserted me after the opening half-hour, during which Piggy had cornered me as I slumped in a chair in the corner of the lounge.

I did recall her attempting a lapdance, which had all the eroticism of a hippopotamus getting comfortable on a shooting stick. Now here I was, in bed with the woman. No matter how hard I strained, I could not remember why. My head pounded, cigar smoke had gone stale in my mouth and I craved water.

She stirred next to me, smacked her lips sleepily, reached behind and extracted my forearm from her bottom. Then she turned over and gazed longingly into my eyes, her cushioned face all dreamy.

"From now," she said, "I call you Mr Pumpy."

A hasty departure was in order.

Heart pounding, I made my excuses to a protesting Piggy, shovelled up a handful of last night's clothes, tugged them on and stepped into the lounge, where comatose Frihedhags and Emo Islanders littered the floor. Empty ale jugs, all toppled, some broken, filled the spaces where humanity was not decaying. Fat cigar butts, extinguished into rugs, lay dotted around like dog turds. The place did not smell fresh.

It was a blessed relief to tiptoe over the snuffling bodies, unlatch the front door and step outside. I closed it behind me, physically escaping the indiscretion of the previous night.

Skaramanger was silent and chill, the sun barely risen. I shivered, clutched arms about my chest and gritted my teeth. Here I was, somewhere in the housing quarter, where the streets were lined with carpeting and the homes all looked the same, praying that I could retrace my steps to Detritos' home. There, I could gather together my few belongings, leave a farewell note stained with guilt and depart furtively.

For once on this journey, my luck was in. Although my turns through the right-angles of Skaramanger were largely hopeful, I found myself at the dwarf's house, having recognised the additional set of windows closer to the ground than everyone else's.

The front door was unlocked and I crept inside, passed through the lounge and peered into the dwarf's bedroom, aware of grunting.

Poking from Detritos's bedclothes was a shock of lurid orange hair, belonging, I could only assume, to a young woman. From the humping going on beneath the blankets, it seemed that the dwarf was engaging in sexual intercourse with her, making a noise I imagined pigs make while hunting truffles.

"Yes, babee!" came his muffled cry. "Detritos fuck anyseeng zat moof!"

The lovers were too distracted to have noticed me so I slunk away to gather my things.

There were the knitted clothes from the Frihedhags, which painful fresh memory would have had me leave behind, but I was desperate. Detritos, too, had come up with some goods, left in his house by passers-through. This included, I noted, two pairs of ladies' bloomers, which would at least fit me and so would have to suffice. There were also five pairs of rough woven trousers that I held against my waist, casting aside all bar two voluminous pairs, a crumpled, stained white collared shirt, a pair of black fisherman's boots, estimated size 14, but which would do, and a grey, coarse-stitched animal-hide jacket, possibly poodle in origin, which fitted well and felt instantly comforting, so I pulled it on.

I scooped everything into a couple of Hessian sacks, also provided by the dwarf. I owed him one, though happily someone else was giving it to him. So I left the room on tiptoe, passing Detritos' bedroom where the moans were increasing in pitch.

Still bewildered, I could not help but glance in once again. The dwarf remained pumping away under the covers, his grunts reaching a crescendo.

Next came an almighty 'Bang!' and the dwarf's lover disappeared is if on a magician's stage. A blow-up doll! The dwarf remained under the duvet, cursing loudly in his mother tongue. The lady had apparently gone down on him too soon.

I left my farewell note in the lounge. It read: '*Detritos. Thanks for your help. Best. Alexander.*'

Then I was gone, with a sigh of relief.

The route from Skaramanger's residential area to its harbour was all downhill, which added a spring into my creaky stride.

It was possible that Piggy Frihedhag was also up, roaming the streets with her sisters, calling after me, at a loss to explain why her love had deserted her. They might be gathered sympathetically around her now, reassuring her that there must be some mistake, that I would return. How glad I was of the carpeting underfoot, silencing each departing step.

It took a short time to emerge from the collected housing into the open cobbled area before the harbour. To my right: a row of wooden shacks masquerading as shops, all shut. To my left: the bleak scenery of the route back to the Unknown Tunnel and Frartsi. Before me… boats ablaze on the sea, a handful of sailing types watching and cheering? That couldn't be right. In my experience, sailors didn't burn their boats, they floated around in them.

"Excuse me!" I hollered, starting to jog towards the scene. That was my transport off the island.

At once the sailors fell silent and turned to stare, perhaps a dozen men, each clad in a uniform of black sweater, thick dark trousers and wellington boots. One said something in Frartsian.

"Sorry, I'm from England," I apologised breathlessly on reaching their group. I forced a smile.

"You are Mister Alexander?" asked one in a grey woollen hat.

How did he know? What if the Frihedhags had been here before me, bitter and twisted, to pass on my description? I wondered, should I lie?

I didn't like the look of my interrogator, a weathered sort lacking front teeth, with straggly dark hair tufting over his ears from beneath the hat. His eyes were ice-blue.

"No, I'm not," I said. "My name's…"

"Meester Alexander! Oh Meester Alexander!" called the dwarf breezily from somewhere behind me. "Forgeteeng Detritos!"

The sailors broke into foreign mutters punctuated often by the words 'Mister Alexander'. Then, unexpectedly, they began to applaud and each, in turn, rested a gnarled head on my shoulder, put an arm around me and slapped my back. A smell of salt and alcohol lingered when they had finished.

Their icy-eyed leader went last. "You kill Borhed," he said. "Everyone now know Mister Alexander, who is hero."

Detritos appeared beside me, rucksack on his back, shiny brown leather briefcase in one hand. "Remindeeng sank John, luffly weekend," he said, gazing doe-eyed.

The fisherfolk clapped. Would I never escape?

I sat with them on the harbour cobbles, sharing a pot of weak coffee brewed over a gas heater. Out on the sea, seven fishing boats continued to blaze, shedding parts into the water with a hiss as the structures weakened. There was nothing I could do.

"This special day," explained the head fisherman, who introduced himself as Parhaghaghed. "One time in thousand year, fishermen of Emo Island make fire boats. All bad luck had gather – fire make go! See? Then build new! Special day, we call Brni Bti, it mean…" he struggled for the translation.

"Burn the Boats," I suggested wearily.

"Yes!" he said, and the fishermen clapped. "Mister is very clever."

"How long will it take to build new boats?" I asked out of politeness.

Parhaghaghed shrugged his shoulders. "Maybe less year. Maybe more!"

"What will you do in the meantime, for money?"

"Emo mayor pay special money so we burn boat, for history. Give maybe ten-time more than make of fish! Hahahaha!" They all joined in his laughter. "So we not rush make new boat!"

I found myself participating in the hysterics. Well, they were a jolly bunch with free coffee. I noticed that Detritos did not join in.

When we calmed down the dwarf addressed Parhaghaghed. "We must goeeng, for Klükamüs."

What did he mean, *we* must goeeng? "What do you mean, *we* must goeeng?"

"Detritos comeeng weez," grinned the dwarf.

"No, you're not comeeng weez!"

"Yes, comeeng."

"No, stayeeng."

"Comeeng."

"Stayeeng."

"Comeeng."

"Stayeeng."

It felt as if we were having a lover's tiff.

Detritos changed tack. "*Pleeze* Detritos comeeng."

"No! You stay here. In Skaramanger."

"*Pleeze*, Meester Alexander!"

"No, Detritos!"

"Yoo-hoo! Mr Pumpy!" came the distant call, wafting across on a wave of cheap perfume.

I turned, horrified. It was Piggy Frihedhag, waving frantically from the edge of the housing estate, craning her neck, looking like someone whose soldier beau was leaning out of a steam train window.

"Run!" I yelled. To my surprise, everyone did.

There was one guarantee: that we would shake her off. Even Detritos, on his dinky pins, made light work of the chase.

We scarpered along the harbourside and caught our breath behind a tall, black-painted hut outside which trawler nets had been hung to dry. The mass escape had induced a sense of bonding and we grinned at each other, catching breath, though I couldn't help wondering why the fishermen had run too.

I cut to the quick. "I need a boat to Klükamüs," I told Parhaghaghed.

"All boats on fire," he pointed out.

The oldest fisherman raised a hand.

"Slthaghedhedhaghaghedhaghed?" said his leader, during which time became precious.

"Hdi brgi," croaked the geriatric.

"Say he have barge," Parhaghaghed translated.

His colleagues applauded.

The dwarf tugged at my trouser leg. "Barge bad," he hissed. "Fuckeeng slow. Klükamüs far. Fuckeeng die."

This much I already suspected. Klükamüs was far enough North that ice might also be a hazard. It was indeed no job for a narrowboat.

The dwarf tugged at my trouser leg again, beckoning me down to his level, and whispered, "Haff uzzer seeng – friend weez balloon!"

He had to be kidding. So petrified was I of heights that I refused to travel by aeroplane, let alone by floating basket.

This vertigo stemmed from a childhood incident. Mother, against Father's wishes, once took me as a six-year-old to the Glibley playground. I urged her to let me play on the slide and she relented. As I made my way gingerly up the steps, however, exuberance deserted me and I lost my nerve. Mother, sensing my reluctance, pushed at my bottom, coaxing me upwards, thinking she was helping.

So I found myself sitting on the platform at the top, staring down the slide, which suddenly seemed like an Olympic ski-jump run. As an impatient queue gathered behind me, others stopped to watch. That was when I wet myself, my river of urine descending the slide. As Mother rescued me, everyone laughed.

"No way am I going by bloody balloon!" I told the dwarf.

"But Meester Alexander, ees queek!"

I would not be swayed, even at the thought of Suzy Goodenough's attentions. Such was my resolve. "Detritos," I said firmly. "No."

I addressed Parhaghaghed: "How many days to Klükamüs by barge?"

Parhaghaghed conversed with Slthaghedhedhag-haghedhaghed. "Mister," he replied, "he say ten week" – the seaman registered my slump – "or maybe nine!"

"And there's no other way off Emo Island?"

Parhaghaghed shrugged his shoulders.

My Quest was over before it had begun. I dropped onto my backside, pushed my head into my hands and moped. The dwarf put an arm partly around me, offered a silver hip flask and said mournfully, "Remembereeng Parees. German een grey, Meester Alexander een blue."

I accepted the flask and took a swig of its bitter-tasting liquid.

Drugged.

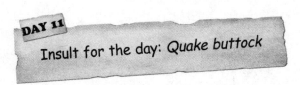

I came around nursing the latest crashing headache, in a balloon.

I was lying in the bottom of a hefty basket, woven plantlife the only barrier between myself and a fatal fall. The dwarf, now dressed in a miniature cream-coloured suit with generous flares, like some Seventies love-god, was perched on a stool peering over the edge. Beside him, bent over and also peering, was a disconcertingly tall, utterly bald man in a fluorescent orange jumpsuit. Above me billowed the interior of a great silver canopy, its burner belching flame.

It took a moment, while miniature miners chipped away at the inside of my skull, to work out what had happened. "You bloody drugged me!" I shouted at the dwarf, who turned in shock.

His co-conspirator turned, too, and I was captivated immediately by his ornate brown handlebar moustache and the flying goggles strapped about his forehead. He must have been eight feet tall. It was he who spoke first, offering a hand to lift me up, which I declined because I did not dare stand up.

"What-ho!" he chirped. "Name's Upper-Crust! Major Lee Upper-Crust, ex of HM Air Force, at your service-ulous! Bally nice day for a flight!"

"No, it bloody isn't!" I snapped, though secretly excited to hear an Englishman.

"Oh," replied the balloonist, clearly put out. "Bang-chip, then."

I turned on the dwarf: "You drugged me!"

Detritos was still perched on the stool. "Watcheeng mouth, keed. Or floateeng home."

I recognised that one, from *Star Wars*. "I *am* floating home, you git!" (Father had always strictly forbidden bad words. But he was dead and I was at last appreciating the freedom.)

The dwarf shrugged. "Meester Alexander bad flyeeng. Detritos *helpeeng* Meester Alexander!"

"You fucking *keednappeeng* me!"

Detritos deflated. His lower lip quivered. "Detritos helpeeng," he protested in a small voice.

He really believed it. Suddenly I felt guilty at haranguing him. Perhaps I might become inured to this heights lark in time?

I dropped the aggressive approach. "How long have I been asleep?"

The dwarf looked shifty.

"A day?" I guessed.

"Maybe."

"More than a day?"

He avoided eye contact. "Ees so."

"Two days?"

"And some!" rejoined Upper-Crust, stupidly jovial. "As memory serves, you were blotto on Emo around elevenses, kipped like a babster all yesterday and it's now near evening the pevening! More than 48 bish-bosh hours. Last time one kipped that length, the guns were locked on 'safety' and the chaps were singing Chrimbo carols, quaffing sherry!"

The fool began to hum *Once in Royal David's City*, waltzing with an invisible partner. I would have stormed off in disgust, were there anywhere to storm off to in a balloon.

"Surely," offered the Major, "if one is scared to fly, it is preferable to be unconscious. To-wit no fear. What?"

He chortled and Detritos joined in.

I covered my ears with cupped hands and began to chant inanities to block out their hysteria.

I felt a hand on my shoulder. It was Upper-Crust's. "Not to worry, young chapter," he spouted gaily. "Should arrive tomorrow morn, provided winds stay tiddly-pop."

It was something. The air had chilled noticeably since Emo Island so we had certainly travelled northwards, towards lands where winters settle into an interminable dusk. Perhaps Klükamüs really was not that far off. The dwarf might have done me a favour, after all.

We sat to feast in the bottom of the basket. (I was yet to muster the courage to stand.)

Above was the balloon's canopy and early evening: a perfectly cloudless sky peppered with the ancient light of the constellations. Besides the occasional roar of the burner, or Upper-Crust talking to himself while tinkering, everywhere was quiet. Detritos was sulking.

Once food touched my lips, I realised how famished I was. Something to do with eating nothing in three days, I suspected, glaring at the dwarf. There were cold meats, salted and rubbery but welcome, with strongly yeasted loaf and dried fruits, possibly prunes. These we washed down with ale, a nutty brew, flat and syrupy. It calmed my nerves.

The balloon's fire illuminated our three faces shades of orange – partly also a reflection from our balloonist's garish jumpsuit – and I studied Upper-Crust's features. His moustache was chestnut coloured and waxed to form points at each erected end; he had a sallow complexion and his head seemed to have been stretched, to keep its dimensions in touch with those of his body. The Major's pate shone.

He must have noticed me ogling his bonce, for he explained, "Too bally tall – kept setting fire to it in the burner, so shaved it all off, what! Make up for lack of brush up top with this bally tish-tosh-'tache! Eh?" He blinked several times and slapped me on the shoulder.

Whatever. "So how did you come to Emo Island?"

Extracting fact from the blather, it went like this. Around a decade ago, the former RAF officer and his wife Binky had taken part in a balloon race that began in England and was supposed to go nowhere near Emo Island. However, Upper-Crust had allowed himself to be blown off-course and had come down in Skaramanger, where the couple were greeted as geniuses in the field of flight by natives unused to strangers arriving by air.

Although they had appeared purely because the Major had missed his destination by some 300 miles, the Emo Islanders, desperate for long-range transport, begged them to stay to run a charter-flight service. Flattered for perhaps the first time in their lives, the Upper-Crusts had agreed and set-up Bally Balloons in Felixtown, outside Skaramanger.

Detritos had befriended the couple because they frequented the same bars, it having become swiftly obvious that few Emo Islanders could actually afford to charter a balloon.

With time on my hands, and not wishing to encourage my fellow fliers into extended conversation, I dug out from my trousers Harrison Dextrose's *The Lost Incompetent: A Bible for the Inept Traveller*.

His entry for Klükamüs began thus:

KLÜKAMÜS

Population: No idea
Capital: Klütz
Currency: Knika
Principle industry: Extortion

By mink, it's cold here. Don't come to Klükamüs.

Which boded well.

We have barely disembarked at Klütz when we are surrounded by natives, the Innit – wide-boys wearing t-shirts, while we freeze in oilskins – offering to take us on snowmobile tours of the arse-end of nowhere, for a fee. When we brush them aside they offer timeshare apartments, moonshine and prostitutes, which raises mine and Shark's spirits.

(According to Tench, the letter K, at the beginning of a name, is silent here. Don't pronounce it or the natives pretend not to have a minking clue what you're on about. They speak a variant of English, so we get by. But remember this: never try to speak the foreigner's lingo; it gives the devious minkheads ideas above their station. Everyone can learn English – that's why we made it so easy.)

By nightfall, having secured accommodation, we find Djüke's Bar, the brashest hostelry in town, run by a young borderline psychotic with whom I establish a rapport. His business is alcohol and his customers are satisfied.

The men here are shaven-headed oafs with biceps. Their women wear high heels and mini-skirts that cause me to salivate. They don't seem to feel the cold, which might be explained by the hordes in Djüke's, numbed by his wares, behaving like a pirate boarding-party. I feel at home.

Shark, ever the moaning scadger, complains of chilblains, but falls silent when I challenge him to tell me what one is.

Caribou Tench, unaffected by anything worse than nuclear war, has been out collecting arctic-type clothing or animal hide from which he sews garments, like a girl.

If I later take comfort from minking whores, dearest wife, it is purely for the warmth.

I leafed backwards, to re-read Dextrose's Emo Island adventures. Now that I knew the place, I hoped to find familiar scenes, to breathe further life into his writings. One section, I suddenly realised, involved characters closely fitting the description of the Frihedhags:

A quartet of tarts sit in one corner, two ancient, one festering, one vast – a feast for any man's eyes. Too minked to chat politely, I whip out the old man, pop him into the huge one's ale and offer to see to her, name her price. Minking dyke becomes irate and pushes me over.

"Mink you!" I tell them all.

Tench says I offered to mink their daughters, at which they turned outwardly hostile, then he carried me home.

"Poor show alert!" bellowed Upper-Crust, as the basket began to shake.

"What do you mean, 'Poor show alert'?" I yelped.

"Hit a dashed anti-thingy!" he replied, frantically tinkering with the burner. Above us, the silver canopy flapped madly like the udder of a space-age sprinting cow. We were now descending faster than was healthy.

I pushed myself deep into a corner and prayed. Upper-Crust became increasingly flustered. Though he twisted valves and held a spanner, mere flickers of flame appeared as we continued our inexorable descent.

Giving up on the burner, he flung his arms over the side and began releasing ballast. With each release our descent slowed partially, but it was not enough. Then all the ballast was gone.

"Need to lose some more bally weight!" he called out.

My life was flashing before my eyes and it wasn't taking long enough. "How much weight?"

"Your guess is as good as a monkey's tink. Maybe 50 pounds?"

"How much do you weigh?" I demanded of the dwarf.

"Dresseeng een best. Prepareeng go down weez gentlemen," he replied. Was he never flustered by anything?

I surveyed the contents of the basket, trying to quell my panic. My two Hessian sacks of clothing, Detritos's rucksack and leather briefcase, a suitcase of the Major's, and a rusty tin toolbox, opened and ransacked.

The toolbox would have to go first, seeming heaviest. I hefted it over the side and heard the muffled clatter of its impact all too soon. Next to hand was the dwarf's briefcase. But when I reached for it, the owner was on me like lightning. "Not toucheeng zees, Meester Al–"

Before he could finish, we hit the ground with a jolt that sent my feet up into my shoulders.

Insult for the day: *Sordid mump*

"Meester Alexander... Meester Alexander..." It was the dwarf sounding tense. A small hand slapped my cheek. I opened one eye and gazed upwards through blur.

"Ugh," I said. His face was right in mine, all quiff, eyebrows, sideburn and concern. Behind that, further beyond focus, was something orange: our inept balloonist, presumably.

"He OK!" hailed the dwarf, clasping my face.

Then he began a little dance of joy, singing, "He OK! He OK!" Upper-Crust joined in, adding a harmony that sounded like, "Tricketty-woo!"

As their commotion continued, I was able to open my second eye. It was daytime, above me was white cloud pockmarked with the most vivid blue sky I had ever seen. When I breathed out, it was as if I were smoking, so I lay there blowing condensation-rings. Though my back twinged when I twisted, nothing felt broken.

Either I had been thrown from the basket, or had been pulled clear after our impromptu landing, because our transport lay some distance to my right. The balloon's deflated silver canopy had become trapped in an evergreen tree, where it radiated the snow's glare. One corner of the basket had shattered, the rest of it was merely battered, and from beneath it protruded a pair of horns, like vast gloves.

We had landed on a moose. The animal's buckling legs must

have cushioned our landing and probably saved our lives. I wondered what were the chances of landing on a moose – size of moose multiplied by number of mooses present, divided by area of land? – but gave up.

I addressed the dancing fools, who were now delightedly waltzing, Upper-Crust clasping a dangling Detritos to his chest.

"Why are you celebrating? We're in the middle of bloody nowhere!"

They stopped dancing and Upper-Crust dropped the dwarf, who disappeared under snow. When he clambered out, they both stood there, gazing downwards like errant children.

The Major coughed. "Bong tinker the wibbly nib," he said, either trying to change the subject or finally becoming certifiable.

I refreshed my face in gathered snow, which tingled like sherbet as the ice particles melted.

Our belongings had been collected together. The dwarf's briefcase, about which he had been so protective, was there, and leaning against it were my sacks of clothing, which I retrieved and disappeared behind a tree to change. It was there that I spotted a wooden sign, topped with a crust of ice and partially obscured by snowdrift. It read:

WOTCHART! EVOL SKWIRLS!

Which meant very little.

I was actually grateful for the Frihedhags' knitting endeavours, managing to squeeze on the following: white collared shirt; two jumpers (penguin motif and cabbage motif), the brown hide jacket, two pairs of Detritos' ladies' bloomers over the boxer shorts I had been wearing since Mdra's, one pair of coarse woollen trousers over my jeans, three pairs of knitted socks, and the outsized wellies.

Walking in that lot felt like attempted escape from pythons, but it beat the perishing cold. I wondered what time it was and looked for my Torquil the T-Rex Dino-Explorer's Watch, then remembered with sadness how the late Borhed had destroyed it. The sun was up there somewhere, so it was daytime.

The night would be colder. We should move on.

Our flight had ended so abruptly in a gently sloping area of half-hearted forestation. No sign of life was about, not even another moose. The dwarf, who seemed unaffected by the weather, had merely put on tan leather gloves to complement the Seventies cream suit.

I turned to Upper-Crust, who was pulling on a dayglo-yellow cagoule over his garish-orange jumpsuit, and wondered whether he might be colourblind.

"Where are we?" I demanded. "And try to talk sense."

"Well blinkety flip, junior rudester! Calm the *crudité*!" he exclaimed as his shiny bonce popped through the top of the waterproof. "By my calculations we're near Klbdow, 100 miles from Klütz. Sensible enough for youdly-who?"

I could only hope that his 'calculations' were wrong, or we were 100 miles off target.

Between the three of us we concocted a plan.

The balloon was beyond repair, particularly since I had thrown away the toolbox. Upper-Crust maintained that Klbdow was to our west, so we would walk in that direction, shouting. Hopefully someone would hear us and offer rescue. In Klbdow, the Major would telephone his wife Binky, who would – not for the first time in her husband's ballooning career – come to his aid bearing supplies. I would find transport to Klütz, while Detritos, Upper-Crust and his wife flew back to Skaramanger.

"Meester Alexander, Detritos comeeng weez."

Was there no end to his persistence? I seemed destined to become the first explorer with a Passepartout you couldn't take anywhere.

We had walked barely 50 metres, still arguing over the dwarf's return home, when there came a distant call.

"Oi-oi?" it went, seeking a response.

Briefly a crystalline silence reigned, followed by indistinct words, then the cracking of twigs underfoot somewhere to our left.

"Oi-oi?"

"Shhhh!" hissed Upper-Crust. "Might be a wolf."

Detritos and I exchanged raised eyebrows.

We reached a collective whispered indecision. Of course it would be nice to be rescued, but one should first know one's rescuer.

The footfalls came nearer, now accompanied by laboured breathing. We sprang simultaneously for cover.

I shimmied up a nearby fir, pressing my way into its dense, thin, annoying branches. The dwarf, I didn't see. He had simply disappeared. Upper-Crust, however, was blatantly visible behind a tree trunk, employing the ostrich's head-in-the-sand approach to concealment. To be fair, his was a lost cause: dressed in glowing orange and yellow; the man might only successfully conceal himself in an outsized display of citrus fruit.

There was no time to call out to him. Two men appeared from between trees, each carrying a hunting rifle. They looked like menacing brothers, curiously similar in appearance: squat, jeans, shaven round heads reddened by the chill, long lace-up brown boots, and arms thick with matted dark hair, protruding from white t-shirts. They looked like Arctic skinheads. So these must be the Innit, as Dextrose had described. At least we really were in Klükamüs.

Now we just had to stay alive long enough to find Klütz, then leave. However, my experiences of foreign travel hardly tallied with those described in the tour operators' brochures. As I had discovered, there is a fine line between hospitality and hospitalisation.

Of course, the Innit pair spotted Upper-Crust immediately. They pointed silently and huddled to plan, though he, head behind a thin tree-trunk, remained blissfully unaware. I was too cowardly to react.

The Innit were hoarse whisperers, such that I could hear every word.

"I fackin' toldja! S'a fackin' alien!" exclaimed Innit One (who was slightly thicker set and squatter than his compatriot).

"Fack orf, mate!" retorted Innit Two. "It were me wot fackin' spottid that shiny silver fing and goes, 'S'a fackin' UFO!'"

"I done that!" squealed Innit One. Their grammar was starting to annoy me.

"I fackin' done that!" retorted his colleague.

"I says, 'Oi, Tjësser, over there – s'a fackin' UFO!' Then you goes, 'S'not, s'a flyin' big football!' Then I goes, 'Footballs ain't that big, you twot!'. Then you goes, 'That fackin' one is, you twot!' An' I goes, 'S'cos it ain't a fackin' football, you twot!'"

"Yeah, Gjüt," replied Tjësser. "An' in the end I agrees i's a fackin' UFO 'cos you stabs us in the fackin' leg wiv a knife."

"'A's exactly wot I fackin' said! You twot! I fackin' said i's a fackin' UFO so stands ter reason, there's an alien in it, innit, an' you goes, 'Nah it fackin' don't!'"

They argued pointlessly like this for some while, agreeing to disagree only after they had run out of enthusiasm for arguments that go round in circles. They laid their weapons in the snow – which was encouraging – and Gjüt called out to the Major, "Oi! Take us to yer fackin' leader."

The Major could not conceive that it was he who had been spotted. So he ignored them, putting his hand to his mouth to silence a titter at his brilliant subterfuge.

This confused the Innit, who began conferring loudly.

"P'raps it don't fackin' speak the lingo?" suggested Gjüt.

"Where's it cam from then?" replied Tjësser.

"I dunno, do I? Probl'y fackin' Mars or summink."

"Where's its fackin' spaceship gorn?"

"Ah-do-I fackin' know? Wod-am-I, fackin' Sigourney Weaver in *Alien* or summink?"

"Sigourney Weaver in *Alien* – luverly!"

"Innit just."

"You'd give 'er one, innit!"

"Yeah, I woot! But you'd give the fackin' alien one, innit!"

"I fackin' wootn't!"

"Fackin' woot! Weaver wootn't give you one, 'less you done 'er cat first, innit!"

"You'd 'ave-ta give 'er cat one, then go up'ill gard'nin' wiv the alien, like some plimpton, 'fore she'd let you give 'er one!"

Gjüt started poking Tjësser's chest. "You'd 'ave-ta give 'er cat one, go up'ill gard'nin' wiv the alien, like some plimpton, then you'd 'ave-ta…"

Happily, before the exchange could become any more distasteful, Tjësser grabbed Gjüt by the throat and began punching him repeatedly in the face, after which they rolled in the snow, carelessly disturbing its virginity while bleeding. Although I was hardly surprised that neither the Major nor I had taken advantage of this situation, where was the rarely daunted Detritos?

Rustling branches aside, no longer fearing detection by the otherwise engaged Innit, I scanned the area. There were just snow-covered trees, bushes and ground. Everywhere was ice-cream from which greens and browns intermittently peeked, but no dwarf.

Then movement high up in a nearby tree caught my attention. It was definitely swaying unnaturally – that was no effect of the wind. There followed a familiar curse, then the dwarf's head appeared from the branches, two-thirds of the way up. His hair, usually immaculately coiffured, was tangled and distressed, and his face contorted with rage. He slipped from his perch and tumbled with an "Aaaaaiii!" down the outside of the tree, pursued by squirrels.

Landing in a snowdrift, he disappeared into a Detritos-shaped hole, followed by six or seven squirrels popping in after him. There was a brief calm, then the group emerged, all flailing fists and rodent snarls.

The dwarf, I surmised, had disturbed the creatures' home while clambering for a vantage point, to which they had taken exception.

Trust him. At least a bank of snow hid the scene from the view of the Innit, who were still busy scrapping. It remained for someone to save the Major... and bags it wasn't me.

Despite my later vertigo, I am used to passing time in trees, having spent much of my early childhood among high branches, which gave me a rare sense of adventure. At the rear of our long, thin back garden in Glibley, we had three evergreens such as the one I found myself in, and which had the same pervasive bittersweet aroma.

From an early age I had forged a route up each of our firs. This involved pushing one's head upwards through the mass of tangled, spiky foliage, breaking off the troublesome, weedy branches and keeping an eye open for their sturdier cousins. Afterwards I would run inside, where Mother would tut and preen the spines and twigs from my hardly styled hair.

The middle tree was always my favourite, as it allowed the highest ascent, and it was there, near the top, that I met Wilf.

Wilf was a tree sprite and my best friend from the age of six until shortly before I was sent away to boarding school.

I recall our first meeting, which did not go well. I had broken my way through to a record new ascent when there he was, perched on a branch right next to my head, drumming fingers on one knee and looking disapproving.

Wilf was 12 inches tall, with bushy ginger hair and beard, and a green tunic and pointy hat with bell attached. Yes, a bit like a leprechaun. His face was red and his nose was bulbous.

Wilf told me that it was dangerous to climb so high and would I leave because anyway this was his tree. I told him that I wouldn't, pointing out that no one can own the trees.

There was a stalemate during which we attempted to stare each other out, until Father called me in to do homework.

The next day after school, eager to discover whether Wilf would still be there or whether he had been a figment of my imagination – the irony does not elude me now – I clambered up the middle fir. And there he was, trousers around his ankles, mooning at me. I called him a rude little man and he blew off.

Rather than being offended, I began to laugh. Wilf started laughing too, and soon we were both in hysterics.

Afterwards, I would visit Wilf every day, sometimes taking him the cheese from my packed lunch (cheese being a tree sprite's favourite food, but not mine). Wilf was terribly irreverent. He had left home, he said, because he didn't like being made to clean his teeth, which were rather brown. Neither did he have much truck with authority – he didn't like the sound of Father and referred to him as The Git.

Wilf could do whatever he liked, which seemed appealing.

For a few years this went on until one evening I overheard Father talking with my mother in the lounge, while I was supposed to be preparing for bed.

"It's not healthy, Mother," he said. "The boy's behaving like a hermit."

She agreed with him (as she always did) and the next morning he confronted me, demanding to know why I spent so much time up a tree. Not wishing him to think me a loner, I explained about Wilf, which failed to placate him.

"How dare you let another child into my garden!" he thundered, so I was forced to elaborate that Wilf was a tree sprite, which also failed to placate him.

"Mother!" he called, and she came running. "Alexander spends all his time up a tree because he has made friends with a tree sprite! Named Wilf!" His temper was rising.

"That's nice, dear," she replied, trying to defuse the mood.

"NICE?!"

Mother persisted: "Perhaps we could invite him in for dinner?"

This seemed madness to me: Wilf could be so uncouth. Yet the fireworks that I was sure would ensue didn't. I spotted Mother wink and Father, on the brink of exploding, visibly calmed.

"I must commend you, Mother," he said, "on a perfectly decent idea."

So it was agreed: Wilf would come for dinner on Friday evening – three days hence – the first time I had been allowed to have a friend visit.

"Pip pip!"

My nostalgic trip was cut short by Upper-Crust's cheery greeting to the still writhing Innit. The idiot must have become bored and was now trying to make friends. He had moved from behind his tree to stand, hands on hips, legs planted apart in the snow, trying to look official. Sadly, with his fluorescent garb, goggles and moustache, he looked like the lunatic presenter of a TV show about inventions.

Just then, the sun broke through the dense cloud and cast one heavenly shaft of gold upon Upper-Crust, who began to fluoresce.

The Innit froze, bloodied and snowy, eyes like saucers, petrified.

"Squeezing the interimptions. Crave tinkle the Binkster on

the old dogster and bowley mahone. Would that clattle the drigster?"

"Wossit sayin'?" Tjësser pleaded of Gjüt, clutching his arm like a distressed damsel.

"Squeezing the interimptions," repeated the Major, slightly impatiently. "Crave tinkle the Binkster on the old dogster and bowley mahone. Would that clattle the nib-nib drigster?"

Like myself, the Innit were thrown.

"Told yer it were a fackin' alien," whimpered Tjësser, now shaking his friend, hoping that it might inspire him into action.

Gjüt lunged for his hunting rifle in the snow and pointed it at the Major. "Let's do 'im an' git artuv 'ere, Tjësser," he pleaded. "E's givin' me the fackin' willies, innit!"

Upper-Crust whipped his arms in the air and let out a very British, "I say!"

Tjësser looked torn. Gjüt seemed more resolved. It was true: they could bump off the Major here and now, in the middle of nowhere, and no one – besides myself – would be any the wiser. Like I would kick up a fuss against two armed and unintelligent men.

"Go on then," urged Tjësser. "Do 'im. Then let's git artuv 'ere."

Gjüt levelled the rifle.

"Leave him alone!" I finally shouted, though it didn't sound forceful, more like the plaintive cry of a cornered gerbil.

Startled, the Innit shot stares in my direction, but I was too well hidden amid the foliage and they gazed blindly.

"Wotwuzat?" yelped Gjüt, firing randomly towards me and missing by a healthy distance, though I imagined I heard the speeding bullet.

"Nah the fackin' trees is talkin'!" said Tjësser incredulously.

Sensing the upper hand, I put on a talking-tree-type voice: *"Put the gun down and go away!"*

"Bollicks! Someone's in the tree!" Gjüt declared.

"*No really, I am a talking tree, you know!*" I called down.

"Bollicks! Trees dan't talk!" pointed out Tjësser, though not entirely convinced.

It was another dicey situation, happily interrupted by the dwarf, who came bowling over a snowdrift into view, snarling and partly concealed beneath squirrels.

This was all too much for the Innit pair, who shouted "Wot the fack!" in unison and turned to scarper, scuffing snow in their haste. Within seconds, they had disappeared back into the dark woodland.

I slid down the tree, through its cluster of thin branches, ignoring the pricks of the pine needles. Upper-Crust stood like a waxwork, numbed with fear or perhaps inanity. Detritos was rolling in the snow, still scrapping, and I mooched over to him, pulling off each determined rodent one by one and lobbing them into the distance.

Suddenly it became obvious. What the sign had meant was: 'Watch out! Evil squirrels!'

When they were all gone, the dwarf lay in the snow, face up, panting intently, suit ripped, hair splayed, skin a mass of bloody scratches. As he gazed into my eyes, a lascivious look crept across his features.

"Ees freedom, babee! Yes!"

It didn't take a trained tracker to follow the trail of the retreating Innit through the snow, though the Major insisted on pointing repeatedly at the blatantly obvious footprints and announcing, "There!"

Of course, we were not desperate to reacquaint ourselves with the unstable pair, but their trail might conclude in Klbdow – certainly in some form of civilisation.

The journey led us through firs mere feet apart that we pushed between, leading with forearms, baggage slung over our backs. As the trees became less densely packed, progress became easier. Falling footsteps and broken twigs echoed into the distance. The sounds made us nervous.

No one spoke. Each inward breath sliced into the sinuses, as if one were inhaling embrocation, and with the early evening came a renewed chill. Though it was dark under the canopy, a departing light peeped through occasionally. My clothing had become dampened by snow melted by body heat and my toes had long since gone numb.

Unprepared for this diversion, Upper-Crust and Detritos had packed no camping gear. We had to make town by nightfall or face possible death in this open-plan freezer.

It was slow going. Our baggage became trapped on bits of tree and the dwarf's strides were not long. The Major was silent – too childlike, I suspected, to be aware of the perils, so instead wrapped up in the adventure.

Darkness overcame us suddenly, like a sooty blanket dropped on our heads. Incredibly, it was Upper-Crust who came to the rescue, producing from his kit an ancient oil lamp that he fired up with matches. The glow was welcoming, inducing a false warmth, though in shadows the forest seemed still eerier.

Things were moving. There were cracks and rustles and the occasional distant animal that sounded malicious. At times, I swore I heard something, or someone, following us – snaps and grunts from behind, like an echo of our progress.

Through fear, I broke wind. The sonorous parp would have alerted any predator within miles but at least it warmed my trouser region. Detritos and the Major feigned disgust in comic holding-of-nose gestures, which broke the tension. We rolled around in hysterics for a good five minutes, taking it in turns to fart, to maintain the good humour.

I have no idea how long we had slogged onward with no concept of direction before the first human sounds reached our ears. But eventually, from a distance, laughing, singing and drunken revelry carried on the faint breeze. We should have been cautious, but cautious people do not generally have blue fingers.

The three of us broke into a pained trot that slowed only as civilisation came into view through the trees. Before us appeared to be some sort of open-air discotheque, all rainbow-coloured lights strung in the darkness.

We began to run, certain that no one would hear our laboured footfalls, until we reached the edge of the bastard forest and gazed as one in wonderment.

Here was Santa's home, a wooden town direct from children's dreams. There were clustered pine shacks, their windows lit by fires within, sloping roofs piled with snow, all draped in multi-coloured fairylights. Between the buildings, footsteps had been driven into the snow. People were singing. As my heart melted, my frozen limbs thawed.

This was no time for reticence. The most imposing of the shacks, from which the main commotion was emanating, had a sign nailed under its eaves: 'Ma's Bar', and beneath that: 'Klbdow's Only Boozer'. Upper-Crust, Detritos and I shared a brief glance that suggested we all fancied a beer and hang the consequences.

As one, we strode towards the establishment. Foolishly, in my enthusiasm, it was I who reached the door first. I flicked the catch and swung it open.

The smell hit me before the heat, as a tidal wave of rancid sweat made a break for the fresh air. Inside, wooden tables and benches thronged with punters clutching beer. All the men were styled – if that is the word – like Innit One and Innit Two, in t-shirts and jeans, with closely cropped hair. They all looked a bit tough. And every woman was bleached blonde and in a bikini top, mini-skirt and high heels, no matter her age.

It was like stepping through the curtain into Santa's Grotto in a department store, and emerging into a beach bar frequented by Club 18-70 holidaymakers.

In movie scenes such as this – night-time, stranger steps into remote pub – everyone falls silent and stares like idiots at the new arrivals. These celebrating Innit, on the other hand, didn't seem to give a hoot. At least warn me about a full moon or somesuch, I thought.

Then the Major stepped into the doorway and stood beside me. Belatedly everyone went deadly silent and stared like idiots.

"S'im!" shouted one, pointing. It was Gjüt.

"Oo?" enquired another voice.

"That fackin' alien wot we toldjer abaht, innit!"

My eyes sought the speaker. There he was, Tjësser, left-hand corner of the bar, canoodling with a middle-aged lady who might best be described as 'brassy', her belly extruding from a crop-top.

"Oo's that wivim?" shouted someone.

"Some ugly geezer!" replied another.

Bloody cheek, I thought, self-consciously combing a hand through my fringe.

"Do 'em!" Gjüt yelled.

But the crowd remained still, staring and indecisive. Then the Innit nearest me – a younger type with mad eyes and fists – began a slow handclap, chanting, "Scrap! Scrap!"

As a ripple, this chant grew in volume, with the rest of the bar joining in. Clap. Clap. "Scrap!" "Scrap!" Clap. Clap. "Scrap!" "Scrap!"

We could have run, but would never have escaped the baying mob. Anyhow, my exhausted limbs felt incapable of flight. Where was the dwarf when we needed him? I glanced over my shoulder. There he was behind us, out in the snow, wrestling furiously inside a rucksack. One hand gripped the stock of his sawn-off shotgun, the barrel of which had become tangled in clothing and would not pull free.

"Hurry up!" I hissed at him.

Detritos leered at me from beneath his lank quiff.

Our aggressors began advancing.

"Scrap! Scrap!" Clap. Clap.

The one with the mad eyes was but three feet away, smacking a fist into an open palm in time to the others' clapping.

"Fackin' SHUT IT!" came the compelling order.

A hush hit, and all eyes turned towards the little old lady stood on the bar at the back, clutching a loudhailer. She alone did not sport the Innit look; instead, she had a thin face tapering towards the nose and wore a light, flowing floral dress belted at the waist, grey hair tied in a bun, and bovver boots. This, I surmised, was Ma.

"Ma!" sang the Major, flinging his arms wide in unsuppressed glee.

"Major!" sang Ma, although still through the loudhailer. "'Ow ya fackin' doin', yer sexy muvverfacker!"

"Bish your tush!"

"An' swish me bush!"

Then she leapt, sprightly for an oldster, from bar to floor, flinging aside the loudhailer, and the Major set off towards her, arms still aloft. The crowds parted, mute with bewilderment. The Major and Ma met in the middle, he sweeping her into his arms as one might hoist a small child.

Behind me came a muffled explosion. Detritos had accidentally shot his rucksack.

Ma had been the key to everyone's mood. She controlled her patrons; if she liked us then everyone did. There had been slapped backs all round and we were offered warmed ale, hot pine-kernel soup and dry clothing.

I had managed a snatched conversation with the loved-up Upper-Crust, keen to know of his previous acquaintance with Ma.

It went like this.

A few years back his balloon had crash-landed on the similarly snowbound neighbouring island Yamda Wolwus. His ankle had broken and he would have died out in the wilderness, had not a passing little old lady on a snowmobile heard his cries for help. This was Ma, who back then was assistant manageress of fast-food joint Yakkity-Yak Burger. While the Major waited to be rescued by wife Binky in the reserve balloon, he had begun an affair with Ma, who must have been at least 30 years older and three feet shorter than the aviator.

A few ales later, my marrow truly warmed and sleep paddling about my eyeballs, I made my excuses. Upstairs were several guestrooms and I was shown into one where a sturdy wooden bed laden with cream-coloured puffy bedclothes awaited.

I stripped in a second and was asleep in two, as the noise of celebration below hammered into the floorboards.

A bleached-blonde lady with the complexion of an over-ripe orange woke me with a cheery "Awight love?" and a mug of warm ale. Inspirationally cosy, I snuggled into the downy duvet and imagined sharing this bed with Suzy Goodenough. I could inform her of my previous bravery while she fondled her own breasts, then take her during a moment of mutual desire.

How far I had come and, contrary to previous events, how well things at last seemed to be going. Moreover, I had made some friends, far more readily than I ever did back home. Had I become more likeable? Or gained a personality? Either now seemed deliciously feasible.

Ma entered without knocking. "Your Major's a right fackin goer!" she announced. "Blew the cobwebs right artuv me minge!"

I brought up and then swallowed some bile.

"Ma," I said, coughing, "I need to get to Klütz fast. Where can I find transport? A snowmobile?"

"Oooo! 'Ark at 'im!" she scoffed, then adopted a mock-posh voice. "A sneuw-mobile, is it? Perhaps sir would care to have his arse wiped?"

She sat on the bed and pulled my hand into hers, all grandmotherly. "Lissen, love. We ain't got no snowmobiles 'ere – too much bleedin' dough. Got some in Klütz, innit. We's just an outpost."

"Is there another way? I'm desperate."

"Luv-a-duck!" she exclaimed, and I wondered whether she did. "Woss all this 'urry, eh? Is it fer a lady?" Her face softened.

"Yes it is. I'm very much in love."

I thought I should play on her sympathies.

"See, everyone's poor 'ere, lives offa makin' fings fer Christmas. Geezer comes along in December, buys 'em up to export. So we ain't got no high-falutin' transports 'ere…" She paused for a few moments, mulling, before slapping herself on the forehead. "'Old on! Fackin' bingo! I mus' be fackin' stoopid or summink! 'Alf the bleedin' tarn's orfta Klütz – s'the fackin' Iditamush today!"

"Iditamush?"

"Annual dog-sled race, innit!"

"From Klbdow to Klütz?"

"S'right! Takes abaht a day."

I became excited. "And I could hitch a ride with someone?"

"Nah, dahlin'! Everyone's got teams, innit. You'd 'aveta drive it yerself, but I can sort-yer art wiv a sled an' some dogs. An' it needs free people – you got the little fella an' Upper-Crust, innit!"

Was I that desperate? "When does the race begin?"

"Noon."

"And what time are we now?"

"Ten-firty."

It was lunacy.

"Find me some dogs!" I declared, at which Ma gave me a little hug before bustling off to action.

While I prefer spontaneity, Tench is an incessant mitherer. Everything must be planned to the last detail. I consider that this takes the spirit out of adventuring, but he insists, and I am too generous to dispense with his services. After all, what would he do without me?

It is for reasons of planning that he rudely interrupts my writing in Klütz, demanding to know about stocks of medicines and elastic. He knows nothing about my journal – this is the first I have produced and prefer to write it in seclusion – and when he sees it he becomes nosy. What am I writing? Why am I writing it? Will it be published? (Of course!) What part does he play in it? He dares even to become immodest, asking whether his contribution will be "appropriately recognised".

Afterwards, though, I consider what he had said. It is why I

have decided here that I should say a word or two about Caribou Tench, my guide and mother.
Mink features.

I threw on yesterday's clothes, which had been hung beside the bedroom's hearth, its embers practically deceased, by some thoughtful intruder while I slept. This would have been wholly comforting, had I not numbered among my underwear a pair of ladies' bloomers, which I opted to leave off today and hang the cold. However, it was probably all around Klbdow by now that I was a fledgling transvestite. Or perhaps the Innit respected one's privacy?

Tjësser popped his head around the door and pursed his lips mockingly. "Awight, tranny mate?"

"Actually, I wore them to keep warm!" I quickly responded.

"Yer, right!" And the sarcy git was gone.

I packed my bags and hurried downstairs, through pine-boarded corridors lined with photographs of regulars: drunken types, gurning.

Incredibly for that time of day, the bar was heaving, though more quietly than the previous night. Innit men huddled around tables studying maps. Teams preparing for the Iditamush, no doubt.

I spotted the Major instantly, he being the gangliest patron and wearing bright orange. He was leaning against the bar, chatting to a pair of ladies. And there was Detritos, partly obscured by this trio, perched on a bar stool, lecherous and still in that now-bedraggled disco suit.

Upper-Crust spotted me and waved. "Morn-mip the Xander!" he bellowed and instinctively I ducked. "Ma says we're orf sledging with the woofters!"

None of the Innit seemed to notice, or mind, that he was a buffoon.

The bar itself was a pleasantly ornate affair, all wooden, lined with columns and decked with fairylights glowing dimly in the daylight. Carved into it were scenes of Innit life, of moose-hunting, paper-chain-making and cheerful boozing.

Rounding idle drinkers, I reached my travelling companions.

"Hey Vasquez," said the dwarf, teeth showing. "Effer be-eeng meestake for man?" He broke into a dirty snigger and the Innit women giggled for the sake of it.

"There's no time to sit around boozing," I snapped. "The race starts in an hour. Ma's finding us a sled and dogs and we need to learn to drive the bugger."

The Major held up a hand. "Calm the precautions, downster. Upper-Crust has ridden the sleds! No probulumptions!"

"And you've flown balloons before, yet manage to crash every time."

His long face fell.

"Leave 'im alone," whined one of the Innit women. She was in her late-twenties and attractive somewhere beneath a plastering of make-up.

But I did feel guilty. The Major's naive enthusiasm would come in handy during hardship and I should not demoralise him with cynicism.

Ma appeared among us, bovver boots encrusted in snow, still wearing that summery dress. "Oi-oi, lads!" she hollered. "Got yer transport out back, innit!"

The bar was emptying. The Iditamush was almost upon us and I would be taking part.

We three travellers gathered up our belongings, bade farewell to Upper-Crust's two lady-friends, and followed Ma behind the bar and out back.

The first sight of snow was blinding. A blue-washed sun offered some heat, though I was glad of my layers and hide jacket. The air was still.

We were greeted by a chorus of wanton yelping. True to her

word, Ma had found us a team of seven dogs for the sled, all straining to be off but tethered, their tongues lolling. It's just that none of them were huskies.

"Ma," I said. "I'm no expert on dogs, but I can't help noticing that one of our team is a dachshund."

"They call 'im Speedy," she said.

"Who calls him Speedy?" I asked. "Talking tortoises?"

"Aw, I dunalf love 'im," went Ma, all gooey.

"She likeeng you," smarmed the dwarf, winking as if I should take romantic advantage of this.

Less than an hour before the off, we attempted to master dog-sledding.

The vehicle, Ma's own and decidedly basic, looked well-used but sturdy. It was a creosote-stained wooden box with shallow sides, perhaps eight-feet long, on steel runners curved at the front. The driver stood on a square of grooved rubber at the rear, either side of which were two vertical metal rods, like ski poles. He clung to these during cornering, leaning with the curve. A third, shorter rod on the driver's right-hand side acted as the brake, cutting into the packed snow when applied.

I would sit at the front of the sled, behind me came our anchorman (Detritos), and cramped behind him, our belongings. In emergencies – when merely braking was not sufficient – the anchorman was to lob out an actual anchor attached to a length of rope. This would halt the sled's progress with minimum subtlety. The driver (Upper-Crust, heaven help us) stood at the back, yelling commands and generally praying.

The mutts were roped into two lines of three with a lone leader harnessed out front. They ran in this order: the dachshund Speedy at the head, twin shaggy grey mongrels, of indeterminate origin, two golden Labradors, father and son according to Ma, and bringing up the rear, a St Bernard and a large black matted-woolly thing, its eyes so obscured by fur as to be seemingly useless.

Ma named them, pointing, "That's Speedy, Mazza, Shazza, Bazza, Dazza, Cazza and Posh."

Had they been required to track down missing Dalmatians, we might have stood a chance. As a crack dog-sled team, they must have wavered somewhere around Beyond Useless.

"Dan't judge a book by its cover, innit," said Ma, sensing my despondency. "All the huskies was gone, right, but these is my dogs. They'll see y'awright."

That half-blind one at the back won't, I thought grumpily.

Relentlessly positive, she posted us about the sled and offered instruction. My only task was to lean at appropriate moments, which was handy, and the dwarf had to be ready with the anchor. However, this left our progress in the hands of the Major, a man wearing flying goggles.

The commands were basic. "Oi-oi!" meant "Go!", "'Old it!" meant stop, and "Bleedin' 'old it!" meant "Stop NOW!"

We practised a straight run. Speedy was a revelation. So short were his legs that they sank fully into the snow when he was stationary, yet when Upper-Crust yelled "Oi-oi!" he was off like a torpedo, zipping across the surface, all silent intent. This compelled the rest into action. Mazza and Shazza put their heads down and were off, tails up, barking like walruses; Bazza practically dragged his aged father behind him; the St Bernard Cazza bounced forwards, all rippling brown-and-white fur and trailing drool; and Posh, the woollen lunk, set off at right angles to the rest and was dragged along on her side for several yards, gathering snow, until she found her feet and direction and joined the rhythm.

Centimetres from the ground at high speed, staring at a couple of bounding dogs' bottoms, the sensation was exhilarating. Already we were out of the yard and in danger of scooting off into obscurity.

I turned to yell at the Major and was confronted by Detritos's petrified features. His black quiff flung backwards by the momentum, leathery skin blotched red by the chill, sideburns flapping, eyes insanely wide, teeth clenched in a deathly grimace, he looked like a man witnessing the removal of his own leg.

"Tell them to stop!" I howled towards the Major.

"Hold it!" he cried, to no effect.

"Swear at them!"

"Can't profane!" he yelled back. "Too dashed rude! Codely-ode of gentlemen's conduct and all that!"

So I screamed at the dogs, "Bleedin' 'old it!"

Upper-Crust's brake ploughed its furrow through packed ice, the dogs howled in protest, my fingernails sliced into the side of the sled, and suddenly everything was still. Addled senses took a few moments to adapt. We had stopped, we were upright and we were alive.

I turned. The dwarf's expression had not changed. Ma came panting after us, stomping through snow, sodden dress hem trailing behind her. Her pinched face was covered with pride.

"You fackin' done it!"

Celebrating, she indulged in a snog with Upper-Crust, which failed to dampen my spirits.

Detritos was carried inside on Ma's back, where the warmth thawed the terror off his face. We sat silently at one of the tables and, with minutes until the start of the Iditamush, gladly wolfed down more pine-kernel soup – quite bitter, actually – with stale bread and warm ale.

Though we hadn't turned the sled by ourselves, and though I might have to be in charge of rude words, the sheer task ahead made me glow with self-satisfaction. Of course we weren't going to win, in fact we were guaranteed to come last, but we should still reach Klütz in 24 hours, which would put me just two days behind Dextrose, whose sea journey from Emo Island had taken five days. I was catching him up.

Suzy seemed within my grasp. And I had become an adventurer.

By mink, I wish I were on dry land. Since we left Skaramanger, the weather has thrown hailstones and the sea is a rollercoaster ride that never ends.

It is now the fourth day of our journey, with no land in sight, not even on the horizon. I sit at the captain's table on 'Dextrose I', my stomach hanging out of my mouth like placenta. I have nothing left to retch on.

If I could lay hands on the mink-faced mutineer Skink, I would wring his neck. The lily-livered codger's pelmet.

We are undermanned. Shark either whines or pukes, going about his tasks with the grace of a cornered hog, so I must trust our fortunes to Tench, who remains accursedly calm. The minker.

Ma came across to the table where Detritos, Upper-Crust and I were in deep thought and handed me a sheet of paper.

"Forgotta give yer this, dahlin'," she said. "Nuffink impowtant."

It read:

IDITAMUSH – ROOLS
NO LITTA
NO SPITTIN
NO CHEETIN (NOT REELY!)

LAST TEEM TO KLÜTZ SPENDS TEN DAYS
MAKIN PAPER CHAYNS

No one had mentioned this before. But what choice did I have? Short of lassoing a passing moose and steering it towards Klütz, this race was my only hope. Yet if – when – we came last, spending ten days making paper chains would ruin any chance of beating Dextrose to Aghanasp.

The situation reeked of disaster. "Ma, what are our chances of not coming last?"

"Nuffink," she said.

As I had suspected.

"Course," she added, "I could always 'elp yer art, innit."

I was all ears. Ma leant into the table, joints cracking. The Major and Detritos joined the huddle, our four heads meeting. Ma took the opportunity to lick Upper-Crust's cheek affectionately.

"I got a plan," she began. "There's this geezer, Tjörd – fat bloke, no 'air, t-shirt – drives the sled fer Tjöm and Tjïm. Superstitious, innit. Every Iditamush, jus' 'fore the race, 'e's in 'ere, wants a fackin' 'ot toddy – ale, stout an' pine kernels. 'Ow abaht, I spike the facker wiv strychnine!"

I needed to get this straight. "Poison a man to death, you mean?"

"Yeah!" Her face was alight.

"What-ho!" exclaimed the Major, raising a triumphant fist.

"Eef Ma no killeeng heem, who deed, sir?" added the dwarf.

I was appalled. "We can't kill a man just to avoid losing a race!"

"Shhh!" hissed Ma, putting a finger to her lips.

"Couldn't we just drug him?"

"Wot? Like an overdose?"

"Or something less permanent?" I offered. "A few sleeping pills?"

There came a banging on the bar, startling us. A plump shaven-headed man in white t-shirt, jeans and bovver boots was staring towards our huddle, his lumpen fist resting on the wooden surface. His forehead was permanently creased, causing a bulge of flesh to hang over his nose like a snowdrift. The man was the size of a portaloo.

"That's 'im," whispered Ma. "That's Tjörd." She straightened up and assumed the manner of a manageress. "'Owd on dahlin'. Be right wiv yer. Fackin' 'ot toddy, innit?"

Ma winked at me conspiratorially.

The whole of Klbdow, it seemed, had gathered in front of Ma's Bar for the Iditamush. Innit people crowded, chattering before the row of Christmas-card buildings. In a trampled white clearing, ten sleds were lined up and tethered to posts, their dog teams straining to forge ahead. Nine sets of seven huskies, like fluffy wolves, keen-eyed, tails curled... and our bunch of misfits, none less excitable. Breath moved in clouds and the air was alive with yelping.

Though it was shortly before noon the daylight seemed tired. The fairylights shed dim multi-colours about the snow and lamps burning in windows made indoors look inviting.

There was one bizarre, very disconcerting incident as we loaded our sled. From out of the crowd, a man wearing a beige raincoat with the collar turned up, brown trilby hat and dark glasses – certainly no Innit – appeared suddenly from among the spectators, marched towards our sled, slapped Detritos across the cheek and ran off into the forest, coat-tails flapping, before anyone could react.

Though the dwarf's ludicrous sideburns had no doubt cushioned the blow, he stood there massaging his cheek with one hand, clinging to his leather briefcase with the other, and thoughtfully gazing after the assailant.

"What the hell was that about?" I asked.

Detritos ignored me. Though there was something funny going on, time was simply too short to dwell on the matter. With our gear loaded, we took up positions in the sled.

Ours was furthest right of the ten; next to us was Tjörd's sled, he at the rear, with Tjïm and Tjöm sat inside. Tjïm and Tjöm were identical twins, but since all the Innit looked the same, different levels of beer-belly notwithstanding, the term 'twin' became largely redundant.

For his part, Tjörd looked unaffected by any form of drug. Had Ma used a slow-working sleeping potion? Or had she let us down?

With moments until the off, Ma came to say goodbye and handed me a bag of goodies. "Summink nice to eat on the journey an' a pair of gloves an' woolly 'at, t'keep yer warm. Me dogs'll see y'awright."

I realised I hadn't paid the lady for my stay. Trouble was, I told her, the currency here was the knicka, but all my travellers' cheques were in sterling.

"Lissen, lover, jus' giz a big snog an' we'll call it quits, eh?"

Lordy, I thought, I'd rather pay cash. Our dry lips met and her cold, slimy tongue forced its way towards mine like a persistent slug.

At that moment, some sort of dignitary took centre-stage, wearing the usual garb topped off with a black tricorn hat trimmed with golden braid. He tried to puff out his chest, but was fighting a losing battle against his belly. Accompanying him was a blonde-haired teenager in white stilettos with matching bikini and fixed grin.

Someone dropped an old crate into the snow. The dignitary hefted himself onto it and held up his arms for hush.

"Oi-oi!" he called.

"Oi-oi!" everyone called back.

"Welcome, you lot, to the fackin' 'undred an' fiff Iditamush, innit," he bellowed, wheezing. "I fink I speak for us all when I says... Bollocks!'"

Everyone found this hilarious.

The dignitary continued, "Nah. Lissen. We 'ave a new team this year, innit. Our friend the Major, some short cant an' some ugly geezer. I don't want no one larfin', right, but I could beat their sled, right, sat on a drip-tray pulled along by Ma!"

Everyone found this hilarious, too.

It was not the first time I had endured mocking laughter. The worst instance occurred at that dinner with Wilf the tree sprite, my childhood friend.

My parents had invited him to dine with us, which I knew was a bad idea, given Wilf's toilet humour. But I could hardly use that as a reason for turning down the invitation. Father would have gone ballistic had he known that I was mixing with someone uncouth.

So I determined to make it the best dinner ever by teaching Wilf some manners beforehand and staging a post-meal, two-handed play for my parents. Posh kids did that all the time, according to Sunday teatime television dramas.

Wilf took to manners like a duck to flames. I spent a full evening after school atop the middle evergreen teaching him to say "Please" and "Thank you" and "May I take your hat?" Also, how one holds one's knife and fork and not to use the fork like a shovel, and practising the art of small-talk.

"So Wilfred," I began. "How was your day?"

"Shit!" he snapped in that voice of his that sounded like a pig snuffling.

"The phrase you're looking for is, 'Very good, thank you'."

"But it wasn't. It was shit," he persisted.

"Well, in what manner was it unpleasant?"

Wilf held up his right leg and peeled off his leather boot. "My foot went rotten."

Indeed it had. It had turned green and was leaking pus. I panicked. His teeth were bad enough; one could hardly take home to meet one's parents someone whose foot had gone rotten.

"How did that happen?" I demanded.

Wilf became sulky. "Dunno."

"Of course you do!"

"Bloody don't!"

My face flushed. "Don't swear, it's rude."

"So's going to a dinner party with a rotten foot."

Then I clicked. "You did this on purpose, didn't you! You made your foot leak pus just so you could show me up in front of my parents!"

Wilf sneered, graveyard teeth appearing between his matted ginger whiskers. So it was true.

"You git!" I snapped.

"Made you swear! Made you swear! Made you lose your underwear!"

I tried to calm matters. "We'll be alright as long as you keep your boot on. And we can stuff some mints down it, to keep it from smelling... Actually, *you* can stuff some mints down it to keep it from smelling."

It was even more difficult to get Wilf to learn his lines for the after-dinner play. It was a piece I had penned myself, though based on one I had seen on television recently about a prince with a skull. At the start of my play, entitled *Danish Village*, a young boy named Hurdy loses his beloved dog, Yorkie, and spends the rest of the time finding it and, later, true love. I would play Hurdy; Wilf would be Yorkie.

We argued over the final scene and Wilf insisted that he write it himself. He had the dog dying in Hurdy's arms, just as his former love, the immigrant girl from Lancashire, returned to our hero's side. Hurdy's closing speech went, "A lass, poor Yorkie! I knew her fellatio!"

I had no idea what it meant, but was sure that a little Latin would impress Father.

I stressed to Wilf how much his good behaviour would mean to me, and he seemed to take this on board. We were the best of friends, after all.

We dusted down his green tunic and trousers, tightened his large-buckled belt around his stomach, poured a packet of Extra Strong Mints down the boot of his rotten foot, combed his beard and I pulled his daft green hat down over his greasy red hair. Finally, we winked at each other and clambered down the tree.

Wilf had never been inside our house. With suspicion, he eyed the dimly lit, austere reception with its framed, faded photographs of haughty, well-heeled types – purchased from antiques shops, though Father claimed the people were ancestors – and the dark oak stairs running upwards into the gloom of our landing. He said it was a smaller version of those castles on hills that princesses are imprisoned in.

Father and Mother were waiting for us in the charmless dining room, he at the head of the dining table, she to his left. They stood as we entered. Father wore his tweed suit with matching waistcoat, the sort of thing Toad of Toad Hall would wear; Mother had replaced her usual apron with a thin sky-blue cardigan. She blinked and looked downwards, more nervous than usual.

Wilf tried to cower behind me but I pushed him into the limelight. "Father, Mother, this is my friend Wilf," I said. "He's a tree sprite."

"Hmmph," said Father. Mother stared uneasily at her placemat.

"Charming," muttered Wilf sarcastically, so I trod on his foot, which squelched.

We sat: Wilf opposite Father – too distant for the smell to carry – myself opposite Mother. She shot me the furtive glance that suggested I tread carefully.

When Mother excused herself to fetch food from the kitchen, we men sat in stiff-backed silence and I watched Wilf nervously, praying that he would behave. He seemed frozen.

Mother returned with four plates of lamb chops, boiled potatoes, peas and weak gravy, placed one in front of each of us, and we began to eat, cutlery clinking over the painful hush.

Eventually, Mother asked me, "Should we call him Wilfred?"

"Don't humour him, Mother," snapped Father.

I gobbled down the food, so that we might move onto my play, which would surely lighten matters. Wilf's plate remained untouched. He sat stock still, staring at Father, either petrified or irate – it was hard to tell.

"Doesn't Wilf like lamb chops, potatoes, peas and gravy?" Father asked accusingly.

Wilf didn't answer. I replied for him. "He likes cheese best."

Father's obsessively groomed ginger moustache curled downwards.

Mother gave me a sympathetic look and I shot a glance at Wilf, who continued to stare at Father. It was like we were playing wink murder, with all of the tension but none of the fun.

"I'll clear away the plates," said Mother.

Father rested his hands on the table. "You do that."

"I've got a surprise!" I blurted out, one knee twitching.

"Another one?" said Father.

"We've written a play, me and Wilf. We're going to perform it for you."

Mother, who was at Father's side, both hands lifting his dinner plate, froze. Her face tightened and she began her dance of nervousness. Father pushed his hands towards me across the table and leaned in.

His thin, anaemic lips contorted into a sneer. His flaky-skinned cheeks burned red.

"*You've* written a play!" Father bellowed, flecking my face with spittle that I dared not remove. "I was hoping that inviting your imaginary friend to dinner would shame you into stopping this nonsense. Instead, you dare to turn up – and then tell me you've written a play."

I shrank back into my chair, shoulderblades against hard wood. "It's called *Danish Village*," I offered plaintively. "I play

Hurdy and Wilf…"

Father sat back down. "*Danish Village? Danish Village?*"

He slapped one hand on the table and the other on my shocked mother's backside, and began to laugh, a whiny, nasal, derisive laugh. He laughed so much he began rocking backwards and forwards in his seat. Mother had gone pale and looked at me with grey, saucer eyes.

Father eventually managed to control his hilarity. "You've written a play! And what use would that be? Plays are for thespians and thespians live in cloud-cuckoo land!"

Mother started crying, still clutching his gravy-smeared plate. "Father…" she barely whispered, biting her lower lip.

He ignored her and ranted, "There are societies in the village that you could have joined; there are schoolbooks you could have read; you could have helped your mother with the gardening. But no. You've written a play! You and your imaginary friend…"

That phrase again. What did he mean? I turned to see Wilf's indignation but he wasn't there. His seat was empty; his meal remained untouched, now cold.

I stood sharply, toppling my chair, and ran from the room as the first tear trickled.

The following morning was a Saturday. Usually Mother would wake me at 7.30am sharp with tea – meaning a long day in which to achieve nothing – but it was almost eleven by the time she came.

As I dressed, I noticed out of the window that the middle evergreen had been felled. Barefoot, in pyjama bottoms and jumper, I went out onto the lawn and stared at it lying uselessly, flattened and already dying. Wilf had gone for good.

"Right!" yelled the dignitary. "Fack orf… NAH!"

Restraining leads were severed; 70 dogs yelped in unison; Upper-Crust hollered "Oi-Oi!" and, to my left, Tjörd keeled over backwards. Ma's sleeping drug had finally taken effect!

With their driver prostrate in the snow, Tjörd's dogs slewed off at a right angle, straight into the path of the other teams. Tjïm and Tjöm clung on for grim death as their sled slammed into the side of Number Eight, while the lines of tethered dogs took out Numbers Seven to One in a tangle of mutts and rope.

Meanwhile, Speedy had his head down, inciting Mazza, Shazza, Bazza, Dazza and Cazza into action, as Posh attempted her sideways sprint. I craned to see the chaos behind us, a heap of cursing, scrapping Innit and frantic dogs. We were only bloody winning!

It would be deceptive to call our progress steady. As we had already ascertained, the Major was at home on the straights, but panicked on a bend of any description, leaning over too far and often toppling the sled. This caused minor injury but no breakages of equipment or limb, as we were yet to master anything approaching a maximum speed.

"You'll get the hang of it, Major," I'd say.

"Really?" he'd reply, genuinely surprised.

The route was well marked. Tall sticks topped with orange flags were arranged at regular intervals along the featureless sections of continuous snow. When we entered forestation, there would be a wide path cut through the densely packed evergreens.

But it was bleak out there. Few birds troubled the eggshell blue of the sky and though a few pawprints criss-crossed our path, we saw no wildlife.

Comfortingly, perhaps half-an-hour into the race, there remained no sight nor sound of any rivals, so it was only our seven mutts that churned up the virgin white. Our progress also made the sole sounds: the insistent, rhythmic panting of the dogs, their feet crunching through the snow's icy crust, the

Major's commands and the Dwarf's whimpers. I sat mesmerised, in awe that scenery so desolate could be so captivating.

The Major was finally getting the hang of steering. Overturning became a rarity and when we took our first sharp bend without spillage, we cheered in unison. Ah, the comradeship.

After a few hours we spotted the first marshal. The race covered roughly 100 miles and Ma had told us we would pass four such officials at 20-mile intervals, offering food and medical supplies if required. There would be one scheduled rest, halfway through the race, in the tiny outpost known as Klona, population: one.

Ma had said that the sole inhabitant, Bob, was a hermit-figure who had departed civilisation several decades hence, to set up shack in the middle of nowhere. His only contact with humanity occurred during the Iditamush, when he traditionally offered hospitality.

The marshal was on a wooden stool, at the bottom of a shallow slope, wearing the regulation t-shirt and jeans, his only sartorial concession to officialdom being a logo across the front of the shirt, in red letters. It read: 'Fackin Marshul'.

"Oi-Oi!" he cried, waving. Then he must have realised it was us, because his mouth dropped open and his knuckles fell as far as his arms would allow.

"Where are we?" I yelled towards him.

He seemed confused. "Klükamüs!"

"No, I mean, where in the race?"

"Fackin' first," he replied incredulously.

I knew this, of course. I had just wanted to rub it in.

Then we were past him and away.

"That showed him!" I shouted.

"Getteeng Detritos!" the dwarf cried. "Geef out weengs!"

"I'm only bally getting the hang of this contrumption!" came the Major's cry as we hit a rock.

When I pushed my top half out of its snow tomb, face burning, the marshal was above me, sniggering.

"You awight, mate?"

As he grabbed an arm, heaving me to my feet, the distant sound of approaching sleighbells reached our snow-burned ears. The marshal cupped a hand towards it theatrically and noted with barely disguised triumph, "Sands like the uvvers is comin'."

The 'uvvers' were indeed coming. Doggie yelps and growled orders became audible among the bells. Hastily, we remounted the sled and were away, back into the white.

"Major!" I yelled. "Can't we go any faster?"

"Well, bam-spit, the junior Xander!" he called back. "Going as bally fast as one can!"

The sky had begun to darken, which would make the going more treacherous. The race organisers had realised this too – as we negotiated the top of one of the steeper slopes, which led down into a bowl-shaped valley, parallel rows of flaming torches stretched into the distance.

We flew easily down the other side, although the sound of pursuing dogs and men then became intense. Someone had crossed over the ridge behind us.

An Innit voice shouted, "Oi!"

"Oi-oi!" I called out, in the spirit of friendly competition.

"Fack orf!" came the reply as a lead husky drew parallel with me. It glanced my way briefly, snarling, followed by six more huskies and two seated Innit.

"Awight, cant?" enquired the front one.

"Fine, thank, you," I replied.

Their driver was bare-armed, a muscley, tattooed beast –

'Simpel and prowd' read his bicep – with a square head. Trails of snot had dripped from his nose and become frozen across his cheeks, then flailed out behind him, like disgusting icicles.

"Posh twot," he snorted.

So much for the spirit of friendly competition.

Within ten minutes, our sled was overtaken on either side by a barking, yelping, grunting, heavy-breathing mass of dogs and men, all too interested in jockeying for position to pay us much attention. Just as quickly as they had appeared, they were gone before us, into the gloom.

It was demoralising. I tried to count them, but confusion reigned. "How many do you reckon there were?" I called back.

"Maybe seex, maybe seextee," the dwarf replied.

"Bally seventeen, I tot-the-totted!" yelled the Major.

The clots.

We crossed another blank plane of snow, flaming torches on either side. In the distance lay a further mass of woodland.

When we reached our second marshal, I asked after our position.

"Dunno. Elevenf?"

"But there are only ten teams in the race."

"You sure?"

"Yes."

"Must be tenf then."

He pointed ahead, to the sled track that sliced between twin clusters of looming pine. "Fru there – right? – you'll see coupla lights an' a titchy wooden 'ouse. Bob's gaff. Stop there. Right? 'E'll give yer summink to eat. An' feed them fackin' dogs. Look fackin' knackered."

I caught this in Doppler effect as we slewed past him, into the woods.

"Thank you very much!" I called back.

"Tosser!" he trilled.

But the wind had been sucked from my sails. Of course it had been folly to entertain the notion that we might maintain our lead in the Iditamush.

It was inescapable: we had to be last. The fairytale was over; our prince had turned back into a frog and his princess was sobbing among female friends who talked of more fish in the sea. I felt the chill as if I were naked. The air was madly cold and the adrenalin that had kept me warm now ceased to circulate. I felt for my nose, but it was like feeling for my nose with someone else's fingers.

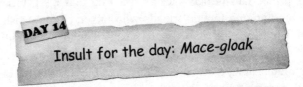

It was the dachshund's delighted high-pitched barking that alerted us to our imminent arrival in Klona. A cluster of lanterns had been hung from branches and to the right of the track stood a wooden signpost with the name of the settlement and, beneath that, 'Population:' with a '2' crossed out and replaced by '1'.

Someone must have died here. I shuddered at the thought of ghosts roaming the wilderness.

Upper-Crust yelled for the dogs to stop and they required no second bidding, dropping onto their bellies in one mass of panting and clouding steam. The Major, Detritos and I dismounted, stretched limbs and stomped, restarting frozen circulations.

There were no other sleds about. As Ma had warned us, some teams wouldn't stop, keen to continue through hunger and the night in the quest for victory. Since we were last, there was nought to lose.

We tethered the sled and fed the dogs with provisions provided by Ma. Then it was time for us to eat.

Bob's log cabin was set back into the forest. It had a flat roof that sloped forward, from which snow drooped like pillows, and from the side protruded a bent tin chimney topped with a conical lid. Set into the front of the cabin was a door and a single window, shuttered. It was a simple existence.

The door swung open and an aged man, naked but for socks

and a pure-white beard extensive enough to cover his private parts, bounded out like a puppet set free from its strings.

"Hee-hee! Hee-hee!" he cackled as he circled us, leaping dementedly.

Bob had aged, clammy-looking skin with patches of wiry charcoal-grey thatch on his calves and forearms. His head was bald, scalp bruised and flaky, and his black, piggy eyes glinted with madness.

His movements were most disconcerting. Imagine an overgrown foetus undergoing electric-shock therapy. Bob's back was so curved that his spine stuck out like a mountain range. As he danced, he brought his knees up so far that he might break his own nose, and his arms flailed.

"Here for the hospital-the-tality!" announced the Major, who, bless him, hadn't realised that our host was several elves short of a grotto.

We gave up on an invitation so made our way indoors as Bob continued to circle, going, "Hee-hee! Hee-hee!"

Inside, a cast-iron stove, topped by a pot, gave out welcome heat. Animal pelts hung from the timber walls, alongside stuffed black birds with beady eyes and bird skeletons. Small bones littered the floor. The only comforts available were a short three-legged stool and grey woollen blanket, rumpled and stained. The place smelled of dampness and decay.

Turning and emitting a shriek, I realised why. In one corner, amid shadows, a decrepit-looking woman with sunken cheeks and tissue-paper skin lay slumped in a rocking chair. Wearing an ankle-length black dress, with wild silver hair splayed about her shoulders, she looked like a witch. Her eyes were closed and gossamer strands of spider's web trailed from her lips. She might have been dead for decades.

It was like walking into a real-life horror movie.

My shriek had alerted the dwarf to her presence, who leapt

into my arms quivering. The Major turned too, performed a short bow and said, "Good evening, madam."

The witch's eyes blinked open. The dwarf and I yelped in unison. She wiped her mouth with the back of her hand, removing strands of drool I had mistaken for cobwebs.

"I'm not dead, you know," she said.

Upper-Crust took one of her translucent hands and kissed it. "Pleased to meet you, Mrs Not-Dead."

Relieved that Bob was merely eccentric, not psychopathic, I dropped the dwarf, who picked himself up and clung to my thigh.

"He thinks I'm dead, you know," she continued indignantly, motioning towards Bob, who was now crouched on the floor toying with bones.

Detritos and I were too horrified to speak, so she continued uninvited.

"I'm his mother!" she screeched. "See how he treats me? Said we should come here after his father died. 'Get away from it all' he said. 'Go stark raving bonkers' would have been more like it!"

Bob sprang towards his mother and leapt up and down angrily, chanting, "She is dead! She is dead!"

"I am *not* dead! I sleep a lot because there's nothing else to do!"

Bob rushed at me, knuckles trailing, and clawed my arm. "She goes a little mad sometimes. We all go a little mad sometimes."

He then scuttled back to his mother and implored her in a child's voice, "Tell them about Daddy."

"I won't speak of that disgusting man!" she snapped.

"Not quite herself today," said Bob, at which the ancient harpy fell asleep.

Detritos let go of my leg. "She scareeng."

Bob stroked his arm as the dwarf shrank between my legs.

"She's as harmless as one of my stuffed birds," he said.

Being famished, we chanced Bob's dubious hospitality. I removed my gloves, hat, hide jacket and oversized wellington boots, which began to hiss as the sweat condensed. Detritos kept on his love-god suit and the Major, who was having to bow down to avoid putting his head through the roof, pulled his flying goggles up to his forehead. He was either impervious to the cold or too barking to notice.

"So, Bob," I said, hoping to spark sane conversation, "where are you from?"

"Oh God, Mother! Blood! Blood!" shrieked Bob in the manner of someone in amateur dramatics, staring at his hands which weren't bloody at all.

Forget the small-talk. "We're very hungry…"

"I hate the smell of dampness," said Bob.

The Major bowed. "One does."

"A very tall man!" said Bob, pointing.

Proactivity was required. Some feeling had returned to my feet, so I went to the stove to inspect the pot, which was empty.

"It's empty," I said.

Bob adopted an expression of pantomime-shock.

I was losing patience. Then I remembered Ma's pine-kernel soup, which was still in the sled, which Detritos begrudgingly fetched.

I handed one bottle of the pine-kernel concoction to Bob. "Could you warm this up, please?"

The hermit fellow held it close to his face, inspected it and then smashed it over his head. Thick brown glop and pine kernels slid off his bonce and dribbled down his face, catching in his beard. One blob dripped from his nose, which he intercepted with his tongue and swallowed.

We shared the last two bottles cold and scarpered.

As I closed the door to the cabin, Bob's anguished cry rose

from inside, "For God's sake don't leave! I'm going mad in here!"

His mother, who must have woken, piped up, "Me too!"

I am not one for foreign food. Mrs Dextrose once cooked me spaghetti and I forced her to knit it into a small cardigan. When foreign food is the only option, I am content to survive on booze, which contains several vitamins and proteins.

The muck I have been offered! Monkey testicles (scooped straight from the scrotum sac!); the braised hump of a camel I had ridden only that morning (so I knew where that hump had been); the indelicate root of something the locals knew colloquially as 'swamp snot'... Foreigners make the most mink-brained assumptions. Eat an animal's brain, you become cleverer (hardly an option for myself!). Eat an animal's eyes, you can see in the dark (I have automatic night vision, evolved over decades of night-time adventuring!). Pork-scratched lunacy.

I recall once being offered a broth of dubious concoction. "What's in it?" I demanded. "Three type of animal penis," I'm told, with no hint of an apology. "Make you more manly!" the minker adds.

"Mink off!" I tell him. "If Harrison Dextrose became any more manly, he'd be... well, anyway... You can stuff it up your mink and mink off, you must think me some mink-headed badger-minker, you mink-stained minkhole! Mink me!" (Later, ruminating on the exchange, as one does, I realised that "Too many cocks spoil the broth" might have made a more eloquent riposte. I shall store it for another time – and, as one who wanders the globe for others' benefit, be sure that there will be another time.)

With foodstuff inside me, the cold felt bracing rather than burdening. Upper-Crust and Detritos were already in their positions, childishly expectant. Speedy, Mazza, Shazza, Bazza, Dazza, Cazza and Posh had their tails up and seemed rejuvenated, too. Was there a chance of catching a straggling rival? Vain hope endured.

Within the hour, we passed our third marshal, asleep at his post. Forty miles to go.

As the journey wore on, our spirits once again began to droop. Amid a sulky silence, the sled took a tumble.

While we bickered, Bazza, the young golden Labrador, somehow escaped his harness, turned on his heel and scarpered towards infinity.

Ma was going to kill us.

Still we pulled ourselves together and were arguing again as our fourth race marshal came into view.

I tried to be positive. "Look, our last marshal! We're almost home!"

"But we last," muttered Detritos.

"We might still catch someone! One of the other sleds might break down... or lose a dog."

"Only way winneeng, uzzers dead."

The marshal began waving his arms violently. "Oi-oi!" he shouted across. "The uvvers is fackin' dead!"

It would have been insensitive to leap from the sled and dance a jig of celebration.

According to the marshal, freak localised temperatures had opened up a crevice on frozen Lake Woowta, a few miles up ahead. The lead sled was thought to have been travelling so fast that it had slid into the exposed water before anyone could react and had sunk into the depths. The battle for second place had been so tight that it was assumed the remaining sleds had been too concerned with race position, and had spotted the danger too late. Only when competitors failed to reach Klütz had a search party been sent to look for them, and the tragedy was discovered.

The dwarf spoke: "Bruzzer, Harry Baylee, breakeeng ice age nine."

There seemed little point in continuing. The Iditamush and my quest had been ruthlessly put into perspective.

The marshal grabbed a scruff of clothing at my throat, lifted me off my feet and spoke into my nostrils. "Lissen, mate. People pop it awl the fackin' time. It's 'ard aht 'ere. We Innits is tough, y'know? When me muvver – gawd luv 'er – give birf to me, she wuz in me Dad's sawmill, right, lyin' on wood shavin's. No lardy-da cotton wool to wrap me in, right. Y'know wot they wrapped me in?"

I didn't.

"San'paper. That's 'ow 'ard we Innits is. Nah, you get aht there an' finish this fackin' race. Give the people of Klütz summink to cheer abaht."

With 20 miles to cover, we set off in mournful silence. A new route, the marshal said, had been marked out, to skirt the hazardous Lake Woowta.

Sunlight wakened the sky and the shifting shadows of clouds blotted the landscape. As we journeyed further towards Klütz, signs of life became evident. Vegetation was growing in patches among previously barren snow planes and bird cries reached our ears.

The sun warmed our cheeks with a deep orange glow. Anyone seeing us would imagine we were adept travellers, at one with this land. Imagine if Father could see me now. Would he be proud? He'd probably drag me home by the ear, tell me to be realistic – "Become an accountant" – and send me to my room. Sod him.

For the first time on my travels, I did not find the prospect of home life preferable. How could I have contemplated vegetating on the sofa, when all this lay out here waiting to be experienced? I had learned more about myself and about the human spirit during these 14 days than I had done during 14 years of daytime television. The explorer's life was for me!

Still, the mutts were weary, as were we, having not slept in almost 24 hours. The Iditamush no longer concerned us, we merely wanted to finish, to leave behind the bastard sled.

When we reached our first smallholding, set some way back from the track, an Innit woman came out, clutching a baby, and waved. She was joined by a young boy, in t-shirt and shorts, who stood and stared. We waved anyway, grateful to have reached civilisation.

Thus distracted, the Major overbalanced and we totalled the sled in front of them. The small boy's happy laughter reached us on the breeze.

As we pulled ourselves together, there came another sound, one shrouded in *déjà vu*: sleighbells.

We strained our eyes back along the route, shielding them from the snow's glare, waiting, until, over the brow of the previous hill, something ominous appeared: a sled.

"Must be locals," I offered unconvincingly.

"Or Santa," suggested Upper-Crust.

But it looked just like an Iditamush sled, pulled by two rows of dogs and manned by three humans – and travelling at speed.

Then it struck me. "Tjörd!"

I had forgotten all about our drugged rival, assuming him to be out for the count. He could never have come around quickly enough to have joined the chasing pack. But, hulk that he was, Tjörd might just have recovered in enough time to warrant a rearguard action. The mood he must have been in, he would have ridden like the wind. Yes, it was him.

Crisis. As the dwarf helpfully pointed out, "He winneeng – we last." Hence, ten days making paper chains.

"Shit!" I yelped, which spurred us into action.

We screamed at the dogs to shift, but needn't have bothered.

They too sensed the urgency.

"Where's Tjörd?" I called to the Major.

"Bally gaining!" he called back.

The Innit spectators were now cheering not waving, sensing a race. Tjörd's sleighbells had become a dissonant clanging in my ears. I heard the Major utter a cheery "Pip-pip!", and the now-traditional "Fack orf!" in response.

As I turned to my right, Tjörd's lead dog, a vicious-looking wolfen thing, had drawn level, teeth bared, eyes silvery, drooling. Unlike our cuddly domestic creatures, *that* was a track animal. Six more hastened past, until our teams were neck and neck.

Their sled slowed to match our pace. Twins Tjïm and Tjöm glared frostily and one gesticulated, suggesting that I might enjoy onanism.

Tjörd barked an order, to which his dogs veered sharply across and their sled clattered into ours. On collision Tjïm (or Tjöm) pushed his palm into my chin. They were trying to force us off the track! Spectators cheered in approval.

"Cheats!" I squealed, aware of the hypocrisy.

Three, four, five more times they clattered us. Each time, I feared obliteration, but our dogs were now snarling back at theirs and wrenching the skidding sled back on course.

A new order from Tjörd and his sled pulled away from ours with ease.

The Major urged on our hounds, who responded with a burst of speed from nowhere. Detritos and I joined in the encouragement, yelling and whooping. Incredibly, we weren't losing ground. The effort required to catch up must have exhausted the huskies.

Just ahead of us, the Innit driver reached forwards to accept something from Tjïm (or Tjöm). A jerry can. I watched with foreboding as, carefully balanced, he unscrewed its lid with his teeth.

Spitting the cap aside, Tjörd swivelled, leered at me and began slooshing liquid across the snow before us, which instantly melted. The git had anti-freeze!

Our runners shrieked as they bit into exposed gravel. The dogs yowled as their feet encountered the same. We were grinding to a halt.

Suddenly, Detritos was clambering onto my shoulders, whirling our anchor on its rope like a cowboy's lasso. He let go and it flew towards the departing sled, one anchor prong catching on the hem of Tjörd's jeans. The Dwarf yanked and the driver's leg shot backwards and upwards, tearing his grip from the sled. The whole contraption unbalanced, his dogs lurched into a heap and the sled cartwheeled. Tjïm and Tjöm flew into space, wailing.

A great roar of approval went up from the crowd.

Meanwhile, tenacity had dragged our dog-team through the defrosted ground onto soft snow and we were again progressing, past our groaning rivals and their howling mutts, between crowds of delirious spectators, towards a banner just yards ahead announcing: "Finnish, Innit".

We had only bloody done it! We three men in a sled plus Speedy, Mazza, Shazza, Bazza (now missing), Dazza, Cazza and Posh. We had won the Iditamush!

Happy, clapping Innit people surrounded us, beginning a period of slapped backs, congratulations and body heat. That we had blatantly cheated seemingly only enhanced our achievement in their eyes.

It was a heady experience, shattered by the sight of Tjörd parting the crowds, followed by Tjïm and Tjöm. They stopped before us as all fell silent. We faced each other off. It was like the showdown at the OK Corral, except there was no corral and this wasn't OK.

But gradually, against the odds, Tjörd's face creased into a grin until he began bellowing with laughter. Tjïm and Tjöm joined in, then the crowd.

Our rivals extended hands to shake. "Gotta 'and it to yers," said Tjörd. "Yer deserved that, yer fackin' cheats!"

"Free cheers fer the cheats!" came the cry.

The Major, Detritos and I were hustled towards a makeshift platform, where a Klütz official, in t-shirt, corduroys and tricorn hat, awaited us with open arms and an insincere expression.

As we mounted the platform, he bade silence from the crowd. "Nah," he began. "As yer know…"

"Yeah, we do, fackin' get on wiv it!" someone heckled.

"Awight. 'Ere's yer certificates," snapped the dignitary and lobbed rolled-up paper at us.

The crowd went ecstatic, leaping and dancing as one, throwing clothing into the air, and we were once again enveloped in a warm mass of well-wishers. It was flattering but too much in my exhausted state.

"I really need to sleep!" I yelled into the ear of the nearest Innit head.

"Cam wiv me!" the head yelled back, and I was clasped by the wrist and pulled through the throng, out into open space and apparent sanity.

"Foller us, sir," said my rescuer, a squat young fellow. "Me name's Yuno. Least 'at's wot everyone calls us, y'know?"

He led me past shopfronts, along slush-laden pavements, into a wooden house with a door, up some stairs and into a bedroom with a bed, where I became dead to the world.

I was surprised to find Yuno cuddled in beside me when I came to, the white brightness of a Klükamüs daytime drenching the room.

I nudged him. "Er, excuse me."

His eyes sprang open. "Wha'?"

"You're in bed with me!"

"Sorry, sir. I ain't never slept wiv the winner of an Iditamush before, y'know?"

"What's wrong with your own bed?"

"This *is* me own bed, sir!"

Oh. "I'd have happily taken the spare bed."

"Wot spare bed?"

There was an awkward silence.

"Well!" I announced, throwing off the single bedsheet, noting with relief that I was clothed. "No time to dawdle! I have a quest to complete!"

"Yer not leavin', are yer, sir?"

"Afraid so. Behind schedule."

"But yer won the Iditamush. Yer an 'ero."

"Thank you. But I really have to go."

"I fink yer an 'ero, sir."

"Really, it was nothing."

"Weren't nuffink. It were sumfink, y'know?"

Though I assumed Yuno to be in his early-twenties, he had a

childish face – flushed, chubby and smooth with eager-to-please eyes. His shaven head was sprouting a fine stubbly black growth. I didn't want to hurt his feelings, but risked it anyway, leaping over him in a single bound to the floor.

"Where's the bathroom?"

I glanced around the room. Whitewashed wooden walls, one bed, one small fireplace, piled high with ash, one poster of a topless woman.

"Er, where are my bags?"

"Dunno, sir. Sleds get taken to Djüke's – 'spect they's there, y'know?"

"Not to worry. So, where's the bathroom?"

"Ain't got one, sir. Got a tub in the kitchin, warmest room in the 'ouse, see. I'll sort yer art a barf, sir."

"Don't worry, I'm sure I can…"

But Yuno was already out of the room and scuttling downstairs.

It was tempting to indulge in a lie-in while Yuno prepared the bath. I stripped off my outer layers and spread them out before the meagre warmth of the expiring fire, shivered a little and climbed back into bed.

So all-consuming had the Iditamush been that it felt weird now it was over. Euphoria dispensed with, the winning seemed to matter less than the taking part. What had I learned? The value of friendship; that even the most inhospitable places have something to offer; that pubs and shops aren't always necessary; self-worth and self-esteem; that those who make rules should sometimes be ignored… This was deep stuff. Too deep for someone who had only just woken up.

Here was my Day 15, late morning. Dextrose had left Klütz on his own fifteenth day – so I had caught him up, yet he would already have been on his way to High Yawl. Still, I had made up some considerable ground and, if I kept up this pace, the

Quest was mine for the taking.

Ah, Suzy. My eyes were drawn to Yuno's poster of the topless lady. She was a touch older than your average pin-up, and less girlish, with droopy, thin breasts like used prophylactics. However, she was clearly a woman with women's bits.

I felt a stirring in a region that had, of late, encountered less stirring than frozen tea. Dare I risk a swift fumble while Yuno was downstairs? My inter-leg region told me that I did.

Lying back on the comfortable feather pillow, I remembered my single sexual encounter with Suzy Goodenough, at a time when she was bored and desperate.

Suzy lived with her mother Sharon, two roads away from me and next-door to my friend Benjamin. Fervent rumour at the time had it that Suzy's father had run off with his secretary.

During school holidays, Benjamin and I had been passing the time cycling around, hoping that something would happen, which it never did. Spins up and down his road were in order when Suzy came out to sit on her gate, swinging her legs lazily, reading or listening to her tape recorder. It was the best we could muster as a teenage mating ritual.

She always pretended not to notice us, so it was to my amazement when, one summer holiday while Benjamin was away on the Isle of Wight, she beckoned me over with a furtive hand gesture.

I stopped and straddled my bicycle, attempting to look nonchalant, and introduced myself, since we had never actually spoken.

"I know who you are," she replied haughtily. "You're the boy whose Father teaches at Glibley Secondary and everyone hates him."

"Do they? I thought –"

"Look, I'm not here to mince words," Suzy interrupted,

swishing her bronze ponytail. "It's my sixteenth birthday today and I need to lose my virginity."

I had turned sixteen only a few weeks previously, and the same thought had never crossed my mind. My tongue went numb. This was Suzy Goodenough. Goddess. Look but don't talk.

"Well, come on then," she said, slipping off the gate and dragging me towards the house.

"What about your mother?" I stammered.

"Mum's out. Will be for hours."

I expected that I'd only need a couple of minutes.

"Right," I said.

I had never seen so much flowery wallpaper and ornamentation in a house, let alone a hallway. Wide, deep-red-carpeted stairs led off to the left, twisting upwards to a landing. At the foot of these stairs stood a life-size neo-classical, rose-tinted statue of a naked woman, with one arm over her head and the other shielding her most private part.

Abject nervousness made me go "Oo-er!" while pointing at it and Suzy, who was already halfway up the stairs, tutted. What propelled me to follow her was a mixture of fear of the unknown and light-headedness.

"I'm in here," came her impatient voice when I reached the landing. Her room was obvious, its door being the only one painted pink with a pony motif. Inside, it was hard to see the walls for the shelves crammed with teddies and dolls. A mute clown stared at me mockingly.

Suzy was sitting bolt upright on her bed, which was also covered in teddies and dolls. Her arms were folded. "I hate these stupid teddies, but Mum won't let me throw then out because she says they remind her of my childhood."

She had on a knee-length denim skirt and white t-shirt, with trainers and no socks, seemingly at odds with the desperate flounciness of the interior décor. I could just about make out she was wearing a white bra underneath.

The prospect of having to remove it filled me with dread, though the thought of her pale, handful-sized breasts would surely impel me to try.

Her mouth was pursed, which it always seemed to be. Caramel-coloured freckles sprinkled themselves in a band across the bridge of her nose, complementing her light tan. Her lips were lipsticked vivid pink.

Having spent my teens at an all-male boarding school, the ways of girls were unknown to me. There had been a briefly reciprocated crush, during junior school, on Sally Brown, but that had involved only love letters and the exchange of sweets.

Here, however, was a girl clearly tinkering with womanhood, bearing none of that Sir-he-stole-my-pencil baggage.

"Go on then, take your clothes off," Suzy ordered.

"Aren't you going to take yours off too?"

"Of course I am," she replied impatiently, making no move to do so.

"Right," I said.

Mother had dressed me in casuals: beige corduroys with an ironed crease and a similarly obsessively pressed shirt in thin blue-and-white stripes, with a collar that made my neck sore. We had argued about the tie and eventually I was allowed to leave it off, the weather being so scorching. But I had been forced into a vest.

I stood there fiddling with my top button, second thoughts running into third thoughts, before Suzy sighed. "God, just hurry up will you!"

"Well don't look, then. You're making me nervous."

Suzy sighed again deeply and covered her eyes with a hand. "Now get a move on. I said my mum would be gone for hours, not flipping days!"

As I unbuttoned the shirt and removed it, then my shoes and

socks, I fixated on one particularly lifelike doll up on a shelf. It was hideously ugly, jaundiced and leering, probably one of those that pisses itself.

After I had pulled the vest over my head, then flattened my hair down, I felt naked. A chill hit my weedy chest and I pulled my arms around me. Suzy looked.

"Come on! Get your trousers off!"

"I feel used," I protested, having heard the same line in a film.

"Oh for God's sake!"

Clearly wanting to get on with it, she launched herself from the bed, undid my belt buckle, unzipped my trousers and pulled my underpants down with them, so they gathered at my feet. Instantly I felt like someone at a medical inspection and covered my beleaguered penis with both hands.

"It'll have to do," she muttered and began methodically to undress. Belt off, t-shirt over head, skirt dropped, down to bra and pants. But before I had a chance to savour those moments, Suzy was naked before me.

White, perfectly smooth breasts shaped like half coconuts, capped by neat conker-coloured nipples, and a thatch of mildly unruly reddish pubic hair. There were tan lines on her upper arms and around her knees. I gazed at her vagina and wondered where the hole was.

It seemed that I should say something complimentary and I came out with, "I like your vagina."

Suzy slumped petulantly backwards onto her bed. "Don't call it a vagina, that's so gynaecological," she snapped. "It's a front bottom."

"Right," I said. "Front bottom."

"Well, stop standing there staring and put it in me!"

"I don't think I'm quite ready," I noted, motioning sheepishly downwards.

"Oh come here. And take your hands away!"

I stood before her, smallness exposed, excruciatingly nervous. She took it in one hand, stretched it violently then let go, as if it were an elastic band. I yelped.

"Why hasn't it stayed up? It's supposed to stay up!"

"Not like that it isn't!" I wailed.

"Oh for God's sake!" Suzy thought for a moment then lay back, in among the sea of soft toys. "Lie on top of me."

Numbly, I did as ordered. Our faces were inches apart and our bodies pressed stiffly together, as erotic as piled corpses. Nothing stirred.

"Now move up and down," she commanded.

With my arms I lifted my torso up and then down, press-up style.

"My name is Miffy. I love you," came a small, tinny voice.

I repeated the motion.

"My name is Miffy. I love you."

Exasperated, Suzy reached behind her head, felt around and extracted a black-and-white panda. "Not now, Miffy!" she scalded, launching it against a wall.

She stared at me, eyes ablaze. "Kiss me!" she commanded.

It was my first ever kiss with someone who wasn't my aunt. Though it started tentatively, teeth clashing, tongues slobbering, something primeval began to kick in. Downstairs I felt a stirring as our rudest regions ground into one another and her breasts squished beneath me...

Suddenly I was back in Yuno's bedroom, eyes tight shut, a noticeable tent formed amid the sheets. Yuno's voice came from the doorway, "You awight there, mate?"

I dressed into warm, damp clothing, cocooned in embarrassment. The winner of the Iditamush, caught masturbating. The story would be around Klütz in a thrice.

When my mind drifted back to the liaison with Suzy, it did

little to divert my attention. We never did consummate the relationship. There had been the unexpected sound of jangling keys and a door opening, then the echoing, coarse tones of Sharon Goodenough. "Suze?"

We had dressed in a panic and, when Mrs Goodenough arrived in the bedroom, were engaged in a hastily arranged dolls' tea party. She was supposed to have spent the afternoon playing bingo, she explained, but a power cut had sent everyone home.

Of course she suspected nothing untoward and I made a grateful exit.

As she showed me out, Suzy hissed in my ear: "You ever tell anyone about this, and I'll spread it round Glibley that you snogged my Mum."

It seemed the unlikeliest of threats, until rumours over the years painted Sharon Goodenough as a bit of a goer.

Down in the kitchen, a functional but homely space of stained pine, Yuno laid out a cooked breakfast while bath water steamed from a tin tub in one corner. A small fire was ablaze in a hearth and something sizzled in a frying pan on the cooker. There were cupboards lined against one wall, beside a painting of a small boy crying because someone in bovver boots has stepped on his puppy.

My host took a seat at the table and began tucking into a steak. Mouth full, he motioned me to take the other chair. I felt sheepish.

"S'awright, sir. I won't tell no one," he said simply.

My hot meal – steak, boiled potatoes and a green bean that was more string than bean – was wolfed down, after which I politely requested seconds.

"Blimey, yer dunalf like yer dog-meat, y'know!" said Yuno, beaming, so I declined the fresh plateful.

Following breakfast, Yuno suggested I take a bath. However,

having already exposed to him more than enough of my private functions, I instead rolled up my sleeves and, removing socks and shoes, washed thoroughly in the hot water. It felt like luxury.

Afterwards, we sat and talked. There were plans to concoct. Yuno had changed from his jeans into brown corduroys, which he said Klütz people did for special occasions. His head was freshly shaved and polished and I noticed three healed parallel tracks of scar tissue across the side of his scalp.

"Bear tried to eat us as a nipper," he explained. "Me dad was killed savin' us. Wrestled wiv it an' bit its froat aht. It swiped 'is 'ead off wiv its dyin' breff."

"What about your mother?" I asked, hoping to lighten the mood.

"Dead too, sir. Gassed to deaf by disturbed skunks in 'er sleep. S'ow I got this 'ouse, y'know?"

It seemed best to change the subject altogether. "Have you heard any news of my travelling companions?"

"Certainly 'ave, sir!" he replied, brightening. "Fetched all yer bags, too. Put 'em in the out'ouse for yer."

"Thank you very much. And my friends?"

"The small one, 'e copped off wiv Tjätia las' night, dahn Djüke's. Ain't bin seen since. The Major's rung 'is wife an' she's comin' to get 'im. In a balloon, I fink. Bleedin' odd, y'know?"

"I certainly do know," I smiled. "Expect her any time next year if she's as good at ballooning as he is."

Yuno forced a laugh. "Yer a real hoot, sir, y'know wot I mean?"

My host explained that he earned a meagre living helping to offload imported supplies from the docks in Klütz. His insider knowledge would be useful. My next stop on the Quest was High Yawl, a testing sea journey across the aptly-named

Dire Straits.

But when I asked after possible transport, Yuno grimaced. "S'only a tradin' 'arbour 'ere, sir, an' we don't do much trade ahtside the Christmas season. Ain't no boats 'spected fer maybe a week, y'know?"

Sensing my sinking heart, he added quickly, "But I've gotta rowin' boat, sir. I could row yer across!"

"That sounds like suicide!"

"It is, sir! But I'd do anyfink to 'elp!"

"It's OK, Yuno, you've done enough already. You're sure there aren't any ships due? I'm desperate."

He sprang from his chair. "Wait 'ere, sir! I'll 'ave a word wiv Tjär, 'e's the 'arbourmaster. 'E'll know fer sure." And off he scooted, slamming the door behind him.

I sat there wondering what to do. I could try to find Detritos or the Major, but would be unlikely to succeed in unfamiliar surroundings. Then a sneaky thought struck me. Yuno had fetched all the baggage from the sled – presumably that included the dwarf's briefcase, which he had guarded with such secrecy…

Outside, the snow was falling like dandruff shaken from the driest of scalps. Yuno lived in a residential street with houses on either side of a narrow, slush-covered road.

These wooden dwellings were detached with random spacing and each was uniquely shaped, as if built by individuals, probably the owners or their ancestors. Some were merely glorified huts while others were more adventurous: one resembling a ski chalet, quaint with ornate eaves and shallow roof; another, an over-grown doll's house, gaudily painted.

The one across the road was by far the most ostentatious, modelled, it appeared, on a gothic castle. The main structure was circular, with small arched windows on two levels and a high conical roof. The front door too was arched: a grand affair in dark, aged wood, criss-crossed with ironwork. Most impressive, though, were the four identical turrets, miniature versions of the house itself, spaced equidistantly around the upper level. Gargoyles jutted out from each, leering.

This was no suburban housing estate, but a declaration of personality. And each property, no matter how modest, glowed with multi-coloured fairylights and festive decorations: neon Santas, reindeer outlined with strings of white bulbs, wreaths and twinkling stars – the usual soul-cheering tat.

Yuno's outhouse adjoined his property. There was a keyhole but no key, and the door proved to be unlocked. Inside were our bags piled haphazardly and nothing else. Yuno was a man of simple means.

The dwarf's briefcase – sturdy, rectangular and deep, bound in scuffed tan leather – was easily extracted. Two gold-coloured clasps held it shut, each secured with a three-digit combination lock. Cracking both codes would take a maximum of 1,998 attempts, I calculated. But how long would Yuno be? I hardly wanted him to catch me breaking into a colleague's belongings.

The left-side combination was set at 289 and the right at 666. I tried both catches at these settings, expected nothing and achieved as much. Logic suggested that I reset both to 000 and painstakingly increase one digit at a time.

Setting the left to 000, I tried the catch, which unexpectedly sprang open. I did the same for the right – and it too sprang open!

What lay within? Weapons? Money? Gold? A dismembered corpse? Nothing at all? I flung back the lid.

Blank, staring eyes and a mouth agape as if in horror... orange hair... and crumpled pink vinyl. It was the dwarf's deflated sex doll, which he had been seeing to so urgently in Skaramanger. I lifted her out by the shoulders and we eyed each other up. That Detritos. "You dirty little sod," I chastised him aloud.

"Em, sir," interrupted Yuno, standing at my shoulder, reddening. "Got some news… But it'll wait till, er, yer finished… Y'know?"

Back indoors, I said nothing. Excuses could only exacerbate matters.

Yuno's news was heartening. According to Tjär, there was a vessel in the area: The Tin Squid, skippered by one Commander Rudi Ptchtikov. It wasn't due to dock in Klütz but Yuno had told Tjär of my plight and the harbourmaster had promised to radio Ptchtikov, to ask if he would take me to High Yawl. Of course, it would cost.

I was to wait at the docks at midnight. If Ptchtikov had accepted the commission, he would be there. If he hadn't, my Quest was doomed.

It was now late afternoon, allowing several hours to kill. I had no intention of seeking out the dwarf only to find him rogering some busty native type. Yuno said I might find Upper-Crust in Djüke's Bar.

"Or yer could visit the observat'ry, up on Klönely Mahntin! Be fun!"

Coincidentally, the stars had fascinated me as a boy. Something about the romance of space travel and the remoteness of the heavenly bodies. A visit to the observatory on Klönely Mountain certainly appealed. It would also be my first stab at doing something touristy. My farewells to Detritos and the Major could wait until afterwards.

"How far is it?" I asked.

"Walk to ahtskirts of Klütz, then yer see it. There's a chairlift ter top. Take abaht an hour, y'know?"

"Sounds good. Just point me in the right direction!"

"I'll take yer there!"

"I'd rather go alone."

"Please let us take yer!"

"Sorry, Yuno. I need some time to myself."

"I won't say nuffink! Yer won't know I'm there, y'know!"

The lad was sadly too needy. "Sorry Yuno. I'm going alone."

"I'll carry yer bags!"

"I'm not taking any bags."

"I'll walk beside yer wiv an umbrella, stop the snow from settlin' on yer 'ead!"

"NO, Yuno!"

He went quiet and sulky. I began to put on my outer clothing.

"There's bears aht there."

"OK, you can come."

Caribou Tench has heard tell of minking star-gazers, on top of a hill around these parts, and has the gall to ask for leave to visit them.

"Leave?" I splutter. "Leave is for cladge-spitters with custard for hearts!"

He mopes away, sulking.

The man is obsessed by the constellations. I remember one late night al fresco in El N'urth when he droned on about the stars, pointing, and I was too far-gone to tell him to minking shut up.

When his ancestors died, he said, their souls rose into the heavens and became stars. The planets are the souls of the greatest leaders and the black holes are those who turned bad. Shooting stars are the souls of his ancestors who have served their time upstairs and are returning to earth, to take the shapes of birds and animals. His great great grandfather, he informed me solemnly, was a water buffalo and his great grandfather was an eagle.

I told him that Mrs Dextrose was a cow, but he didn't get it.

Though I managed to wrestle the umbrella out of Yuno's hand before we left, he insisted on walking a few paces ahead of me, to shield me from the oncoming wind. I gave up trying to stop him.

The sun was beginning to set. We walked along Yuno's road, which he said ran parallel to Klütz's main street. There were lights on in houses and sounds of unseen people arguing.

We hit the edge of Klütz, where the buildings simply ceased to be. To our right, an imposing incline stretched upwards, trees rooted into it at treacherous angles, areas of grey rock exposed where the gradient had been too steep for the snow to take a hold. This must be the Klönely Mountain. Just visible among vague rows of trees were twin dark wires, supported at intervals by pylons.

"Cable-car's up 'ere, sir, y'know?" said Yuno, heading off towards the base of the mountain.

The man-made route had ended, forcing us to wade through virgin snow more than a foot deep. It spilled into my wellingtons, chilling cosy feet. The clouds of mist we generated billowed larger as our breathing grew more laboured and faint sounds of revelry drifted in on the breeze from Klütz's bars.

Eventually we encountered a functional wooden hut confronted by a huge horizontal cog. This supported the taut wires from which a steel-and-glass car hung lifelessly, clinging to a single bow-shaped support.

Light illuminated the inside of the station. Above the door hung a large rectangular clock that read '20.21'. Yuno knocked. No response. He knocked again and hollered, "Oi-oi!"

A key rattled in a lock and the door opened to reveal a bleary-eyed, shrivelled Innit man. His jeans hung baggily on bowed legs and he was bald by design. The skin on his face framed his skull like cling-film. His arms were white, hairless and skeletal. Though he patently needed a decent hospital meal inside him, he wore the regulation white t-shirt, which hung limply over wasted muscles.

"Oi-oi," he greeted us in a raspy whisper. "Bin asleep."

"Goin' to the observat'ry," Yuno explained, as if that weren't obvious. "Me mate 'ere, 'e won the Iditamush."

Wizened Innit brightened faintly. "I done that... Nah, when wuz it?" And he stood there trying to remember for several minutes while we waited patiently, shivering. Eventually he shrugged. "Nah. S'fackin' gorn."

Yuno ushered me towards the cable-car. "When yer ready, Granddad," he called out.

We mounted a short flight of steps onto a wooden platform, level with the twin doors. When Yuno pushed a button, these slid inwards accompanied by a hydraulic hiss.

The car swayed as we entered. Yuno and I sat on opposite sides to distribute our weight, on wooden slatted benches for two. The roof and floor were metal, and there was glass all around from waist height to afford a panoramic view. My companion pressed a button inside and the doors hissed shut.

Vertigo had already begun to infect me, though we were still on the ground. Should I bale out? Or at least cower on the floor, gibbering? I remembered the childhood incident on the slide... But that was many years ago, when I was immature. If I could defeat Borhed and survive the rigours of the Iditamush, a cable-car ride was nothing. Surely?

I twisted around to see Wizened Innit lofting a thumb and returned the same. The ancient man pulled two-handed on a lever, exerting all his strength. Machinery screamed in protest as our car was launched, jerking, into the void.

It was a slow, peaceful ride, up above the trees and a fall that would incur certain death, towards the heavens. Everywhere seemed unnaturally still. Even over-eager Yuno was, for once, more intent on gazing than chattering.

As the car negotiated each pylon with its run of guiding cogs, so came a troubling clatter and we were bounced up and down on our seats. I clung to the wooden bench with whitened knuckles, as if that would save me should we part company with the single supporting wire.

Once this fear had partially subsided, I dared to peer downwards through the window – we were way, way above the ground – shrieked, returned to the very centre of the bench, rigid, and decided not to do so again.

"How many times have you visited the observatory, Yuno?" I asked, hoping to divert my thoughts from terror.

"Firs' time, sir, y'know?"

I wondered how he knew it would be such great fun.

"At least we haven't seen any bears."

"Nah, they dan't ride the cable-cars, sir."

It took a quarter-of-an-hour before sky came into view above the Klönely Mountain, cloudless and mauve, sprinkled with starlight. And there, framed before it, the observatory, a silver-domed construction camouflaged by reflections and shadows. Imagine living there, away from the rest of the world with animal shapes and mythical beings traced into nothingness for company. The thought rather appealed.

At the top of our ride, the car slowed noticeably before being dragged onto stabilisers and coming to an automated halt with a clunk. No one manned the station. Yuno opened the doors and we stepped out into an alien snowscape of startling silence, not even a whisper of wind.

A short pathway had been cleared to the observatory entrance, a single red door stamped into the looming cylinder of stainless steel. The mind boggled at how the construction materials might have been brought here, let alone something as vast yet delicate as an astronomical telescope. Surely the Innit didn't possess the capability?

Yuno and I reached the door. There was a sign on it that read:

Klükamüs Astronomical & Geothermal Monitoring Station
AUTHORISED PERSONNEL ONLY
Our security guards are armed and lack humour

"Jesus, Yuno!" I hissed. "We're not supposed to be here!"

My guide blushed. "I told you I ain't bin 'ere before, sir, y'know?"

The red door suddenly opened inwards on slick hinges. Standing before us was a man wearing a beige raincoat with the collar turned up, brown trilby hat and pitch-black glasses. A sense of *déjà vu* hit me – it was the same garb worn by the mysterious figure who'd slapped Detritos before the start of the Iditamush. Yet this was a different man. The dwarf's assailant had been of average build; this fellow was over six-feet tall and wiry. His face was clean-shaven and his cheekbones spiky.

"Vot do you vont?" he demanded in a voice with militaristic overtones.

I attempted to blag it, surprised by my own temerity. "We were hoping for a tour."

I tried to peer behind him but he moved forward into the doorframe, blocking my view.

"Can you not read?" he enquired with unnecessarily shrillness.

"Yes I can."

"Zen vot dus der sign say?"

"It says, 'No Unauthorised Personnel'."

"NO IT DUS NOT!" The raincoated man's face turned purple. "It says, 'Ausorized Perzonnel Only'!"

Talk about splitting hairs, I thought, shrinking backwards. Yuno was already cowering several paces behind me.

A second man appeared behind Raincoat One. He too was dressed in the same bizarre uniform, but with an extensive gut and his piggish face shone with grease. His nose was pock-marked and bulbous, but his most disconcerting feature was a vivid purple scar, running the length of his right cheek, from jaw to temple. Worse, it seemed to be moving.

Raincoat Two noticed my stare, plucked the scar from his cheek and held it towards me in a pudgy opened palm. "You admire my pet vorm?"

He slapped the creature back on to his cheek and smiled.

A nutter, clearly, though hard to take seriously in his clichéd spy garb.

Unlike his excitable colleague, Raincoat Two oozed insincere charm. "Zo, yunk friends," he purred greasily. "I am askink, how may I help you?"

Yuno thrust himself between me and our interrogators. "Leave 'im be! 'E won the Iditamush, 'e's an 'ero." He turned to me. "I'll save yer, sir."

"I'm not sure we need saving, Yuno," I countered, gently pushing him to one side and addressing Raincoat Two, "We were hoping to visit your observatory, have a look at the stars."

He shrugged. "Ah. If only it coult be. But, as you are seeink, ze Aztronomical and Geosermal Monitorink Station is top zecret."

"OK, so it wasn't to be," I replied. "We'll be on our way. Come, Yuno!"

The fat scientist butted in. "No, please, vait. I am askink, you are friend off ze dwarf, ze Green Sparrow, yes?"

The who? And how did he know that I knew Detritos? I had never seen the man before in my life.

"Who?" I offered cagily.

"Surely, I haff seen you togezer – in ze sled race, yes?"

Well, I certainly hadn't seen him, and he wasn't someone you would miss easily. Most disconcerting. "When was that?"

"Ah. Perhaps you did not see me. I vos perhaps in trees. You see, I vos…" He faltered and turned to Raincoat One. "Vot vos I doink, Footz?"

Footz looked put out. "Collectink sqvirrel droppinks, Colonel Tomasz?"

"You fool, Footz! No vun collects sqvirrel droppinks!" The worm on Tomasz's face began to pulsate, but calmed as he regained composure. It was as if the creature tapped directly into his moodswings. He continued, "No. I vos... takink zeismic readinks. Yes, zis is so. So now I am askink, vill you be seeink ze dwarf again?"

"Probably not," I lied.

"You see, your friend has somesink of mine, vhich I am vontink back. Has he mentioned anysink to you?"

No, he bloody hadn't. Detritos, the secretive git. Now madmen in hats were on his case. I suspected I should keep them guessing. "No, nothing."

"I coult make it vorth your while to find zis sink for me." Tomasz had become simpering. "You vish to go somevhere in a hurry – I am tellink you, I haff helicopters and speedboats. You coult use zese."

"But I don't know what I'm looking for."

"Vhen you see it, you vill know."

"It's not an inflatable sex doll, is it?"

The worm throbbed. "No! It is not an inflatable zex doll! You sink I am interested in ze animal vorkings off ze puny human body? I am sayink, zis disgusts me! Ve, ze Candid Ablicans, ve shall..." He caught himself mid-rant, as he was pounding a fist into his shiny palm, and smiled the smile of someone offering a small child sweets. "Zuffice to say, you vill know." He actually fluttered his eyelids. "Vill you help me? Pleeeeaze?"

"Of course I will," I lied wholeheartedly.

The psychopath leant forward and puckered his lips. "Goot. Now you may go." His breath smelled of pickled onions.

The door slammed shut.

Yuno maintained a healthy lead as we sprinted the short distance back to the cable-car, and was already inside, panting, as I threw myself opposite him. "Close the bloody doors!" I gasped.

The doors connected, the car jolted to an automatic start,

accompanied by a mechanical cacophony.

Yuno and I stared at each other wordlessly and wide-eyed. I was the first to recover composure. "What the hell was that about?"

"I dunno, sir, y'know?"

"Well, who are these... Candid Ablicans?"

"Dunno, sir. We 'ardly ever sees 'em. 'Ccasionally, one comes inter tahn, buys some stuff, then facks off back up the 'ill, y'know? They never says much."

A noise distracted me. Yuno heard it too – his ears pricked. Footfalls on metal... It couldn't be? As one, we raised our eyes. There it was again.

"There's someone on the roof!" I hissed.

"Y'know wot I mean," he whispered back.

"What are we going to do?"

There was no time for a reply. Hitherto I had failed to notice the door cut into the roof, secured by a single catch – which was now turning.

"I'll save yer, sir!" Yuno cried, and grabbed me around the waist.

"What are you planning to do? Hold my body parts together as the gunshot peppers my body?"

"It's all I could fink of, sir."

"It won't work."

In a flash the skylight swung outwards, legs dangled from the opening and down beside us dropped a triumphant figure wearing a cream-coloured suit and a canvas rucksack. It was the bloody dwarf.

Casting Yuno to one side, oblivious to the hazardous rocking motion of the cable-car, I picked up Detritos in twin fistfuls of collar and pulled his head next to mine. His beady eyes were full of mischief.

"What the fuck were you doing on the roof, scaring the crap out of us? Why, whenever I turn around, are you there? And what do you have that the blimp on the hill is so keen to retrieve?"

I set the dwarf down. He flashed teeth at me. "Off all geen joints een all towns een all place, ees walkeeng eento mine."

His glibness was too much. I picked him up and flung him backwards. In a flash, one of his flailing arms hit the Open button, the doors slid apart and the dwarf sailed into thin air, shock frozen into his leathery features.

It all happened in an instant. As he was travelling outwards under momentum, still level with the cable-car, his expression switched to something cockier. His hand pulled on a tag at chest level and as he began to drop a bundle of silk unravelled above him.

Throwing myself at the aperture and clinging to either side of the doorframe, I looked down. There he was, floating to the ground beneath a dinky orange parachute, lighting a cigar.

"Detritos, I'm sorry!" I yelled, the apology echoing back towards me off the mountainside and sounding insufficient.

The dwarf looked up. "Talkeeng to hand, Meester Alexander, face no wanna heareeng."

I slumped back into my seat with my head spinning. "What have I done?"

"Well, sir. That short feller wot you won the Iditamush wiv – you frew 'im aht the door an'–"

"I know that!" I snapped. "It was a rhetorical question!"

"I was only tryin' ter help, y'know?"

I sighed. "Don't worry about it, Yuno; it's my fault."

"Yer, t'is," he replied sulkily.

The doors were still dangerously open though neither of us made a move to close them. Outside, the cold air slid past. Somewhere to our rear, the dwarf would be landing in a snowdrift, or a precariously placed tree, halfway up the Klönely Mountain.

As usual, I was left with more questions than answers. What

had Detritos been doing at the observatory? What did he have that the mentally unbalanced man wanted so badly? When had the two of them crossed paths before, and why? And just who were those sinister Candid Ablicans?

"Have you heard of Ablica?" I asked Yuno.

"Nah, sir, y'know. Wot is it?"

"Another country, I guess."

"Wot, you mean there's uvver places, not jus' Klükamüs?"

I was dumbfounded. "Yes, of course there are. Where did you think I was from?"

"I fort you wuz from that posh estate in Klöcushun."

"No, I'm from England."

"Where, sir?"

"A country many miles away across the sea."

Yuno looked frightened. His baby-soft cheeks drained of their colour. "But, sir, if you sail aht to the 'orizon, you'll fall off the edge of the world."

I tried a little test. "Yuno, if I have five biscuits and you have two biscuits, how many biscuits do we have?"

"Why've you got more biscuits than me?" he wailed.

He had not been taught well. One day, I decided, when I had become as famous for my travels as Harrison Dextrose, I would return to this place and set up a school for Innit orphans such as Yuno. I supposed I should name it after myself.

As our ride clunked to an automatic halt, the ancient Innit operator could be seen through the window of the cable-car station, slumped across his control panel, either asleep or finally deceased. The clock now read 21.55.

"Come on, Yuno," I urged. "We're due at the harbour in two hours. I can't afford to miss Ptchtikov – if he even turns up."

Yuno, who had been lost in thought, piped up. "Sir, 'ave you bin stealin' my biscuits?"

I slapped him on the shoulder light-heartedly but he just

looked puzzled, so I confirmed that I hadn't.

Given the clamour arriving from the direction of the town, the inhabitants of Klütz were in full celebratory mode. Women shrilled, men guffawed, and several songs played at intense volume mingled into a distant drunken buzz.

I passed the time attempting to discern individual tunes while we hastened back to Yuno's. The loudest, sung by a chorus of geezers, went like this: 'My old man makes tinsel/'E wears a Santa 'at/Keep yer 'ands off my bird/Oi, wot you starin' at? Oi!'

Though I did not believe in any god, I was happy to go along with the whole Nativity scenario, since it was rather touching and had resulted in presents several centuries down the line. Not, of course, that Father believed in the commercialisation of Christmas. Each year, without fail, my stocking would be filled with a succession of oranges and a new school uniform, accompanied by a note that ran along the lines: 'Don't go falling over in this one. Mother has better things to do than darn your trousers. Hohoho. Santa.'

Djüke, the esteemed landlord of Djüke's Bar, is a man after my own heart, in that we both understand the benefits of alcohol (escape, relaxation, increased charm and frankness, to name but a few) and the uselessness of other people, particularly those in one's employ.

On my third successive night in his hostelry, when we are both the worse for wear, one of the slag-chompers who passes for bar-staff leaves a beer tap running, then starts chatting up some micro-skirted minker stool-side. Djüke watches with amusement while the precious ale cascades over the sides of the drip-tray and pools on the floor.

The slag-chomper eventually realises his error, mimsies like a plook before the towering Djüke, and offers to wipe up the mess, whining that any wastage can be deducted from his wages.

"You fink I pays yer enough ter cover that, cant? There's 14 fackin' pints on the floor!" Djüke growls.

"What shall I do, sir?" grovels the petrified mink.

"Lick the 'ole fackin' lot up, you fackin' plimpton!"

Djüke and I watch while this seven-stone nerd with zits slurps the floor clean, gushes golden vomit untroubled by lumps and passes out. Djüke wipes up the mess using the unconscious minker and lobs him into the street.

"Drinks on the 'ouse, I fink, 'Arry!" he announces on return.

Had I feminine tendencies, I might well have kissed him.

On reaching Yuno's, I retrieved my bags – noting that Detritos' and the Major's were gone – and we headed for the harbour. I was nervous. Ptchtikov had to show, or I would be trapped in Klükamüs.

We diverted through town, tiptoeing past bodies in the street – the drunk and the dribbling. Ahead of us, a tottering man boasting a family of beer bellies took a wee in the middle of the road. "Fuggoff, yer bastas!" he ranted at us, shaking a fist that overbalanced him and caused him to fall into his own pool of part-frozen urine.

There were a handful of bars next-door to each other on the main drag, these being the hub of the general commotion. Central, and brashest, was Djüke's Bar, where I hoped to encounter the Major, to say our goodbyes. A young couple in the doorway were attempting a mutual tonsillectomy while a flashing neon sign above them promised: 'If our staff can't drink you under the table – we'll give you the table!!!!!'

I couldn't believe that Upper-Crust would be in there, among the lagerati. A glimpse inside confirmed my belief and I was ready to quit the half-hearted hunt.

However, Yuno was cheerily persistent. "Cam on, sir, we'll go ask Djüke wevver 'e's seen 'im, y'know?"

Djüke had received numerous mentions in Harrison

Dextrose's *The Lost Incompetent*, none of which made him sound amiable or even level-headed. I was not desperate to make his acquaintance.

But Yuno was already inside and waving me towards a bar at the far end of the establishment. If I now tiptoed away, I'd look like a right ninny. So I found myself threading past men and women with biceps, whose white t-shirts and skimpy dresses glowed neon under ultraviolet lighting. Though a handful noted our progress, their eyes failed to focus. A bespectacled man soaked in booze lay under one table, clutching a wooden leg to his breast and sucking his thumb.

It was obvious which staff member was Djüke, being the only one whose t-shirt bore the slogan, 'I'm Djüke! You gotta problum wivvat?'

His shaven head resembled a fist, so battered was his skull. Half his left ear was missing, displaying teeth marks, and his nose was a fleshy splat. To steady his swaying bulk, the sozzled landlord rested his hands on the bar. Across one set of knuckles was tattooed 'HATE', and across the other was squeezed, "MORE HATE". He had arms the size of beer-barrels.

Stacked behind were curious bottles of luridly coloured alcopops, backed by a mirror and trailed through with fairylights. There were pumps at the bar, advertising brews such as Ply the Missus, Head Spin and Porcelain Prelude.

"Let's just forget about the Major," I suggested to Yuno.

"S'awight, sir. Djüke won't 'urt yer. Long as yer don't say 'Please'. Or 'Fank you'. Djüke 'ates politeness, y'know?"

The great oaf's bulbous, bloodshot eyes wandered in their sockets and rested on us. His chin, like a brick stuffed under skin, shifted outwards.

"'Ow yer fackin' doin', Yuno?" he asked in a growl. "An' 'oo's this cant?" He stabbed a finger across the bar to poke me in the shoulder.

"'E won the Iditamush – 'e's an 'ero, y'know?"

Djüke wasn't suitably impressed. "So? I won the fackin' teddy in las' night's raffle. Big fack. Wha'choo want, *cant*?"

He spat out the last profanity, spraying 70 per cent proof gob across my face. I shuffled my feet and offered a frozen grin.

Sensing my weediness, Djüke directed his next question at Yuno, "'S'e a fackin' plimpton?"

Yuno, now a little perturbed himself, shook his head.

Without warning, my voice worked. "Have you seen the Major? Tall man. Orange jumpsuit."

Djüke grabbed me by the nose and pulled me across the bar, my shoes making a 'sssssstttkch' sound as they were prised off the booze-sticky floor. Dregs seeped into my clothing off the counter.

"You wot? *Cant*."

"Dall. Oridge," I whimpered nasally.

"They teach yer 'ow ter swear where you cam from? *Cant*?"

I tried to nod but it proved impossible while being held off the ground by my nose.

"So swear you facker! Swear like a fackin' man!"

"Bleedid' Bajor. Dall bad. Oridge fackid' jubsude."

Djüke released my throbbing hooter and I slid off the bar back onto my feet.

"'At's better. Yer, I fackin' seen 'im. But 'e's fackin' gorn, innit. If I see the cant, I'll tell 'im yer called. Where yer gonna be? *Cant*."

"At the harbour."

Djüke glared at me, the veins across his forehead becoming purple mountain ranges.

"At the fackin' harbour," I corrected myself.

"Right!" Djüke folded his great arms across his chest and leaned towards my head. "Nah piss orf!"

"Is he always like that?" I asked Yuno as we hurried past darkened shop-fronts towards the oily reek of the harbour.

"'E is, sir. But 'e don't mean no 'arm."

"Absolutely, Yuno. Beneath that violent exterior beats a

puppy's heart."

"I don't fink I'd go that far, sir."

There wasn't time to explain the nuances of sarcasm. Ahead of us lay the harbour, all sea, concrete seawall and eerie-looking machinery bathed in the stark luminescence of a full moon. The air was still.

Set back from the quayside was a row of tall wooden buildings coated in snow and creosote, mostly warehouses with vast double-doors. These dwarfed one building, the only exuding any light, outside which was a sign: 'Harbourmaster'. Everywhere felt unwelcoming.

With mere minutes until midnight and Ptchtikov's supposed arrival, I scanned the sea for likely vessels. But there was only one out there, a crappy little submarine, surfaced some 50 yards out, with a man in its conning tower, waving. Hold on…

"You're joking!" I exclaimed.

Yuno spotted it, too. "The Tin Squid! 'S'ere! Told yer, sir!" he sang, slapping my back. "Told yer 'e'd turn up! I done yer proud after all, sir, y'know!"

"Yuno, I said I was desperate, not that I had a death wish!"

He looked hurt. "'S' not that bad, y'know."

"My chances of survival in that thing must rate only slightly higher than those of Elvis on his last toilet trip."

"'Oo's Elvis, sir?"

"Fat singer in a sparkly suit… Look, it doesn't matter. I –"

A loud report rang out and echoed across the sky. Yuno and I looked around, startled. Was that a gunshot?

Furious barking ensued and a series of variously sized dogs appeared from the direction of the town, followed hotly by a tall man in an orange jumpsuit spouting drivel. Another report came. Upper-Crust ducked while running. Was someone really firing at him? Why would anyone bother?

Dazza reached us first, followed by Posh and Mazza, and they began drooling expectantly. From The Tin Squid came a muffled 'Whoomph!' and I turned as a missile arced towards me followed by snaking rope.

The man in The Tin Squid's conning tower – Ptchtikov, presumably – had fired a grappling hook.

"Don dry cadge!" came his cry, or at least what I made of it. Moments later, a large hook flew past my head and landed with a clank, before scooting across the cobbles. Ah. "Don't try catch!"

As the dogs gathered to stare, I stared back at them, hardly decisive.

"Die robe!" shouted Ptchtikov across the distance.

"Die robe?" I called back.

"Yes, die robe! Die robe!"

That's what I thought he's said.

"Er, I fink 'e's sayin' 'Tie rope! Tie rope!' sir, y'know?" said Yuno.

Of course! I raced to the hook end and found a harness clipped to it. A plan began to take shape: attach the hook to something solid, put on the harness and use the rope slide to reach the submarine! Easy!

My concerns about travelling by sub had vanished amid the possibility of being shot.

I stepped into the harness, pulled it over my shoulders and clipped it shut at my waist. So far, so good.

What next? As I dithered, Upper-Crust arrived, took the hook off me and clipped it to a rusty iron derrick at the harbour's edge.

"Just give it a tug-the-bug, check it'll hold-the-bold!" gasped the Major, breathing heavily and pulling on the rope… which immediately parted from the grappling hook, knot undone. "Oh!" he said.

"What are we going to do?" I squealed.

Another report came, as two Candid Ablicans appeared from the direction of town, waving pistols.

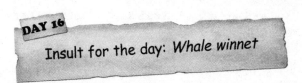
"I'm hopeless at knots," I told Upper-Crust. As, it seemed, was Ptchtikov, despite being a seaman.

"Never fear, the Major's here!" he sang. "Quick Upper-Crust balloon knot-the-bott and nattle-grat's your boomster!"

Oh Christ. An Upper-Crust balloon knot? However, the Major was already at work and the Candid Ablicans were getting nearer.

What did they want? The one in the lead was unmistakeably lanky Footz, with Colonel Tomasz huffing and puffing some way behind. Unable to run any longer the fat one eventually stopped, wheezing for breath.

"Vait, Footz!" I heard him shout.

Footz stopped, 20 yards from us.

Tomasz called across to us, "Ve do not vish to harm you. It is ze dwarf ve vish for. I am sayink, shop ze dwarf ant you vill all live."

"Dwarf?" the Major muttered to himself. "What bally dwarf?"

"He isn't here," I replied. "We don't know where he is. We haven't seen him since the end of the race."

"'S'true, y'know," piped in Yuno.

"Lies! All lies!" shrieked Tomasz, at which Speedy started and leapt into my arms.

Footz raised a pistol and fired. I felt a thump, staggered

backwards and fell to the ground, as the dog shrieked in pain. My face was warm with blood.

A bullet had ripped off half of the little dachshund's neck.

"At last, I hit somesink!" cried Footz. "I haff killed ze dwarf, Colonel!"

"You fool, Footz!" shrieked his boss. "Zat is not ze dwarf, zat is a small dok!"

I needed no further encouragement. While the Candid Ablicans argued, I snapped the harness onto its line and with Speedy still pumping blood over my shoulder, I ran towards the sea. I could only hope that the Major had finished tying his knot – and that it would hold.

"Bim whip the tog, junior Xander!" the Major shouted as I ran, which could have meant anything.

At the edge of the harbour I jumped out into thin air, squeezing my eyes tightly shut. Down Speedy and I fell.

We hit the water and went under. The shock of the cold felt like a cocoon of steel needles. All at once, the strap attached to the centre of my harness yanked us upwards and the rope slide dragged us back out of the water. Suddenly we were sliding forwards towards The Tin Squid, the sea inches below us.

"Wo-hoooooooo!" I yelled, delirious with success.

We reached the sub in a matter of seconds, Ptchtikov's black bulk looming larger and larger. As we made the conning tower our momentum ran out and we were in danger of sliding back towards the sea, until his giant hand whipped out and grabbed me by the shoulder.

In that split-second, the Major's 'special balloon knot' gave out, the rope behind us went slack and snaked into the depths. But we were safe.

I clambered over the conning tower, still clutching Speedy to my chest, and turned to see Footz and Tomasz reach the harbour wall. They began firing in our direction but were lousy shots and Footz had exhausted all his luck for one day.

I could at last turn my attentions to Speedy. "Stay with me, old pal," I whispered to the dog, whose chest still pumped, weakly, though his eyes were glazed.

The Commander pointed at a notice sellotaped to the inside of the tower. It read:

RULE OFF TIN SQUID
No smoke
No fart
No wounded pet

"What?" I exclaimed.

Ptchtikov clutched his sides and emitted a deep, rumbling laugh. When he calmed down, he said, "I made dis quick when I see you have hurt dog! It not for real!" And he laughed some more.

Idiot. I ignored him and waved towards the Major and Yuno. "Bye Major! Bye Yuno!"

Their goodbyes rolled back across the brine, interrupted by Tomasz, "Vere is ze dwarf? I am sayink, zis is your last varnink!"

I snapped back, "I told you, we don't know where he is. Now bugger off!"

As I looked down to negotiate my way into the bowels of The Tin Squid, the grin came back up at me.

"Hello, Meester Alexander."

Conditions were necessarily cramped inside the ill-lit interior. As my eyes became accustomed to the perpetual dusk, I made out two beds with grey blankets, set opposite each other at the rear of a single, long room. The dwarf occupied one of these, purportedly already napping.

Between the beds, at their heads, was a metal door bearing a central, circular handle. Behind that, an idling engine sounded like industrial indigestion.

The place reeked of oil and sweat. The ceiling, of hard steel, afforded only Detritos any appreciable headroom.

Ptchtikov was up at the front, seated at a control desk straight out of Jules Verne, manipulating levers. He was a hulk of a man, who appeared to have been constructed from a series of large boxes. His head was a perfect cube, ruined only by sticky-out ears and nose, topped with a woollen beanie hat. He had tiny, beady eyes and wore all black: roll-neck sweater, jeans and big boots.

Stacked behind him on either side, seemingly without order, were piles of cardboard boxes from which variously coloured tinsel was spilling – the Commander's cargo, I surmised. In one of these, flat-out and unmoving, lay Speedy, where Ptchtikov had set him.

A circular window up-front afforded the Commander a view of the undersea, illuminated by a spotlight on The Tin Squid's exterior.

Ptchtikov yanked downwards the largest of his levers, notching along a semi-circular dial with his other hand, and the engine-noise rose to a muffled cacophony. Fuel fumes invaded the senses.

"Prepare sub-berge!" he barked, and ordered me, "Sit!"

I made for the free bed, tripped over a wooden box full of tools and hit my head on a metal cupboard door, narrowly missing a handle that might have holed my brain. It hurt enormously and I lay there moaning, rubbing the burgeoning bruise vigorously.

"SIT!" yelled Ptchtikov.

I crawled to my bed, slithered onto its blankets and continued to moan. The prone dwarf opened one eye. "Hard to see, dark side ees," he quoth, sniggering.

"You little shit!" I hissed. "I want a word with you about a certain 'Green Sparrow'."

We were travelling downwards. I sensed the water lapping around us on all sides as we became potential corpses in a tin coffin. Ptchtikov's bath-tub creaked and groaned. Claustrophobia threatened to overtake me and I fought for breath, clutching at itchy blankets for comfort.

For several minutes I lay there waiting to die but, when death failed to arrive, my fear subsided. With a cease in downward momentum, we completed our dive. Then came an increase in the pitch of the engines close behind my head and we were off, gathering speed towards High Yawl.

Another minking sea journey. How I despise the water and its perpetual colic. It does not help that we are no longer aboard the sturdy 'Dextrose I', which I lost gambling back in Klütz to an accursed native with more than tricks up his sleeve. Instead, Tench, Shark and I have chartered a vessel crewed by minks, but it means we can laze and dream of the next knobbing.

I cannot get Tench's tale of the giant whorehouse in High Yawl out of my head – unless it's interrupted by a vision of Mrs Dextrose with a rolling pin. He says they call it 'The Pleasure Dome' and it stretches as far as the eye can see: cubicles, soft lighting and women with no clothing or morals. Let me at 'em!

Of course, Tench, the streak of wasted jism, never took advantage of the facilities. He boasts – boasts! – that he is celibate and is saving himself for Miss Right. I have saved myself for Miss Right, Miss Left and all the other minking tarts in between! My money is always legal tender in their ports.

My teeth began chattering. I was still wearing soaking garments. Sodden layers came off, one-by-one. Half an ocean sloshed from my wellington boots and transferred itself to the floor of the submarine.

The Commander, who had been making his way towards us,

stooping, stopped and glared at the pool of water. "Clean ub!" he growled.

He looked as if he belonged to an unsavoury militant army, and had a sense of humour to match. I began mopping, using my discarded jeans.

"Could I borrow some dry clothing?" I asked. "Just for the journey?"

"Twenty bound," said Ptchtikov. "And for Tin Squid, anudder dree hundred."

Before I could protest, he added, "And one-hundred-fifty bound for friend – he half size!"

Ptchtikov shook with mirth like a monster wired into the mains.

I stared across at Detritos in dismay. Not only had I not wanted him to come along, but now I had to pay for him.

"Meester Alexander cash, he good at bar," said the dwarf.

"That's daylight robbery!" I blurted out, all British affront.

Ptchtikov stop laughing and loomed dangerously.

I began fumbling through pockets. "On the other hand, if I can just find my wallet..."

The Commander purred into my ear, "You don'd find wallet, I find head in cook-bot."

I sat there in saggy boxer shorts and socks feeling abused.

I knew that my wallet and *The Lost Incompetent* were somewhere about my clothing because I had kept them close ever since the Ogr incident. And yes, there was the book, in a back pocket, its pages sodden, wrinkly and stuck together. Reverentially, I laid the tome open on the bed, praying that the warmth of The Tin Squid might return it to life.

Inside the right hip pocket was my wallet, which I recovered with audible relief. It too had become drenched. The tan leather weighed heavy and was stained dark. Inside, my folded passport at least opened up and would survive. The signature on my credit card had run in the style of a school chromatography experiment. I would have trouble getting that past any wary shop assistant. The book of travellers' cheques didn't look good, either. When I tried to prise the pages apart, they began to rip, but I reasoned that they would dry out. So I lay them also on the bed, with an apologetic grimace at Ptchtikov.

"I can pay," I offered. "Just not yet. My cheques must dry out."

He glared and thrust out a grasping hand. "I dake book. And card."

I wasn't exactly in a position to argue – one hardly wants to be chucked out of a submarine. "OK, but please take care of them."

Last out of my wallet were the two photographs of my baby-self and my parents, which I kept for sentimental reasons. Again, sodden but dryable. These I gazed at, hoping for a nostalgic whiff of home, but none came. I felt detached from that past, which was probably a good thing.

As I was changing into hired dry clothes – sweater-and-denims uniform, the black disguising the oil stains – a pathetic whimper reminded me of Speedy's plight and I rushed to attend his tinsel sickbed.

The once-sturdy dachshund was in such a pitiful state that I could not bring myself to study his wound. His breathing was shallow and erratic, but he was clinging to life.

He managed once to wag his little tail but could not even raise his head and his yellowing tongue lolled like blanched ham. Occasionally he shuddered, scrunching his eyes tight-shut. It was heart-breaking. However, my sausage-dog companion was a fighter and therein lay hope.

I stroked the top of his bony head. "Hang in there, Speedy. You'll get better – just you see," I puffed, realising they probably said the same to Lord Nelson.

Speedy needed proper medical attention. In the absence of that, I would have to still my churning stomach to dress his wound. I tapped Ptchtikov on the shoulder. Up ahead, shoals of small silver fish darted to and fro as one, apparently following a lead fish that was hopelessly lost.

"Excuse me," I said. "Where can I find some water?"

Ptchtikov snorted. "Water all around! Hahahahaha!"

The Commander clearly fancied himself as a comedian.

"You really are a hoot," I said, hoping he wouldn't get the sarcasm.

"Hey, small man!" Ptchtikov called towards the bed-bound Detritos. "Your friend dinks I am owl-noise! Maybe he more mad den me! Hahahahaha!"

Detritos laughed along like the class swot.

"Water?" I reminded Ptchtikov.

The walking barn stiffened, harrumphed, and pointed back down the submarine towards a cupboard amidships. "Go, also where we do business."

The Tin Squid's closet was an inadequate space containing a thick-rimmed tin bucket: our toilet. A red button protruded from the floor beside it, which I assumed operated the flush.

I tested the mechanism. Stepping on the button, the sound of angry, frothing water echoed from below as the bottom of the bucket flipped downwards to reveal a wide pipe leading into darkness, presumably the sea itself. The instant I stepped off, the flap slammed shut and the disturbing racket ceased.

I imagined the untreated progress of our excrement and became concerned for passing sea-life.

Stacked behind the toilet were green military-looking jerry cans. The first one I picked off proved to be filled with water, which I hefted over to Speedy's bedside.

The dwarf was there, peering in. "He dead," he said.

Ptchtikov swivelled around in a flash.

"He nod dead!" he declared theatrically. "He resding!"

The dwarf clapped his hands in glee at this cue. "Hey meester, Detritos know dead dog eef lookeeng! Ees lookeeng dead dog!"

Ptchtikov didn't miss a beat. "No no, nod dead! Resding. Remarkable dog, de dachshund. Beaudiful plumage!"

"Plumage not seeng." The dwarf was giggling. "He dead!"

"No! Resding!"

"Shut up!" I wailed, to no effect.

"Eef resteeng, Detritos wakeeng up!" The dwarf lifted the dachshund's left lobe and shouted into the hole, "Hello Meester Speedee! Haffeeng doggee food!"

Ptchtikov joined in and kicked Speedy's bed. "Dog move!" Tears were streaming down the man's perpendicular face.

Appalled at their heartlessness, I clutched at Speedy's box while Detritos jolted it with the palm of his hand, crying, "Testeeng! Testeeng! Testeeng!"

"Stop it!" I shouted, trying to push the dwarf away. But he was wiry and strong, and, twisting like an eel, kept eluding my grasp.

With a lunge, he had Speedy's floppy, pathetic form in his hands, which he lobbed into the air. We watched as the lifeless bundle reached the apex of its ascent, before plummeting to hit the steel floor with a sickening slap.

"He dead dog," noted Detritos, deadpan.

I pushed him aside, scooped up the dachshund and stormed to the rear of The Tin Squid.

"Hoi," Ptchtikov called after me. "Whad about pining for fjords?"

I sat on my bed, cradling the deceased Speedy in my lap, disconsolate. Detritos and Ptchtikov stayed at the other end of the vessel, muttering and occasionally giggling.

I was horrified. The indomitable Ma had entrusted Speedy

into my care. And this dog with its legs surely too ridiculous to propel a sled, had not only endured its task but had inspired others.

Yet here he was, torn and lifeless. Speedy's death seemed to me like a metaphor: the idealistic little person taking on the system – and losing. I felt very sorry for us both.

There was someone sitting on my bed. Speedy, who had been cradled in my arms when I drifted off, was gone.

I opened my eyes. The dwarf was lying next to me, above the blankets, his face so close that I could feel his breath on my cheek. As I winced, his eyes opened. At so short a distance his features became one blurred oval of unlikely concern and hair.

Seeing me awake, Detritos beamed. "Here lookeeng for heem, keed!"

He sat up, rested his hands in his lap and said with sympathy, "Hello. Meester Alexander ees sleepeeng beeg. Poor seeng."

He asked whether I wanted some food. The Commander had cooked a meal, he explained, before offering to reheat the leftovers for me.

What was his game, all this toadying?

I sat up too. "Where's Speedy?"

The dwarf looked pious, head lowered, big eyes, quiff drooping over his nose. "Meester Alexander. Detritos beeg sorry playeeng weez dead doggee. So geef good bury."

"So where is he?"

The dwarf seemed shocked that I should question further. "Een sea, Meester Alexander!" he protested. "Putteeng een flag, sayeeng pray, then bye-bye Meester Speedy." He waved solemnly as if replaying the moment.

I remained suspicious. "So you've buried him with full

191

honours at sea? How?"

"Meester Alexander, *pleeze*. Detritos good. Rudi haff… he sayeeng… excape hats?"

"Escape hatch?"

"Excape hats!" Detritos slipped off the bed to perform a sort of can-can. When he stopped, he threaded his hands together in mock prayer. "Pleeze, Meester Alexander. Beeg sorry. Meester Alexander good friend. Detritos OK?"

Although his humility seemed rife with insincerity it would have been churlish to drag out any hostility. The dwarf had been good to me in the past, and life in a submarine could surely drive anyone to acts of folly. However, here was a bargaining tool, which I was prepared to use.

"Alright," I offered. "But first I want some answers. Like, who are the Candid Ablicans, and how do they know you? Who is Green Sparrow? And what's in your briefcase?"

"Pleeze, pleeze, Meester Alexander!" he replied laughing, beating back my questions with paddling arms. "So much seeng! Detritos telleeng, but now eateeng. Ees good?"

It was 5.30am, Ptchtikov informed me, so I had slept solidly for 15 hours. I used to do the same before setting off on my Quest, while unemployed, but this time the extended slumber felt good because I had deserved it.

Detritos arrived with a plate of gristly meat and indeterminate vegetables, which Ptchtikov had attempted to disguise with a fiery garlic-and-chilli sauce. Aware that regular meals were elusive I shovelled down the lot, oblivious to the health consequences.

The dwarf sat beside me wearing a fixed grin. His green suit was now enormously crumpled and stained. He resembled a bad child with good intentions and sideburns.

When my plate was empty, Detritos washed it in the tiny galley area next to the toilet. He returned, lay on his bed and made as if to sleep.

"Hold on!" I said sharply. "You owe me some answers…"

He slapped his forehead. "Aaii! Ees so! Pleeze comeeng weez." He patted the blanket beside him. "Rudi no heareeng. Beeg secret."

I took my place, folded my arms and raised an eyebrow. "Well?"

The dwarf drew in a deep breath and said conspiratorially, "Detritos ees beeg spy, saveeng world."

I exhaled a derisory snort. "You're a big spy saving the world?"

"Pleeze, too beeg noise. Rudi heareeng," he hissed frantically – so frantically that it seemed the dwarf might at least believe his own story.

"Alright, so how do you plan to save the world?"

"Eef Detritos sayeeng all," he whispered, "haff keel Meester Alexander."

"Rubbish!"

He shrugged.

I persisted. "How do you know Tomasz and Footz?"

The dwarf tightened his lips and shook his head.

"Come on! You owe me. I've let you tag along since Emo Island and all you've ever done is get us into trouble. When we get to High Yawl, that's it – I'm on my own."

"Pleeze, Meester Alexander! Detritos stayeeng!"

We had been here before. "So who are Tomasz and Footz?"

He stood on the unsprung bed, put his mouth to my ear, and whispered, "Veree bad. Wanteeng keel world."

"A likely story!"

Detritos clamped a sweaty small palm over my mouth. "Shhh, Meester Alexander," he hissed. "Eef Rudi heareeng, Detritos keel heem also."

I stared at him, seeking truth in his dark, determined eyes. He was serious. The dwarf had psychopathic delusions of philanthropy.

"What's in the briefcase?"

He appraised me long and hard. Eventually he growled through clenched teeth, "Knoweeng, Reeck. Many friend een Casablanca."

I was above his silly quotes. "What's in the briefcase?"

"No sayeeng." And he leapt off the bed and headed towards Ptchtikov.

Well, he could get stuffed. I hadn't wanted to become involved in his mysterious playing-spies shenanigans, anyway. Only curiosity had forced me to enquire. It was the increasing lure of the Quest – how enlivened my soul had become – that compelled me onwards. That and Suzy Goodenough's pants-region.

Life aboard a submarine is no hoot. The trick, I discovered, is to find things to do.

I checked out the engine room, a dark, manly place of overpowering odour and noise. One false move in the darkness and I would have become cog food. So I wandered up to the other end of The Tin Squid, where the Commander was taking readings from a navigational gadget. Before him was a bank of controls that cried out to be toyed with.

"What do all these knobs and levers do?"

"Nudding," he answered.

I stared out of the window at the occasional passing fish, some of whom stared back.

To pass time, I went to relieve my bladder. A godawful stench – the chilli diet, no doubt – had set up an exclusion zone around the door, so I braved a swift eyes-shut, breath-held raid on the bucket and emerged gulping for air.

With Detritos already asleep, I lay on my own bed attempting to do the same just to pass the time. But the land of nod proved elusive.

I tried counting sheep but became obsessed with the staring bovine eyes. Was that terror in their gaze, or inanity?

A phone rang, which I answered, and a female voice said, "Before you say anything, is your pronunciation of 'bottom' up for sale?"

My eyes pinged open. A dream! I had slept after all.

"We arrive!" Ptchtikov was shouting in my ear, shaking me awake.

At last, my heart soared.

"What time is it?" I asked the Commander.

"Time you god a watch!"

How I would miss his quick wit.

The dwarf stirred, tugging tangled quiff from beneath his eyelids.

"Yes, but what time is it really?"

"Eighdeen hundred hours."

Good news indeed. By boat, the same journey from Klütz to High Yawl had taken Harrison Dextrose almost four days. In The Tin Squid, it had taken just over a day-and-a-half, having avoided the turbulent surface of the Dire Straits. Clearly there was something to be said for undersea travel, ambience notwithstanding.

I was actually ahead of Dextrose for the first time on the Quest, and by some 36 hours. It felt good – as if I had served my explorer's apprenticeship and was now deemed worthy of competing with the best.

Having stuffed my now partially dry and rumpled copy of *The Lost Incompetent* into a back pocket, I accosted Ptchtikov for the return of my traveller's cheques and card.

"Dodal is 600 pound," he monotoned, retrieving the books from a strongbox with a broken lock.

"Dodal?"

"Yes, dodal."

I focused instead on the '600 pound' bit.

But hold on. I calculated that 300 (my fare) plus 150 (Detritos) plus 20 (clothing hire) totalled – ah, total! – £470, a fact I pointed out.

"The clodes are *now* dirty and musd be cleaned," he countered.

"What do you mean, the clothes are now dirty – they were oilier than a car mechanic's when I put them on!"

He pointed at my chest. "You drip chilli sauce here."

It was going to be pointless arguing, and anyway he was huge. "Alright, how about I keep the clothes for 30 pounds more, so 500 in total?"

On the sly, I admired this all-black look. It made me feel secretive and interesting. Plus I could afford to splash out. After all, this was the first time I had raided the traveller's cheques and an easily sufficient £1,500 would be remaining.

The deal was sealed.

A thought struck me. "Where's my credit card?"

"The who?"

"Credit card. The plastic card I gave you."

"Why you want?"

"Because that's my money too!"

"This card is money?" Ptchtikov bellowed with laughter. "Fool! Money is paber and dinsel and sometimes podadoes!"

"Can I have my credit card back, please?"

"OK."

Ptchtikov retrieved it from the metal box.

"Hang about!" I spluttered. "You've cut out the hologram!"

"The shiny ding? It was lovely decoration, I dink. Look," he said, pointing at his hat, "I have glued to hat!"

For heaven's sake... At least I still had the travellers' cheques.

"How do we get to shore?" I asked, resigned to another lunatic rope slide.

"We dake row-boat."

"What, there was a boat all along? Why didn't you fetch me at Klütz?"

Ptchtikov glared. "You wand hero, don'd ask man who export dinsel."

The dwarf was checking his belongings. As I walked past the toilet, the stench had become unbearable. Whoever had used the facilities during my latest slumber was in dire need of medication.

Worryingly, I became aware that my own previous evening's meal was pounding at the exit, demanding evacuation.

At the window end of The Tin Squid, where the air was freshest, I drew in a vast gulp and ran for the closet door, swung it open, slammed it shut, cheeks already bulging, and involuntarily glanced into the bucket.

The flush valve was jammed open. By a dog that had been stuffed down the toilet. Speedy's glazed eyes stared up at me. It was the decaying corpse that was causing the unholy stench.

My evacuation would have to wait; instead, I rushed to vent my spleen.

Detritos denied any knowledge of the crime.

"How then did Speedy end up lodged down the toilet?" I demanded.

"Maybe runneeng and treep?"

"But he was *dead*."

"Ees true," the dwarf agreed, rubbing his chin.

"Just forget it!" I snapped. "We're finished."

Ordinarily he would have protested. This time he did not.

HIGH YAWL
Population: No idea
Capital: There isn't one

Currency: Token
Principle industry: Retail
Feet: Minked

High Yawl is situated on the eastern coast of the Economican continent. Once it was farmland but they developed that many years ago, and then someone covered the buildings in domes because everyone was getting sunburnt. Don't ask me when that happened. Ask Tench. He's the know-all with the caring interest in history.

I have embarked on this Dextrosian Quest for two reasons: to track down my drinking buddy Livingstone Quench, with whom I have whiled away many a purposeful hour, and also in the spirit of adventure. There's a third, now I come to think of it: to escape Mrs Dextrose's ceaseless moaning. The woman's a saint's back-door.

I am not here to recount historical tales that may or may not be true. If that is what you're after, you have come to the wrong book. Mink off.

As we arrive, there is scaffolding everywhere, indoors and out. A pair of guides dressed like butterboxes apologise for the mess and tell us that High Yawl is being refurbished and new air conditioning installed. I tell them I'm not interested and ask where The Pleasure Dome is.

Like myself, Shark hangs on their every word. When they have finished telling us, Tench asks if there is a museum.

Everyone laughs.

The Tin Squid surfaced and we emerged into a balmy, still evening with its merciful fresh air. Purple streaks of cloud drifted in the sunset sky.

Two hundred yards across the water awaited High Yawl: a strange sci-fi landscape of clustered, reflective domes, varying in size from very large to ostentatious. Beneath these, as

Dextrose had forewarned, lived a community paranoid about holes in the ozone layer and the negative effects of natural radiation.

To either side of this sprawling conurbation, off into the distance, was a barren, sun-dried landscape. Many years ago, High Yawl had grown out of the desert. Far more recently, someone had covered it in giant umbrellas. The effect was dazzling.

I savoured this moment as the beginning of the final leg of my Quest. No more journeys across water. On the other side of High Yawl I would pick up the dusty trail north-west towards Frank Lee Plains, where the land would become more fertile. From there, a short rainforest trek into Aghanasp and my ultimate goal.

Dextrose had taken five days to complete that stage of the journey. I hazarded that I could take a day or two off his time, simply by leaving out the whoring.

Ptchtikov rowed us wordlessly ashore, myself at the prow and the dwarf astern, who clutched his belongings and looked shame-faced.

High Yawl became increasingly impressive as we approached. The domes were giant mushroom-shaped structures in high-tech plastic, anchored to the ground by wires, like guy-ropes. Beneath each of these, along the coastline, lurked a single building of concert-hall dimensions, constructed entirely from panes of mirrored glass.

The one we were headed towards was by far the most imposing, fronted by red curtains some 20 metres high, so gaudy and shimmering that it seemed there might be a harem of 18-metre-high leggy blondes waiting within.

Above the drapes, outlined in flashing neon, were the words 'HIGH YAWL!'. This was the entrance to the town – and most entrancing it was.

I realised that the dwarf was calling me with a series of unsubtle "Psssts".

He beckoned me over. "Pleeze, meester, comeeng queek!"

Not only did I not wish to speak with the oik, but Ptchtikov's bulk was between us, rowing.

I shook my head, pointing at our oarsman.

He only beckoned more furiously.

After much unbalanced huffing, I sat before the dwarf and he produced his leather briefcase.

"Before goeeng, zees Detritos doeeng for friend Meester Alexander."

With a glance to check that Ptchtikov wasn't peeking, he flicked open both catches.

Both set at '000', I thought smugly, wondering what I could possibly have missed inside.

"Ready, ees he?" asked the dwarf.

He lifted the lid, shielding the contents from my gaze, hastily removed the vinyl floozy and sat upon her. "Neffer useeng zees!" he muttered with a disingenuous grin.

From his pocket, Detritos removed a Swiss army knife – in fact *my* Swiss army knife, which he must have retrieved from the penguin park on Emo Island – and began cutting into the lining.

"That's my –"

"Shhh!" he hissed.

A brief tinkering later, the dwarf twisted the case around, so that I could see inside.

The beige plush lining had been peeled back to reveal a false bottom of foam. Cut into the centre was a round compartment almost two inches in diameter, in which nestled a blood-red jewel.

"Jesus!" I gasped.

The dwarf put his finger to his lips, folded back the lining, replaced the inflatable sex doll and closed the case. "Detritos doeeng for sorry."

I was gobsmacked. "What's it worth?"

"Not money. Bad seengs. Telleeng no one, Meester Alexander," he hissed, his dark eyes intense.

With a jolt and the scraping sound of timber across pebbles, we beached suddenly on the shoreline of High Yawl. The dwarf gathered up his belongings and held out a hand, which I grasped.

"Goodbye, Meester Alexander."

Before I could respond, he let go, turned, skipped onto the stern of the boat, and jumped into the shallow water, falling flat on his face. He cursed, picked himself up with tattered dignity, and strode into town, dripping.

What the hell was he doing, carting around a ruby the size of a sheep's bollock?

There was something in my hand. I looked down. It was my Swiss army knife. Though, to all intents and purposes it was mine and the dwarf had stolen it from me, it felt like a parting gift.

Some yards from the looming curtains marking the entrance to High Yawl, red carpet had been laid over the sandstone ground. This would have seemed glamorous, had the extended rug not been a well-worn affair, bleached by the sun.

As I trod the pile, with Ptchtikov already on his way back to the submarine, two men appeared from behind the curtains. They wore identical suits of rainbow glitter and matching top hats. Each carried a golden satchel slung over a shoulder.

One grabbed my hand and shook it vigorously. "Hello there, sir. My name is Stetson Wolfwhistle…" He wafted an arm in the direction of the other gentleman. "And this is Fenton Clench."

In unison, they pointed at outsized name-badges pinned to their lapels.

"We'd like to welcome you to High Yawl," Wolfwhistle continued. "Your visit is sponsored by Yap! No Gristle! dog food. Please take a free sample." He handed me a single-serving sachet of pet food.

"Did your son come through here not minutes ago, sir?" asked Clench. "Loved his hair!"

"Erm, no," I managed to mumble. The reception was rather overwhelming.

Still odder, the pair appeared identical – fine facial bone structure, perfectly tanned, icy eyes, full lips, same muscular physique, same height even – yet they had different surnames.

"Excuse me, are you twins?"

Wolfwhistle and Clench laughed falsely. The former replied, "No, no, no, sir! We liked each other so much, we had appearance enhancement surgery to look the same!"

"I was three inches taller than him, sir, so had the respective amount of bone removed from each tibia," explained Clench.

"Sure brought you down to size, partner!" chuckled Wolfwhistle and the pair of them laughed heartily during a brief embrace, flashing teeth whiter than washed linen.

"And my facial structure was all wrong, sir, so I had my whole skull removed and replaced with a plastic cast of Mr Clench's."

"Here's looking at me, kid!" quipped Clench, at which they both bent double to hoot.

Stetson Wolfwhistle and Fenton Clench were giving me the creeps.

"Can I go inside?" I asked.

"Why, surely, sir!" chirped Wolfwhistle, swishing aside the curtain. "This entrance through The Drapes is sponsored by the Bags Me First! candy assortment. If you would, Mr Clench…" And Clench handed me a bag of sweets from his golden satchel.

"If I may say so, sir, you are rather dour-looking," said Wolfwhistle. "We know just the store for you, don't we

Mr Clench!"

"We surely do, Mr Wolfwhistle."

Without warning, my escorts grabbed a hand each and skipped me into High Yawl as if I were Dorothy in *The Wizard of Oz*.

Inside was an awesome space of canopy up to the heavens, about which bland piped music echoed. It would have required binoculars to see the other end of the ludicrous building. The acreage of unending floor must have made the cleaning staff weep.

Around the sides stretched hundreds and hundreds of shops and restaurants, and in the centre of the floor area someone had constructed a rollercoaster ride.

People milled around, dwarfed by the sheer space, while among them slid silent vehicles topped by amber flashing lights. Each car was in the shape of a tacky product and plastered with logos, the windows built into the design so as not to detract from it. Better to offer total promotion than adequate visibility, it appeared. Nearest to me were a motorised hamburger, advertising 'Burger Bill's 57% Beef Patties – Nutritio-licious!', a soft-drink carton complete with swirly straw and desert-island design ('Paradise Pops – Three Sips to Heaven!'), and a gold television set with 'Square Eyes – Rounded Education!' emblazoned across its screen.

Although the sheer dimensions alone were disorientating, there was something else flustering me that I couldn't place. My brain gently throbbed, my face flushed and I began to panic.

Wolfwhistle and Clench stopped and studied me, feigning concern. Their ridiculous suits began to swim as a rainbow-coloured swirl before my eyes.

"Don't worry, sir," said one, whose name-badge I could no longer discern. "You will faint shortly. It's not uncommon."

"Not uncom–" I began to protest, and fainted.

When I came around, my head was propped in Wolfwhistle's lap and he was stroking my hair. There was something covering my nose and mouth that made me feel claustrophobic. I swiped the object aside. It was a plastic facemask, attached to a canister held by Clench.

"There is no cause for alarm, sir," smarmed Wolfwhistle. "Your lungs have now adjusted."

"In High Yawl we don't breathe the air outside," explained Clench. "Nasty common air, Mr Wolfwhistle."

"Yes, all those nasty germs, Mr Clench."

"We High Yawlians breathe a sanitary chemical equivalent of everyone else's air, sir. We call it Nectair."

"Mmm, Nectair, Mr Clench!" said Wolfwhistle, inhaling deeply.

"Ordinary lungs take a short while to adapt. I have given you a quick boost," Clench indicated the facemask, "which means you will now be able to function as normal. Please rise."

"Oooh, Mr Clench!" camped Wolfwhistle.

Obediently I rose, still feeling light-headed, and tottered a little before gaining composure.

"Now, time to get sir some more appropriate attire."

My stomach turned over. I remembered my curtailed expedition to The Tin Squid's toilet. "Actually, I may need to excuse myself first."

"Oh how quaint!" squealed Wolfwhistle, clasping his hands together. "He wants to *excuse* himself!"

Clench smiled. "People who use euphemisms for dirty habits are always welcome in High Yawl, sir!"

It took ten minutes just to reach the public convenience, in the corner nearest The Drapes. The two doors were painted the same bright white as the walls, disguising their existence. Only their outlines and a single letter on each – 'M' and 'W' – gave them away. I made for the 'M' but my guides gasped in unison and Stetson Wolfwhistle ushered me towards the other door.

"W for Winsome, M for Macho, sir!"

The pair of them followed me inside, which sounded my internal warning bells.

Along one wall was a row of stainless steel sinks and, opposite those, a row of cubicles with polished metallic doors. I could see no urinals. Perhaps the people here deemed visible urination gauche?

The white wall ahead of me suddenly sprang to life as a giant, previously concealed video screen filled with the head of a rat-faced man with straggly black, over-greased hair spilling from beneath a white peaked cap. It seemed as if his head had been stretched outward by someone pulling on his nose.

"Welcome, sir!" sang Rat Face, then broke into a nasal ditty, "I'm your janitor/Name's Linden Twine/You does your business/I does mine!"

"Very good!" I exclaimed, applauding without meaning to.

Twine continued, looking smug, "Visitors may be used to an antiquated flush mechanism. In High Yawl, simply remain seated. You will be cleansed and dried automatically – once your task is completed."

Then his face was gone, replaced by the blank wall.

"I'll be a short while," I said to Wolfwhistle and Clench, making for the furthest cubicle and eyeing my guardians suspiciously. They remained near the entrance, simpering.

It felt good to lock the door behind me and to be alone. So much of my journey had been spent in the company – often enforced – of others. Without the time to reflect, events seemed to have tumbled past.

My stomach performed another somersault. Reflection would have to wait. I lowered the necessary garments and slumped down with a sigh. The toilet seat was blissfully cushioned and seemed even to be heated. In High Yawl they thought of everything. I might begin to enjoy it here, I mused, once I could escape Wolfwhistle and Clench.

"Comfortably seated, sir?"

Such was the start that I shook my head, cartoon-style. The cubicle door had become a video screen from which Linden Twine once again appeared to be staring. So close was he now that I could see stains on his teeth.

"Please go away," I whimpered.

"Certainly, sir," said Twine, and the video screen went blank.

I was so paranoid I could barely crap.

"Don't worry, sir," came Wolfwhistle's echoing lilt from across the room. "Voice recognition as standard!"

My performance concluded, I paused as instructed and felt a gush of warm water spray my nether regions, not unpleasantly. The toilet then flushed itself as a blast of air began the drying process. A slot opened in the wall to my right, through which a slip of paper appeared, accompanied by a hushed printer sound.

Somewhat mystified, I pulled it free. It read:

Complimentary Stool Analysis

Composition (%)
52 meat (poss horse)
20 root crop (prob turnip)
9 chilli
6 garlic
5 carrot
5 sweetcorn
3 worm

Your diet is: unsavoury

Enjoy your stay in High Yawl
Happy bowel health!

Who the hell had put worms in my food? It could only have been from the meal on The Tin Squid. And horse meat? Perhaps the worms hadn't been added, but had been living inside the horse? My stomach turned over once again.

Identical heads beneath glittering top hats appeared above the cubicle door. A hand followed, clutching a small green aerosol.

"Sir," announced the one holding the can, dispensing a fine liquid mist in my direction, "your bowel movement has been proudly sponsored by Odour-Be-Gone Personal Air Freshener!"

"You can't flirt – until you squirt!" sang the other.

"Would you mind if I continued my journey alone?" I asked immediately when we were outside.

Wolfwhistle and Clench looked staggered.

I added, hopefully, "I'm sure you have other visitors to welcome…"

"But sir, Mr Clench and I pride ourselves on a personal service, tailored to the individual. There are other New Visitor Facilitators to take our place at The Drapes." Wolfwhistle seemed genuinely hurt, but their persistence was beginning to rile me.

"I do appreciate your help, but I'd really prefer to tour High Yawl by myself," I said.

"But sir's dark, unseemly attire…?"

"So point me in the right direction and I'll pick up some new clothes."

"Hmph," went Clench.

"Ungrateful little shit," snarled Wolfwhistle. From his golden satchel he pulled a leaflet that he thrust into my hand. "Here's a map, hope you get lost."

Noses in the air, the glitter twins turned on their heels and sashayed away.

Alone at last. I guessed it must have been late-evening, yet all the shops were still open. The new clothes would have to wait; my priority was to find accommodation for the night.

I unfolded the map that Wolfwhistle had handed me so ungraciously. It represented the domes, in aerial view. They were arranged in a semi-circular fashion, the straight edge tracing High Yawl's coast. Each was numbered and there was a key along the left-hand side, which went up to dome number 78.

The largest dome, my current position, was numbered 1: the 'Welcome Dome'. I scanned the rest of the list: Designer Dome, Video Dome, Pamper Dome, Sensory Deprivation Dome, Sycophancy Dome… ah, the Pleasure Dome, number 69, where Harrison Dextrose had frittered away his days… There were at least ten Retail Therapy Domes and still more Nutritional Domes, offering different styles of cuisine, from Super-Spicy to Mama's Own.

Handily, the domes on either side, numbers 2 and 3, were each labelled 'Luxury Accommodation'. I could certainly do with a little baby-soft linen after a night in the Tin Squid.

Though how was I to get there? The distances in this place were mind-boggling. I looked around and became aware that a shark on wheels was making for me. When it was close enough, I could spot the driver peering through its gaping mouth, his head appearing to nestle neatly between the teeth. He swung the vehicle broadside and stopped.

It was a boxy, misshapen shark, presumably to accommodate the passenger seating and workings, but boasted the requisite dorsal fin atop. The slogan along its side ran: 'Al's Aquarium – come see the Great White!' then below that, 'Don't worry – the other fish are just as great!'

The gill section swung open and the driver, a silver-haired gent in neat navy-blue matching short-sleeved shirt and shorts, leaned out.

"Wanna ride, sir?"

He had a pot belly the size of a prize pumpkin and a skin-tone that verged on orange. "Are you a cabbie?"

Pot Belly chuckled briefly. "I guess that's what we were called once, sir. These days we're 'route facilitators'."

"I'm afraid I don't have any cash on me."

"No need for that, sir. 'Anywhere you please – for free!', that's our motto." It wasn't a great motto, but the sentiment suited me fine.

"Hop in!" offered Pot Belly. "Handle's above the pelvic fin."

The shark shell was light, constructed of fibreglass. The inside, however, was incongruously plush: all black leather and instant comfort. All it lacked was windows.

Pot Belly twisted around, pushing aside the glass screen that separated us. His teeth were so white, they winked. I felt dentally inferior.

"The name's Trenchant Malaise. In the control panel in front of you, you'll find a video screen with full menu and sponsor messages, a soft drinks dispenser – 'So-Lush Lemonade – You'll Turn Tart For Us!' – Nectair conditioning regulator, back and thigh massage control, games console, automatic route-tracer, solarium activator –"

"There's a solarium – in the car?" I spluttered.

"Sure. Just hit that button marked 'Solarium'."

I did so and became bathed in an electric-blue light emanating from a panel in the roof.

"Goggles in the side pocket, sir. Along with electric shaver, promotional vouchers – 'Proud Mary's Diner – You won't find finer! Ten tokens off the Cholesterol Surprise!' – freshen-up towelettes, deodoriser, depilator…"

Pointedly, I switched off the solarium. The gimmickry was becoming a little obsessive. "Actually, I'm just after a hotel; it must be getting late."

"You don't have a watch, sir?" Malaise sounded horrified.

"Not really, no. I *did* have, but –"

"Then we should take sir to buy one this instant! Trenchant Malaise knows just the place! 'Chronos Watches – For the face that fits!'"

"Surely it's closed," I protested weakly.

Malaise chuckled. "Sir, High Yawl's open 24-hours-a-day, seven-days-a-week, 367-days-a-year!"

"Don't you mean 365?"

"Sir, we added two days to ensure everyone could get their Christmas shopping done. In High Yawl, you can buy anything, anytime."

"I'd rather buy a watch tomorrow, if that's alright."

Malaise twisted his head, to look me in the eye. His age-dried jowls thus taut, he resembled a sincere lizard. "Sir, it'd be remiss of me if I didn't find you a watch right away."

Before I could protest further we were off, on slick electric motors.

Malaise was not one for small-talk, unlike the British taxi drivers I had encountered.

"First time I've ever been driven around in a big fish," I offered.

"Not for me it isn't," the driver replied, failing to appreciate the humour. "Been driving Al's Great White nigh on 40 years."

Awkward silence. I leaned forward. "Must be difficult to see pedestrians through that mouth."

"You get used to it, sir. Never hit anyone yet."

Further silence. "Tell me, you mentioned tokens – is that the currency here?"

"Sure is."

"Because I'm stuck with Sterling travellers' cheques."

"You can change them any place in High Yawl."

"Right."

I surrendered to his lack of social skills and sat back. This was a strange, captivating place, unlike anything I had encountered before: a self-sufficient, environmentally cocooned haven for shallow consumerism. And slightly tacky, of course.

Imagine if Suzy Goodenough could see me now, chauffeured around in a fibreglass shark... And Benjamin. What might he be doing right now? Something less interesting, no doubt.

"Chronos Watches!" announced Trenchant Malaise, as the Great White slowed to a halt.

My door swung open and I was greeted by a grandfather-clock... or rather by a man in a foam grandfather-clock costume, his face painted white with black numbers, the hands showing a-quarter-to-two.

"Good evening, sir," he said, bowing. "Welcome to Chronos Watches – for the face that fits! Please step inside."

I looked to Malaise for support, but none was forthcoming. He sat there staring forwards like a crash test dummy.

"My! Sir is very darkly attired!" said the grandfather-clock. "It would be my honour to recommend 'Garish Gear – If you look bright, people will think you're bright!' in the Retail Therapy Dome: Casualwear."

"Well, possibly... Let me just look at the watches first." Still, I was secretly excited at the thought of buying a whole new outfit. Rudi Ptchtikov's offcasts, which had once seemed so mysterious, now just whiffed of oil. These High Yawlians seemed to have the right idea with their dazzling-white teeth and crazy ways.

Grandfather-Clock led me into Chronos Watches, a well-lit, white-walled showroom, with perspex display cases framed in neon. Row-upon-row of wristbound timepieces, of all descriptions, lined the walls. Never had I wanted a watch more.

When I turned around to compliment Grandfather-Clock, he had vanished into thin air and, as I turned back, a young blonde lady in a futuristic metallic-blue mini-dress and ankle socks was standing before me.

"Oh, hello," I said, flummoxed.

"Welcome to Chronos Watches – for the face that fits! My name is Mimsy Flopkins. How may I help you?"

She had a ponytail and cheekbones that could have skewered windborne litter. Her skin was perfectly tanned, she had a little upturned nose with freckles across the bridge, and eyeshadow that matched her dress. I guessed she was in her late-teens. Mimsy Flopkins was gorgeous. I decided there and then that if she tried to sell me a concrete sundial, I would buy it.

"I'd like to buy a watch," I said.

"Sir, has anyone told you that you have lovely eyes?" she asked, fluttering her own.

"Nnno," I replied, sounding like a skid.

"We stock a range of more than 2,000 watches, as you can see. The basic design starts at 190 tokens… but I can see that sir requires something more elegant. We have watches with alarms, timers, depth gauges, height gauges, pedometers, speedometers, barometers, anemometers, voltmeters, heliographs, dictographs, spirographs and girographs." Finally, she drew breath. "However, for sir I would recommend the Timeco Z112.2 XG."

"What's that?"

"It's a very special watch, sir. Please follow me."

Mimsy led me towards the rear of the showroom, to a perspex tube that ran from floor to ceiling, containing just one watch. She produced a plastic card, slid it into a slot beneath the timepiece, a hidden door fell away and she retrieved the product with some reverence.

"Before you try on the Timeco Z112.2 XG, I am obliged to warn you, sir, that should you attempt to steal this product, you will be traced by one of High Yawl's Security Counsellors within 13.3 seconds."

I was a little taken aback. "I can assure you, miss, that I had no intention…"

She smiled. I laid the watch piece in place. Two curved metal arms moved automatically inwards, wrapping themselves around my wrist with just the right pressure, and secured themselves with a click.

"As you can see, sir, the Timeco Z112.2 XG fits itself."

"Wow!" was all I managed.

It was a stunning timepiece, the size of a small tin of shoe-polish, silver rimmed, with seven buttons around the outside. Within the face were four dials of varying sizes and two digital readouts.

"That's time here, time anywhere in the world, time on other planets and timer," said Mimsy Flopkins, pointing a blue-painted fingernail at each dial in turn. "You do not need to adjust the main readout – the Timeco Z112.2 XG knows where you are in the world and adjusts the time difference accordingly."

A facility that would prove useful during my Quest.

"These digital readouts," she continued. "One is a directional thermometer. Point the Timeco Z112.2 XG at any object and it will indicate its temperature, up to 10,000 degrees centigrade…"

"Handy," I lied.

Mimsy glanced at me blankly, which was still attractive. "The other monitors your blood pressure. If it flashes red, you are about to die."

It was the most wonderful watch in the world, boasting more functions than I would ever require. I wanted it.

"How much is it?"

"It's 6,000 tokens, sir; however I can offer it to you, this evening…"

Wondering what time it was, I glanced at the Timeco Z112.2 XG but was none the wiser.

"...for 5,600."

"How much is that in Sterling?"

"Ten tokens to the pound – £560! A bargain, you'll agree!"

I did. "I'll take it."

Thus did I leave Chronos Watches with £940 remaining in travellers' cheques, and a timepiece that could predict my death. I turned to wave goodbye to Mimsy Flopkins, who glowed amid the neon.

"Your premature departure has left a hole in my soul," she trilled.

"To the Luxury Accommodation Dome, sir?" enquired Trenchant Malaise, who had dutifully waited for me in Al's Great White.

"Actually, I was thinking of visiting the Retail Therapy Dome: Casualwear."

"I understand, sir," said Malaise.

I spent the entire journey – an estimated 25 minutes – trying to work out the Timeco Z112.2 XG, which came with a manual heavy enough to require a dedicated carry-case.

The instructions were written in 57 languages, with English at the very front. Having failed to understand even that, I began flicking through some of the foreign pages and was amused to note that the Umbongon for 'watch' was 'titwanq'.

As Malaise signalled our arrival inside the Casualwear dome, I had finally worked out how to tell the High Yawl time, and reasoned that I was unlikely to need world or outer-world time, at least for the moment. The respective hands showed, to my mild horror, twenty-past-eleven. Almost midnight – I really should have been in bed.

"Which retail therapist, sir?" asked Malaise.

"Actually, Malaise, I think I'll have a wander. Maybe check out a few stores... retail therapists. Could you drop me off anywhere here and wait for me?"

The driver craned his face towards mine and smiled a sickly smile. "Anywhere you please – for free!"

I window-shopped for several hundred metres, in a state of awe. All these retail therapy outlets were lit like ostentatious UFOs, and most were patrolled outside by promoters in costume, cajoling me to step inside. I was accosted variously by a pair of jeans, a baseball cap, matching wellingtons and a girdle. Frankly, I didn't know which way to turn next – it was all so enticing.

It was amid this indecision that I chanced upon Garish Gear, as recommended by the grandfather-clock. I didn't even wait for an invitation.

Like the others I had passed, the store had its goods stacked around the walls, leaving the floorspace completely clear. This, I found, gave one the room to breathe, indeed, to feel excited.

Sifting through a selection of t-shirts on perspex rails, I sensed someone beside me. It was Mimsy Flopkins again, dressed now in sparkling green.

"Hello!" I chirped, oddly delighted. "How did you get here?"

"I'm sorry, sir, I don't think we've met before. My name is Miranda Flam-Tintin. How may I be of service?"

Yet she looked exactly the same as Mimsy: same face, same nose, same hair... same everything, except the dress colour.

"This is a nice garment, don't you think?" said Miranda Flam-Tintin, holding out a hideous tie-dyed t-shirt bearing the slogan 'Love me, love my wardrobe'.

"Hmm," I replied, too English to contradict.

I emerged from Garish Gear wearing blue denim bell-bottoms, a red-and-white striped tanktop bearing a happy-tortoise design, and a pair of Supa-grip™ green spangly trainers, Miranda having offered to incinerate my previous togs.

In my carrier bags, I had six pairs of pristine boxer shorts, the same number of pop socks, two t-shirts (orange and lemon coloured, with pictures of the respective fruit), a cagoule (camouflage pattern, in white and sky-blue) and silver baggy trousers that I bought because they made me feel like a spaceman. The lot totalled a bargain 2,100 tokens (£210). Miranda threw in a free sombrero, for her "favourite customer". She was easily as nice as Mimsy Flopkins.

Next door was Bottom Shop – 'Making your butt attractive' – which exclusively stocked underwear and was staffed by another Mimsy lookalike who introduced herself as Marcella Flib-Nibster. For some reason, these identical shop assistants failed to faze me; indeed, in High Yawl the concept seemed perfectly reasonable.

I bought six more pairs of boxer shorts and a bra-and-pants set for Suzy Goodenough, in preparation for our tryst. Marcella helped me choose the latter and we plumped for the most expensive one in the store – pink satin, featuring a discreet electric bottom warmer – priced at a thoroughly reasonable 1,200 tokens. Though I was forced to guess Suzy's bra size, which conjured up a pleasing mental image, the assistant noted that I could bring the garment back if it failed to fit.

"But I live in England," I pointed out.

Marcella admitted she didn't know where that was. When I tried to tell her about my homeland and its relative geography, she seemed more interested in selling me some tartan socks, which I bought.

When I left Bottom Store, I realised that my purchases had become unwieldy. As if by magic, Trenchant Malaise appeared in the Great White.

"Nice outfit!" he remarked, and seemed to mean it.

I took my seat in the back, gratefully offloaded the numerous bags, and checked my money situation. Only £560 remained in travellers' cheques, which sent a shockwave up my spine.

Already I had spent £940, and I had only been in High Yawl for a few hours.

A curious sensation overtook me, as if I had physically stepped out of a dream. What had I been thinking of? I had arrived in High Yawl with £1,500 remaining of the inheritance money I had set aside to fund my Quest – a significant proportion of which I had spent on new clothes, an excess of pants and a watch that cost more than the average fridge-freezer.

Then the sensation passed. Hell, I owed myself some guilty pleasure.

I glanced at the Timeco Z112.2 XG and could not resist a tinker, allied with my latest consultation of the instruction manual. I was slowly getting the hang of the thing and concluded the following: my blood pressure was some way above normal, but that I was still very much alive; Trenchant Malaise's body temperature was 98.8; and the time on Alpha Centauri was 6.17 in the morning, in the year 3,146,237,928. It was by chance that I noticed, with a sharp intake of breath, the High Yawl time: midnight.

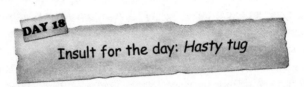

To a hotel, sharpish!" I ordered the driver.

Malaise swivelled. "Sir, I think we should get you some food."

I swore I spotted panic sprint before his eyes. "Really?"

"You must be hungry."

Come to think of it, I was.

"I know an excellent place, sir, in the Nutritional Dome: Home Cooking. The Carnivoral – 'Food to diet for!'."

Well, I thought, a few more tokens on a meal could do no harm, and eating was, after all, a human necessity.

When Malaise dropped me outside the restaurant, I noticed for the first time that my fellow consumers were a portly bunch, quite at odds with the lithe shop assistants I had thus far encountered.

The couple nearest me were checking out the menu at Just Fries – 'One Potato, Two Potato, Three Potato... 10,000 Potatoes!' They wore jeans shaped like funnels so voluminous were their waists. She had a stringy blonde bob, he a pink baseball cap. Their chins were folds of saggy flesh that might double as interesting bibs.

Aware that I was staring, they faced me in unison, smiled and waved a chubby hand each. I hurried into The Carnivoral.

At the far end of the restaurant was an open-plan kitchen in which cooks wearing unblemished white outfits prepared food on stainless steel surfaces. The place certainly seemed clean and I swore I could smell lavender, which was strange.

All around, outsized diners' buttocks spilled either side of shiny four-legged stools as they tucked into plates piled high with slabs of meat and chips. It wasn't all that inviting and I considered sneaking out, until I realised that the floor was moving.

The entrance mat I had stepped onto was transporting me silently up the aisle between tables.

Should I step off? "Please do not step off the mat," said the mat. It spoke… and possibly read minds. I decided to do as I was told and to avoid subversive thought.

The mat took a sharp right between obese diners, who failed to pay my progress any attention, performed a nifty zig-zag and stopped before an empty table. "Please alight," came its electronic voice. Again I obeyed, perching myself on one of the four stools available.

The tablecloth was vinyl and red-and-white checked – a concession, no doubt, to traditional home cooking – already set out with knives, forks and napkins. Also on the table were a jumbo bottle of GM Relish – 'Full Flavour, All Year Round!' – which was bright red, and a large glass sugar dispenser with silver spout.

A waiter appeared at my side, wearing a white shirt, black waistcoat and trousers, and a white apron. His face was long, thin and haughty looking, and his slicked-back dark hair was counterpointed by a thin moustache that travelled neatly along his upper lip.

"Hello, sir," he said, and staring pointedly at my stomach added, "I see we are not a regular. My name is Quickly Verbose and I shall be your nutritional consultant for your visit. Would you care to see a menu?"

Verbose was so tall that he was peering down his nose at me.

"Yes, please," I replied, intimidated.

The waiter handed me not a laminated card, but a digital device bearing a small blank screen, Up, Down, Left and Right depressible arrows, and a Start/Select button.

"Hit Start, sir," Verbose sniffed, already gliding away towards the kitchen.

However, within seconds, while I was staring at the menu like a man whose brain has seeped out through his nose, he returned.

"I'm not quite ready yet, Quickly," I said.

"Sir, I am not Quickly. My name is Quaint Vernacular and I am your beverage consultant."

Quaint handed me a second computer-menu and flounced off. This, I put to one side. One technical conundrum at a time.

When I pressed Start, the bloated face of a beaming lady suffering from sunbed-overexposure filled the screen. "Welcome to my establishment! I'm Duchess Daisy and I trust you'll enjoy your visit to my Carnivoral! Remember, if it's got four legs, we serve it!"

Duchess Daisy's face was then replaced by a list of options:

Appetiser Appetiser
Appetiser
Starter
Starter Seconds
Main Course
Side Orders
Other Side Orders
Main Seconds
Main Thirds
Water Ices
Dessert
Dessert Seconds
Cheese & Biscuits

The Whole Meal Again

The system seemed user-friendly enough but the choice was overwhelming. I plumped directly for main course to save confusion, at which I was offered a list of alphabetic letters. I selected 'A', because it came first. The screen became filled with a list of names that began:

Aardvark
Aardwolf
Abert's Squirrel
Aceramarca
Acuchis
Addax
Afghan Mouse-like Hamster

None of these appealed. Scrolling down, some 300 names must have slid past. The 'A' list concluded:

Audacious Mole Rat
Aurochs
Aye-aye
Azara's Agouti
Azara's Night Monkey
Azara's Tuco-Tuco
Aztec Mouse

Bewildered, I returned to the main menu, found Main Course again, selected 'C' and sought Cow from among the Cottontail Rabbits, Coues's Climbing Mice, Cowan's Shrews, Coyotes and Coypus. I wondered whether Duchess Daisy's Carnivoral alone might be responsible for the worldwide mammals facing extinction.

I selected Cow. Instead of being presented with a list of

steaks, what appeared was a video of cows in a pen. What was this about? I peered towards the kitchen, spotted a waiter and hoped that it was my nutritional consultant.

Raising a finger, I coughed and called across apologetically, "Um, Quickly!"

The waiter sprinted across, knocking over a small child as he did so.

"You didn't need to rush," I said.

"I know, sir," replied Quickly. "That was my idea of a joke."

I let it pass. "Could you explain, please; I selected Cow and this video of cows appeared…"

"Sir, at the rear of the establishment, Duchess Daisy's zoo contains every mammal known to man. The menu provides a direct camera link. Simply place the cursor over the beast you wish to eat."

I stared aghast at the screen. One of the cows looked straight at the camera with an endearing nobody-home expression, leaned in and licked the lens, leaving behind a smear of drool and cud.

"But that's horrific!" I blurted.

"Don't worry, sir, we'll clean the lens."

"No, I mean condemning an innocent animal to death!"

Pointedly, I placed the menu on the table. "I don't think I fancy meat tonight."

The waiter stiffened. A smile flickered on his thin lips and he stooped to whisper in my ear, "There is one item that you may enjoy, which we prefer not to publicise on the menu. The Vegetarian Surprise, sir."

"And what would that be?"

"Cow also. It surprises the vegetarians."

"Quickly, you're a snide person."

"Thank you, sir."

"I think I shall pass on dinner."

"As sir wishes. Don't expect a lift to the door."

I rose with dignity, brushed imaginary dirt from my happy-tortoise tank top, nodded formally at Quickly Verbose and took my leave. As the waiter marched towards his kitchen, a thought struck me.

"Tell me, Quickly, is that lavender I can smell?"

He swivelled and sniffed. "It is, sir. Scent pumped into the Nectair conditioning. You wouldn't want to smell roasting Gundlach's hutia."

My experience in The Carnivoral had disturbed me and I told Trenchant Malaise as much when he asked after my meal. As usual, the driver knew just the place for me. "Sir, I should take you to the Pamper Zone. You need to learn to realise your worth."

"You think so?"

"Sure. I'll take you to That's Charisma! – 'We're great, but then so are you!' If anyone can make you interesting, they can."

I wasn't sure whether to take this as an insult.

To pass the time on the journey, I pulled out the map of High Yawl and traced the route from the Welcome Dome, via the Retail Therapy Dome: Casualwear, to the Nutritional Dome: Home Cooking. It turned out that we had travelled in an arc almost around the left edge of the undercover country.

"Where are we now?" I asked.

"Number 63, sir. The Touchy-Feely Dome."

I looked for it on the map and found it. However, there was something odd about dome 62. It was the only one not labelled in the key. I mentioned this to Malaise.

"We prefer to forget that one, sir," he said, and offered no more.

"Could you remember it for me?"

The driver sighed. "You've seen how consumer-friendly everything is in High Yawl, sir?"

"I have."

"So when the celebrated lesbian lovers Amanda Void and Antonia Grin announced their intention to develop 62, everyone predicted a triumph…" He sighed again. The tale seemed to hang like a plumbline through the driver's heart.

"I have to take you back to the beginnings of High Yawl, sir. Some 200 years ago, this area was unfertile. Crops barely grew and the cattle wilted in the heat. There was a scientist named Inherent Myopia. Experimenting with fertilisers, he developed a crop called nitrogen-enhanced maize, or NEM. It grew like wildfire and made the tastiest bread. Soon our ancestors were milling it and selling it all around the world. There were fields and mills everywhere to meet the demand. The High Yawlians became rich and it was through that wealth that this great nation you witness today was built, sir."

"So where does that fit in with number 62?"

"Amanda Void and Antonia Grin announced they would built a monument to our great nation and its bread-making heritage – with a vast potential for merchandise – and everyone became excited. Only they commissioned a young High Yawlian artist, Concepta Stoat, to fill the place."

"Yes?"

"We queued around the block for the Grand Opening, sir. Some camped out for days. And when we got inside there was just one exhibit: a 300-foot-tall white elephant, carved from a giant sugar cube!"

"What was that about?"

"You tell me, sir. You tell me. People stayed away in their droves and the place was boarded up within the year. These days it's just a deserted monument to fiasco."

The Pamper Zone, number 77, was next to the Souvenir Dome, number 78, the final dome in High Yawl at the far end of which, according to the map key, were the 'Anti-Drapes', which I assumed to be the exit.

Of course, I had no intention of leaving. At that moment my Quest was running a firm second to the prospect of purchasing. Anyway, I was still ahead of Dextrose, who had spent so much of his time in the Pleasure Dome.

I glanced at my shiny Timeco Z112.2 XG. Half-one in the morning. "You know, Malaise, I haven't bought anything for almost two hours."

"That's too bad, sir," replied Malaise.

"I know it is," I found myself replying. "How much do you think I'll manage to spend in That's Charisma!?"

"Therapy doesn't come cheap, sir. And you'll probably be able to pick up some books there, and maybe a mug."

I settled back into the leather seat. "You know, Malaise, if they do sell mugs, I'm going to buy two."

"Good for you, sir."

Our fourth day in High Yawl, my fourth day immersed in its Pleasure Dome. I have never seen a whorehouse like it. All the tarts look identical! Legs up to heaven and breasts like medicine balls, naked as the day they were born, offering services even I had never countenanced.

I pay by the hour and the booze is free. Every luxury is offered.

They all have the strangest names. I have visited more than I care to remember. There was Phoenicia Splay, Priscilla Split, Penelope Strain, Philomena Stretch, Poppy Seed... As I said, I cannot remember them all. Stop pestering me.

I sleep here, too, for half-price, at last free from my crew of minkers. Tench would not dare show his face in here. Shark ran out of money after two days and begged for an advance of his wages. I told him to mink off. When will he be advancing me his services?

According to Paloma Slaver, whom I am currently knobbing, he was spotted skulking around the Boot Sale Dome, trying to

flog ship models carved from matchsticks.
I fear I may only leave this place when I too am out of money.
By which time, the old man will be on crutches.

That's Charisma!'s open-plan interior was painted solid purple. Two men with expressive arm movements were conversing on stools at the far end while the piped sounds of cash registers emanated soothingly from hidden speakers. I noted with excitement a merchandise stall, selling not only branded mugs but t-shirts, scarves, hats, gloves, slippers, books, paperweights, snow-globes, corkscrews and what looked to be a That's Charisma! hostess trolley.

I made straight for these products and was intercepted by a very short lady wearing a cardigan and half-moon spectacles. She took my hand, looked up at me from chest height and winked.

"I know why you're here," she said in a deep, undulating voice. "My name is Aureola Zarathustra and I am here to help. I shall be your Personal Personifier."

"Great," I said. "Can I buy some mugs?"

Aureola extended a finger across her lips. "All in good time. Worldly goods are all very well. It is charisma that will complete the self. Tell me your name."

"It's Alexander," I said.

"As I had imagined."

I was led to a purple-cushioned stool and bade to sit. Aureola perched opposite me, pressed a thumb into each of my palms and gazed into my eyes, as if trying to spot contact lenses. I noticed how old she was. Her skin was brown and papery, stretched taut over her a neat skull. The myriad wrinkle lines around her thin lips made her mouth look like a millipede.

"Alexander. I want you to go on a journey for me. A journey to yourself. What is your route?"

"Left then sharp right," I guessed.

"Good," she said. "Now what do you see?"

"I'm sitting in an armchair watching television."

"As I had imagined. I want you to take part in an experiment for me. Will you be my guinea pig?"

"Eee!" I screeched rodent-style – an attempt at humour.

I could tell Aureola Zarathustra was not impressed, because she slapped me across the face. "Aversion therapy," she explained. "The fool may make people laugh, Alexander, but he is first to forfeit his dignity."

I knew what she meant.

"Now, you see my colleagues there?" My Personal Personifier motioned towards the two gentlemen at the rear of the room. "They are your Charisma Litmuses. I want you to sit and talk with them. See how they react to you."

Still in thrall of Aureola, who seemed terribly wise, I took a stool beside the conversing men and offered a hand to the one in the heavier spectacles. He ignored it and continued chatting.

"The ego and the id are comparable only in their contrivance," he stated solemnly.

His partner nodded. "And the superego is merely a vestige of disinterest."

They were both very bearded and wore comfortable suits.

"I'm Alexander," I butted in. "How do you do?"

Heavier Specs deigned to notice me. "The question is not 'How do you do?' but 'Why does one be?'"

"Naturally," added Lighter Specs. "If the goal is attainment of the self then the quintessential purpose of existence must be acknowledged. Now, would you go away?" He made a shooing gesture.

"But Miss Zarathustra said…"

"*Miss* Zarathustra?" snorted Heavier Specs. "He uses labels based on sex and servitude!"

"How crassly gendercentric!" his partner agreed. "Go on, piss off!"

"How did it go?" asked Aureola gently.

"Not that well," I admitted.

"As I had imagined." She paused and eyed me meaningfully. "I shall give you the gift of charisma. It must cost you 3,500 tokens. This price includes my book, *You're Great, You Just Don't Realise It*, and a That's Charisma! cheque book and pen."

"You have a deal," I replied.

Aureola Zarathustra shook her prune-head. "I deal only in people."

From her cardigan pocket, she produced an egg. "I want you to cradle this in both hands. It represents the Current You. Nurture it, because You are important."

Gingerly, I held the egg as if in prayer. Aureola placed her hands lightly around mine.

The therapy began. "Repeat after me… I am Alexander."

"I am Alexander."

"I am great."

"I am great.

"No really, I am."

"No really, I am."

"Everyone likes me."

"Everyone likes me."

"I have the gift of the gab."

"I have the gift of the gab."

"When I speak, the world stops to listen."

"When I speak, the world stops to listen."

She removed her hands from mine, bowed briefly, and said, uncharacteristically vehemently, "Now crack the egg over your head!"

Inspired, I did just that. Yolk and albumen mingled with my hair and began to drip before my eyes. Aureola rose with a beatific smile, hugged me and air-kissed each of my cheeks. As she puckered up to the second cheek, she spoke into my ear, "The breaking of the egg represents the destruction of the Current You and the birth of the New You. Consider yourself charismatic."

She retook her seat, still beaming. I noticed that a bit of egg yolk had transferred itself to her nose. "Now return to the Charisma Litmuses and discover the success of your treatment."

I had not even reached Heavier and Lighter Specs before they were out of their seats and heading towards me, arms extended, mouths agog, excited about something.

"How wonderful to see you, Alexander!" Heavier Specs greeted me, pumping my hand vigorously.

"Really?" I replied, slightly confused.

"Such modesty!" declared Lighter Specs, pumping the other hand. "The domain only of the confidently popular!"

"I'm not sure I understand," I said.

"He toys with us!" boomed Heavier Specs.

"Because he is so much more intelligent!" added his partner. Heavier Specs at last released his grip. "Well, we must be going. Time waits for no man… though it may well wait for you. Genuinely, Alexander, it was a privilege to meet you."

"Indeed," Lighter Specs agreed. "You have made us feel small. We envy you your depth of personality and your inevitable popularity."

On the way out, I picked up two That's Charisma! mugs (100 tokens each), as I had promised myself, and a tea-towel (150 tokens). I was likely to be hosting some well-attended parties in the future, which would mean plenty of washing up.

"How was the treatment?" Trenchant Malaise enquired, as I retook my seat in the back of the Great White.

"Brilliant!"

He twisted and pointed. "There's some eggshell in your hair."

"I know! That represents the New Me!"

"You sure are a character, sir," said Malaise.

My newfound charisma was working and never had I felt more confident. And it was all thanks to this place and its freedom to express oneself via the beauty of shopping. "Where to now then, Malaise?" I trilled. "I feel the need to spend, spend, spend!"

The driver explained that we were tantalisingly close to the Souvenir Dome, a favourite haunt of visitors to High Yawl. "Sir, there's a retail therapist there I just know you'll love: Oh My Cod! – 'Novelty fish-masks for every occasion!' They do shellfish too!"

I imagined myself as party host, regaling guests with tales of my adventures then reducing them to hysterics disguised as a creature that is half-man, half-halibut. I could picture Suzy Goodenough laughing uncontrollably in a state of heightened passion, and Benjamin witnessing this scene jealously, now that I was everyone's idea of fun.

"Malaise," I said, "you know me too well. Onwards to Oh My Cod!"

Just to be on the safe side, I checked my financial situation. Travellers cheques to the total of £175. Whoops. I appeared to have spent rather a lot. "How much does the average mask cost?" I asked.

"It varies, sir. Average price, maybe 800 tokens."

Eighty pounds sterling... Excellent, I thought, I have enough for two.

While I was pondering the relative comedic merits of the flat fish, Malaise butted in. "Sir, we're approaching the Anti-Drapes so I should warn you about the Self-Satisfied Ikeans."

"The who, Trenchant?" I now felt comfortable addressing him by his first name.

"Bunch of grimy, funless folk, led by a guru named Ike. They travel here once in a while, steal in through the Anti-Drapes and kidnap tourists."

"Whatever for?"

"The Ikeans try brainwashing people to their simple tastes: living off the land, having no fashion sense, that kind of thing. They're very anti-commercialism, sir. Get this – they equate buying stuff with greed."

"Preposterous!"

"I know."

Although this was unnerving news. High Yawl was such a haven for happy shoppers – to think that people were prepared to ruin this perfectly respectable state of affairs.

"You're sure we'll be fine, Trenchant?"

"No problem. Oh My Cod!'s real close, and the Ikeans never hang around. Once the alarm goes, our Security Counsellors are on them in 13.3 seconds. Course, you're lucky you're with Trenchant Malaise. One or two of my route facilitator colleagues can't be trusted. They set up a kidnap and sell their customers for a handful of tokens and some stupid trinket."

It felt good to know that I was in safe hands. "Are we there yet?"

In reply, Malaise slowed the Great White to a halt. His driver's door opened and a hairy arm appeared, handing over to him a bundle of tokens and a plastic model of a monkey having a wee.

It couldn't be... "Trenchant," I yelped. "What's happening?"

He turned around, his great orange face beneath that silver thatch a picture of smarmy deception. Suddenly, my rear door was yanked open and a wild-eyed man with stubbly cheeks and tombstone teeth lunged at me. His dusty brown hair looked like a keratin explosion.

"Why, Trenchant, why?" I implored, flailing arms to elude my kidnapper.

"Sir, I got bills to pay and a wife to feed."

Other Ikeans joined the attack. Hands were clamped on all parts of me, tugging at my clothing. I tried to wedge my legs in the footwell before realising that struggle was futile. I was outnumbered. Wildly, I looked around, seeking some form of weapon, only to catch sight of my lovely bags of shopping.

"My purchases!" I wailed. "My free sombrero!"

This wasn't how it was supposed to end. After the bleakness of Frartsi, the raw survival instincts required on Emo Island and the hardships endured during the Iditamush, I had finally discovered some kind of luxury. When people read travel brochures, they aren't faced with pictures of holidaymakers chained to pipework or warily inspecting toilets for discarded dachshunds. They see carefree sunbathers and sightseers, people visiting department stores in glamorous cities.

My experiences in High Yawl had been no less than I deserved, yet here I was being unceremoniously dragged away by a series of unwashed types who preferred the puritan lifestyle.

"Leave me alone!" I shrieked.

"But we've come to save you!" a nearby hook-nosed kidnapper replied breathlessly.

"I don't want sav..." Someone stuffed material into my mouth.

Alarm bells began to ring, echoing around the empty spaces of the Souvenir Dome. Ha, I thought. The incursion had been noted. Security Counsellors would be here in moments, then we'd see who was leaving High Yawl. I would take great pleasure in shopping Trenchant Malaise.

"Get him out of here!" the quisling blustered.

With an almighty tug, I was ejected from Al's Great White and plopped onto the floor like a newborn. Behind us, Malaise was already on his way.

As I was dragged along the polished tiling on my back at high speed, like a human sledge, I craned to see my kidnappers. They were a group of men and women in sackcloth smocks, so unkempt that they looked Stone-Aged. How undignified this was.

"Six seconds!" shouted one Ikean, who must have been timing the arrival of the Security Counsellors.

Come quickly, I prayed, my heart set on a latex prawnhead.

"Five... four..."

I could make out two crusty Ikeans just ahead at the Anti-Drapes – black, not red like The Drapes, and much smaller – holding the curtains apart. I tried to back-pedal but it was hopeless; even my Supa-grip™ green spangly trainers could not gain a hold on the ceramic surface.

"Three... two...!"

My kidnappers sprinted through...

"One!"

...Followed by myself. All was lost. My heart sank.

And so we were outside, in sunshine heat, my back being dragged through dust and pebbles. I howled as a wave of nausea overcame me. The world turned shades of orange and purple, peppered with sparks of light like disorientated fireflies. I tried to breathe but my mouth was stuffed with sacking and my throat felt as if it were full of balloons.

The kidnappers stopped and concerned, hirsute faces, already blurring, crowded my vision. Someone – a woman – pulled the gag from my mouth. "For how long were you breathing Nectair?" she asked, her voice sounding like part of a dream.

"How much for the prawn?" I heard myself mumble, and that was all.

It saddens me to report that there was a mutiny, that bane of the adventurer, Tench, aided by Shark, raided the Pleasure

Dome and overpowered me while I was at my least decent, with the former crowing in my ear, "This for your own good! This for your own good!"

Those gradient horticulturists have plumbed the depths of cowardice. A man cannot fight back when his hands are tied (by Perdita Spit, who later whipped his genitalia).

They carried me under their arms, undressed and cursing, past gawping minkfaces, out of High Yawl and dumped me in the boot of a hired jalopy. I had to promise not to fire them before they would release me, which they did finally on the outskirts of Frank Lee Plains. The minkers chose to believe my word. Mutiny is the final act of the reckless.

The voice of an angel was humming an ethereal tune in my ears, while a waterfall cascaded over my fevered brow. My eyes were closed yet aware of light and I wondered whether I might have died and reached some higher plane, populated by golden-haired goddesses in flowing robes.

I blinked open my eyes. Leaning over me was a dirt-ravaged middle-aged woman with matted, shoulder-length auburn hair, absent front teeth and three prominent warts lined along her forehead like queuing raisins. She wore a sackcloth smock, belted at the waist, and was dabbing my forehead with a dampened cloth. For some reason, she had a dry bone, perhaps a foot long, tucked into her belt.

She ceased humming and gasped.

"Oh," she said. "You are awake at last."

My brain refused to function logically so I resorted to the first thing recently unconscious people say in films, "Where am I?"

"You're in Frank Lee Plains. My name is Jane. You are safe," she replied.

Was I really? Harrison Dextrose hadn't seemed keen on the place, for reasons he chose not to elaborate upon. Trenchant

Malaise had painted a picture of these people as fanatical members of an ill-conceived cult... But then, Malaise himself was hardly to be trusted.

I took in my surroundings. I was inside some sort of hut constructed of bare, crudely fashioned planking. Daylight shone through gaps where the joins failed to meet. A single window had been set into each of the four walls.

Above me was a roof of dry, closely woven thatch over rafters forming an inverted V-shape. The walls were bare and only a couple of simple chairs troubled the sparseness.

As my head cleared, it let in a glimmer of hope. Malaise had failed to mention that the home of these people was Frank Lee Plains – also the penultimate destination of my Quest! Such a happy coincidence. If the Ikeans turned out to be merely deluded, rather than dangerous, fortune might have favoured me after all and I could continue with my journey...

But something was amiss. Travelling here by hire-car from High Yawl had taken Harrison Dextrose almost 24 hours. I had not registered a journey at all.

"How long have I been asleep?"

Jane looked pityingly. "For almost three days. The effects of the Nectair. We brought you here by mule and cart and I have tended you for some time while you were uncon."

DAY 19

Insult for the day: *Last train to Bognor*

Evidently comatose.

DAY 20

Insult for the day: *Donkey drool*

And here.

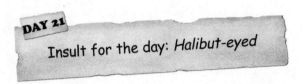

"Uncon? You mean unconscious?"

My nursemaid, who was kneeling, removed the bone from the belt at her waist and rapped me three times over the head with it.

"Ouch!" I protested, clutching at the damage. "What was that for?"

She bowed her head. "You have used a word that is forbi."

"Forbi? Eh?" Far from being safe, I was being set about by a toothless harpy with a large bone.

Jane replaced the weapon in her belt and rose. "Come," she said. "It is time to meet Ike. He will explain. First, I have made you some mash."

As I pulled myself up, I realised that my beautiful High Yawl clothing had been removed. I was wearing the de rigueur Frank Lee Plains smock, which itched considerably, and sandals. It meant they had my wallet and copy of *The Lost Incompetent*, as well as my Swiss army knife, only recently recovered from the dwarf. On the verge of a renewed howl, I checked my wrist and saw that the Timeco Z112.2 XG remained in place.

It was a start.

I wolfed down a sizeable helping of mashed potatoes, which were watery but filled a gap, followed by a mug of water. The time was shortly after noon.

Jane and I emerged into an empty square of dust and sand, surrounded on all sides by sizeable wooden buildings, in various states of hasty workmanship. All rested a couple of feet off the ground on stilts, with steps leading up to their doorways. Not one was painted and most were sun-scorched, cracked and bowed.

To my right I saw the tops of trees above the huts, some bare, others clinging onto their foliage.

Behind those huts ahead of us, a single structure dominated the skyline. It looked to be a church. While all the other buildings were a modest storey high, this one boasted at least three levels. Central was a square wooden tower rising to a spire. This alone was painted, in glossy white, and bore elaborate stained-glass windows. At the very top, resting on scaffold, was a carved wooden statue of a seated, powerfully built man in a tuxedo, gazing benignly downwards. Ike? But why was he in full dinnerwear when everyone else made do with sackcloth?

Tall stained-glass windows were visible in the lower section of the structure, as well as a foreboding set of high, arched double doors. Above these a sign read, 'Keep it simple', and on either side stood two more statues of (presumably) Ike, erect in natty attire, gazing on those who entered.

Frank Lee Plains seemed a sinister place. No wonder Dextrose had come and gone without pausing to unzip his fly.

A small girl with wayward blonde hair, wearing regulation sacking, skipped from one of the huts, took the steps in a single leap and landed in a satisfied heap. She picked herself up, spotted Jane and sat solemnly to read a book that had been cradled under one armpit.

We continued onwards, towards a gap between buildings that led to the church, as butterflies played kiss-chase in my stomach.

Beyond the gap, Frank Lee Plains opened out into an expanse of fields in shades of yellow and green that rolled down into a shallow valley. Across from these was another settlement of wooden huts and, behind that, hills where livestock grazed.

Dirt tracks criss-crossed the area, on which ponies-and-carts lumbered, topped by stooped riders. One woman was working a field behind an actual horse-drawn plough. Technology did not trouble this place and High Yawl seemed a world away.

Jane led the way inside the main building. The house was full: a good 500 of them, a sea of sackcloth and hair. Like Jane, they wore sandals and had a bone tucked into their belts. No one had given me a bone. Most noticeable was the stench: sour body odour that hung in mid-air, a visible mist.

There were no chairs or pews. The congregation knelt in rows, listening intently to the chap of the statues, who occupied a platform towards the rear, preaching beside an altar. Behind him, a tall stained glass window depicted the man himself handing out corncobs. Followers were shown tying these on top of their heads and there was an inscription beneath which read: '*Ike has a good idea*'.

When he saw me, Ike stopped talking – something about the dangers of seeing shapes in clouds – and beckoned me forwards. The congregation turned to stare and a hushed rumour-mill cranked into action, which he halted with a raised hand.

"My Ikeans," he announced. "I give you our new recruit, rescued from the evils of High Yawl."

Recruit? I didn't like the sound of that.

"High Yawl is not high at all/But lower than someone who's small," the people chanted in unison.

My mind, which had been fogged, cleared rapidly. This lot were serious.

Ike spread his arms open wide, as someone might of a

religious bent. "I call upon you all to relinquish worldly goods in favour of subsistence farming and basic clothing that some may find uncomfortable. Such is the path to self-satisfaction."

Came the unanimous response: "We pledge you this, to keep it simple/And worry not of boil and pimple."

I reached the steps beneath Ike and fumbled for words.

"Sit!" he thundered, pointing at his feet.

I lowered myself down cross-legged.

The congregation gasped.

"When I say 'Sit!', I mean 'Kneel!', shameless coveter who has worshipped the false gods of small-screen advertising!"

Ike's brainwashed followers worried me more than the man himself. The statues portrayed him as far taller and more imposing than he actually was. No doubt he had been bullied at school.

He stood a little over five-feet high, in his shiny tuxedo that strained at the buttons, and had pulled wispy strands of hair from left to right, across his shiny pate. Perhaps as a hair decoy Ike also boasted a full, sandy-coloured beard and tendrils hanging from his nostrils. His skin was pale, his cheeks pock-marked red and he looked to be in his late-forties.

A short, fat, middle-aged ugly bugger, basically – and yet these hundreds of people were in his thrall. Anyway, I knelt. The numbers were against me, and dictators are known to be easily irritated.

"There are rules here, probable user of *eau de toilette*. One, all your worldly goods shall be forfeit, and that includes your watch," Ike glared at my Timeco Z112.2 XG with undisguised envy, "which we could not wrest from your wrist. Two, you shall learn by heart the teachings of our Ikean bible, *What Ike Says, Goes*. Three, you shall recognise the Syllabic Ban, whereby you shall use no words longer than two syllables, as they are considered ostentatious. Only I may use big words; you will abbreviate. There are exceptions to rule three: when quoting from *What Ike Says, Goes*, because you are reasonably spreading the words of Ike; and the words of songs about me, because all the best compliments are lengthy.

"Finally, for now, we take names that are but one syllable long, since we are all equals and mine is Ike." He sneered. "What is your name, snazzy wristwatch owner?"

"Alexander." There came a communal intake of breath. Quickly I added, "You can call me Al."

Everyone rose to their feet and broke into song. It went like this, accompanied by much arm-swaying, "I was con-sid'ring washing my hair/Nits larger than shrimp feast on the grime/Howev'r if I be con-strued as vain/Then egoless Ike, pray give me a sign."

It was somehow worse than their chants. Steeling myself, I decided to mention that I really should be off. "Um, actually..."

"He uses *four* syllables!" announced Ike. "Now he shall discover our punishment. I shall bone him before you!"

Eh?!

Ike clicked his fingers. "Bill, bring my Ceremonial Bone of Bonking."

He clicked again and motioned towards me. I was restrained by a series of hands. As I turned to remonstrate with my captors, one stuffed a tangerine into my mouth.

Bill, a kowtowing youth with lengthy dreadlocks, scurried onto the stage, lowered himself onto one knee and presented to Ike, in upturned palms, a gold-painted bone that might have come from a rhinoceros. I struggled pathetically.

"I shall rap you over the head with this four times – once for each syllable you have used. Consider yourself fortunate; he who uses five syllables is boned to death."

I tried to scream, succeeding only in choking on tangerine juice. Fingertips dug into my under-developed biceps. Ike stood before me and raised his weapon.

There came a kafuffle to my rear, murmurs and people

shuffling. A woman appeared at my side and prostrated herself before Ike. It was Jane.

Lying there, she put one finger on her nose and with her other hand contorted her fingers into the shape of a shadow-puppet rabbit. "Great Ike," she said, her voice muffled by the floor. "I beg you spare this unbel. He is new to our rules. Let me teach him."

A dirty look spread across Ike's features, like Marmite across toast. "So, she pleads that he is spared and makes the rabbit-head gesture of lust." He paused, no doubt thinking unspeakable thoughts, and turned to Bill. "Bill, fetch my Large Wishbone of Inevitable Regret."

Could my situation get any worse? Jane perhaps had a crush on me. Dare I accept her affections, this complete stranger – to both myself and hygiene – or face being hit four times over the head by a bone the size of a Yule log?

Ike smiled malevolently.

Bill reappeared, breathing heavily, carrying a red box with an ornate clasp, which he opened before Ike. Inside was a wishbone-shaped compartment, from which he removed the Large Wishbone of Inevitable Regret, which was painted silver. Ike raised it aloft.

The Ikeans bowed their heads. "When you wish upon a star," they chanted. "Your wish will have to travel far."

Jane, who was still eating floor, was bidden to rise and manhandled beside me. The tangerine was removed from my mouth and my captors backed away.

"Mim!" called Ike.

A woman with healthy sideburns appeared and took her place next to Ike, holding a leather-bound book. What deviousness could he have in mind? I appraised the flight situation: hopeless.

A hush descended; the chief Ikean's head slumped forward,

as if someone had switched it off. Immediately he threw it backwards, raising high the wishbone in both hands. He stayed that way for a good minute, so that I could see his scaly neck, while his Adam's apple bobbed up and down.

"Yu fui dledqok sno duko!" Ike suddenly roared. He was now facing Jane and me, his eyeballs rolling in their sockets. With the wishbone, he was clawing at his own cheeks. I began to understand why the Ikeans deferred to him.

"Ike speaks in tongues!" announced Mim.

Shit, I thought.

"Cnolo carr as roek?" Ike growled.

"On your knees to Ike!" intoned Mim, who seemed to think she was translating, though the beaky crawler was clearly sneaking peeks at lines in her book.

With the uniform shuffling of a school assembly, the Ikeans sank to their knees. I fear I did so too, caught up in the mindless zeal. Jane's hip touched mine as we sank. She was trembling – and she knew what was going on. I wished I were back in High Yawl, just shopping.

"Cnes det as *zoet*?"

The '*zoet*' was uttered with such venom that I winced.

Mim continued to 'translate', "Can love be FOOLISH?"

Ike had drawn blood from both his cheeks with the wishbone. It trickled downwards and pooled in his pockmarks. "Aqoy tisy hf sno cef!" he continued, teeth bared.

"Ike is your father *and* your lover!"

"Fui cuirkts cets!"

"But he needs more Ikeans!"

"Su atbaso naz *luitk*!"

"Loins must bear *fruit*!"

Ike's growl disappeared, replaced by something more matter-of-fact, "Fuil xres xul yivvol."

Mim copied his intonation: "By which I don't mean real fruit."

"Ho xalys su, ozear…"

"Such as pears, grapes…"

"Zo, es…"

"Oranges, melons…"

"Ketqofgw…"

"Lychees..."

"Es nuszear kus du kus iq."

"And so on and so forth."

The blood had made its way onto Ike's tuxedo, forming red rivulets down his starched white collar. He closed his eyes, chest heaving, lowered the Large Wishbone of Inevitable Regret and began to calm down. When his eyelids sprang open, his pupils were focused on me. I saw in them a mixture of dislike and ill-humour.

He offered Mim one arm of the wishbone while keeping the other and, in a twisted take on the turkey-based tradition, the two pulled and the bone snapped. No guesses who got the 'wish' half.

Slowly, Ike raised the bone portion to his mouth, closed his lips over it, sucked it in and began to chew, not once removing his gaze from me. As his lower jaw ground the wishbone into shards, I imagined the damage he must be doing to the inside of his mouth. He didn't flinch.

The Ikeans remained silent and captivated; I, increasingly disturbed. Anyone prepared to do himself that kind of damage in order to assert control was a danger to society – and this was Ike's society.

Two Ikeans came to the stage, a crusty gent and a bedraggled blonde, to stand before Jane and me. He held out a carrot for me to take and she gave Jane a bagel.

Ike swallowed the last of the wishbone with a showy gulp. He threw wide his arms and cried out with feeling, "I pronounce you man and wife!"

My jaw dropped. Ike shot me a gotcha smile. Jane tugged at

my coarse clothing. I looked down at her, for she was a good six inches shorter than me, and she mouthed three words that made me wish for a complete inability to lip-read. "I love you."

Ike dismissed the congregation and made towards a flight of stairs at the rear of the church. I looked once again into Jane's eyes, which were the only clean part of her body, and caught something childlike.

What on earth was I supposed to do? The delusional woman had saved me from a severe beating and now imagined to have fallen head over heels for me. How could I hurt her feelings? I would have to play along for now. Something would surely come to me.

Jane took me by the hand and walked us out of Ike's church. I chewed distractedly on my carrot. Outside, in the sunshine's glare, she turned and took both of my hands.

"Al," she said, with a little shudder of excitement. "Now we are married, Ike will let us live among the married quarters. I shall take you there. Before I shared with thirty-seven others; we will now have a house to ourselves. Be wary as we talk along the way; Ike will not have the word 'l-o-v-e' spoken aloud, though I can see that it dances in your head and longs to be given voice."

The only word dancing around in my head was 'Help!'

"I need a drink," I suggested.

Jane was guiding us around the church. Through a line of scorched horse chestnuts I could make out another settlement: row-upon-row of wooden huts.

"I can make us some deli tea," she offered.

"I don't want tea; I want alcohol!"

She braked sharply and squeezed my wrist. "Al, my husband," Jane hissed, glancing around conspiratorially. "I should bone you three times for that, but I cannot bring myself to. Please remem, it is alco. And Ike does not allow such intox substan in Frank Lee Plains."

"Such what?"

"Intox substan…" She grimaced in frustration. "Drinks that make you drunk."

"Why not?"

"It is decreed in *What Ike Says, Goes*, chapter 27, paragraph 16: '*Alcohol shall be banned from all of Frank Lee Plains, for it can give delusions of grandeur…*'"

"Bloody hypocrite!"

Jane clamped one hand over my mouth and went for the bone in her belt with the other. "I cannot warn you again, my husband. If I am seen to not punish you, I will be boned to death. Then the Ikeans will do the same to you."

"How very self-righteous!" I snorted.

Jane would have to learn to see the hypocrisy inherent in her society, and the sadistic arrogance of her leader. I wondered how to explain this to her in words that would not see us boned alive.

Jane studied me with compassion. "Be calm, husband. It also took me time to adjust to living here. You do not yet under our ways, nor Ike's goodness and gener spirit."

"Pffft," I replied, in the absence of a multi-syllabic riposte.

Undaunted, Jane brightened. "I know!" she trilled. "When we have settled in, we can read *What Ike Says, Goes*! Then," she winked, "we can make l-o-v-e. Ike says that married couples must do so twice each day, and three times each day in the week that the woman is most fertile."

Suzy Goodenough suddenly seemed a long way away.

It was mid-afternoon and Jane led us into hut number 2541, next door to Geoff and Gay in 2540, whom she explained were the last couple to be married in Frank Lee Plains. Three weeks later, Gay had joyfully announced her pregnancy.

I noticed a glint in Jane's eye. Was I expected to sire the

woman's children? I wanted to cry out, "I'm too immature for fatherhood!" but two of those words were forbidden.

A thought struck me. "Where are all the children?"

"Those over the age of two attend always-Sunday school out west, between 7am and 8pm, unless they are ill, in which case they may read quiet while seated. The babies are cared for in the married quarters. They may cry between 11am and 11.10am. Other times, the mothers give them dummies made of cotton soaked in hooch."

"Sorry?"

Jane became impatient. "*What Ike Says, Goes*, chapter 27, paragraph 17: '*Children under the age of two, not yet being susceptible to delusions of grandeur, may be given hooch whisky, which has a calming effect. Be sure to do this if your infant cries, as high-pitched sound disturbs Ike's concentration.*'"

"You can't give babies alcohol!"

"Ike says it helps them sleep."

"I'm not bloody surprised! It's a wonder you're not breeding alco... people depen... addicts!"

"Al, my husband. Any Ikean over the age of two caught drinking the hooch is boned to death, so that's not a problem." As she spoke, her voice tightened. She seemed uncomfortable with the idea. Was there some residual sanity, a memory of life away from this place, which might help me communicate with her as normal human beings do? It was a small hope.

The interior of hut 2541 was, as I had come to expect, functional: bare wooden walls; grey rug for a bed; miniature chest in one corner, providing room for perhaps three hankies; and kitchen area in another, comprising wood fire upon stone slab, over which a single pot was suspended. Beside this were stacked: two plates, white, and two mugs, white. And by them, a pail of water. The single window in each wall offered an excellent view into the huts around.

No one seemed to consider curtains necessary. The lack of any form of lighting would hamper peeping-tom instincts, though I could not help but pick out Geoff taking with-child-Gay vigorously from behind, in hut 2540.

I let myself fall to the floor, back to a wall. I desperately wanted to go home, and sod the Quest. At that moment, I would willingly have passed by Suzy Goodenough, and supped bromide, for one quick go on a matter transporter.

Before, there had been adrenaline and survival; here was a slow death by self-righteous cruelty.

Jane, sensitive flower that she was, noticed that I was upset. As she crouched down before me, my tears began to flow and she wiped the salty solution from one cheek, thereby cleaning the inside of her index finger for the first time in perhaps decades.

"What ails you, my dearest Al?" she asked.

My cries became heaving sobs and I pulled her towards me in desperation. A lock of her unruly hair became sucked into my mouth and I feared I swallowed a nit. It didn't matter. I craved comfort. I wanted my mother. Suddenly I understood what bonded these Ikeans together: their absolute need for each other.

Jane spoke softly into my ear. "Don't worry, my husband. I can tell that your l-o-v-e for me makes you sob."

I didn't want to hurt her feelings. "It's. Not. Just. That," I managed to reply between chest-heaves.

There was a long pause. "I know," she said. Then she stood up and said she was off to retrieve her things from her previous residence (but in shorter words).

"I'll be back in five minutes, my husband. Wait for me."

The door opened and closed and she was gone. I could have made a break for it, I realised, but the blubbering fool makes a conspicuous fugitive. Before I could fully compose myself, Jane returned breathless, carrying a twig.

"What's that?" I asked.

"My things," she replied.

"But it's a twig."

She looked hurt. "Ike allows us to own one thing, which must be of the earth. This is mine. I call him Tim and we speak to each other in whispers at night."

We seated ourselves cross-legged on the rug-come-bed and gulped down water (being all out of tea) and Jane produced from the miniature chest a snugly fitted copy of *What Ike Says, Goes*. I should have guessed.

The paper was thick and ragged. The cover bore simply the title of the volume, and below that: 'By Ike'.

I went to take it from her but she pulled back.

"Let me read it, Al," she said. "It… It…" Jane's chin dropped and then raised again. "It feels good to speak big words."

Chapter One was titled '*The Origins of Frank Lee Plains*', and it began like this:

In the beginning, there was Frank Lee. Frank was a spoiled child whose parents, Hector and Jocelyn, had become bloated on greed. As he grew older, Frank came to realise that less is more.

Aged 18, Frank rejected the trappings of consumerism, gave away all of his possessions bar one set of plain clothing, some seeds (and a credit card), and travelled the Earth on a mule he had liberated from its owners, until he found a disused land that he named in his own image. This was Frank Lee Plains.

Frank lived alone there for many months, living on vegetables. He then realised that others might care to share his way of life, his vision of self-sufficiency. So he placed an advertisement (a necessary evil, just this once) in Lost Souls – Incorporating The Dispossessed – Magazine. *Thousands, possibly fewer, joined Frank in Frank Lee Plains. And they formed a community.*

Everything they needed, they would make or grow. Except for saws, which are difficult to fashion, and corkscrews (likewise). Livestock were rescued from farms on the Outside, and came to live there, where they became much happier. Frank's people were happy, too. They built a place of worship in honour of their leader, where he would preach to them, and they placed a statue in his likeness at the very top.

Then Frank took a wife, whose name was Felicity, and she bore him a son who was named Ike. Soon, procreation became a habit and many other children were born of Frank's people. These children were deemed fortunate for they would never have to encounter the evils of convenience foods, or televisions, or motorised transport, or sprung mattresses.

As Ike became older, Frank allowed him to take a hand in leading his people, which Ike seemed to enjoy. Ike passed a law that the people should burn their casual clothes, which were remnants of a consumerist society, and replace them with simple sackcloth garments. This they did willingly.

Then tragedy. Frank's body was discovered in a shallow grave among the cornfields. Ike, who was distraught, investigated this terrible crime while the people grieved. After much detective work, Ike gathered the people and explained that his father had been bitten to death and interred by ants, which can carry many times their own bodyweight.

Shortly afterwards, Felicity was found dead in her bed. Ike said that she had died of a broken heart, though there were unsubstantiated rumours that she had been found with her head stoved in by an axe.

As heir to his father's leadership, Ike reluctantly took charge. And so a new and still happier time began in Frank Lee Plains. Ike found an old tuxedo of his father's, which was shortened at the sleeves, and which he wore as a symbol of suffering, because the shirt collar was very stiff...

I felt fit to burst. "Jane, can't you see what really happened here?"

She looked puzzled. "Yes, it is as it says in *What Ike Says, Goes.*"

"What, Ike's father was killed by ants?"

"Yes! That is what Ike says!"

She went quiet then continued, "Ike is good to us. Before I came here I was homeless. My father was a drunk who beat me and my mother. One day, Mum went to Iceland and never came back. So I ran away from home. I was forced to steal from others. I was a *thief*, Al."

"I starved and I became ill and people walked past me. I would have died on the streets, but for an Ikean who came to my town with leaflets about life in Frank Lee Plains. I went with him and met Ike, who was kind and gave me a bed and a roof, and now I work for my keep, which is just."

She breathed deeply. "You don't know us, my husband. The people here were lost before Ike took us under his wing…"

I spotted a flaw in an otherwise persuasive argument. "But I wasn't lost. The Ikeans *kidnapped* me from High Yawl!"

Jane threw her arms up in despair, wafting odours my way. "But that is the most evil place in the world! The people there are prisoners…" She stopped and clamped a hand across her mouth. Then she removed the bone from her belt and hit herself over the head with it three times.

"Stop it!" I pleaded.

"No, you stop it, Al! You think you know better because you are from the Outside. You judge us when you do not –"

"Jane, listen! Please. I wasn't a prisone… prison in High Yawl. I was free to move as I pleased. I liked spending! Some people do!" My voice had become whiny.

My reasoning did not have the desired effect. Jane stood abruptly.

"Ha!" she spat. "You think you know it all. But you don't.

Yes, people did once come and go as they wished, but that did not please the leaders in High Yawl. They wanted the people to spend more and more. That is why they devel Nectair – it controls the mind; it makes people buy. And when people have breathed it for more than a day, they cannot leave. If they tried to breathe normal air, they would die.

"Why do you think you were uncon for so long? Nectair was taking over your lungs. You might have died, Al, but I nursed you to health with a balm of lilac, parsley and horse dung."

After this outburst she stormed out, weeping. I didn't try to stop her. She had won the battle but not the war. Now I was determined. I wasn't going to put up with this; I would force Jane to see through Ike's treacherous caper. Somehow. Whatever horrors these Ikeans had escaped from, that did not excuse Ike's methods.

But how best to make Jane realise that? I picked up her copy of *What Ike Says, Goes*, seeking ammunition. Let the bastard fall on his own sword.

The latter half was devoted to a calendar, with each day assigned a name. The Ikeans were obliged to perform a specific daily task, as decreed by their leader. These tasks were eccentric, to say the least. I shuffled through a few at random:

January 22
'The Day of Unlikely Conversation'
Bring up with a friend a subject of conversation
that has not been previously discussed. This
will promote new thinking.
Some possible examples…
"What are your views on tin?"
"Why is blue always blue? Who are the colour fascists?"

*Or: be controversial. If your neighbour does
not own a goat, ask him…
"How is your goat?"*

April 7
*'The Day of Avoiding Steep Gradients'
Have you ever wondered why we make things difficult
for ourselves?
If, on this day, you encounter a gradient greater than
1:5 within Frank Lee Plains (for instance, Ike Hill, the
Great Ike Valley (north side), the area left of the potting
shed), do not toil upwards – walk around it! Even if
this involves a detour of several miles.*

September 13
*'The Day of Wearing Corncobs as Hats'
When you lived on the Outside, evil marketeers told
you what to wear. You were a slave to branding. Thankfully,
that doesn't happen here. Rejoice in your freedom to do
as you please!
On this day, tie a corncob on top of your head and
declare that it is a lovely hat. Raise two fingers to your
old way of life! (Anyone caught not wearing the corncob
hat will be boned to death.)*

While I mused, Jane returned, looking calmer. As she opened
the door, I heard explosions in the distance.

"What are those bangs?" I asked.

She laughed. "The people are shelling peas."

"Sorry?"

"Today is The Day of Shelling Peas. Ike has collect weapons,
should others attack our way of life, and today we Ikeans have
target practice on small vege."

"Ike has amassed weapons?"

She pecked me playfully on the cheek. "It's nothing, Al. They are just guns: rifles, mortars, the odd bazoo."

"...ka?"

"Shhhh!" She looked stern. "You must never complete an abbre word. Ike deems this wanton and you will be boned."

"But the madman has high explo!"

Jane sighed deeply. "Why do you contin to deride all I hold good?"

This was a tricky one. Though I wanted to put considerable distance between myself and our relationship, I also felt sorry for her and, perhaps, a small fondness. "I'm just trying to help you," I persisted. "Can't you see that Ike is an egom and a hypo?"

"A what? A hippo?!" she laughed, childlike.

I struggled for shorter words for 'egomaniac' and 'hypocrite'.

"Husband, I thank you for your twisted caring, but I do not need to be helped! I am happy. And now that I have you, I am happi... more happy than any woman in the world!"

I tried so hard not to deflate, but I stood less chance than a punctured lung. Jane chose not to notice.

How could I make her see sense? Clasp at straws, perhaps! Expose the stupidity of a few of Ike's rules! "Tell me, why do the Ikeans not wash?"

She exhaled petulantly. "Because we must not worship false gods! On the Outside, we were told that cleanli is next to godli. Ike proved this is not true. He held up a diction before us and the words were many pages distant! So we do not wash." She giggled. "You are so silly, Al!"

It was hard to know where to begin dissecting such garbled logic, so I tried a different tack. "Alright, what day is tomorrow?" Something ludicrous, no doubt.

"It is the Day of Greeting a Chicken as a Long-Lost Friend. Why?"

Ha! "You don't think that might be a bit daft?"

"It is explained in *What Ike Says, Goes*: '*The Day of Greeting a Chicken as a Long-Lost Friend. Have you ever noticed how dislocated and wary the chicken looks? Just imagine that you provided eggs for people yet were treated with indifference. All of Ike's creatures are deemed equal yet chickens have been labelled as poultry – paltry by another name! Therefore, on this day, embrace a chicken and mean it. Show your appreciation for her daily abortion.*'"

I shook my head. The genius of Ike's pronouncements was in their seed of sense, planted in a mud of madness.

A bell rang, deep and insistent, echoing through hut 2541.

Jane shivered noticeably. "That is the Bell of Bedtime," she said, fluttering her eyelids, though one set became stuck together and she was forced to prise them apart. "We must remove our clothes at once and lie down."

I consulted my Timeco Z112.2 XG, which Ike was yet to get his mitts on. "But it's only 5pm!"

"Of course, my husband. The Bell of Breakfast wakes us at 4am so that we may work the fields before sunrise. As Ike tells us in *What Ike Says, Goes*: '*Early to bed, early to rise, makes an Ikean healthy and wise, though not wealthy. That is the price we pay for purity.*'"

"Welcome to Ike's pithy world!"

I would have laughed bitterly, had I not noticed that Jane was standing before me naked, sackcloth around her ankles. I sighed and turned away.

Fingers gently touched my back.

"Al, my husband, you do not need to turn away. All of this is yours."

Precisely why I turned had away, I thought. This just wasn't right. I wondered when the last time was she had experienced a man. Come to think of it, when was the last time I had experienced a woman? Were we as sexually naïve as each other?

Suddenly, Jane was nuzzling her head against my chest. She let her tongue emerge from her mouth and licked me in one swoop from chin to eyebrow. "Was that nice?" she asked.

No it wasn't! I imagined all manner of germs drying out across my cheek and, having been released from their saliva bonds, throwing a party. I could not bring myself to reply.

She looked up at me, hurt and slightly bewildered. "Husband, do you not find me attract?"

"It's all been such a… shock… Everything. It hasn't sunk in yet."

Not terribly convincing. She looked hurt and puzzled.

"I really think I should leave," I said quietly, rubbing her shoulder in a caring-not-sensuous way. "It isn't right for me here. I'm an adven… and explo… I travel the world seeking new sights. I'm a free spirit who cannot be caged…"

Hey, the Dextrose-style guff was just tripping from my tongue! Jane couldn't fail to be taken in.

"Touch me down there!" she growled passionately, suddenly a wanton woman, grabbing my hand and thrusting it between her legs. I tried to pull away but she was determined.

My fingers encountered something stringy, dangling between her legs. I could imagine what it was, not being entirely untutored about women's workings, and the thought made me queasy.

We struggled, Jane's hand wrapped tightly around mine, any semblance of sensuality having long since leapt out of the window. With much grunting, I managed to pull away and realised that the string was still in my hand. The horror. I could not help but look down.

I shrieked.

"Where did you find that?" Jane yelped.

"What the hell is it?"

"It's a vole."

With a shudder I dropped it and jumped into a far corner. "A what?"

"A vole. I found him in the fields; he was cold and ill…" She slapped her forehead. "I remem now! I had nowhere warm to put him, so I snuggled him down there!"

I dry-heaved. "How long has it… been… there?"

She counted mentally. "Two months… But… Is he dead?"

"Well I'm not bloody looking!"

Jane bent towards the vole and placed it in the palm of her hand, now quietly sobbing. Seconds later, she started. "His eyes opened! He's alive!"

I was speechless.

She continued her tale regardless. "He must have popped his head out and taken food every time I crouched! And water too, when it rained!"

That was quite enough detail. I hoisted myself up and made for my clothing. "I'm going outside," I said. "I may be some time."

"No, Al!" Jane urged. "If you are caught outside after the Bell of Bedtime, you will be boned to death."

Hands on hips, I eyed her resolutely. "Either the vole goes, or I do."

She lowered her head. The rodent, somehow recovered, scuttled up her arm and settled on her shoulder. We faced each other off, me against her and the vole.

I won. Jane sighed and, without looking at me, took the creature from her shoulder and carried it to the door. Opening it, she kissed the vole and placed it on the top step. "Bye-bye. Be safe," she called softly.

Wordlessly she returned to the mat, lay down and curled herself into a ball facing the wall.

I felt terrible. Guiltily I slunk to bed but dared not touch her.

I lay there on my back for hours while the sun sank outside, thinking swirling thoughts of home, departed family, missed friends and my situation. I should not be here. I resolved to escape the following day, the Day of Treating a Chicken as a Long-Lost Friend.

"Do you think he'll be OK?" I heard Jane whisper, though still faced away from me.

I said nothing.

"I think so, too," she continued.

She was talking to Tim the twig, which made me feel worse.

Shifting slightly, I cupped her bare shoulder and squeezed. Jane remained unresponsive. But eventually she rolled over and we searched out each other's eyes in the darkness.

"I'm sorry," I said.

"I know," she replied.

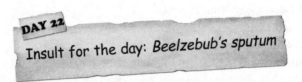

The Bell of Breakfast was not a welcome sound, being the same volume as the Bell of Bedtime, but at 4am. It was still dark. There was no Jane beside me.

I raised myself up on stiff elbows and saw her already dressed, busying herself in the kitchen area, humming.

"Mmph," I mustered, by way of a greeting.

"Al, my husband, you are awake!"

"Hmm," I replied groggily. "I just can't sleep through the tolling of the bells of hell."

She actually laughed and came across to kiss me on the forehead.

"I have been to collect pota from the store. I shall boil them in cabbage water, which we can drink." She smiled, aiming to please.

"Lovely," I said.

Jane lit a fire and I dressed, which took all of ten seconds. She tended the pot and every so often would turn and beam at me.

Last night's resolve had not deserted me: I had to escape Frank Lee Plains.

After breakfast, we left hut 2541. Darkness persisted. Jane led me past the church and down a dried mud-track between potato fields, to an area of coops where the air was rent with gobbling. It was time to hug a chicken.

A queue of silent Self-Satisfied Ikeans had already built up, emanating dust. We joined its rear and I tapped my wife on the shoulder to ask a question, but she put a finger to her lips. The gesture suggested, I assumed with some weariness, that anyone who talked in the queue for poultry hugging would be boned to death.

Jane went first. She walked through the gate into the chicken coop, scattering bemused ginger birds as she did so. The nearest, she lunged at and, scooping the feckless creature up in her arms as it squawked, hugged it to her breast and spoke soothing words that I could not discern.

My turn. Feeling stupid, I faltered and was nudged onwards by impatient types to my rear.

The ground inside the coop was lathered in chicken-shit and seed. As expected, my prey scattered. I looked around for a bird that might be lame and so easily caught, but they all seemed perfectly able – my criteria being squawking and the possession of two legs.

After some time, during which I stooped around in circles, it became obvious that there was one bird cockier than the others. It stayed closer than its friends dared come, pretending to peck at food while taunting me with its proximity.

I made a lunge for it, slipped in shit, clawed the air for a handhold and managed to fall flat on my back, staring at the sky, which was beginning to lighten.

Before I knew it, my quarry had climbed onto my chest and was pecking at me, performing a passable impression of a woodpecker. "Ow! You little bastard!" I yelped, grabbing my attacker by the throat.

There was a collective gasp from the direction of the queue.

Swiftly, I let out a cheery laugh and began to speak to the thing as if it were a small child. "...Aren't you, eh? Such a tease! Aren't you, eh? Chubby chicken. Chubby,

chubby chicken."

This seemed to appease the audience.

I picked myself up, still clutching the bastard. "So," I concluded, patting the bird on the head while squeezing its bastard throat. "Great to see you again. Must be off. Bye."

Jane was waiting for me. "You poor thing," she soothed, brushing crap and chicken snacks off my back. "That one is Alf. He can be quite touchy."

I pulled on my sackcloth décolletage, as a lady might do to inspect her boobs, and noticed that the bird had pecked several, tightly clustered holes in my flesh, which were seeping blood. It was too demoralising to contemplate.

"What now?" I asked.

"Now we work in the fields until the Bell of Sermons."

This perked my spirits. If I were outside, preferably obscured by tall cereal crops, I might feasibly be able to make a break for it.

Jane continued, "I spoke with Rod, who details our tasks. I shall milk cows. You are to split lentils with nine others in the Small Exposed Hut, so named because it can be seen for many miles around."

Escape would have to wait until after lunch. I sighed. "What on earth for?"

"Ike says lentils should have one perfect flat side. He says the twin curves may cause impure thoughts in men."

Sarcasm billowed from my lips. "I've often been aroused by a complete lentil!"

It went right over Jane's head and she patted my hand and gave me a 'you're-in-safe-hands-now' look.

I gave up. "So how am I supposed to split them?"

"With a barely sharp knife and patience."

It might have made a decent punchline, but Jane wasn't laughing.

She gave me directions: back towards Ike's church, then left past the vegetable plots, follow a narrow stone pathway up to the top of Ike Hill, upon which stood the Small Exposed Hut.

I wondered aloud why this single building had been erected on a hilltop, expecting in return some typical Ike twaddle, so Jane's reply chilled me, "All newcome, who may be daunted, work there during their first week. It can be seen for miles around, so they will not think of leaving. It does take a while to settle in."

With a peck on my cheek, she set off down the dirt track, heading towards the livestock fields beyond.

Now I felt alone and nervous. Jane was my sole ally. The other Ikeans seemed a ruthlessly obedient army of dead hippies returned as zombies.

I checked my Timeco Z112.2 XG. It was shortly after 5.30am. I also checked my blood pressure, which was higher than normal, though I was still alive. I tried out the directional thermometer; the temperature of the Ikean woman just passing me, bent double under a bale of hay, was 98.6. She would live, too. Anything else, I would have failed to work out – the instruction manual, along with any other purchases that I had not been wearing, had been left in Al's Great White. Once again, I longed to be back in High Yawl, Nectair or not.

Oozing trepidation, I began the uphill journey towards the church. Escape required planning, which I had conveniently overlooked.

Ikeans hurried past in either direction, never looking at me. One, a young man in his early-twenties, appeared tidier than the rest and I wondered whether he might be a fresh intern like myself. His hair was manageable enough still to hold a parting and his skin had not yet been caked with the medium of his toils.

As he approached, staring resolutely groundwards, I chanced

a raised palm and a "Hello!" He glanced up and smiled, then shuddered, lost the carefree look and scurried away. Ike ran a tight ship. It might only be a matter of days, perhaps even hours, before his peculiar brainwashing gained its hold over me.

When I reached the Small Exposed Hut, atop a sizeable hill on which the grass had been pointlessly trimmed, there were no other people around. They had all reached their places of work and were beginning their exercises in self-sufficiency.

I paused to take in the panorama and sadness struck me that was for once not self-centred. From up here, closer to the sky and as the sun began its ascent, Frank Lee Plains was a beautiful land. What a waste.

It might almost have been England, deep in countryside. Stretched shadows fell among patchwork fields that reached towards each horizon. People were at work, dotted among the crops, all arms and outmoded implements. The breeze carried distant birdsong.

So much familiarity. But what of me?

"Ouch!"

Someone had hit me over the head with what I assumed was the business end of a bone. Turning, I was met by a windblown battle-axe whose shoulders had grown wispy brown hair. Her eyes were mean and her teeth pointy; she was shaven-headed, her scalp marked with weals and blisters.

She eyed me unhumorously, clutching the bone, knuckles tending towards the dirt.

"What was that for?" I demanded, rubbing the throbbing area.

"You're late, twinkle!" she barked in a strangely shrill voice, the sound of a dog having its tail stepped upon.

"And how would you know?" I wasn't about to be downtrodden by some heathen fanatic.

She replaced the bone in her belt and folded her arms, tensing muscle. "The name's Fletch, twinkle, and you'll do well to remem that. I be tell you when it time for your bed, when it time for your baby bottle, when…" She spotted the Timeco Z112.2 XG and lunged. "How be you keep this instru of evil from Ike? Give it me!"

Her grip was iron. With one hand she held my wrist and with the fingers of the other she clawed around the watch, trying to rip it off. Happily the strap held. One gets what one pays for.

"Stop, you'll break it, you lunatic!"

Like lightning she had the bone from her belt, batting me over the head three times with meaning. I dropped to the ground, whimpering.

"Please. I really don't know how the strap works and I've lost the instructi… instruct… manu."

She sneered down at me. "Maybe Fletch be cut off your hand, then, twinkle."

I could tell she meant it. "I'll work it out. Promise."

"I be give you one day, twinkle. I see that evil on your wrist tomo and…" The huge sadist made a sawing motion, smiling. "Now, work!"

Inside the Small Exposed Hut was one long wooden table, at which seven Ikeans were labouring, heads down, piles of pale green lentils stacked before them. Three stood out from the others: two middle-aged women, one male in his teens. They looked almost normal; their transformation into dishevelled robots must have been just beginning.

There were two spare seats, one on the end of a row, among the new intake, the other at the head of the table. The latter was Fletch's, no doubt, where she could cast a mean eye over us.

A shaft of sunlight beamed in through one window, picking out the clouds of dust rising from sacks of seeds piled in one corner, and from the four well-established Ikeans.

Fletch came in behind me, prodding my back like a prison guard.

"Be sit!" she thundered.

Everyone flinched.

"Don't flinch! Work!"

If there was no time off for flinching, I saw little hope of a tea break.

The time was just after 6am. I sat and glanced to my left, at the teenaged newcomer. His features were keen, his hair still glossy if matted, and there were five holes in his earlobes where rings had recently been. From his stubble, I guessed that he must have been in Frank Lee Plains for just two or three days.

He didn't look up, instead concentrating on the single lentil pressed between two fingers, which he sliced open with a crude knife blade bound to a stick. There were lacerations all over his fingertips where he had previously missed.

"Here be the rules, for twinkle here," announced Fletch. "No be talking. No be eating the lentils. No be skiving. You split one hundred lentils each hour, or it be the dropping for you."

Hands resting on the back of her chair at the head of the table, she leered at me.

What could she mean by 'the dropping'? I could tell she wanted me to ask, to titillate the madwoman inside of her, but I wasn't sure of the procedure for questions. Nervously, I raised a hand.

"Yes, twinkle," said Fletch sweetly.

"Please, Fletch, what is the dropping?"

Ike's foot-soldier pointed towards an Ikean at the other end of the table. "You be ask Todd there. Go on, twinkle, you may speak."

Todd looked to be one of the long-term inmates. His arms were sun-blistered and his face scabby.

"Em, Todd…" I uttered softly.

He did not respond, too intent upon a whole lentil. The others shifted nervously in their seats but did not stop working.

"To-odd!" I sang, more loudly. Still no response.

Fletch moved to put a hand on each of my shoulders and massaged menacingly. "Go on, twinkle," came her voice from above. "Ask him!"

"TO-ODD!"

The Ikean split his lentil and smiled to himself with satisfaction, lost in his own little world of dried seeds.

Fletch dug in her fingertips and laughed. It was a strangled, high-pitched thing that went, "Ktchktchktchktchktchktch!"

As she calmed down, she clasped her fingers around my throat and tightened gently. "Todd can't be hear you, twinkle, that be the twist. He did speak seven times, and each time I did push one rabbit dropping into his ears! That be the dropping! Ktchktchktchktchktchktch!"

We sat there labouring while Fletch toyed with rabbit droppings, occasionally launching one towards the roof, catching it in her upturned gob and crunching. She was no slacker in the art of intimidation.

There was a knack to lentil-splitting with a barely sharp knife, which I discovered only after slicing off several fine layers of my left thumb and forefinger, coating everything I touched in blood. It required the seed to be squeezed tightly on its end and the blade to be forced carefully between the pressed flesh. This ideally guided the knife onto the rim of the lentil, which could then be halved with a meaningful stab.

Repeating this procedure took mindlessness to its conclusion. One time I sighed too audibly and Fletch inserted a rabbit dropping into my nostril. Not daring to touch it, I tried to squeeze it out by tensing a sequence of nasal muscles, but it would not budge and only worked its way further towards my sinuses. Mercifully, it was too dry to smell.

And so the hut became filled with my laboured breathing and a series of dull clunks, as knife blades forced their way successfully through seeds onto the table below. Every so often, our warder would become bored and rose to circle the table, to taunt one of us physically with a slap on the cheek or an elbow in the spine. Still no one uttered a sound.

It would have been comforting to let my mind wander, but each time my thoughts drifted to escape or home, I would carelessly slice off a further layer of flesh. Eventually, I was forced to swap hands and to master the procedure all over again.

At 11am, a cacophony of infant bawls reached our ears from the direction of the married quarters. The babies were being allowed to unbottle their cries. It was like being subjected to white noise on headphones. Only Todd remained blissfully untroubled.

When the racket ceased ten minutes later, Fletch nudged me and smarmed. "I be want a babbie, twinkle. Maybe I choose you, yes?"

'Thtnk!' went my knife, removing a substantial portion of my left forefinger. "Aaaaagh!" I screamed.

She grabbed my ear, pulling me towards her, at the same time aiming a rabbit dropping towards my lug, as the darts player aims his dart. Instinctively I raised my left hand to ward off the perfectly spherical turd, just as an electronic female voice emerged from the Timeco Z112.2 XG.

"Welcome to the world of Timeco," it said. "Congratulations on making such a prestigious purchase."

I didn't even know that the watch could speak – Mimsy Flopkins had failed to mention this facility.

There were gasps from my peers. Even Fletch seemed stunned.

"His hand speaks!" declared an aged female Ikean across the table, which caused further gasps.

"It's not my hand!" I chuckled. "It's the watch!"

"This is your alarm call. It is 11.11am. Have a nice day," said the woman in the Timeco Z112.2 XG.

Fletch must have somehow set the alarm as she pressed buttons arbitrarily while trying to wrest it from my wrist.

"His hand speaks!" repeated the Ikean crone, her voiced quaking.

"It is the sign!" announced another voice, and three of the established Ikeans slid off their chairs to cower beneath the table, joined shortly by a confused-looking Todd, leaving we new intakes swapping bemused expressions. Fletch remained in her seat but even she was mute and shaken.

Something sinister was brewing.

Fletch slammed a fist onto the table, keen to reassert her authority. "Rise!" she shrieked.

One-by-one, the four Ikeans raised their heads above the tabletop, like woodland creatures emerging from burrows.

"Sit!" commanded Fletch.

Now we were all rapt, and to hell with the lentils.

"Remem what it be say in *What Ike Says, Goes*," she began, her face already contorted with concentration. "Chapter 127... I be think. *'One day shall arrive in Frank Lee Plains a man whose hand does talk. This shall become known as the Day That is not Good...'*"

"Really, it was the watch," I protested, holding up my hand. "See, it doesn't speak!"

"Please enjoy the rest of your day," said the watch, as if on cue.

"We're doomed!" quailed the old woman who had appointed herself hut soothsayer.

Fletch pounded the table. "Silence!" she ordered. "Ike be say more. *'This man shall have a third nipple, set in between the usual two...'*"

That was alright, then, since I didn't have a third nipple. Disaster averted!

All eyes were on me. Eager to cease the scary nonsense, I

pulled aside the shoulder straps of the sackcloth smock and tugged the garment down to my midriff.

Everyone gasped.

The soothsayer pointed. "The third nipple!"

"Rubbish!" I spluttered. But when I looked down, there it was: a dark red circular scab, right in the centre of my weedy chest. To the willingly deluded, it could easily resemble a nipple.

"That's not –" I began to protest.

Fletch cut me short. "Silence! There is still more. Ike does contin: '*And that third nipple shall be removable*'…"

Like lightning, she struck out a hand, poked a fingernail at the side of the scab and flicked, prising off the clot which then hung by a thread beneath the opened, raw wound.

I squealed like a pig and clutched at the pain. Frantic, I explained: "It's not a removable third nipple. It's where I was pecked by a chicken this morning."

"A likely story. He thinks us gulli," tutted Fletch, then turned to the others. "So it be true. The Day That is not Good be upon us. Ike says, '*If such a man does come among us then the world shall end before night falls.*'"

Armageddon. Great. I knew it wasn't going to happen, but how would the Ikeans react, believing that it would? My hopes weren't high.

Fletch continued reciting Ike's words, straining her brain: "'*But the Earth shall not take us, for we Ikeans are too clever for that. Oh yes. We shall forfeit our own lives, long before the fire and brimstone rain down from the heavens.*'"

Sated by the sense of occasion, she grabbed me under the armpits and threw me over her shoulder fireperson-style, which winded me, though it did at least make me snort out the rabbit dropping.

"Come!" she called to the others. "We be tell Ike. It be time to toll the Bell of The End!"

It had all happened too quickly for me to become loose-bowelled. One moment I was bored witless, the next I was being carted off by Captain Cavewoman, with the sole intention of having my bucket kicked for me. So bizarre was the Ikean logic that my own mind was blurred, trying to make sense of it.

Our little group skipping down Ike Hill towards the church seemed wholly chipper at the prospect of mass suicide.

As we reached the bottom of the hill, Fletch hollered towards the Ikeans working the vegetable plots, "Be pass it around: today is the Day That is not Good!"

They stood, looked briefly blank, then cheered and rushed off to spread the word.

By the time we neared the church, from my vantage point atop Fletch, I could see people scurrying through the fields towards us, waving their arms in delight. The place had come alive with a sense of celebration.

Ike was at his altar. Fletch hefted me off her shoulder and dumped me at his feet like rolled-up carpet. Already, a healthy congregation had gathered, respectfully silent, palpably tense.

"He is the one you wrote of, egoless Ike. The Day That is not Good is upon us," she announced, and went on to recount the story of the talking hand and removable nipple.

"It is good," said Ike, making his fingers into a spire shape. "Bill! Ring the Bell of the End! Let everyone come to take their final rest." He pointed at me. "You, come with me. You must be prepared."

I'd had enough of the little twerp. I stood up. "Sod off Ike, you –"

I was promptly boned from behind by Fletch and went down in agony.

"Ike is wise and Ike is kind/Ike saves us his bacon rind," chanted those gathered.

"Enough!" bellowed Ike.

A bell began to ring: three short clangs, pause, four short clangs, pause, two short clangs, then one that reverberated. The pattern was repeated over and over.

Ike kicked at me. "Come, chosen one," he sneered. "Or I'll have you killed here and now."

I followed him towards the rear of the church, to the door that he had used after the previous sermon. Short and squat in his tuxedo, he waddled like a penguin.

He pulled a keyring from his pocket, unlocked the door and we walked through. He locked the door behind us. We were in a stairwell at the bottom of a steep flight of stairs with walls on either side. A stained-glass window halfway up offered kaleidoscopic light.

Ike smiled at me, pulled a jewelled dagger from his inside pocket, and snarled, "Get up the stairs, you pestilent turd."

I stumbled upwards and on reaching the top tried the door. "It's locked."

"I know it's locked, face-fuck." He handed me the key and jabbed me in the side with the dagger. "Open it!"

Inside was one giant loft space, the same area as the ground floor, and as high. Four vast stained-glass windows dominated the wall space, shedding multi-colour around the room. A central spiral staircase led up to a trap door, which must have opened into the tower. Hanging down its centre, and continuing through a hole in the floor, was a rope, which was rising and falling in time with the tolling of the Bell of the End.

And everywhere were boxes stacked high from which treasures spilled. Jewellery, gilt-framed paintings, leather jackets, TV sets, microwaves. A plush case had been knocked over near my feet. Watches, pearls, gold chains and rings lay scattered across the floor.

"The confiscated possessions of your loyal followers, I presume."

Ike sneered. "No shit, Sherlock. Over there!" He motioned towards a desk and chair set against the front wall of the church. "Sit, so I can talk down to you."

"Do you know how long it took me to build this empire?" Ike's dagger was hovering at my nose level. He looked fit to burst. It would be wise not to toy with him.

"No."

"Thirty fucking years. *Thirty fucking years.* And you come along and destroy it all in one day. I knew you were trouble the moment I set eyes on you, you dolphin cock."

"It's not my fault!"

"Not your fucking fault?" He pressed the point of the blade onto the tip of my nose and pushed upwards, breaking the skin. "When I wrote *What Ike Says, Goes*, I knew I had to include Armageddon, because all the best religious books do. But because I didn't actually want an Armageddon, I made the conditions for it happening so ludicrous that it need never concern me. A man with a talking hand and an extra, removable nipple!"

I tried to reason with him. "But my hand didn't talk, it was my watch. And it's not a nipple, it's where I was pecked by a chicken."

Ike slapped me hard across the face. "You know that and I can only imagine it is the case, because it's too fucking stupid to comprehend, but those dumb twonks don't. If I told them my shit smelled of perfume, they'd dab it on their necks… Hang on… I did that last year!" He laughed fruitily. "They think you're the man, the chosen one that ends it all, because it says so in *What Ike Says, Goes*. If I try to change their minds, I undermine the whole operation. Result? Anarchy. So all because of you, we have to go downstairs and commit suicide."

With the dagger pointing at me, he rummaged around in the mass of paperwork on the desk and uncovered a cardboard box, opened it and took out a pill. "Take this and put it in the pill pocket of your smock."

I couldn't say that I had noticed one.

Ike became impatient. "There, on the left below your belt, you myopic monkey's menstruation."

There it was, a tiny square of sackcloth sewn onto the clothing. I pushed the pill inside. "Cyanide?"

"Right again, Sherlock. Nasty, painful death, like someone spilled acid down your gut."

"And you'll be joining us?"

"Oh sure." He tapped his own pill pocket, sewn at his left breast.

"Not so poisonous?"

"Vitamin A. Worst that'll happen is I get better night vision." Ike reached out and slapped me playfully on the arm. "No one'll miss these people – they haven't spoken to anyone besides each other in years. Most are presumed dead, anyway. I'll have to re-recruit, which is a pain, but Frank Lee Plains'll be up to quota in a couple of years."

He swung his arm around the room, triumphantly. "And it means I get to double the loot! I guess I should thank you really, Al. You wart on the shrivelled scrotum sack of a ram's personal pieces..."

It's funny, but I didn't feel fear as Ike frogmarched me downstairs at knifepoint. It all seemed too unreal, like I was watching myself from above in a dream.

But as the seconds passed and I didn't watch myself from above in a dream, reality began to kick in. What to do?

I could elbow Ike aside and tell the assembled Ikeans that their leader was a fraudster, that his suicide pill was a fake, and that he had all their belongings hoarded upstairs... But I had already tried to talk sense to Jane and had failed. No one would believe me.

Perhaps I could make a break for it?

Ike opened the door at ground level and we walked out into the church. The place was heaving. Everyone from Frank Lee Plains had gathered there – men, women and children, one sprawling mass. An aphid would have had a problem making a break for it.

All eyes were on me. Someone waved from the front row. It was Jane, flushed with excitement. I mouthed at her, "We're going to die!"

"I know!" she mouthed back. "Isn't it great!"

No, there would be no talking these people around.

Ike took to his altar and made me stand beside him.

"My Ikeans," he began, "Armageddon is soon upon us. But we shall beat it!"

"When it comes, the end of the world/I won't be screaming like a girl," they chanted.

"It has been my privilege to lead you all these years. Do not be afraid. We shall meet in another world, where we can continue the practices I have taught. Now, does anyone not have with them their Pill of Predestination?"

A hand up at the back, accompanied by a small voice. "Em, Ike, I gave mine to a sickly bantam."

Ike sighed. "Wise sentiment, Bob IV. Have the person next to you break theirs in half so that you may share. Anyone else? No? Good. All my Ikeans, take out your Pill of Predestination."

This really was it. Blood pumped to my brain, which was fit to explode. I wondered what Ike planned to do with all these bodies. Would he burn down the church and build a new one? Hang on, why was I worrying about that?! But, wait!

What if I merely *pretended* to take the pill? Played dead, and when Ike was away counting his loot, ran for the hills! A shiver of adrenaline electrified my spine.

Ike spoke. "Since Al here is the chosen one, he shall take his pill first so that we might all witness his journey into the other world."

I groaned, a weighty, hideous groan. Ike laughed.

"Take out your Pill of Predestination, Al."

I did so, and stood staring at it. There was no way I was going to take it. I would just have to run. What other option was there?

Suddenly there was an almighty sound of breaking glass. And there, swinging on rope through a great hole in the *Ike has a good idea* stained-glass window was a noticeably short man in a turquoise suit. Detritos!

As the dwarf reached the furthest extent of his swing, he let go of the rope and flew through the air to land on Ike's face, wrapping his arms and legs around the back of the git's head. The pair of them toppled to the floor.

It was a daring, beautiful gesture on Detritos's part, though clearly flawed. He would not be able to fight off swarming Ikeans; he didn't even appear to have a weapon.

Then, through sheer necessity, I was struck by my most brilliant idea yet. With Ike indisposed, a dwarf sitting on his head, I slipped two fingers into his pocket, took out his fake pill and swapped it with mine. It was a stroke of genius!

As predicted, a series of Ikeans swarmed over Detritos and pulled him off while he snarled. Ike regained his feet.

The dwarf, held aloft by several pairs of arms, looked at me and grinned. "Detritos leettle short stormtroopeeng, Meester Alexander."

Now was my chance. I raised my arms for attention. "Ikeans!" I called out. "Your leader is a charlatan!"

People booed. Many pulled out the bones in their belts and surged forwards, but Ike, arms folded, cockiness across his face, held up a hand. "No, my Ikeans, let him continue."

"I have seen his hideaway upstairs, where he has hoarded all your belongings, for his own purposes."

There were cries of "Lies!"

"But I can prove to you that he is a charlatan!"

"This, my people, I have to see!" taunted Ike.

Everyone laughed. Some shouted, "Show us!"

I played my hand. "If Ike was truly planning to join you in the other world, then let him take his Pill of Predestination before us all! I believe that his pill is a fake! If he lives, he is a charlatan!"

A murmur rose. Would my plan work?

Someone in the crowd put up a hand. "Why don't you take Ike's pill? If you are right, you will live and we will know that you speak the truth. If, as we believe, you do not, then you will perish."

"Yes!" called out a few others.

A chant grew: "You take Ike's pill! You take Ike's pill!"

Bollocks. My plan had backfired spectacularly. I cursed my own ingenuity.

Ike held up his hand. "No, my Ikeans! If you can even believe that I might be lying to you then I am distraught. So I shall prove to you that my word is good. I shall take my Pill of Predestination. Once I am dead, you shall all take your own pills. That is how it must be."

What could the tuxedoed fox have up his sleeve? Not knowing of the swap, perhaps he would believe he had to take his own and play dead? Boy, was he in for a shock.

Being one to stand on ceremony, Ike made a play of removing the pill from its pocket and placing it between two fingers to show everybody. He popped it in his mouth, smiled at me, and swallowed. I smiled back.

You could have heard a pin drop.

It was obvious when Ike began to realise his mistake. His pock-marked skin grew redder and his eyes widened. Terror cavorted around his features. His nostrils twitched and he clutched at his stomach, bending double. He looked up at me, all twisted loathing. "You faecal matter in the small intestine of a copulating camel."

He pitched forward, let out a death rattle, and was gone. Hurrah.

"He killed Ike!" came the cry.

"Ike did not lie!"

"Lynch Al!"

Clearly my plan had only been thought through so far.

"Wait! Please. Listen…" What was I going to say? In desperation, I resorted to the truth. "I swapped my Pill of Predestination for Ike's! When my friend landed on Ike's head, I reached out and exchanged our pills. You didn't realise that's what I was doing but someone must have seen me… Please? Anyone?"

No one. Seconds passed while the hysteria grew. Then a woman stepped forward from the throng. It was Jane. She hooked her arm in mine and addressed the Ikeans. "I saw him. You must have too."

Some people nodded. Then more. Someone shouted out, "If that is true, then take Ike's pill. Prove it was a fake."

No problem. The Vitamin A tasted just fine. So too did the victory.

So Detritos had saved me from Ike, Jane had saved me from the Ikeans, and I had saved the Ikeans from themselves.

Yet the mood of the people was not one of celebration. A few refused to accept the truth, causing arguments and scuffles; the remainder seemed dazed. Trust was a precious commodity and theirs had been systematically abused. It would be some while before they could leave behind the hurt and begin to rebuild their lives.

I stood upon the stage, lost in contemplation, my arm around Jane. The dwarf joined us and I picked him up and kissed him on each wire-wool cheek.

"Thank you."

"Seenk Detritos goeeng weezout goodbye keess?" he replied, planting a smacker on my lips.

I shrugged him off. "How the hell did you get here?"

"Followeeng."

"Since when?"

"Beeg time."

"So why wait until I was knocking on death's door to save me?"

"Sinkeeng Meester Alexander haff fun weez ladee!"

Before I could wring his neck, a voice came from among the congregation. "What do we do now, great Al?"

A group of Ikeans had gathered to beseech me.

"That's up to you," I replied, slightly loftily. "You're in charge now. Stay here. Go home. It's your choice. But find some water, have a wash, get a haircut and change out of those smocks. All your belongings are upstairs. And my name's Alexander. And I'm not great."

"Al is great and Al is brave/He saved us from an early grave," they chanted.

"He very beauteeful," announced the dwarf.

"Yes, well, thank you, but that's quite enough," I stuttered, wondering whether all the compliments were true. Perhaps they were? If so, my character had undergone a sea-change as a result of Harrison Dextrose's Quest. From drifter in life's slow lane to hero. It seemed odd.

"Jane, Detritos, I'm going to find my things upstairs. Ike has… had my clothes, my wallet and a book I need back. Then I'm going to sleep for ages. I've been up since 4am, and saving people takes it out of you."

There came a chorus of "Three cheers for Al!"

As this giddying adulation went on, Jane clasped my hand.

"My name's not Jane," she said. "It's Deborah."

Tears welled in her eyes.

I awoke in 2541, lying on the rug, with Detritos straddling me, shaking me by the collar. Deborah lay next to me, lightly snoring.

For the first time since my arrival in Frank Lee Plains I was dressed in comfortable clobber, my own rescued from Ike's hideaway. There had been hundreds of us there, sifting through the boxes as if at an anarchic car-boot sale. My clothes were easily found, being stupidly colourful. The wallet and book had been wrapped among them. Holding Dextrose's great work again made me feel warm.

I had returned to the hut, quaffed water and stuffed down mashed potato, then lapsed into the deepest of sleeps.

"Get off me, you fool!" I snapped at Detritos, who refused to budge.

Deborah snorted and stirred. She had washed and changed into a beige swirly-design dress that was noticeably more exciting than the previous sackcloth.

I checked my watch. It was 9pm. The sky was dark and outside were sounds of merriment.

The dwarf bounced up and down on my chest until I threw him off.

Blearily Deborah opened her eyes. "Wha?"

"Ignore him," I sighed.

"Your breath smells," she said, wrinkling her nose.

Detritos was tugging on my ear.

"What do you want?" I asked impatiently.

"Meester Alexander, we must goeeng. Someseengs wickeed zees way comeeng."

"Listen…" I restrained my temper, recalling the dwarf's most recent heroics. "What? What's coming?"

"Pleeze hurryeeng."

"Why, what's the rush?"

"Tomasz and Footz!"

This pricked my complacency. "What? Jesus! Where?"

Deborah put her arm around my shoulders. "What's the

matter, Alexander, my husband?"

"Hussband?" yelped Detritos.

"Yes, it's a long story. Where are the Candid Ablicans?"

"Lookeeng Detritos een..." He struggled for the word, gave up and pointed away towards the cornfields.

How could Tomasz and Footz have possibly tracked Detritos here, even if he was wearing the sort of outfit favoured by outlandish country and western singers? We had left them flailing at Klütz's harbour.

I strained my brain until it hit me: they must have a tracking device! I shook the dwarf unnecessarily. "Where are your things?"

"Seengs?"

"Yes, your things. Your bags."

"Leef uzzer."

"Other what? Place? Where? High Yawl?"

He nodded.

"What, even the leather briefcase with the…"

He winked, though it was more of a dirty squint. "Ees so."

It came to me from the recesses of my memory, while Deborah busied herself washing her single pot. The figure in the raincoat and trilby who had appeared from the woods in Klbdow, as we prepared for the Iditamush, who had slapped Detritos and then slunk away…

It had seemed bizarre at the time, though apparently harmless, and had become forgotten amid the tension of the race. That had to be it.

"Give me your left sideburn!" I ordered, pulling the startled dwarf's head towards me and peering into the sprawling bush. So dense was it that I was forced to preen him like an amorous monkey.

"Mmmm!" he drooled. "Detritos likeeng."

Among the exterior contents of the sideburn were several

nits, a woodlouse, an uninhabited spider's web and a chewed toothpick. Delving further towards its interior revealed a piece of stale cucumber sandwich – which the dwarf grabbed and devoured – the missing spider (deceased), three baby earwigs, a foreign coin and a dried spiky seed pod. So I was wrong.

...Or was I? I pulled at the seed pod, which had become entangled in the mass, causing the dwarf to squeal. When it finally came loose, closer inspection revealed the thinnest of pins, inserted through the centre, holding the halves together.

While Detritos and Deborah peered, I prised the shell apart with two thumbnails. Inside: a tiny silver electronic device.

"Meester Alexander clever."

The dwarf snatched the device from the palm of my hand and, dropping it to the floor, stomped on it with a hob-nailed heel before baring his teeth. "Beengo! Gone! Now Detritos clever!"

I clutched my head in my hands. "You fool! We could have given that to one of the Ikeans, who could have taken it to the far ends of the earth, with the Candid Ablicans in hot pursuit!"

"Oh," said the dwarf. "Ees true."

Again I had become inveigled into the dwarf's plans. He had a sneaky habit of managing that. Tomasz and Footz didn't want me; they wanted the ruby. And since Detritos claimed to have left the briefcase behind in High Yawl, I could only assume that he had it on his person.

What to do? For starters, get out of Frank Lee Plains. Though Dextrose had undoubtedly dallied among the whores of High Yawl, all the Ike palaver had put my Quest on hold.

I flicked quickly through the pages of *The Lost Incompetent*:

FRANK LEE PLAINS
Population: Hundreds of the minkers
Capital: No idea
Currency: They barter!

Principle industry: Preaching piffle

It is early afternoon on the 23rd day of my Dextrosian Quest to find Livingstone Quench. Fully clothed and desperate for a drink after my mutinous incarceration in the boot of the jalopy, I order Tench to stop the vehicle and wind down the window to accost a native to ask after the nearest bar. The pious minksack goes slack-jawed and tries to sell me a book that he claims will turn my life around. I open my car door sharply on the minker's head and he falls like toppled reliquary.

So we find our own way into town, where a dusty, mindlessly grinning crowd develops around our vehicle, inviting us to a service. "What sort of services do you offer?" I demand, and they become confused. One gobswill offers to trade vegetables for my hat.

Frank Lee Plains is no place for Harrison Dextrose. I order Tench to drive like the wind. Speaking of which, those minking oysters of Perdita Spit's have been repeating on me.

So I was still ahead of the game even though Dextrose had continued directly to Aghanasp. The time was shortly after 9.30pm and my final destination was in sight. Victory could still be mine.

If I were honest with myself, however, the whole Suzy Goodenough thing was beginning to feel rather shallow. Dextrose's great boast that he was a philanthropist was surely twaddle – he would always help himself before anyone else – yet I, having saved the Ikeans from Ike, could genuinely consider myself to be humanitarian.

The Alexander Grey who had set off from Blithering Cove barely three weeks ago had become a stranger to me. I actually felt rather snobbish towards him. How could he have frittered away all those years, with no nose for achievement? What a lonely, pathetic character, how lacking in ambition and devoid of fortitude. Travel truly did broaden the horizons.

That said, a shag wouldn't hurt.

"Well, I'd better be going," I announced.

Deborah was standing in a corner, hugging Tim the twig.

"I'm sorry, I…"

"I know," she said quietly.

"I don't think our marriage…"

"I know."

Ike's authority wouldn't mean a bean in the outside world, and anyway my token of marital bonding had been a carrot, which I had eaten.

"You'll be alright now," I said.

She bit her lip. "I should have known you were right." Her voice was quivering.

"Don't blame yourself. How could you have done?"

"I'll miss you, Al… Alexander."

"I'll miss you, too, Deborah." Such conversations, I gathered, did not require originality.

"What shall I…?"

"You're much stronger than you realise. You should leave this place, build your own life." Hang on, I was lecturing someone else on moral fibre.

Her mouth curled into a smile. "Should I lose the twig?"

"I think you'll find more handsome suitors."

Deborah's shoulders shook with disguised mirth. A sparkle had begun to inhabit her eyes.

The dwarf joined our *tête-à-tête*, fit to burst. "Kisseeng Deborah, Meester Alexander, not talkeeng to deaths!"

It would have been churlish to refuse. I leaned in and pecked her on the cheek. She touched my arm and pecked back. I raised my hand; Deborah raised hers.

"Bye."

"Bye."

"Good luck."

"You too."

Detritos stepped outside, peering cautiously through the fire-illuminated gloom. Cheers wafted skywards. The air smelled of bonfires and tasted of freedom.

"Ees OK," he hissed.

Ducking as he ran, as if he could get any lower, he beckoned me to follow him towards the rear of the married quarters, away from the church. I glanced back. The building was ablaze. Flames licked at the feet of Ike's statue. I raised two fingers to him, inhaled deeply, and scarpered.

When I caught up with Detritos, he whispered, "Deborah very beauteeful."

"Well – ish," I retorted, and immediately felt shallow. What was a wart or two between bonded friends? How pathetic of me. "Actually, Detritos, I think you may be right."

We passed over a dirt track, looking right and left several times, like children trying to impress with their knowledge of the Green Cross Code. On the other side, we were into a copse of horse chestnuts, where fallen conkers cracked open underfoot. An orange glow from the flames consuming the church spire provided enough illumination to pick out a route between the eerie trunks.

A little way in, Detritos gestured me towards a pile of leaves, which he began brushing aside. When he was finished he waved an arm in the direction of the object he had uncovered.

"Findeeng zen hideeng."

"It's a battered old tandem."

"Ees so."

"And?"

"Detritos not fuckeeng rideeng! Not reacheeng fuckeeng pedal!"

So that was why he needed me. Could I let him down? "How

far are you expecting that to take us?"

"Not beeg."

"You know I need to get to Aghanasp?"

"First Monserratum. Small seeng. Aghanasp, he near!"

I didn't believe him for a second.

"Pleeze! Detritos haff map!"

The dwarf picked up a stick, cleared an area of leaves and drew a line in the crumbled earth. He pointed to one end of the line. "Zees now." He pointed to the other end. "Zees Monserratum." From there, he scored a second short line and pointed to the end of that. "He Aghanasp. Seemple!"

"That's not a map! That's two lines in the mud!"

So: Detritos's delusional mission to save the world, somehow involving a giant ruby? Or mine, to complete a daft Quest quicker than an ancient braggart, for fornication's sake? This time it was a no-brainer. The dwarf needed me.

Anyway, what if he were right about the Candid Ablican threat? In my new guise as philanthropist, it would look good on my CV: 'Saved planet'.

I offered him my hand and we shook. "Don't let me down."

"Heheheh," he chuckled.

I set the tandem, a rusty, heavy old black thing with a bell, upright, and wheeled it out of the woods. I climbed onto the front saddle and felt Detritos clamber onto the back. When I looked around, he was leaning forward precariously, clutching the centre of the handlebars, his feet a clear foot or so from the pedals.

"Alright Eddy Merckz. Which way?"

"Who?"

"Famous cyclist from… Oh, it doesn't matter. Which way?"

"On," he said, pointing forwards and nearly falling off.

"Do we stay on the roads?"

"Ees so. But shhhhh."

There was one problem with that: the aged boneshaker squeaked like a mouse enjoying orgasm.

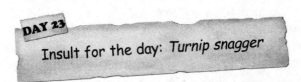

After an initial freewheel down Ike Valley, the dirt tracks in Frank Lee Plains seemed to comprise uphill struggles. The tandem offered no gears. Shortly, I was spitting phlegm.

Complicating matters was the darkness. I was navigating by moonlight, so every hidden stone and branch on the route jolted non-existent suspension, causing sore buttocks. The dwarf seemed unusually vociferous in this respect.

On the positive side, there was no one about, since the former Ikeans were all raving in town and, though we kept alert, there was no sign of pursuing Candid Ablicans.

After an hour's exertion, we reached a crossroads and a sign. It read:

> **You are leaving Frank Lee Plains**
> **Are you authorised? Be sure!**
> *Ike is tall, handsome and thin*
> *Is that a bone? Or are you just pleased to see him?*

Turning left would take us downhill; right, uphill.

"Right!" commanded the dwarf.

"Sod… off," I wheezed, dismounting.

Wheeling the bike towards a thicket of bushes, I lifted off Detritos.

"Here's the deal," I began, gathering breath. "You tell me

287

everything... Or here we stay... I want to know... Why the Candid Ablicans are after you... Where you're from... Why we're here... And the significance of the ruby." Deep inhale.

"So much seengs!"

"Yes, so much seengs. And unless you tell me them all, I'm off to Aghanasp, on my own, and you can walk the rest of the bloody way."

He shrugged, calling my bluff.

"I mean it," I persisted. And I did. Pedalling that ancient boneshaker was like Chinese coccyx torture and I wanted to know what I was letting myself in for. I had the dwarf by the short and curlies – and he knew it.

After silent contemplation, Detritos sighed. "Ees so."

From a pocket of his shiny turquoise jacket he took out a silver hip flask and offered me a swig. I had never tasted petrol, however that is what I assumed the liquid to be. It removed a layer of my mouth and sent it down my throat.

"Agggggh!" I shuddered.

"Ees good!" beamed the dwarf. Then he began his tale.

Translation from Detritos's pidgin English proved hazardous, since his vocabulary was limited, and we were forced at times to resort to sign language and mime. This is what I gathered:

The dwarf was born in a country named Green Golan. He had a twin brother who was unusually tall. ("He beeg beeg beeg!" – such was the material I worked with.)

Aged 16, deemed too short to go into the family business – professional basketball – he had left home, something of a black sheep ("Baaa baaa", points enthusiastically at hair colour). Detritos moved from country to country and odd job to odd job until he was handed a business card by a shady sort in a bar in San Dymphna.

He called the number. It turned out to be the worldwide spy

organisation SHH! (Secret Heroes Ho!), who were looking for a discreetly small agent. They trained him in the martial arts, in covert operations and how to ride a kangaroo (I may have misconstrued the dwarf's mime there).

This is where it all comes together. Detritos was sent to Emo Island, to mingle with the natives. From there he would make regular forays – in the balloon of Major Lee Upper-Crust (another SHH! agent!!!) – to Klbdow. There, agents of Candid Ablica, intent upon world domination, were rumoured to be building a weapon of mass destruction ("Beeg boom!").

According to the dwarf's intelligence, the observatory atop the Klönely Mountain housed not a telescope but a giant laser trained on the moon. If fired, it would send the moon out of orbit to crash into the earth under gravity. Thus did the Candid Ablicans plan to hold the world to ransom.

Before the construction of this laser could be finished, however, Detritos had infiltrated the observatory and had stolen the very heart of the weapon: its ruby. That is why Tomasz and Footz wanted it back so badly. They had sighted him once, but Detritos had given them the slip by disguising himself as a bush – thus did they codename him 'Green Sparrow', because he had hidden in vegetation and had flown from them like a small bird.

It sounded like utter bollocks, but he believed it.

"You are winding me up, aren't you?" I chortled.

But he was utterly serious. "Meester Alexander knoweeng James Bond?" he asked. "Uzzer bad peoples, maybe doeeng zees? Ees so?"

"You're telling me that the Candid Ablicans, inspired by Bond villains, have built a laser that could shoot down the moon?"

The dwarf shrugged. "Maybe ees so. Maybe no. Can takeeng..." He didn't know the word, so mimed...

throwing dice?

"Dice!"

"No no! Eef doeeng zees…?"

"Gamble!"

"No no!" He egged me on, excitedly.

"Chance! Would you take the chance!"

"Ees so!"

Though his story seemed to be rooted in madness, there was fuzzy logic in there, deep down. What if the Candid Ablicans truly did have the capability, the technology, to build the world's first interplanetary laser weapon? Who could tell what type of scientific genius might be at work behind by the sinister buffoons Tomasz and Footz?

The Candid Ablicans might of course be deluded overgrown children playing at war games, and could be left to their own devices. But, as Detritos had so rightly pointed out, could the world take that risk? No, I thought, and felt rather important.

"So what do we do with the ruby?" I asked.

"We?"

"I'm not just here to play tandem driver and miss the great ending. In fact, I'm not going anywhere unless you make me an honorary agent of SHH!"

This was so much fun – it was like my boyhood had never ended! I realised that any detour would hinder my chances of beating Harrison Dextrose's Quest time, so lessening my chances of sex with Suzy Goodenough, but this seemed far more exciting and important. "Come on, we're in this together!"

No response.

"I'm not going any further unless you do it."

He remained silent. I folded my arms. We had reached a stalemate.

Crickets chirruped and something among the trees made a

noise like a man polishing a chalkboard with a kumquat.

Eventually, defeated, he reached into the breast pocket of his turquoise suit, bade me kneel before him and pinned something to my tank top. Then he performed a strange salute, waving index finger and middle finger in front of his mouth while whistling.

I looked down. I was the proud owner of a black button badge featuring a cartoon depiction of the lower half of a face, with a finger to the lips, and the logo "SHH!"

My heart sang.

"So what do we do with the ruby?"

Detritos beckoned me closer. "Monserratum, ees two heel. One heel, he heel. Uzzer heel, he..." the dwarf mimed an explosion.

"A volcano!"

"Shhhh! Ees so. Rubee goeeng een vol...seeng. Beeg beeg hot!"

"Wow!"

"Ees so. Goeeng?"

"You bet we goeeng!" I performed the SHH! salute.

Detritos raised his eyes to the skies.

The early hours of the morning had brought a fierce chill to the air, though my renewed enthusiasm for the cycle ride had increased my exertions, which kept me toasty warm.

The relentless squeaking of the tandem troubled me, now that I knew what was at stake. There remained, at least, no sign of pursuers.

Our dirt track was bordered either side by uninviting scrubland. Its shallow uphill climb carried on towards the horizon for further than I cared to contemplate, playing psychological games with my stamina. I put my head down and sought a rhythm.

How often I had daydreamed of England and my friends, wishing that they could witness my escapades. This, though, was the *piece de resistance*. I was an actual honorary spy, on a mission. (I checked for the SHH! badge, which was still there, so it had to be true.)

Of course, as a child I had played at being a secret agent. Father had not encouraged my making friends – he did not enjoy the sound of repeated footfalls in the house, nor that of childish banter – but there was one boy who lived up the road, whom I bumped into on rare occasions during holidays, and we formed the loosest of bonds.

His name was Gareth and he was a sour-faced youth. He wore a dental brace and a fringe that all but obscured his eyes. He spoke in a mumble and his favourite word was "Turd". Our interactions usually involved sitting on a wall, making dwindling conversation, or my kicking a football to him, which he failed to return.

I recall one summer, when we were both aged around 12, I suggested building a camp in Glibley Woods and playing spies. There had been some big action movie on television the previous afternoon.

"Turd," Gareth had replied, though I could tell that he was keen because he had a habit of clenching his fists when he was excited. Gareth always wore shorts, come rain or shine.

I suggested that we put together a secret-agent kit and reconvene within the hour. I rushed home, found an old shoe box and, with elastic, secured inside it: a magnifying glass, tablet bottle filled with talcum powder (I had seen the fingerprint experts on television), secret code cut from the back of a cereal packet, sunglasses (borrowed from Mother), and a plastic picnic knife (Father wouldn't allow any sort of gun in the house, not even toy ones).

Gareth was already waiting for me, carrying his own shoebox. Excited that I had at last inspired some form of creativity in my acquaintance, I sprinted to the woods. Gareth caught me up 20 minutes later, having ambled all the way. At least he came.

I found a fallen tree, at such an angle that I could crawl beneath its trunk, and began to prop branches against it to form a natural tent. After an hour of my exertions, Gareth joined in. It seemed that my enthusiasm was infectious. He was emerging from his shell.

When the structure was complete, we went on the hunt for flooring and discovered a rancid old mattress, dumped by people in clear contravention of the Forest Code. This we dragged to our fallen tree and, by chance, it fitted perfectly. That it was water-sodden and populated by creepy-crawly families did not bother us. We were boys.

Inside, our 'base' felt secretive and cosy. Light passing through the woodland camouflage had a pleasing dappling effect. Wind rustled the den's leaves. It all seemed real in my childish imagination. I was an actual spy, plotting the downfall of evil with my moody sidekick.

"Right, Secret Agent Gareth, let's kick baddie butt!" I declared, opening my shoebox. "I have a magnifying glass, fingerprint kit, secret code, dagger and disguise. What do you have?"

He opened his own secret-agent kit. "Turd in a box."

To my horror, it was true. He had Sellotaped one of his own faeces to the bottom of a shoebox.

I tried to avoid him after that. The last I heard of Gareth, through local gossip, was that he had been sent to a home for disturbed youths.

I dared not consult the Timeco Z112.2 XG during the climb, as the laborious passing of time would have played havoc with my mind. When we finally reached the hill's apex, dawn had broken.

Detritos and I were confronted by a breathtaking vista.

Ahead of us were, undoubtedly, the twin peaks. These were not substantial in height, fortunately, though steep enough in parts to elicit a shudder. Their sides were the reddish-brown of scorched earth. All around were lesser hills cloaked in green, above which groups of birds were circling.

A wide river the colour of rouged cheeks ran though the foothills to the right of the peaks. To the left, began a vast area of dense forestation, as far as the eye could see, lush green in colour. Cut into it, like crop circles, were three substantial clearings, distant from each other, which I imagined must house some forms of settlement.

From here, our dirt track ran mercifully downhill, where it ended directly between the two hills.

We dismounted, the dwarf fresh from his passenger ride, myself systematically shattered. I collapsed in a heap and the dwarf handed me a billy-can of water. I gulped at it voraciously, unable to speak, otherwise I would have asked irately why he had not offered it to me previously.

The liquid was cool and sizzled on my tongue. He grabbed it from me before I could guzzle the entire contents.

Detritos pointed. "Monserratum," he said, stating the bleeding obvious.

He motioned right of the peaks, in the direction of the rising sun. "Zees way, Green Golan. Detritos home." Then left, towards the dense forestation. "Aghanasp. Meester Alexander goeeng zees."

So he hadn't lied about the proximity of our two destinations. There it was, my journey's end, among enough trees to make an environmentalist moist. Which of those three potential settlements might be Mlwlw, I wondered, my excitement levels rising.

This development also meant that I might feasibly kill two birds with one stone: save the world *and* beat Dextrose's time to Gossips, so getting the girl too. It seemed audacious.

After more than 23 days of travelling, I could have reached out and touched the finish line... given arms the length of the Pennine Way. Harrison Dextrose had reached Livingstone Quench's bar, Gossips, at 1.32am on his 24th day. It being currently 6.52am on my 23rd, I had just over eighteen hours in which to better his time. Making this target might well depend on which of the three clearings housed Mlwlw. Sod's Law stated that it would be the furthest.

And, of course, there was a small volcano to climb first.

Still, this was no time to become despondent.

"Hop on, then," I told Detritos, already mounting our rusty steed. "It's all downhill from here, apart from the big hill at the other end."

"Hoppeeng on good foots zen doeeng bad seengs," he replied, slapping me on the bottom.

The sun was climbing and the hazardous high-speed freewheel brought a pleasing draught to my exposed flesh. Feeling devil-may-care, I lifted my feet off the pedals and stretched my legs out ahead of me, as rosy-hued children do in books by Enid Blyton. I glanced quickly behind, to see Detritos doing the same. The next I knew, we were both going, "Wheeeee!"

Damn, but we were in fine spirits.

The journey downhill covered at least a half-mile and we gathered a frightening speed, one that our boneshaker was unaccustomed to. I applied the single brake. With a twang, the cable snapped. Something in my heart region did the same.

I could see ahead to the point where the dirt track simply ended, to become an area of lightly inclining screed.

"Stoppeeng!" yelled the dwarf.

"I bloody can't!" I yelled back.

I could only keep going, over the dreadful rocks and pebbles, and pray that the incline would eventually bring us to a halt.

It didn't work. As we started upwards the front wheel hit a minor boulder, sending the back wheel up and around.

Detritos, unprepared for this sudden manoeuvre, went flying off with the verve (though not the helmet) of a human cannonball. I clung to the handlebars as the ground flashed towards me, offering up a short prayer to the saint of cycling disasters.

My thigh hit first, followed by my shoulder, sending the tandem and myself spinning out of control. Then I was still.

I lay there gulping breaths, still clinging to the handlebars, mentally checking for broken bones. The whole of my left side was burning.

When I eventually picked myself up, there were rips and scuffing all the way up the leg of my bell-bottoms and along the sleeve of my happy-tortoise top. Blood was seeping through the material.

Both of the tandem's wheels were buckled to buggery. The machine was a write-off.

And the dwarf? He had already picked himself up and was limping towards me, hair a tangled mess, his suit ripped and tattered, blood seeping from an impressive gash across his forehead. He looked annoyed.

Detritos shook a stream of stones from one suit sleeve and glared. I prepared for the verbal assault. Instead, he broke into a delighted grin.

"Zees beeg fun! Doeeng one more?"

We stood at the feet of the twin hills of Monserratum, gazing upwards, shielding our eyes from the sun. At close range the slopes did not seem as daunting as they had from our previous vantage point.

Their surfaces were earthen and cracked by heat, littered with grit, pebbles and rocks. Little vegetation grew there. Certainly uninviting, though hardly too much for an honorary agent of SHH!

My geological knowledge was admittedly limited, but even to the amateur it was plain that Monserratum had lain dormant for many years.

"So which one's the volcano and which one's just a hill?"

"Hmm," said the dwarf, chin in hand, looking from one to the other. "Sinkeeng zees one," he suggested, pointing to the right.

"Are you guessing?" There was no way I was walking up the wrong one.

Detritos became sheepish. "Ees so."

"Jesus. So what are you going to do?"

I let him stew before holding my Timeco Z112.2 XG under his nose. "Directional thermometer," I said. "Measures up to 10,000 degrees Centigrade. I thought all secret agents had them."

Pointing the lovely watch towards the peak of the right-hand hill and pressing the button labelled 'therm', I checked the digital readout: 30.3. Then the other peak: 46.5.

"It's the left one," I announced, and began walking.

The going was arduous if not treacherous. There was no call for ropes and crampons, which was a shame as such palaver would have suited my new action-hero image.

Detritos was still limping after our tandem wipeout and my left side felt terribly sore, but I was too squeamish to inspect the damage.

And so we ventured higher. A small lizard scampered between rocks up ahead, which I pointed out excitedly to the dwarf, who just shrugged.

"See-eeng one, see-eeng all."

"Oooh, hark at the lizard king!"

It was banter of sorts.

Eventually, exhausted by dehydration and exercise, we

rested a couple of hundred metres from the top, sitting on rock that felt significantly cooked, saying nothing, glugging the dwarf's warm water. The scenery was truly awesome, wavering in a heat-haze. I made out the track we had tandemed down and pictured our descent, chuckling at the recklessness.

The dwarf looked across at me. "Meester Alexander. Keeng off world!"

"Zo!" came the voice from behind us. "I am sayink to you, ve haff needleverked you like zis pair off kipperz!"

There they were, legs apart, waving pistols, having appeared from nowhere on the slope above us. Still in those raincoats and hats despite the persistent rays. Tomasz and Footz.

"Ze Green Sparrow ant his cursed friend." The chief Candid Ablican rubbed his hands together. "Fallink into my brilliant trap!"

Footz patted his boss on the head. "Brilliant indeed, Colonel!"

"Get off me, you fool Footz!" snapped Tomasz, swatting away the arm. "Do somesink useful ant tie zem up." He pointed at us with the barrel of his gun. "Any funny bizness ant ve shall shoot."

I looked to the dwarf for inspiration. He seemed unconcerned. Was there a plan up his sleeve?

Detritos and I were bound at the wrist and those bonds attached to a length of rope that the Candid Ablican pair used to half-drag us the remainder of the distance to the crater of Monserratum.

I puzzled over the dwarf's calmness. Did he not have the ruby on his person? If not, why had we trudged all this way? He must have it. Yet he had left behind all his possessions, including the leather briefcase.

It struck me that, despite being an honorary SHH! spy, I had hardly been taken into the organisation's collective confidence.

What struck me harder was, at the edge of the volcanic crater, a large pulley wheel. Rope had been slung over it and disappeared into the depths. It looked ominous. I reasoned that spies might divert their minds to avoid focusing on danger, so tried to spot more lizards. But there weren't any.

The crater itself was roughly ten metres in diameter, from which heat-haze was emanating. The air smelled slightly sulphurous.

Nearby, the Candid Ablicans had piled supplies and, beside those, a grey motorbike and sidecar, camouflaged under netting. That we had not heard any engine during our journey here suggested that they had arrived well ahead of us. That stupid bloody tandem.

"How did you know we were coming here?"

"Hahahahahaha!" laughed Tomasz cheesily.

"Yes, hahahahahaha!" went Footz.

"I am sayink to you, vot did you find in ze Green Sparrow's sideburns?"

"A tracking device. We crushed it."

The worm on his cheek performed a figure-of-eight loop. "Vot else?"

I cast my mind back. "Nits… sandwich… earwigs…" It was like a grotesque version of *The Generation Game*. "Dead spider…"

"Aha!" boomed Tomasz. "You did not look inside zis arachnid?"

I wrinkled my forehead.

"It vos ze second bug! A bugged bug, if you are likink! Ant zo it zoon became obvious vitch vay you vere headink – here, to destroy ze ruby! Zo ve beat you here by anuzzer route!"

So that was it – foiled by my lack of diligence, by the dwarf's lack of a decent map and by the uselessness of our transport. A conclusive defeat.

"Bind zeir footz, Footz," ordered Tomasz.

Footz grinned foolishly. "Viz zis rope, rope?"

"BIND ZEIR FOOTZ OR I KILL YOU FIRST!" The familiar madman had emerged. The worm on his cheek reared up and lunged for the gangly henchman. Footz shrunk away and scurried to fasten our bonds.

"Now," smarmed Tomasz, "for my next cunnink plan."

"Tie ze blond to vun ent off ze rope."

At pistol-point, I was frogmarched to the pulley. Footz hauled up a few metres of rope from inside the volcano and bound my wrists tightly to its end. I had a terrible inkling of what the Candid Ablicans had in mind but dared not contemplate it. There was no way I was peering down into the crater, imagining a drop into the core of the earth.

I took several steps in reverse, stopping only when my spine made contact with Footz's gun barrel. I looked round at him, catching my reflection in his sunglasses. I looked duly petrified. He sneered.

Even my SHH! status failed to give me courage.

Tomasz addressed Detritos, who was whistling a gay tune. "I am askink you zis vunce, Green Sparrow: vere is ze ruby?" The facial worm writhed to form a question mark.

The dwarf continued to whistle.

"Footz, remoof his clozink!"

Detritos started. He was very proud of his turquoise suit. Tomasz pointed the gun at his head and cocked it. So the dwarf complied, backing towards me as the garments were pulled off.

When he was naked, taut and hairy, the Candid Ablicans stared, rubbing their chins. "Very impressive, Green Sparrow. I am sayink to you, vun cannot tell a man's manhood from hiss foot size. Now, Footz, giff me his clozink!"

The glistening Candid Ablican went through each item, feeling in pockets and around seams. When he was satisfied that the jewel was not there, he ripped the cloth and flung the item aside.

It was while this went on that I noticed something unusual on the dwarf's left buttock... A fresh, bulging scar, two inches long, with clumsy ends of string poking out on either side. So that was it! He had sewn the ruby into his own bottom!

Such dedication to duty. No wonder he had complained during the tandem ride. Was there no pain he would not endure for the SHH! cause?

Tomasz let out a roar of anger as he tossed the final sock into the volcano. "Zo. You are forcink me to place into practise my cunnink plan." He motioned Detritos towards the pulley. "Green Sparrow, take hold off ze uzzer ent off ze rope!"

The dwarf did so, standing with his back to the drop, so avoiding exposing his buttocks to the Candid Ablicans. We looked at each other, I numb with fear, the dwarf confident and as naked as the day he was born. Tomasz moved towards us, patting Detritos on the head. "Are you holdink tight, Green Sparrow?"

Before the dwarf could reply, and before I could react, he lunged at me. Taken unawares, I tripped backwards over the edge, into the volcano of Monserratum. I screamed as my brain pulsated.

The dwarf let out an almighty grunt as my body slammed into the volcano's inner wall. For a moment I was stationary, then fell a little further downwards and tried to scream again but no sound came. Then I was still. Detritos must have found his grip, though how long could it last?

My arms were taut above my head, stretched horribly, but the pain was the least of my worries. I could sense the darkness beneath me and saw the brilliant blue sky above. Gravel that had toppled into Monserratum with me still continued its descent. So dizzying was the vertigo, coupled no doubt with the shock, that I blacked out.

When my senses reawakened, and the terrible fear returned, I heard Tomasz gloating.

"Zo, Green Sparrow, it vill not be lonk before you tire ant release ze rope – zen your frent vill die! Hahahahaha! However, I am sayink to you, tell me vere is ze ruby ant ve rescue your frent."

"Tell them where it is!" I yelped.

"Ah, you zee?" said Tomasz. "Your frent agrees wiz me."

The dwarf began to whistle.

Had I been too hasty? No real spy would give up secrets under any threat. But then, was I a real spy? "Please, Detritos!" I grovelled. "Tell them where it is!"

The dwarf continued to whistle.

"Zo. Zis is how it shall be, even ven your cowartly frent begs! Hey! Cowartly frent! Beg zum more!"

It was tempting, so I did. "Let me out of here, please."

"Goot! I am sayink to you, cowartly frent, you are vise!"

I still dared not look down. The heat was intense. Sweat streamed into my eyes and down my sides from my armpits.

I knew where the ruby was. Should I tell the Candid Ablicans? But who was to say that they could be trusted? Surely I should trust Detritos, who did seem able to sustain his hold on the rope, and who had taken us this far?

I knew one thing: I didn't like being referred to as the 'cowardly friend'. I would rely on the dwarf just a little longer.

Minutes passed, during which my discomfort increased manifold. My biceps ached as if scored by razors and my hands had gone numb. I moved my legs slightly every so often, to keep them awake, careful not to cause myself to swing precariously.

At the crater's edge, the silence was broken by someone pacing around and by taunts from Tomasz or Footz. Things like:

"You are tirink, yes?" or "Mmm, zis water, it is zo nice."

Detritos seemed to have shut himself off from the world, concentrating on the task in hand, Zen-like.

By the time the sky began to darken, I had become blasé. My body had gone numb, so there was no pain, and it seemed that the dwarf would be able to hold me safe for several weeks.

I also suspected that Tomasz was beginning to realise the same, as I heard him prowling angrily, kicking at the ground, muttering.

I actually nodded off and awoke to discover that night had set up camp.

I was shivering, hungry and horribly thirsty. Should I plead for water? I tried to rub my tongue over my lips but they felt like fat biscuits. I needed liquid badly. However, I realised the dwarf was winning the psychological warfare with the Candid Ablicans, and if I grovelled now it might dramatically shift the balance. As I pondered this, veering once again towards capitulation, Tomasz's voice came from above.

"How do you do it, Green Sparrow? Ze cowartly frent must be ten times your body veight. Are you a zuperman?"

No reaction.

"Footz! Come here!" he ordered.

"Yes, Colonel. Your vish is my commant!"

"Footz, how much bigger would you be zan ze cowartly frent?"

I nearly called out, "Alright, I think we've got the message with the 'cowardly friend' thing."

Footz hmmed a while. "I am guessink, six stones taller?"

"You fool, Footz!" snapped Tomasz. "You shall svap places viz him! Zen ve shall see vot zis Green Sparrow is made off!"

"But, Colonel, I –"

"Do it, Footz! Ve shall tire zis so-called zuperman yet!"

I screamed as the rope was tugged; it felt as if my muscles

were under attack by electric eels. Then it became apparent: I was actually being hauled upwards, out of that hideous cauldron. Safe! My pain was superseded by cool waves of whale-sized relief.

"Oh thank God," I whimpered.

I was dragged over the edge of the Monserratum and experienced the delight of horizontal land. Detritos stared down at me, caked in concern.

"Ees OK? Meester Alexander?" he said softly.

I managed the briefest of smiles.

Tomasz dragged me to one side and I watched, barely conscious, unmoving and aching, as my bonds were untied and transferred to an ashen-faced Footz.

Detritos clutched his end of the rope, his buttocks still concealed from the Candid Ablicans. As I marvelled at his fortitude, I realised that my tongue had lolled out of my mouth, gathering dust, and I sucked it in, spitting.

Footz was at the edge of the crater, looking pleadingly at the Colonel.

"Step off zen, Footz!" ordered Tomasz impatiently.

Obedience was his imperative. With a grimace, he stepped backwards and dropped.

For a second time, Detritos braced himself. As the rope went taut, his biceps seemed to pop out of his arms. Sinews strained in his neck and chest, even his willy twitched, but his expression remained stoical.

Tomasz slammed a fist into the palm of his hand. "Curse you, Green Sparrow!" The worm on his cheek writhed into a ball.

Footz's head suddenly appeared over the top of the crater, as he pulled himself up on twitching arms. Sweet relief and residual fear were etched into his features. "Footz reporting, Colonel. Everysink is O—"

Then Detritos let go. "Oop," he went.

"Aaaaaiiiiiii!" went Footz.

"Ha!" went Tomasz, clapping his hands in delight. "Zo! It is proofen! Ze Candid Ablican is too much for ze puny Green Sparrow!"

"He too beeg," the dwarf protested innocently.

There came a small, echoing voice. "Em, Colonel! It is I, Footz. I am clingink to zis letch."

"You fool, Footz!" shrieked Tomasz, waddling apace to the crater's edge, where he knelt down and peered in.

I shot a glance at Detritos, who had the same idea. It was down to him. I could only have moved swiftly if fitted with castors and a motor.

As the dwarf darted towards the Candid Ablican, Tomasz realised his mistake, began to turn and levelled the pistol. Detritos hit the great raincoated behind like a sprinter from starting blocks. With his free hand, Tomasz scrabbled for a hold and with the other he fired a hopeful shot in the dwarf's direction. The worm reared up. Its master's bloated head pitched forwards, followed by his torso and the gathering momentum took both he and his shiny invertebrate friend over the edge.

Defiant to the end, Tomasz made no sound as he fell, though I heard Footz stammer after his disappearing form, "O-over here, Colonel".

I listened for the thud but heard none. Tomasz had plummeted to the centre of the earth, where he could continue his insane ranting to atoms responsible for the beginning of time.

I looked for the dwarf, already beaming. He was lying dead still, arms sprawled out, on his back. A pool of blood had collected beneath the ragged, gaping hole in his side.

I scrambled to him on hands and knees, my pain now incidental, and scooped up his limp form in one arm. His eyes were closed and his quiff was plastered to the side of his face with the sweat of his exertion. I brushed it aside.

"Detritos!" I urged. "Detritos! Don't bloody die."

He opened his eyes.

"You git! I thought you were dead!"

But I could see it in his face, the first time he had ever worn such an expression – of resignation. His body, coated in blood, slipped in my arm.

"No," I said quietly.

"Ees so," the dwarf whispered. His eyes were upon me, peering inside. "Keess heem, Hardy," he gasped.

This had better not be a trick. I released my tears without shame. They splashed onto his face, resplendent in its anguish, as I leaned in to touch my lips against his cheek.

At once, he struggled against me and with awesome effort rose to his feet. Innards hung like butcher's shop sausages from the hole in his left side. This was the last of his strength.

Stumbling, he backed the few feet to the crater's edge and forced a smile. Detritos was acting out his final scene as I watched helplessly through salt-water blur. It was not my place to interfere in his destiny.

"Bye-bye, Meester Alexander," he wheezed. "Beeg friend, ees so?"

He waved and stepped backwards.

"Yes, we big friend," I whispered to the night.

What made one person help another, I wondered, as I lay there among the silence? I had been a stranger to the dwarf yet, annoying as he could be – very annoying, in fact – he had been there for me more than once, even when I had rebuffed and rubbished him. The memory made my stomach turn.

Father, a close relative, had always been far less helpful. So what compelled a person towards altruism?

I didn't have any answers but I knew that random acts of

humanity provided hope and made life worth continuing.

And so a different kind of numbness consumed me. I did not move for many minutes after Detritos took his own life, destroying the Candid Ablicans' ruby in that same sacrificial moment. Thoughts battered against my skull, dousing me in confusion.

I looked at my watch. Almost midnight. Was it pity I was feeling, or self-pity? It was lonely up there on that punctured rock. Footz's campfire had burned out and a cold wind had developed.

Should I stay forever, to starve indelicately, or coax my functions into action? Detritos was gone. At least there had been a point to his actions. He had saved the world, or at least he imagined himself to have done so – we would never know. What of myself? A stupid journey, for what? A pathetic shag... Albeit with Suzy Goodenough.

Life went on, I supposed. Indeed, to finish the Quest, thus to liaise romantically with a lady... Well, Detritos would have approved.

I should finish my Quest in his honour.

I had one-and-a-half hours to descend Monserratum, into Aghanasp, to find Mlwlw and so Gossips, to catch Suzy Goodenough's telephone call. It seemed unlikely that there would be sufficient time. On the other hand, there was Tomasz's motorbike and sidecar, and one should never say die.

Urging my damaged limbs into action, I hobbled to the vehicle, climbed astride its mechanical manliness and found the key in the ignition. Fortune was on my side.

I had ridden a motorbike just once, at Benjamin's house. The machine had been his father's and it had run away from me, depositing me in a low-speed heap after which I had vowed never to ride again. At least I vaguely understood the principles and the pedals.

"Hello? Anyvun up zere?" came the tiny voice of still-stranded Footz.

I turned the key and pulled back on the accelerator. First time, it gunned into life, sending the sound of giant hornets coursing through the valleys. They were efficient types, those Candid Ablicans.

I found the light switch. Its beam cut though the gloom. People must be able to see me up here for miles around, I realised. It was a feeling of omnipotence.

We arrive in Mlwlw in the speeding jalopy during the small hours, scattering natives among trees.

"Where's Gossips?" I roar. One of the minkers points and runs.

So there is such a minkhole. Can I really have found Quench?

Tench pulls up outside the first hovel that looks like a bar and I tumble out, eager to use the line, "Mr Livingstone Quench, I presume?", which will sit well in the history books. I consult my timepiece for posterity. It is 1.32am.

I spot the barman immediately: a clean-shaven, upstanding minker in bowtie and dinner suit, smug in his sobriety. It can't be Quench, who was often mistaken for a tramp and dragged to soup kitchens by do-gooders.

He throws out his arms. "Harrison, my dear old chum!"

"Mink!" I declare. "What the mink happened to you?"

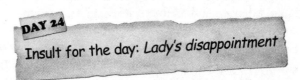

There was no trackway leading down off Monserratum, so it was a matter of staying in first gear, twitching at the brake and picking out the path of least resistance. The progress was dangerous, but it beat walking and anyway I was forced to make up time.

The dwarf's demise flashed back to me. I replayed over and over again in my mind his final moments and shed new tears. I felt them snake along my cheeks, blown backwards by my speed, and trickle down the back of my neck, where they gathered at my collar and grew cold.

When I reached the base of Monserratum I encountered two dirt tracks. One skirted the volcano, the other headed off towards the dense forestation of Aghanasp. I checked the Timeco Z112.2 XG: 1.02am. Half-an-hour to go.

As my greasy, stringy hair flapped in the slipstream, I shifted up through the gears. The foot-high dry grasses either side of the track bowed and scraped as I passed. I clocked the speedometer at top speed: 46 mph. Was that all? It felt more dangerous.

Then I was in among the trees – clustered, elegant creations with smooth, towering trunks and foliage stretching for sunlight.

The trackway was in poor shape and made slippery by fallen vegetation. I was forced to slow down or face ignominy off to one side.

The motorbike roar disturbed all manner of wildlife. I made

out bird shapes flitting among the canopy. A monkey swung between branches, howling as it went, gathering others until they were a gang and felt safe enough in numbers to calm down.

And there were eyes among the tree trunks, bright yellow, blinking and then gone. The place was alive.

I glanced again at the Timeco Z112.2 XG: 1.16am.

Eventually the trackway widened out and I saw flaming torches up ahead. As I drew nearer, two human shapes blocked my route. They held rifles against their chests, presumably soldiers, and I could only hope that they were friendly.

"Hello!" I said as breezily as I could, reducing the revs to idling. I did not switch off the engine. Behind them, tantalisingly, I saw buildings.

"I'm a tourist," I said. "I'm looking for Mlwlw. Is this the place?"

Each man wore baggy t-shirt and shorts, bearing sports branding I failed to recognise, and white trainers that all but shone. They were both in their early-twenties and lanky. One had a golden front tooth; the other had a whistle in his mouth.

"Speak English?" I enquired hopefully. "I'm looking –"

The chap with the whistle blew a tune on it and the pair of them started a happy, loose-armed dance. I was obliged to wait, itching with impatience, until they stopped.

"Speak English?" I repeated. "I'm in a bit of a hurry."

And off they went again, on the whistle/dance routine. It was mindlessly exasperating. They were hardly the most professional of soldiers, but I dared not risk their armed wrath.

They stopped again.

"What you want?" demanded Gold-tooth.

"You do speak English! Great. Thanks. Is that Mlwlw?" I asked, pointing up ahead.

"Yeah."

"Is it alright to go in?"

"What you askin' us for?" replied Gold-tooth.

"You're not soldiers?"

"Nah, man. We off shooting things. You wanna come?"

Oh. "No thanks. Any idea where Gossips is?"

"Second left. Third building on right. But it's shit."

I checked the Timeco Z112.2 XG: 1.25am. Seven minutes to go.

"Gotta dash."

I gunned the engine between rows of white-painted, rough-walled buildings with roofs of sloping, tightly packed reeds. People sat out front under electric lanterns, drinking, chatting, and cheered as I sped past.

Reaching the second turning on the left, I swung the motorbike sharply around and skidded sideways. I gritted my teeth and closed my eyes, expecting to go over, until the sidecar whumped into a veranda, the machine tottered, changed its mind and deposited me upright. I exhaled deeply, leapt off without bothering to turn off the ignition and scanned the buildings for sign of Gossips.

There it was, right above my head: 'Gossips', in horrible Eighties type, the sign still swinging after my impact. Harrison Dextrose might have bumped into Livingstone Quench. I had bumped into Quench's entire bar.

I was checking the Timeco Z112.2 XG even as I tugged open the door: 1.30am. Two whole minutes to spare, after all that journey! I forced down my elation, mindful that I should not celebrate until I actually heard Suzy Goodenough's mellifluous tones.

A tanned man with long grey hair pulled back into a ponytail was sitting on a high stool behind the bar. He was of medium height, lean, his skin was tanned, taut and moisturised, and he wore an old dinner suit. Could that healthy-looking chap really be Livingstone Quench?

There were no beer-taps or optics behind him and he was leaning against the wall, hands behind head, eyes closed, lacking custom. The place looked like it had last been busy some while back.

He shook himself awake as I staggered towards him breathing heavily.

"Are you Livingstone Quench?" I gasped.

"The very same. And you must be Stanley?" His voice was rich and beguiling. He offered a hand and shook mine firmly. He was an athletic sort, having obviously cleaned up his act since the Dextrose days.

"What would you like?" asked Quench.

"Does your telephone work?"

"You don't stop for breath, do you young man? Phone's over there." He motioned towards an ancient callbox hanging at an angle from the wall. "Of course it works."

"Great. Do you accept travellers' cheques?" I had a few left over from my ludicrous High Yawl shopping spree.

"I'll take anything you've got."

"A cold beer?"

He winked.

As he bent down to locate the booze, I surveyed the charmless interior and noticed for the first time that there was someone else in Gossips: a shabby figure hunched on a stool in a darkened corner. He had his head in his hands and his shoulders were moving in spasms.

The time was 1.33am. Suzy was always late.

Livingstone Quench reappeared clutching a brown bottle and prised off its crown cap. While rifling through my wallet for payment, I nodded towards the sobbing drunkard. "What's the matter with him?"

"Oh, don't mind him," boomed Quench insensitively. "That's Harry. He's a regular. Always starts weeping around this time.

Eh, Harry?"

Harry didn't look up.

And I wondered: Harry? I peered into the corner as my eyes accustomed themselves to its darkness. That mop of shaggy curls, greying, the bloated, crimson hands, the age-old khaki explorer's suit, such that television naturalists sport. It couldn't be…?

I took out my copy of *The Lost Incompetent: A Bible for the Inept Traveller.* Quench saw me doing so. "You've got his book, eh? Bloody good read. I'm in it, you know. Call them 'my erstwhile days of insobriety'."

I was stunned. "You mean that's him? Here – in this bar? Harrison Dextrose?"

"Yeees. Been here for a while. Often visits since the exploration business dried up. Keeps trying to convert me back to the booze but I'm not for turning."

With shaking hands I fumbled for payment. "He seems upset."

Quench beckoned me closer. "The drink, you know. Makes him morose. Starts wailing about losing his wife and son."

"I didn't even know he had a son. And I thought he loathed his wife."

"Between you and me, he and the missus patched it up when he realised he had no friends left back in Blighty. She joined him on his last expedition, he got sozzled, left her behind somewhere and can't remember where." He continued at a whisper, "And I shouldn't really talk about his son – very personal, don't you know – but yes, he and Mrs Dextrose had one… oooh, good thirty years ago now. She had him adopted. Said she couldn't cope with two babies in the house. Hit him hard. Or it did when he occasionally sobered up."

I looked across at him, the lonely, hunched figure. *That* was the man I had practically worshipped for the past 15 years? He looked so insignificant, pathetic even.

Quench was burbling on, "Did you know, when he was here last, he –"

"Yes, er, thanks," I said, heading towards Dextrose.

I didn't know whether to feel pity for his situation or be furious at his potential fraud. Losing one's way was acceptable; losing one's family surely was not. Still, that was him. *The* Harrison Dextrose. Blimey.

It was funny, I had finished my Quest but the elation I should have felt was marred by the sad specimen before me. Had all those years of hero-worship, my own incredible journey, really been inspired by *that* man? The Dextrose of my fevered imagination had been a manly, upright, if booze-addled sort. Of course he had exaggerated in *The Lost Incompetent*, but I had always thought that was for the sake of a good yarn. What if the whole thing had been a vast exaggeration, even lies?

I reached Dextrose's table and looked down at the lost figure. Something inside quelled my indignation. He was old now, into his seventh decade.

I tapped him on the shoulder. His chest heaved and he looked up.

His eyes were rimmed vicious red and his chin was covered in a full growth of hair registering spillages. "I've lost the wife," he moaned. His voice was heavy and troubled by catarrh.

"Well don't worry. Have a drink," I suggested glibly, still unsure whether to laugh or cry.

As I took a seat across from him, Dextrose grabbed my beer and downed it in one while I looked on enviously.

"Got another?" he asked.

The man was ravaged by the effects of his hedonism. His face sagged like melting wax. He reeked of alcohol and stale tobacco. He lurched at me, throwing his arms towards me across the table. "I love you," he slurred.

"Thank you," I said, appalled by his breath. Five minutes

earlier, had someone told me that Harrison Dextrose would declare his love for me, I would have swooned with delight. Instead, I had to cover my nose.

Gently, I pushed him away, but his body kept on going and his head slammed against the wall. He didn't seem to notice.

"I weren't unfit! I were pissed!" he cried, shadow-boxing.

"Where's your wife?" I asked.

"Minking lost her!" he shouted, slapping both hands into his lap.

How bizarre, I thought. The editor of *The Lost Incompetent: a Bible for the Inept Traveller* had censored Dextrose's swearwords using the word 'mink'. And he had adopted the same affectation. He had become a parody of his literary incarnation, presumably keen to rekindle the old days, or perhaps just to be recognised.

"Where did you lose her?" I asked impatiently. I wasn't taking any flannel from this bumbling old charlatan.

He waved an arm backwards, hitting it on the wall. "Somewhere. How do I minking know? I thought she were following. Turn around, minking gone. What shall I do?"

This was awful. My hero, this alcoholic vagabond, was asking me for advice. It wasn't supposed to be like that.

Suddenly, Dextrose was rummaging for an inside pocket, missing and starting again.

"Can I help?" I asked politely.

"Mink off!" he snapped, poking a finger into my chest.

That did it. "Alright then, I will do!" I huffed, beginning to rise.

He grabbed my arm and pushed me back down. "What's the hurry? It's a jungle out there." Dribble performed a tango down his beard.

He eventually retrieved a pair of heavily battered photographs, haphazardly folded and with corners missing. He passed them to me and pointed at the top one.

"That's her. Minking cow."

It depicted a young, not unattractive, woman swinging around the mast of a decently sized yacht. She wore a headscarf and summer dress that showed off trim hips. She looked late-thirties. If Dextrose were over 70 now and had married someone of a similar age, the photograph must be some 30 years old. That he carried it around with him showed he had a heart somewhere. The front and bluster had not deserted him, at least.

I flipped Mrs Dextrose to the back and looked at the other photograph, of a bawling baby, perhaps six months old. It stopped me in my tracks.

"Me minking son, poor little mink!" He was crying again, great heaving sobs. Dextrose pointed at the picture. "S'the last I saw of him."

"But…" I reached for my own wallet and, in a trance-like state, pulled out the photograph of myself as a baby, also bawling, which Mother had so treasured. "But it's me."

The photographs were identical.

Harrison Dextrose looked up, almost lucidly. "Minks!" he spat.

I held up his photograph of the son in one hand, and my baby picture in the other. He sat there studying them for many moments, focusing.

"It can't be," he said quietly. Sobriety seemed suddenly to have kicked in.

"Mr Dextrose," I said, "I've no idea how, but I think I may be your son."

He lurched forward once again, to envelop me in a drunken bearhug. His tears were tears of happiness. "Me son! Pilsbury! I minking found him!"

Familiarity breeds contempt, they say. Familiarity with Dextrose's work had bred only contentment for me. With each read, I had noticed new details, added nuances to speech, and the pictures in my head had grown more vivid.

Literature had always provided my escape from reality while my parents had been alive – ticking off the hours of solitude in my bedroom to avoid Father downstairs – and Harrison Dextrose's odyssey had been like nothing I had encountered before.

And I had never grown out of *The Lost Incompetent*. Quite the opposite. Having been inspired by the boy's-own adventuring with adult themes, I had begun to seek the author's unspoken motivations and inspiration. What had made him tick? What had gone on beneath the gung-ho? I had never been able to decide and instead had returned, giggling and wide-eyed, back to the surface of Dextrose's stories.

In Gossips, I believe I found some answers.

Dextrose would never admit to being an outsider, at odds with the world. But he was. Colleagues, lovers, acquaintances – he paid for them all, in wages, fees or rounds of ale. He knew they'd be off when the remunerations ceased, and he brazened it out. He feared isolation.

Dextrose kept moving, because to stand still only exacerbated his loneliness. He was a shy, introverted man, sheltering those defects beneath a brilliant disguise. Attack had been the best form of defence, and that was why he had been quite the combative curmudgeon.

Deep down, Harrison loved Mrs Dextrose; she was the only human being to stick by him despite his myriad flaws. Petrified that she would leave him after the baby was adopted – his failure – he had left her instead, time after time. (This is guesswork of the amateur psychologist, but it fits nicely.)

How, in their old age, he had persuaded her to accompany him on an adventure I have no idea, nor why he would want her to. Whether he had lost her on purpose... it was possible.

Why had Dextrose so appealed to me, then? I had been

apathetic. Instead of seeking new surroundings, I had sat in that house, with its ghosts and ill memories, for 15 years, funded by my inheritance, portraying those times to myself as one great student lark. But in darker moments, the sense of alienation had crept up on me.

I had grown accustomed to my own company. Yet I'd always had self-belief, enough to know that one day I would do something. It had just been a matter of energy.

My Quest, inspired by *The Lost Incompetent*, initiated by Suzy Goodenough, had not only brought me to life, it had given me a glimpse into the alleged world of Harrison Dextrose. I began to understand the adrenalin buzz of risk, the point of even annoying companions, the thrill of the chase. It was about building a world, a false one that lasted only as long as the journey, but which consumed one's thoughts and gave a point to one's existence.

There was one particular section of *The Lost Incompetent* that came back to me, as I sat beside Dextrose in Gossips, trying to make sense of what had gone before. It had always jarred with the rest of his writing, which had been resolutely macho, concerning the after-effects of a night on the tiles in Klütz. If no profound self-analysis, it was as much truth as Dextrose had been prepared to expose.

By mink, last night's booze was fearful: colour of phlegm, flat, and with a taste of stagnant bile. Djüke maintained it was peculiar to the region ("Only fackin' brew it 'ere, innit!") and had named it Bottom Baffler. It has certainly baffled mine, which knows not whether it is coming, going, or going quicker than that.

I maintain the brew was merely peculiar. It has given me a debilitating sense of melancholy, such that I dare not venture outside, lest others witness me shed a woman's tears. So black has it made my mood that I am missing Mrs Dextrose. The last time I missed the triple-bagger, it was with a hunting rifle!